Queensborough Rock

Stephen Shaiken

Crosswinds Press

Published by Crosswinds Press

Visit Stephen's website
http://www.stephenshaiken.com/

Receive Stephen's newsletters
http://eepurl.com/dBomIX

Follow Stephen on Twitter
https://twitter.com/StephenShaiken

First Edition: September, 2022
ISBN: 978-1-7321474-7-8

Contents

Foreword

New York City consists of five counties known as "boroughs." Queens is the largest in size and borders the Borough of Brooklyn on its south and suburban Nassau County to its east. All three are part of Long Island; the only borough situated on the mainland is the Bronx. Across the East River, west of Queens, lies the island borough of Manhattan. (The fifth borough, Staten Island, does not appear in the novel.)

For unknown reasons, the spelling "borough" is used in every governmental instance except one. While it's Queensborough Community College, Queensborough Public Library, Triborough Bridge, and Borough Hall subway stop, the famous Fifty-Ninth Street-Queensboro Bridge uses an alternate spelling. When you see the two different spellings, it's not a mistake. The word "borough" is capitalized only when it is part of an official name, just to add a little more confusion.

Chapter 1
January, 1971

T he receptionist at Luna Records summoned Bernstein with a wave of her hand. She was petite and pretty, long brown hair complementing her soft, dark features. Bernstein smiled, hoping for a friendly response.

"Mr. Schwartz will see you now," was all she said. Bernstein shrugged and asked where to find his office.

"Down the hall, fourth door to your right," she instructed, rising from her desk as she pointed to the imposing mahogany door behind her. Bernstein caught a glimpse of her thigh as he walked to the door. The bright green and yellow pastel colors of her skirt contrasted with the cool, dark blue of the reception area. The walls, the furniture, the carpet, even the florescent lighting was that same color. Bernstein associated the color blue with sadness and pain, mostly because those were the most common themes of his favorite music, named after the color. The color blue would normally be of no consequence, except Bernstein considered it an inauspicious sign for a meeting of such enormous consequence.

Bernstein passed through the door and ambled down the long hallway. The carpeting was still blue, but the walls and lighting were white. Doors were evenly spaced along both walls of the corridor.

Glass-covered albums by Luna's top stars hung between the doors. Most had gone platinum.

The fourth door on the left displayed a large plaque reading "*D. Schwartz, Artists & Repertoire.*" Bernstein knocked and waited. The lock clicked, and the door opened slightly.

"Come on in!" a slightly high-pitched male voice called out. Bernstein pushed the door and entered.

He found himself in a large office, mercifully devoid of blue. Bernstein considered this to be a good sign. A few overstuffed chairs and a huge, pillowed couch were scattered about, following no particular style or design. Two large windows looked out on the Manhattan skyline from thirty-five floors up. A shelf ran the length of the inside ledge, holding an amplifier, turntable, and tape deck.

A large oak desk sat in front of the windows, facing the door. The desk was cluttered with record albums, some sticking out from sleeves or covers. An assortment of magazines, stray papers, empty coffee cups, and strange gadgets of varying sizes filled most of the remaining space. Bernstein spotted his tape amidst the confusion. He recognized his handwriting on the exposed paper label.

Duke Schwartz, head A&R man for Luna Records and one of the most influential people in the business, sat behind the desk. His job was to decide which artists won the brass ring of a recording contract with one of the largest and most important record labels in the world. Schwartz squinted at Bernstein as if trying to decide if he recognized him. Bernstein stared back without needing to squint or sort through his memory bank. Bernstein knew if he had ever met Schwartz, he would never forget him.

Schwartz emerged from behind his desk and lunged at Bernstein, a heavy hand extended. Bernstein felt its clamminess as he shook, at the same time, studying the animated, roly-poly, five-foot two-inch ball of flesh before him. Bernstein, at five-eight and average height at best, stood almost a head taller. Duke's clothing ensemble was at least five years behind the times and evidenced no more strategy than his furniture arrangement—green and white polka-dot shirt with an oversized white collar, white leather vest open and showing his protruding belly, green and gray striped bell-bottoms, and black patent leather boots. Several rings holding large stones of different colors graced his thick fingers.

"Duke Schwartz," he announced in that high-pitched voice. "Really glad to know you."

Bernstein discreetly wiped his hand along the side of his pants. "Jack Bernstein," he said, smiling and hoping it didn't look like he was laughing. Schwartz went back to his seat and told Bernstein to pull up a chair. As soon as Bernstein was seated, Schwartz asked what he could do for him.

Bernstein hadn't considered the possibility Schwartz wouldn't remember why he agreed to see him. As he sat there, it dawned on him —men like Schwartz made their fortunes through endless meetings with people who had something they wanted to sell. There were too many to keep track of. Bernstein was just one little man on a conveyer belt running past big men like Duke Schwartz. Big in influence, anyway. Men with Schwartz's power just sat behind their desks, listening to tapes as promoters quivered before them.

This is what they mean by "the pitch," Bernstein realized.

Bernstein wanted to tell Duke he had it within his power to make Galahad a star with the fame and fortune spilling over to Bernstein as well. As an old agent once told him, "Money and power—the vitamins and nutrients of the music business." Duke Schwartz had an abundance of each to dispense as he saw fit.

Bernstein also wanted to explain how he had put every penny he had into the studio tape, and on top of that had begged, borrowed, and even pawned a friend's guitar. Those loans had to be repaid sooner rather than later. Pawnshops had a buyback deadline, after which the guitar could be sold. That would not be easy to explain to his friend. Missing a payment to a loan shark would be even more problematic. Striking out with Galahad was not an option.

Of course, he said none of this. Record label executives heard such stories every day and had survived the same to get where they were. Bernstein knew it was suicide to beg or plead. A manager or agent who has faith in their talent never does. The folks at the top treat the folks at the bottom like the hired help at best. At worst, they get treated like indentured servants, maybe even slaves. Bernstein regularly assured himself that when he made it, he wouldn't treat anyone that way.

Bernstein explained why he was there. A certain respected studio engineer hired for Galahad's tape suggested, after the mixing, Bernstein call Luna and ask to see Schwartz. "Tell them I sent you and I guarantee you get a hearing," the engineer had assured Bernstein as they smoked a joint to celebrate the final edit. "I've sent them a whole bunch of artists they signed."

Schwartz nodded as if to signal, "Yes, now I remember." The engineer had called, and Duke's secretary made the appointment with his approval. Bernstein pointed to the tape.

"Ah yes, a tape!" Schwartz cried as if it were the first time he'd ever seen one. He moved over to the tape deck on the shelf by the window and told Bernstein to join him.

"Watch this critter swallow the tape," he squealed as he placed Bernstein's tape on the spindle of a Wollensak reel-to-reel tape recorder, among the world's best and most expensive tape machines.

"Top of the line," Schwartz said.

For Bernstein, it was more than a tape—it was a labor of love, the magnetically reconstructed record of his dreams and hopes, the most important possession he ever owned. This moment was the culmination of all he had worked toward over the three years he had been a manager. For Duke Schwartz, it was just another day at the office.

"Just place the reel on the deck, press the button, and off we go!" he shouted. He leaped back into his seat like a large, fleshy frog, landing on his rump as the first notes sounded through the big speakers attached to the tape deck.

Whatever someone outside the music industry might think of Duke Schwartz the first time they met him, Bernstein knew the little round fellow was nobody's fool. He wouldn't be sitting in this office wielding such power if that were the case. The story of Luna Records was imprinted in the mind of every music industry professional, and Duke Schwartz's role was hardly a secret. Luna Records was started by eighteen-year-old Bill Krumpert in his parents' garage in Newark, New Jersey. His first hire was Schwartz, his best friend since grade school.

Elvis was in the Army, Buddy Holly and Richie Valens had just been killed in a plane crash, and the ever-changing world of music was wide open. The teenagers roamed the Garden State, stalking the best groups at Battles of the Bands, signing them, and recording them on a beat-up old four-track tape recorder Krumpert bought cheap from a soul station that had been forced off the air to make way for another top-forty clone.

Krumpert was the brains and motivating force behind the fledgling operation with the drive, business sense, and brutal focus needed to succeed in an industry so cutthroat, one rock critic had opined, "It makes piracy look humane."

If Krumpert was the brains and the brawn, Schwartz was the ears. Since the time they were grade-school kids, Schwartz had never failed to pick the next number-one hit. Krumpert relied on Schwartz to tell him who was really the best and most popular band at any battle, and which bands they caught at clubs were worth their time. Neither Krumpert nor Schwartz cared about anything other than whether they could land the band a recording contract.

Krumpert was an energetic and compelling figure who persuaded wealthy investors to loan him the money needed to stay afloat in the early days. He wisely gave them interest-bearing notes secured by future royalties on any Luna artists, which he paid in full, keeping ownership of Luna to himself alone, though many suspected Duke had a small piece as well. Suppliers were cajoled to advance credit, and most importantly, Krumpert persuaded several established groups their destiny lied in abandoning their major labels and getting on board with a nascent operation, one in the process of leaving its garage for a small office in a strip mall above a pizza parlor. They did so because it was Krumpert, and it proved a wise move for all of them. From those humble beginnings, Luna enjoyed ongoing moves to more impressive quarters, finally settling into this battery of offices, a full three floors high above Broadway in the Music District. The thirty-fifth floor was where the decisions were made, where Krumpert ruled his universe with the aid of Duke Schwartz's ears.

On the floor below the corporate suites was a spanking new thirty-two-track recording studio. Every artist, producer, and engineer dreamed of working in that studio, where Luna Records pumped out a steady stream of breadwinning singles and albums that made them a force to be reckoned with.

Duke Schwartz held Bernstein's fate in his pudgy little hands. Bernstein knew this, and he also knew Galahad's music bore little similarity to Schwartz's tastes. Luna did have some acts under contract of whom Bernstein approved, but their empire was funded by a large catalogue of what Bernstein termed "rock choir boys"—clean, well-produced, noncontroversial pop music with an audience that potentially included anyone whose musical appreciation was frozen at the age of twelve. Their bread-and-butter was usually called bubblegum music, but Luna also had some genuinely talented musicians. Luna didn't hold talent against an artist so long as they made money. It was just a fact of life talent didn't always translate into sales, just as sales were not always indicative of talent. Luna's artists were played on AM bands across America, and on turntables in every city, town, and village. They didn't include stars like Jim Morrison, arrested for exposure on stage, or groups promoting use of any drug. If there was ever a trace of a political message, Krumpert and Schwartz made sure it was scrubbed.

Duke Schwartz had no musical background, played no instrument, lacked any knowledge of studio production, and had no idea how to promote a group. What Schwartz possessed was an uncanny, intuitive insight into which groups would capture that top-forty market. He instinctively recognized who would succeed and thus was worth Luna's time and money. It was an established myth in the business that Schwartz would listen to a song and decide right on the spot whether the artist made the cut, but Bernstein sensed it was no myth. Schwartz referred those groups to Bill Krumpert, who had the final say in making them rich and famous. Krumpert was unconcerned he was gambling on the word of a man who could not discern a Gregorian chant from Dixieland jazz. He knew Schwartz was almost never wrong.

Bernstein silently prayed Schwartz would listen to the tape the with full concentration, so he would feel Galahad's voice merge with the melody and his lyrics. The kind of music Schwartz was most familiar with did not require such close attention, as its listeners didn't demand much out of a song other than a catchy tune and easy-to-remember words.

The first song was "I'll Dream Tonight," a soothing melodic piece —a good, solid composition, tasteful and thoughtful while sustaining a rhythm and melody with commercial potential. He glanced in Schwartz's direction, searching for some reaction. He was disappointed when halfway through the song's second verse Schwartz reached into a desk drawer and pulled out a small box, which fell to the floor. Schwartz followed it, dropping to his knees and scrambling across the rug like a crab.

"Let's play marbles!" he squealed. "Just picked this set up in Hollywood. Heard Neil Young has a set, and I just had to get one." He reached into the box and withdrew a plastic case of marbles and several small cups of varying colors. He set the cups on their sides in a wide circle on the floor so they looked like the entrances to miniaturized Lincoln Tunnels. A small ramp was molded into the bottom of the cups to allow marbles to roll in. Schwartz arranged the cups.

"Choose your marbles," Schwartz ordered as he held out the small box. Inside were four sets of marbles of different colors, somewhat larger than the ones Bernstein recalled playing with as a child. They looked more like semi-precious stones than cheap glass marbles. He doubted they were cheap.

Bernstein feigned debating which color to choose, settling on turquoise. Schwartz plucked them from the box just as the instrumental break began. Bernstein felt his stomach spiraling. Schwartz did not appear to be paying attention to Galahad's vocals or the backup band's tight playing, especially Ed Stern's soaring leads. He prayed again for a sign of acknowledgment from the pudgy powerhouse. Bernstein was not religious and rarely prayed, but this was an exceptional circumstance. He wanted to leave the building with a contract, not a debt load he couldn't manage. It was starting to look like that might require divine intervention.

Schwartz snatched an amber set of marbles. He looked up at Bernstein, who followed on his knees. Schwartz set up his marbles in groups of two or three between cups. Hoping to curry favor, Bernstein did the same.

"The idea is to knock the other guy's marbles all over the place while shooting your own into the cup. You get two shots every turn, one to do each. Got it?" Bernstein hoped it looked like he was paying attention as he envisioned his time and his money floating around the circle, Galahad and him disappearing into the ether where failed bands and managers dissolve. He made halfhearted efforts to play the game as "I'll Dream Tonight" yielded to "Cosmic Ways," Bernstein's least favorite of Galahad's songs.

"Cosmic Ways" was a quasi-spiritual number Bernstein believed would disappoint those looking for spiritual music but draw no one else into its orbit. It was too slow, too preachy, too irrelevant for rock fans. Managers and artists constantly argued over what to record and in what order. The conflicts usually entailed a manager's need to bring in money versus the artist's desire to express their feelings. Galahad refused to set foot in the studio if "Cosmic Ways" wasn't included and placed second. Bernstein feared no one would listen to the remaining songs after hearing "Cosmic Ways." He considered having the order of songs rearranged on a separate tape and playing that one for interested parties, but he had heard too many stories of artists accusing their managers of mishandling their career, or worse, betraying them. He was well aware that there were no secrets in the music industry. Bernstein knew how strongly Galahad felt about the song and its message and resigned himself to acceding to his client's stubborn insistence. As the producer, he worked with the engineer and Ed Stern to create a final version of "Cosmic Ways" that emphasized Galahad's voice and Stern's blues-based, emotive guitar work. All three thought they made a silk purse out of a sow's ear with the song, but Schwartz would decide. Bernstein searched Duke's face for a hint.

"You shoot again," was all he got. Bernstein pinged a few more, flicking his index finger off his thumb as he'd done as a young boy playing on the streets and playgrounds of Queens. *Maybe it's better that I distract him while this one plays*, he thought. A few more marble shots later, "Cosmic Ways" ended, and the third song began, an upbeat blues rock number, Stern's Strat lead paying homage to his hero, Muddy

Waters. Duke hummed the tune of Luna's latest bubblegum millionaire as he eyed his next shot. After twenty-seconds, Bernstein knew he had either lost Duke or the garish music maven had already decided to recommend signing Galahad. *Somehow, I don't think so,* Bernstein thought.

The third song yielded to the last, and then the tape was silent. Bernstein explained how much he enjoyed sporting with Duke, but he had an appointment back in Queens to hear a new band with a hot reputation, and he wanted to sign them before someone else did. *I've got to have some clients beside Galahad.* He hoped Duke, who started his career in a similar way, would understand. Bernstein added he'd appreciate Schwartz's on-the-spot appraisal. They walked back to Schwartz's desk and sat.

Schwartz deliberated for a moment, stubby fingers curled and pressed against his temples, elbows propped on the desk.

"You're a nice guy, and I'd like to see you make it," he said. His hands dropped from his head and reached into a drawer for a bag of candy. He offered one to Bernstein, who accepted, though he rarely ate candy.

"It didn't sound bad. Actually, the first song was really good, but I've got forty-five ears, and Galahad ain't forty-five music. It's a different league, and I'm not safe playing there. Sort of rock, folk, and blues mixed together with some other stuff I just don't understand. So, I can't sign off on it, but it's too interesting to just toss aside. What I will do is send it on to Bill, which I don't usually do if I pass, and believe me, if he likes it, you've got it made."

Bernstein nodded. *Like a stay of execution,* he thought.

"Now, I ain't promising you anything," Schwartz added, his voice more reserved. "And, needless to say, if during the course of your wanderings you come across a band you think might be for me, give me a call. I'll make it worth your while."

Bernstein rose, torn between despair over the debts and the hocked guitar and relief that the final word would not come from this amiable clown with enormous power. They shook farewell, and Bernstein scraped a finger on one of the rocks on Schwartz's fingers. As he walked back along the corridor, he realized Luna had one copy of the tape, Ocean Records another they had been sitting on for weeks, and Bernstein had a copy at home. The master was still at the studio, where it was safe and could be copied again for a small price. Schwartz struggled to shake the thought that if things didn't go well with Bill Krumpert, even a small price would be out of reach.

Soon Bernstein was back in the reception area. The pretty receptionist paid him no heed as he walked past. She was speaking to a young man with long black hair and a ratty brown corduroy jacket. Her voice was sweeter than it had been to him. *Maybe she likes long, straight hair better than my Jew-fro*, he thought.

"Mr. Schwartz will see you now," she said. "Down the hall, fourth door to your right."

Chapter Two

Bernstein hurried the three blocks to the parking lot. While waiting for a light, he asked a fellow pedestrian for the time. He had six minutes before he would owe another hour. *Should be no problem*, he thought. These days, even that small amount of money made a difference. He sprinted the last block and avoided the extra hour's charge by less than a minute. *Good thing my parents told me to never smoke cigarettes.*

Managing Galahad was a full-time project. Bernstein thought about the calls he had to make, hoping some would lead to paying gigs. He thought of the next day, when he would be at the library all morning, searching the newspapers and telephone directories of Queens and Nassau for any clubs or coffee shops he hadn't seen before. It was tedious, boring work, but no one else was doing the same, plumbing the depths of Queens and Nassau for bands under the radar of the big music machines in Manhattan. *I better start doing more plumbing*, Bernstein thought. There were several known instances of such discoveries—fellow Queens College graduate Paul Simon and Queens native Leslie West of Mountain being the most renowned. "They say a lotus grows in the mud, and let's not forget truffles live in dirt and get sniffed out by pigs," he liked to say when former girlfriend

Jennifer questioned his strategy and suggested taking a more traditional job. "No way," was his inevitable response. They broke up almost a year ago, and he hadn't found anyone else.

Bernstein's black 1963 Volvo stood out among the Cadillacs, Lincolns, Corvettes, and foreign cars favored by the music business executives and lawyers whose offices filled the towering buildings in this section of Manhattan. He got behind his steering wheel and started the engine. The choke was as temperamental as always, but the car started on the second attempt. *First time this heap fails me will be the last*, he told himself. *But then how would I get around?*

Bernstein knew buying a car was out of the question. He had no money and owed enough to buy two decent cars. Funding Galahad, especially the tape, had drained Bernstein of almost all his savings. Managing Galahad took all his time and caused him to give up managing other acts. Everything was riding on Galahad getting a record contract with its royalties and concert tours. *And it's all in the hands of an idiot like Duke Schwartz.* Bernstein had heard a lot of good things about Bill Krumpert, but maybe it was wrong. *How sharp can he be if his right-hand man is a clown? A clown who doesn't know good music when it smacks him in the face.*

And who holds my entire future in his hands.

～

Midtown traffic was least congested mid-afternoon, and it wasn't long before Bernstein was driving across the Queensboro Bridge. The Midtown Tunnel was faster, but it charged a toll. When things were as tight as they were at that moment, fifty cents mattered.

The Volvo had an FM band on its radio, not common in American cars. When he was over the bridge and entering the Long Island Expressway, Bernstein tuned in WNEW, which was playing "Tales of Brave Ulysses," by Cream, off their *Disraeli Gears* album.

When the song ended, Bernstein was a few blocks from the basement apartment he rented in Bayside. Apartment might be too generous, Bernstein often thought during the almost two years he'd lived there. It was a finished basement, entered through the vestibule, then a door, and down a staircase. It had a bathroom and a primitive kitchen—nothing more than a short counter with a hotplate and coffee maker. A small refrigerator was squeezed beneath it. There were no windows or air-conditioning, making the famously hot and humid New York City summer most uncomfortable even with a fan. It was cheap, but he couldn't invite music businesspeople over aside from his good friend Ed Stern.

The landlady, Mrs. Bardoni, was a hawk-faced, unsmiling woman with gray hair tied in a bun. She lived with a daughter named Anna, who seemed close to Bernstein's age. He had never spoken to Anna, and he rarely had to deal with her mother since he left his rent on the vestibule table every Friday.

A positive feature of living in Bayside was the ability to park for free on the streets. Bernstein pulled into a spot a block from the house. He was about to turn off the car and radio when he heard the disc jockey—now calling themselves "hosts"—tell the audience he was taking a brief commercial break, and after that, he'd play "A Rainy Day in Memphis," the title song off the recent album by Tennessee Eddie. "If you haven't heard the name before, you'll be hearing it a lot from now on," the host assured the audience. Bernstein turned off the engine and radio and sat in the Volvo in silence.

Tennessee Eddie. I try not to think about him since I found Galahad.

He thought about nothing but Eddie as he walked to his basement, and it continued well into the night.

Chapter 3
July, 1969
(A year and a half before Luna)

Whenever he was asked about Tennessee Eddie, Bernstein said it hurt too much to think about. Truth was, for quite some time, that was all he thought about and traces always lurked in the background, like a sore muscle one comes to accept while wishing it would be gone.

Bernstein had graduated Queens College the month before and was free to devote all efforts to his management career. He printed cards announcing himself as "Jack Bernstein Management" and signed a contract with the same answering service used by Bill Graham when he started out. At least, that's what the service told him.

It was the night before the Fourth of July 1969, the Thursday before a three-day holiday. Anyone able to leave town had done so, and the streets of Manhattan and Queens were deserted. None of this meant anything to Bill Graham, who could fill the Fillmore East any night of the year. Bernstein and Jennifer were driving home after a bill headlined by Jeff Beck, the British guitarist greatly admired by Bernstein and Ed Stern. The opening act was Jethro Tull, another English group featuring the intense Ian Anderson, who sang and played flute, often while standing on one leg. Bernstein was in awe of him. There weren't many rock stars who made it on the strength of their flute playing.

Bernstein considered Queens Boulevard "the Broadway of Queens," notwithstanding Queens had a Broadway running through densely populated Jackson Heights and Astoria. That Broadway had none of the charm, legend, or excitement of the real Broadway in Manhattan, so Bernstein designated Queens Boulevard as his Broadway, the Champs-Élysées of the borough of Queens. One could live their entire life along the Boulevard and never need to leave. Its five or six miles were lined with apartments, groceries, medical clinics, schools, houses of worship, restaurants, appliance stores, accountants, and what Bernstein deemed the crown jewel of Queens—the White Castle drive-in.

White Castle served hamburgers slightly larger than a silver-dollar pancake. Anyone in the grips of the "marijuana munchies" or "hash hungries" would find succor at the Castle, open twenty-four hours, suitable for any size hunger or budget. The Castle was ideal for those occasions when one was too stoned to want to leave the car. Bernstein was usually satiated with three burgers, a cardboard box of onion rings, and a soft drink. Ed Stern, thin as he looked, could down a half dozen of the square patties in their soft buns, topped with chopped onions and a slice of pickle, then order a half dozen more. Many were the nights Bernstein and his friends pulled into a spot and gave their orders to the attractive young ladies, known as "carhops," who sometimes roller-skated to the car windows. They would be certain to ogle the carhop's legs and comment on them. Sometimes they'd munch and sip on the way home, other times, they devoured their orders in the car while listening to the radio or tape deck. Barry Tarpol, his friend since grade school, became friendly with one of the carhops over the course of many visits and eventually wound up in a strange relationship where she would drop by his basement after her shift ended at midnight. Barry's basement was in his parents' home and was more comfortable than Bernstein's, having a separate door to the street and air conditioning. Barry had been granted exclusive control of the basement of the large family home in Bayside as a consolation prize for not being sent to an out-of-town college. Any member of his little crowd could pop in and out at any time, so long as Barry was awake or could be awakened. After Barry and she tired of each other, Bernstein met her at a party when Jennifer was at home dealing with her monthly visitor, and they wound up spending the night in his basement apartment. When he told Barry, his friend laughed.

"She must really like basements," he said.

JENNIFER HAD no interest in a quick stop at the Castle, so Bernstein passed it, enjoying the empty stretch of Queens Boulevard. At that time of night, drivers hitting the right stride with the metered lights would cruise along as if on a freeway. He approached a Queens treasure, Sunnyside Gardens, once a renowned boxing arena whose best years were behind it. Bernstein remembered watching boxing matches on television fought just a few miles from home. His father told him they used to hold the Golden Gloves matches there. The fights with the big names were now all at Madison Square Garden, and Sunnyside Garden's current fame was on account of the big clock out front.

The Volvo sailed through one green light after another, but Bernstein pressed down on the brakes when saw a double-parked car, hazard lights blinking. As he drew closer, he saw a tall man standing by the driver's door and waving his hands. Bernstein pulled up ten feet behind the car.

"Let me see what this guy wants," Bernstein told Jennifer.

"Do you think it's safe?" she asked. "We're on a dark street in the dead of night."

"There's streetlights, and it's not like no one ever drives by. Besides, look in the back seat. A guitar." The upper part of a guitar case was barely visible. "Anyone with a guitar must be all right." He left the car with the engine running.

"What seems to be the problem?" Bernstein asked the tall man, who stood over six feet, dressed in worn jeans and a short-sleeved white shirt. He wore his black hair like Elvis Presley, slicked back and held in place by some sort of gel; Bernstein could see the shine of it under the streetlights. He was too thin to pass for Elvis, but that was what the hair suggested.

"My heap just stalled out on me and won't start. My battery's died on me a whole bunch of times lately. I was hoping for someone to come along and give me another jump. Just enough to get me going." The man spoke slowly and with a deep Southern accent. Bernstein scanned the car. There was enough illumination from the streetlight and the Volvo's headlights to show the butter-yellow color. A dog stretched out on the back seat, lifting his head.

"Caddie?" Bernstein asked.

"Sure is," the man replied. "Fifty-nine. Bought it last year with a hundred thousand miles on it. Put on another twenty-five since."

"That's a lot of driving," Bernstein said. "If you have the cable, I've got the jump."

The tall man smiled and extended a hand. "Eddie Wayburn out of Marvin, Tennessee, but everyone outside my state calls me Tennessee Eddie. Wandering musician and perpetual tourist. That's Fred," he added, tilting his head in the dog's direction.

Bernstein shook Eddie's hand. "Jack Bernstein, and that's my girlfriend Jennifer in the car. I manage musicians, and this has to be the craziest introduction ever."

"Well, Mr. Bernstein, if you can manage us out of this mess, you may have first rights to Tennessee Eddie."

"Get your cables," Bernstein said.

THE JUMP WOULDN'T WORK. Bernstein knew his battery was fine since he had just paid good money for it at Sears, and everyone knew Sears made the best batteries. Tennessee Eddie stood hunched under the hood while Bernstein turned the ignition key, and a timid whine of three-seconds signaled the death of the battery. After several tries, they gave up. Bernstein told Eddie to wait a minute while he walked back to the Volvo. He got behind the driver's seat and told Jennifer his idea.

"That clunker isn't going anywhere without a new battery, and I doubt we're going to be able to get one at this hour."

"Why not?" Jennifer asked. "There's an all-night gas station farther down, maybe a five-minute ride at most. Why can't we drop him off there and let them handle it?"

Smarter than I figured, Bernstein thought. He went straight to the point.

"I saw some paperwork when I was sitting in his car. This guy's been hanging around at all the places you want to be if you're going to make it. Maybe showing up for open mic nights, perhaps just listening to what working musicians are up to, or just trying to get his face known to other musicians." Bernstein had seen matchbooks, napkins, and receipts from Max's Kansas City, The Gaslight Cafe, Gerde's Folk City, and several venues Bernstein didn't recognize, most likely very new or very short-lived. Perhaps both. The lifespans of clubs mirrored those of the artists. Some came and went with a good memory or two, others survived the tempestuous winds of change in the music industry.

"And?" Jennifer asked.

"This could be fate. Coming home from a concert, I meet a struggling artist who's good enough to play in the name spots in the city."

"What makes you so sure he's ever played in the city?"

"Why would he be lugging his guitar with him?"

"Probably open mic night."

Bernstein squeezed her hand. "I know you're trying to watch out for me, but trust me, it's a small world out there. An artist makes a fool of himself at one place, not much chance they let them get on the stage anywhere else. It's true even for open mic night. Last thing a club owner wants is people bitching the music isn't good. Good musicians line up to play for free at these places. I'd bet this fellow has something. A sharp manager figures that out and gets the clubs to start paying. A little at first, but the idea is to get them used to paying for the music. I'd bet anything he's halfway there at least. If he can keep getting attention at these open mic nights, or whatever he's doing to make himself known, it's only a matter of time until someone signs him. I just can't let him disappear into the night. I have a feeling about this guy. Something about his personality and the way he looks. He's coming home with me. If it turns out I'm wrong, so what? I helped out a struggling musician."

Jennifer was silent for a moment.

"So, you're telling me we won't be spending the night together because this total stranger is staying with you?"

"In a manner of speaking, yes," he replied. "Just this one time. How often does something like this happen?"

Jennifer squeezed his hand. "Just this once, okay? But I never want to be second to your dreams."

"Never, Jenn. Never. You can count on that."

AFTER BERNSTEIN and Tennessee Eddie pushed the Cadillac into a legal space—fortunately the next day was a holiday—the musician climbed into the back seat with his guitar and dog. Bernstein helped him empty the trunk of a large duffle bag and Fred's food and bowls for the next day, placing them in the Volvo's trunk. The sound of Jennifer's AM station filled the Volvo. She turned the volume up so loud that conversation would have meant shouting, so no one said a word until they dropped Jennifer off. Eddie bade her a good night. She smiled and returned his greeting but said nothing to Bernstein.

MRS. BARDONI the landlady was sound asleep by the time Bernstein and Eddie arrived. That was good because two of the many prohibitions she insisted upon were overnight guests of more than one night and pets.

"That sofa pulls out into a bed," Bernstein explained. Somebody's aunt was getting rid of it when Bernstein moved in, and he took it. The sofa bed proved handy when Barry or another friend was too tired or stoned to leave. Eddie had no problem pulling out the mattress while Bernstein grabbed bedding from a closet. Fred lay silently next to a bowl of water. Eddie assured him his dog wasn't much of a barker. "Hound dog, but he ain't noisy," Eddie said.

"Hope I didn't cause you any problems with your young lady," Eddie said after he had made his bed.

"Not at all," Bernstein said, thinking Jennifer's failure to kiss him goodnight wasn't a sign she was angry but merely a flesh wound in the war of the sexes.

Bernstein remembered he had two beers in the refrigerator. They weren't hard to find, as there was nothing else inside except for a small container of milk. Bernstein opened the bottles and handed one to Eddie. On impulse, he asked if Eddie would care for a joint as a chaser. The musician laughed and said of course.

They sat on the couch bed, alternating between slugs of beer and tokes of grass. Bernstein learned that the town of Marvin, Tennessee had no more than a thousand people and was miles from anywhere, which was why, with his parents' permission, Eddie joined the Air Force at seventeen. He spent his four years servicing cargo planes in Texas. "Did get myself a GED, which made my momma proud," he said. He learned guitar from fellow service members and discovered he had a talent for playing and singing. When he received his honorable discharge, he hit the road with his dog and his guitar and had been on it ever since. "Three years last month," he said. "On my second vehicle. First was a fifty-three Caddie. Traded it in when I bought this baby."

"Can you play me a song?" Bernstein asked.

"Won't I wake up your landlord and get us all tossed out?"

Bernstein explained her bedroom was on the second floor, and they were in the basement. He wasn't worried at all about her daughter, Anna. Six months ago, Bernstein returned home a day early from an out-of-town trip, and when he arrived, he discovered Anna and a neighborhood guy *in pari delicto*. Bernstein said nothing, left, and when he returned a half hour later the basement apartment was empty, the bed made, and a note on the pillow read "thank you." He told Eddie it was all right, and the Tennessean opened the black hardshell case.

Eddie's guitar was a Gibson Hummingbird, the model used by Keith Richards and the late Brian Jones on several Rolling Stones albums. It had that beautiful sunburst finish, but there were several small dings around the body. Not unusual for musicians, especially on the road. It had nothing to do with how the instrument sounded.

"Got this at a pawn shop in Chattanooga," he told Bernstein. "Paid a luthier ten bucks to set it up so it plays like new."

"What are you going to play for me?" Bernstein asked.

Tennessee Eddie thought while he tuned his guitar.

"I got a song I learned off the newest Dylan album," he said, referring to *Nashville Skyline*, which had been released a few months before. "'I Threw It All Away.'"

Eddie strummed softly, picking a short riff every now and then. He captured the remorse and regret of the song, but seasoned it with a touch of anger, presumably at himself for letting go of the perfect woman. Eddie captured the spirit of the Dylan version but made it a different song with his own take on the lyrics. Eddie's voice was a steady tenor, tinged with the accent of his native Tennessee countryside. Bernstein saw something very important to a manager— Eddie loved playing and singing. He was anything but arrogant, but he knew he was good. Bernstein had worked with enough musicians to learn that a pleasant and easygoing manner usually meant a better working relationship, but more importantly, it was a strong indicator of the kind of stage presence audiences liked. Beneath the laid-back Southern demeanor, Bernstein sensed a very ambitious man.

When Eddie was done, Bernstein applauded lightly so as not to wake up Mrs. Bardoni. He struggled to restrain his hands from clapping faster and louder.

"That was mind blowing," he told Eddie. *All he needs is the right manager*, Bernstein thought, and he did not believe he was the only one who would realize this. Most young artists are oblivious to the business side of the music industry, and even the most talented need a smart manager to guide their career and protect them against record labels and concert promoters looking to cheat them. Eddie struck Bernstein as just such an artist.

"Why don't you and your lady come see me next time I play?" Eddie asked. "I'll dedicate a song to you two. Just let me know in advance so I make sure I know the chords."

"I want to be there as your manager," Bernstein replied.

∼

EDDIE DIDN'T HAVE A MANAGER. He didn't have other critical things either, like a place to stay or a dollar in the bank. He explained this to Bernstein over breakfast the following morning.

"What I basically got is my guitar, my Caddie, Fred here, and a few changes of clothing. Oh yeah, I also got a hat to pass around."

They were seated in a booth at the Island Diner. The Long Island Expressway and its service road, Horace Harding Boulevard, lay to Bernstein's right, the diner's counter to his left. Bernstein studied Bob, the short order cook, as he juggled the various orders on a huge griddle, stirring scrambled eggs and grilling cheese sandwiches, pancakes, and burgers while waving his arms, spatula in one hand, scraper in the other. He was Toscanini in an apron. The Island was a hop, skip, and jump from the Queens College campus, and Bernstein had spent as much time there as in class. He continued frequenting the place after graduation, more because of Bob than the cuisine. If food was the issue, the place to go was the Blue Bay Diner, minutes away. The food at the Island wasn't bad, but it was limited to basic diner food—eggs, sandwiches, burgers. The Blue Bay offered such exotic dishes as baked sole, grilled lamb chops, even eggplant Parmesan and lasagna. The problem with the Blue Bay was that Bernstein had twice encountered an ex-girlfriend there in the past year. One time, she was with her current boyfriend, and he was alone, the other when she was alone, and Bernstein was with Jennifer. Jenn didn't like Bernstein seeing the ex, even though they had broken up a year before they met, so to play it safe, the Island was his go-to greasy spoon. Bob compensated for it all.

The Island Diner was open all day, every day, Fourth of July included. Fortunately, so was the gas station a few blocks away, and they just happened to have the very battery Eddie's Caddie needed. It was a used but fully recharged battery pulled from a wreck, and it could be returned within a week if it died out. Bernstein handed the attendant a five-dollar bill, and Eddie carried it to the Volvo's trunk, where it sat while Bernstein and Eddie were in the diner.

Bernstein and Tennessee Eddie were waiting for Marnie, the waitress, to bring their breakfast. She spoke with a deep German accent, and many Queens College students believed the rumor she had been a Nazi war criminal who worked in a concentration camp. Bernstein believed this was due to a genuine Nazi war criminal being discovered living in Queens just a few years ago, a woman named Hermine Braunsteiner Ryan. She was married to an unaware American citizen and lied about her past to get a green card and citizenship. Bernstein never believed for a second Marnie was a Nazi or a criminal. He figured after the government discovered Braunsteiner, they checked out every other German woman immigrant. Besides, she had once asked Bernstein to drop by her place after work, and a real Nazi would never seek out sex with a Jew, not even one at least twenty years younger.

"Do we really need a contract?" Eddie asked. "Where I come from, a man's word is good enough or it isn't. No piece of paper makes it good, and we seal everything with a handshake."

"Believe me, Eddie, right now, we're not where you come from. A manager who can't produce a contract won't see the light of day from a club owner, promoter, or record label. You may not think contracts really make all that big a difference, and I sort of agree, but everyone else in the business wants to see them. That's because nobody trusts each other, and for good reason."

Eddie looked down into the coffee he had toyed with while waiting for his food.

"I guess so," he said, but he didn't look very happy.

Chapter Four

Walter Blickner wasn't in his office when Bernstein arrived. Dan Picarelli, the criminal lawyer who shared the cramped space with Walter, explained Walter had a house closing a few hours earlier and was probably stuck there.

"People always come up with some bullshit to fight over at a house closing," Picarelli said. "That's why I prefer criminal law. That's all I do."

Bernstein was surprised to hear this. Walter had told him his experience as a prosecutor was of little value in Queens because there just wasn't enough crime. "Good thing state law requires an attorney at every house closing," Walter once told Bernstein. "It's the full employment law for New York attorneys."

"Is it hard to make it just with criminal?" Bernstein asked Picarelli. *How much crime can there be? Don't people live here to get away from crime?*

"South Jamaica, buddy. There's a lot of business for a White lawyer who can put up with the yoms."

Bernstein stiffened. He had enough familiarity with Italian American culture to know their derogatory term for Black people.

"That's assuming they want to deal with a wop like you," Bernstein said. He didn't like using ethnic slurs, but sometimes it was necessary to make a point.

Picarelli snorted a laugh.

"Don't think it doesn't come up every now and then. Just yesterday I quoted some yom drug dealer a fee, and he looks at me and says, 'For that money, I can get me a Jewish lawyer.'"

"Wow, that sounds like a bummer," Bernstein said, not certain if Picarelli was being straight with him. "What did you do?"

"What did I do?" Picarelli asked. "I dialed this phone here," he said, pointing to a black phone sitting on the desk to his right. "Called my best friend, Rick Hymowitz, who went to law school with me and Walter. He's doing real well. Has a nice little setup over on Queens Boulevard, right across from the courts, a few doors down from Pastrami King. I ask him if he wants a drug case with a good fee, and of course he says, 'Sure, what do I have to do?' And I tell him, 'put on your yarmulke.' He sent me a nice referral fee."

"How ecumenical," Bernstein said.

"Hey, guy, I'm all for that ecumenical stuff. You know, back in sixty-five, Pope John the Twenty-Third finally got around to saying the Jews didn't do anything and stop hating them. About time, you know? Anyways, Rick's the best."

What's with these greaseballs and Jews? Bernstein thought.

Walter returned from his closing and went over the contract between Bernstein and Eddie. It provided for the standard 10 percent of all sales and concerts and carried a steep penalty, should either terminate without good cause, in the form of a five-thousand-dollar payment to the aggrieved party.

"Really protects you if he screws you in any way," Walter explained. "Unlikely he would sue you if you dropped him. If he's any good, someone will grab him, and if he sucks, he can't claim he lost anything."

Bernstein nodded but added, "If you ever met Tennessee Eddie, screwing his smart Jewish manager is not likely to occur."

Walter handed him three copies of the contract in a manila folder. "Then this provision will never be tested," Walter said.

~

EDDIE SIGNED the contract after Bernstein reminded him twice. It wasn't hard for Bernstein to locate his client, who was still living in his basement and sleeping on the sofa bed. When they were both up and around, Bernstein kept the television, radio, or stereo on so Mrs. Bardoni couldn't tell someone was living with him.

As Eddie's stay grew longer, Bernstein and Jennifer had to plan ahead to enjoy sex. Eddie occasionally spent the night away, if he met a like-minded young lady. When he was able to get word to Bernstein, Jennifer spent the night. Other times, they suffered the indignity of the worn and dingy Mets Motel on the industrial stretch of Queens Boulevard.

Bernstein wasted no time putting Tennessee Eddie in front of audiences. He was confident the big venues in the city would eventually pay once Eddie built a name and following. Bernstein believed in a secretive pathway to success based on access to exclusive pipelines and connections. If a manager persuaded one club to hire their artist, other clubs suddenly did the same. Bernstein knew a manager must carefully develop their talents. Making it through one or two songs on open mic night was very different from playing a full set, but it was ideal preparation.

Bernstein passed hours at the main branch of the Queens Library on Main Street, Flushing, poring through the Queens and Nassau Yellow Pages and the entertainment section of every newspaper the library carried, looking for new venues. He visited Queens College, where he perused the campus newspapers—*The Phoenix*, the alternative *News Project*, even the fraternity and house plan newspapers. House plans were a more democratic alternative to fraternities, as they accepted almost anyone. They yielded a few additional coffee shops and tiny clubs. Whenever Bernstein found a new venue, he updated his blue spiral notebook in meticulous detail. Without the advantages of backstage concert passes to help keep him in the loop and quickly gather intelligence, Bernstein was forced to do his own legwork and create his own version of insider information.

If he couldn't reach a place by phone, he drove there. Sometimes he managed to speak to someone with authority to book. Bernstein knew if he could tell them Eddie had played open mic nights at Max's and Gerde's, it would catch their attention, and it often did. Other times, he was summarily dismissed. The blue notebook grew into a compendium with tenfold the entries it had before. Each entry contained the names and numbers of the right person to call, what each club wanted, and Bernstein's appraisal of the place.

Whenever Eddie landed a gig, no matter how small or obscure the venue, Bernstein prepared a flier with the help of an old friend with a BA in art who was always willing to spend a half hour drawing up an ad in exchange for a few joints and the implied promise of an album cover. Bernstein tacked the fliers onto as many telephone poles, laundromat bulletin boards, and coffee shops as he could find, and on every college campus in Queens and Nassau. The Volvo piled on the miles, and every time the choke faltered, Bernstein suffered a mild anxiety attack.

The fees weren't much, but they allowed Eddie to put gas in his car and feed his dog. Bernstein's share helped delay the inevitable depletion of his bank account, but not more. There wasn't time to waste on lesser talents for the pittances they might bring. The road to success was with Eddie. Fred was staying with Barry until Eddie was settled into a place that allowed pets. Bernstein couldn't risk Mrs. Bardoni knowing there was a dog on the premises. Barry's parents permitted their son to do anything legal, so long as he stayed in college, where he had been for the past five years and at least two more in sight. Eddie drove over to see Fred at least once a day, often taking him for long walks in Cunningham Park.

"Good luck with him, Jack, but I think he's weird," Barry said about Eddie. "Can't put my finger on it though."

Bernstein invariably picked up the tab at the Island or White Castle, and they drank coffee by the gallon in the basement. Bernstein saw it as an investment at first, but as time passed, he came to believe that he and Eddie had a relationship beyond manager and artist. Eddie's own words confirmed this to Bernstein.

"Jack, you're doing just great as my manager, but you're doing just as good as my friend. My best friend. Actually, may I call you my brother? I had a brother, named Henry. Two years older than me. Back in the small town I come from, family is everything, and me and Henry were real close. We did everything together. Fishing, tossing baseballs and footballs, later on, fixing up cars. He was my older brother, and he was always watching out for me, making sure no one gave me a bad time and that I didn't go off and get myself in trouble. I could always talk to him about anything. When Henry turned eighteen, back in sixty-two, he enlisted in the army. Two years later he was killed in Vietnam."

"I'm sorry to hear that," Bernstein said. "You must miss him."

"Every day of my life," Eddie said. "I think he's still looking out for me, Jack. I think he set it up so I met you. You're my brother now. You treat me like a brother. I feel I can talk to you just like I talked to Henry. Can't be just the money you're hoping we make, brother. You know, most times it never happens. You're treating me like family."

Bernstein was moved by Eddie's unburdening himself.

"In this business, we don't get a lot of artists liking us as people," he explained. "I'm honored to have you as my friend."

"I haven't discussed Henry with anyone since he died, not even my family back home." Eddie's eyes glistened with the moisture of tears he held back. "I probably enlisted because he did. Army never sent me overseas."

"Anytime," Bernstein said.

"And I know this is causing you a lot of problems with your lady, and I really feel terrible about it. The day you tell me to go, I'm gone."

"Don't even think about that," Bernstein replied. "You're causing me no problems at all." *Aside from it being hard to get laid these days.*

Eddie's guitar playing and singing improved rapidly. "Working and practicing regularly can do that," Bernstein told him. He encouraged Eddie to write more songs. "That's the trend," he counseled. "You won't go far doing only covers."

Practice presented a logistical problem. There was no prohibition of acoustic guitar among Mrs. Bardoni's rules, but loud noise was banned. Eddie could strum his guitar or fingerpick softly and sing if he wasn't loud. Stern was generous in allowing Tennessee Eddie to practice often in the soundproofed studio he built in an extra room at home. Sometimes they played together, Stern's short melodic riffs enhancing Eddie's strumming. Eddie would occasionally fingerpick a melody, in which case Stern would strum chords.

"He's really good," Stern told Bernstein one afternoon when he paid a surprise visit to the basement when Eddie was out. "My only complaint is that we have the same name, and that would drive people crazy. When I do his studio guitar work, I'm Ed and he's Eddie. Jack, you've gotten your hands on the real thing. Don't forget me when you're rich."

Bernstein smiled. He knew Ed had no interest in touring, content to be a well-respected and well-paid studio musician. He rarely played live shows but perhaps would make an exception to help Bernstein advance Eddie.

"Ed, I can't make you rich yet, but I can pay you something to appear with him a few times. You're well known, and insiders will realize that if you're willing to play with this guy, he must be worth hearing. Plus, you'll make him sound like a million bucks. When he gets a record deal, you're the studio guy all the way."

"I don't want your money, not for gigging. I'm making good money in the studios, and that's what I like doing. But anytime I'm free to jam with Tennessee Eddie, send him over. It's fun, and I'm helping him become better. I promise that much. And when he gets his first gig in a name place, I'll appear with him that one time. Only because it's you."

"I'll drink to that, except I really don't like drinking. How about I roll a big fat one in honor of that promise?"

"Sprinkle in a little hashish if you have any."

WHEN BERNSTEIN TOLD TENNESSEE EDDIE that Stern would play at least one gig with him, Eddie was exuberant.

"I heard that name a few times when I was bumming around the city on my own," he told Bernstein. "I was impressed to learn you and Ed Stern were close. He's helping me because of you. Same reason Barry takes care of my dog. I owe you more each day."

"Brother, when you hit the big time, I'll be right there with you," Bernstein said.

May it be sooner rather than later.

Chapter 5
Mid-January, 1970

Bernstein was pleased with his management of Tennessee Eddie, especially his telephone strategy. Since most clubs in Manhattan knew Tennessee Eddie from the open mic nights, auditions weren't necessary. The clubs wanted to make sure he wasn't a flash in the pan who had one good night. Regular gigging, including venues outside the city, increased the odds of being taken seriously and paid to play in the Big Time. After several months of appearing before small audiences—Bernstein preferred the term "intimate"—and with dozens of hours playing with Stern, there was no question about Tennessee Eddie being ready to gig in Manhattan.

Bernstein traded messages with club answering services, eventually managing to speak with a few where Eddie had played at open mic night. When they heard Eddie was gigging regularly and now had a manager, most were receptive. *Discovering new talent is what they all brag about*, he thought.

"Hey, this is Jack Bernstein calling about booking Tennessee Eddie," he began every call. He knew three out of four music industry people would be afraid to ask who he was, fearing it would make them appear ignorant. He'd remind them Eddie had played at one of their open mic nights.

When asked where Eddie had been gigging, Bernstein knew what to say.

"He's been working with Ed Stern. You know Stern has his home and studio out in Queens, so Eddie's out there a lot to jam and drop by a few clubs and test out his material on a live audience." Dropping Stern's name gained attention.

Bernstein lined up three gigs for Eddie to open for better-known acts—first, Max's Kansas City, then the Bitter End, and then the Gaslight Cafe, all places Eddie had performed for free. He was far down on the bill and low paying, but they were gigs at famous places.

Bernstein was most excited about the Gaslight because of its fabled history. It helped launch the careers of several guitar playing singer-songwriters, including Richie Havens, José Feliciano, Joni Mitchell, Tom Paxton, Eric Anderson, and Carolyn Hester. Eddie would be on the club's promotions and signs as well as in the *Village Voice* and *East Village Other* musical listings. Bernstein's management skills had Tennessee Eddie on the fast track to stardom.

Max's Kansas City, the first of these gigs, hired Tennessee Eddie as an opening act on a Tuesday night bill of four. The booking manager remembered Eddie from open mic, and he liked Bernstein's account of what Eddie had done since. He would start at eight o'clock, before the crowds filled the room. Bernstein couldn't do much about that except to call every A&R person, rock journalist, and the few B-list acts he knew. Stern invited several musicians and engineers, hoping for a positive buzz in the industry. A paid gig was important for more than money. The people who can make or break a new act don't come out for open mic nights; they trusted the clubs to do the first level of vetting. They would be there for a night with a headliner. Bernstein hoped they showed up early when opening acts played.

～

TENNESSEE EDDIE WOULD PERFORM four songs. "I Threw it All Away" was an absolute must as was his rendition of the blues classic "You Got to Move," one of Bernstein's favorites. It was first recorded by the Reverend Gary Davis in 1962, and three years later by another great bluesman, Mississippi Fred McDowell, who played it on slide guitar as did Eddie. Bernstein initially pigeonholed Eddie as country or country rock, but he was more than adept at blues and especially gospel-oriented numbers. When Bernstein mentioned this to Eddie, he laughed and explained, "I lived my whole life in the South, got the accent, went to church every Sunday. What's the big surprise?" The third song was his own, titled "A Rainy Day in Memphis," a sad country ballad about a man who lost his job, his wife, his car, and his dog—everything but his guitar. Eddie's songwriting needed some improvement, but with his voice and Stern's leads, Bernstein felt no one would care.

They filled out the playlist with "Expecting to Fly," a haunting folk-rock number composed by Neil Young when he was with Buffalo Springfield. Their album version was lushly orchestrated with strings and woodwinds, but Tennessee Eddie and Stern played a stripped-down rendition. Eddie strummed the chords and picked the opening notes on his Hummingbird, while Stern's tasteful and soft melody lines filled in when Eddie wasn't singing. Eddie's tenor was a few octaves deeper than Young's semi-soprano and sounded better to Bernstein.

BERNSTEIN AND EDDIE picked up Stern at his home the night of the gig. Stern carried his Stratocaster in its hardshell case. Bernstein knew at Max's, Stern would remove the instrument from the case and not allow it out of his hands until they departed. Both knew how many musicians lost their instruments to thieves who managed to get near the stage, waiting for an opportunity to grab a guitar or bass and make their way to the nearest pawnshop or street corner to trade the instrument for quick cash or drugs.

The music director at Max's Kansas City recognized Eddie from the open mic nights and cheerfully ushered them backstage. He offered a small room for privacy, which Bernstein suspected was for snorting cocaine. Bernstein and Stern were extremely infrequent users of the white powder, preferring the milder and more controllable marijuana high. Tennessee Eddie wouldn't even smoke weed before a performance.

Bernstein preferred mixing with the cognoscente when he had the opportunity. He remained in the large backstage area while Stern and Tennessee Eddie prepared for the moment of glory.

Lou Reed of The Velvet Underground, a favorite of Bernstein, stood off to one side, in animated conversation with a tall, vaguely familiar Black man. Bernstein's mind scanned the countless album covers in his memory bank, and the name Richie Havens emerged. Bernstein had no idea those two knew each other, but then again, why would he? Bernstein knew little about professional relationships beyond the borders of his Long Island fiefdom.

A few minutes before eight, the manager tapped Bernstein on the shoulder.

"Your boy's up now," he said.

Bernstein looked at Eddie, fine-tuning his guitar a few yards away, and nodded. Eddie turned the last peg and walked onstage. Bernstein sat to the side of the stage in a chair reserved for him as Eddie's manager. *Never dreamed I'd be here so soon.*

Max's was at two-thirds capacity at least, far more than Bernstein predicted. He knew there was a back room where only the most privileged upper crust of rock and roll were permitted entry, and he had no idea how many ventured out. Scanning the audience at tables and standing, he spotted Lester Bangs and Robert Christgau, two of the best-known rock writers in America, seated together. Lou Reed was still deep in conversation with Richie Havens. Bernstein wondered if they would watch Eddie, though they would certainly hear him. Ed Stern told Bernstein that at Max's, the high and mighty were often seen in the company of ordinary human beings. Perhaps one of them would decide to strike up a conversation with him. *This is what they mean by a big opportunity.*

Seeing established stars trod the same ground as he and Eddie made Bernstein feel relaxed, and his confidence rose as he watched the scene around him. People were dressed in every conceivable fashion: men in tuxedos and women wearing evening gowns, stalwart members of the remaining hippies of the East Village, lawyers and stockbrokers in custom-tailored suits, even a few who looked like street people who slept in Tompkins Square Park in the spring and who knew where to stay warm in this cold time of year. *They could be eccentric stars*, Bernstein thought.

When the master of ceremonies announced Eddie, Bernstein took a deep breath and exhaled slowly as if breathing out too quickly might bring bad luck. *Showtime.* The atmosphere of Max's Kansas City put him as much at ease as he ever imagined he could be at such a moment. Bernstein struggled to think of a word that described the ambiance. *Welcoming*, he decided, but knowing how much was on the line, he remained nervous.

Eddie's opening song was "You Got to Move." Bernstein didn't want him to start with the Dylan or Neil Young songs; he didn't want the first number to create the perception of one more clone. Bernstein didn't think Eddie's own song, "A Rainy Day in Memphis," was strong enough to open, but would resonate well as the third song. Bernstein was certain, once the crowd warmed up to Eddie, they would accept his interpretations of other artist's work.

Eddie appeared solo for the opening number; Bernstein wanted him to display his slide guitar and establish him with the audience as a serious musician. Stern would accompany him for the remainder of the set. On the final number, Eddie's interpretation of "Expecting to Fly," a bass player and drummer would join them. Stern knew both musicians, who agreed to play the set for twenty dollars each, more than Bernstein was making. He was losing money on this gig, but couldn't imagine a better investment. His return was going to be enormous.

Eddie walked on stage and stood in front of the microphones. One was set high for his voice, the other set lower to amplify his acoustic guitar. He strummed the Hummingbird softly, while he spoke in his Tennessee drawl.

"Hello, my name is Eddie Wayburn out of Marvin, Tennessee. My friends call me Tennessee Eddie. Some of my enemies call me that, too." Bernstein saw smiles on the faces of at least half the audience. He was unsure what it meant. *Are they laughing with him or at him?* Bernstein was worried it was the latter.

"My first number was written a few years back and recorded by some great bluesmen, Reverend Gary Davis and Mississippi Fred McDowell. I love singing this song 'cause it gives me a chance to pay my respects to two guys whose spirits helped bring me to this stage tonight. Also gives me a chance to show off my slide guitar."

More soft laughter flowed through Max's Kansas City. Bernstein caught Robert Christgau and Lester Bangs seated across the stage nodding in synch in a most serious way. Bernstein had been around long enough to know what music critics love, which ones know the bluesmen and regularly pay them tribute in their writings and gaining fans for the artists. Their approval worked wonders for the Yardbirds, Clapton, and the Stones. *Maybe they're looking for someone who doesn't show up with a Stratocaster and plays blues the old-fashioned way.* Bernstein no longer felt the earlier touch of trepidation.

A few chairs away sat Danny Goldstein, who Bernstein knew from Queens College. Danny had been the star of the Queens College radio station, hosting a rock show several times a week. Danny was as good a deejay as anyone in the newly emerging FM galaxy. Stern had once mentioned Danny hosted a show on a station in Westchester County. If all went well with Tennessee Eddie's performance, he would make contact with Danny the next day. *First my guy has to do well tonight.*

The resonating sound of Tennessee Eddie's slide guitar filled the room. Diners set down their knives and forks and listened. Eddie's emotive tenor played against the drawn-out slide notes, and when he flat-picked between verses, it was as if there was a second acoustic guitarist in the wings. When he finished, the place broke out in applause. The rock writers and the A&R men had their eyes fixed on the stage. Bernstein's eyes were fixed on them. *He's really good, and everyone here sees it. My plan is working.*

When the applause ended, Eddie told the audience that "famous guitarist Ed Stern" was joining him for the rest of his set. Stern came on, Strat in hand, and he strapped on the guitar and plugged into the amplifier as the audience applauded. Ed Stern was well known to industry professionals, and everyone else wanted to look like they were in the know.

"Here's a beautiful Bob Dylan number off his latest album," Eddie announced. The room grew quiet, and he began strumming the chords of "I Threw It All Away" as Stern played a soft melody line. When Eddie sang, Stern's leads filled the gaps between verses. Bernstein's eyes stayed on Eddie, aside from a few quick glances at the audience. When the song ended, the audience remained still for a few seconds, until a man's voice called out, "You did it better than Dylan!" When the entire room broke out in applause, Bernstein felt as if he had just smoked a joint of the best Panamanian Red on the planet.

When the room was quiet again, Eddie said, "No, Dylan is Dylan, and there ain't no other. I'm Tennessee Eddie Wayburn. Proud to be." The audience applauded again.

This is what they mean by having them eating out of your hand, Bernstein thought.

"Now, for a song yours truly wrote, like the title says, one rainy night in Memphis, sitting in a fleabag hotel with nothing but half a bottle of Tennessee sour mash and my guitar."

"A Rainy Night in Memphis" was not in the same league as the blues number and the Dylan song, but the audience didn't care. It wasn't a bad song, but Tennessee Eddie wasn't a songwriter in the same league as Bob Dylan, and the song lacked the raw power of the opening blues number. Eddie's composition conformed to the basic rules of country song—a story, preferably sad, a very relatable central figure, a broken heart or promise, or just being broke, but George Jones had nothing to worry about. *Not yet anyhow.* It didn't matter. Stern's guitar more than compensated, and the audience adored Tennessee Eddie. Had he stood up and read from the Manhattan phone book, they would have gone wild. They applauded even more for this song than the others. *Go figure,* Bernstein thought.

I knew he was a country boy from the minute I laid eyes on him, Bernstein thought. *That's really who he is, through and through. When he says we're brothers, he means it.*

During the applause, the bass player and drummer came onstage. The drums were already set up as far to the end of the stage as possible, a simple kit consisting of snare, bass, and small and large tom-toms.

"I haven't made it out to Los Angeles yet, but God willing, that's on the agenda," Eddie told the audience. "Because I wanna play in that

Whiskey a Go Go and The Troubadour, where so many bands I admire became known. One of the best was Buffalo Springfield. Here's my last song for tonight, by the great Neil Young, off the *Buffalo Springfield Again* album."

Bernstein thought the original album version of "Expecting to Fly" was creative with its lush production, but it was more string or woodwind arrangement than rock song. Tennessee Eddie's stripped-down version was folk-blues. Stern bent a lot of notes and squeezed out a mournful vibrato as the bass and drums kept a subdued blues rhythm. Eddie sang a melody fully recognizable as the Neil Young song. The audience stood on their feet when the song ended. They called for more, but the rule at Max's was strict—the opening act never got an encore. It might make the bigger acts nervous if they didn't receive the same demand. Eddie asked the audience to thank his band, and they gave them a hearty applause. The four musicians returned backstage. They would enjoy a fifteen-minute break before the next act.

"You crushed them," Stern told Eddie when his Strat was back in its case. "Hit it out of the park."

Eddie blushed. "I couldn't have done it without you guys," he said, sweeping his arms in the direction of the band and Bernstein.

"Oh yes you could," Stern replied.

Bernstein wandered about backstage looking for a knot of people with at least one person he knew. He spotted Stern over in a corner talking with men who looked like a band, especially since one had a guitar strapped around his neck.

"This is my friend Jack Bernstein," Stern told the others. "Lucky bastard manages that incredible talent we just heard. Oh, and Jack, meet the members of Long Pants. Third act tonight. They're recording an album for Epic Records. After that, they're going on a national tour, opening for Grand Funk Railroad and Steppenwolf." They all shook hands like octopi waving their tentacles.

"Next to top billing," Bernstein said. "Pretty damn good at Max's. We'll be hearing from you guys for sure. Give my compliments to your manager."

"If we can find him," the guitarist snapped, his tone a sharp contrast to Ed and Bernstein's exuberance. "Bastard disappeared with the advances from the record company and the down payments on the tour. Turned out IRS is after him for fraud. He's somewhere living well on our dough. Why the hell do you think we're opening for a band no one ever heard of and getting peanuts? Because, just like everyone else, we need to eat." He glared at Bernstein.

"Jack's not that kind of manager," Stern said, with a firmness that replaced his joyfulness.

"Every manager is that kind of manager," the guitarist answered. He feigned spitting when he mentioned a manager the second time.

Ed Stern was having none of this, and leaped to his friend's defense.

"Tennessee Eddie was playing for free until Jack started making him some money, and whatever Jack gets, he puts right back into Eddie's career. Just because you were burned doesn't mean every manager is a crook."

The guitarist looked into Bernstein's eyes and then extended his hand. The two men shook again. He spoke in a softer voice.

"Mr. Stern's right as usual. I'm sorry. I had no cause to insult you. It's just that I'm pissed."

"So am I," Bernstein said. "That manager had no right to steal from you. I'm ashamed to have someone like that in my line of work. I'm sorry there's so many. But I'm not one of them, so here's my card, and when you're ready for a new manager, let me know." He felt bad for the members of Long Pants, knowing as well that thieves like they hired created problems for all managers.

Bernstein felt he had defused the situation and decided it was time to do more mingling. He nodded to the others and started to leave. The guitarist called out to him as he walked away.

"And the bastard even stole my girlfriend. Took her away with him!"

Bernstein waited until the angry guitarist was out of sight.

"That didn't go very well, did it?"

Stern patted him on the shoulder with his free hand. "Don't take it personally, Jack. What do you expect? Guy just lost everything to his last manager. Happens all the time. That's why I'm happy as a studio guy, waiting for calls. Maybe right now, getting a new manager isn't on top of his list of things to do."

"Well, it should be if he wants to keep working."

"Nice if it worked that way," Stern said. "But if musicians were logical, guys like you wouldn't be needed."

Bernstein and Stern made their way back to Tennessee Eddie. He was surrounded by people, some of them musicians and others, men in suits. When Eddie saw Bernstein and Stern, he called them over.

"This is my manager, Jack Bernstein, and the handsome guy over here is my kick-ass guitarist, Mr. Ed Stern. Same first name as me, but he uses the grown-up version."

"We all know Stern," a man in a tight suit said. "Don't believe we've had the pleasure of meeting Mr. Bernstein yet," he said and extended a hand. It was weak and clammy. He gave his name as did the other suits who did so without offering handshakes. The musicians broke off, and Tennessee Eddie and Stern left to join them.

"Are you on the bill often?" a portly fellow in a muted plaid suit asked. Bernstein explained that he mostly worked on the Island, but he and Tennessee Eddie would now be regulars on the Manhattan circuit.

A third suit, a Brooks Brothers classic, older than the other men, weighed in. "You've got to get yourself an address in the city if you want to keep people like this one."

Bernstein smiled at the man. "Appreciate the advice, but I'm not worried about Tennessee Eddie. We're like brothers."

The Brooks Brothers man arched his eyebrows. "Young man, if I had a dollar for every time I heard one of us say something like that, I wouldn't have to be working at this age. Unless you're the Allman Brothers, the Chambers Brothers, or the Righteous Brothers, the term doesn't matter in this business."

Bernstein thanked him for the advice and went back to his friends, who were deep in conversation with the group of musicians. He pointed to his watch, then to their designated seats.

Bernstein and Eddie didn't know any of the next three acts, aside from Long Pants, who they had just met. When the last act finished with the encore that only they were allowed, Bernstein told his friends it was time to leave. He didn't like the men in suits, and Long Pants had brushed him off for now. *As long as the audience likes my guy, the others can all go screw themselves.*

"I'm going to stick around a little longer and hang out with the musicians," Tennessee Eddie said. "I think I earned enough tonight to pay for a cab home." No doubt. The manager handed Bernstein an envelope of cash during the third act. After Bernstein withdrew his ten percent, he gave the envelope to Eddie.

"Leaving's not a bad idea," Stern said. "Mission accomplished. You two can go home in the Volvo. Two producers told me to call them about some studio work. I can afford a cab."

Tennessee Eddie would have none of this.

"Let Jack drive you home, Mr. Stern and then he can go get some sleep himself. He's got things to do during normal business hours. There's nothing going to happen here that two pros like you haven't seen before. Probably gets boring after a while. Me? I'm just a country boy musician, and this is all new to me."

"You played here before," Stern reminded Eddie. "They remembered you from open mic night, and your smart manager used that to get you a paid gig tonight."

"I guess that means I'm officially a professional musician," Eddie said. "It's time I started to get to know some others."

"You're also a little fish swimming among sharks," Stern said. "You don't want to wind up like that guitarist."

Eddie's face froze for a moment. "What are you talking about? I got Jack here to protect me. He's a good guy, like you said. He's my manager, so I ain't worried one bit."

"I'm also worried about Jack," Stern replied. "Those guys in the suits were sizing him up, seeing how much of a fight he would put up."

"Fight over what?" Tennessee Eddie asked.

"Over them stealing away one of his artists," Stern said.

Bernstein placed a hand on Stern's shoulder.

"Come on, Ed. Let's not get carried away. This is like a family."

"Damn right," Eddie looked at Stern, his eyes blazing with anger and more force in his voice than Bernstein had ever seen. "I trust Jack with my career and my money. Like the man said, it's family. We're brothers. I talk to him just like I talked to my brother Henry, rest his soul. I'm sure you mean me no disrespect, and you're just watching out for Jack, who's your brother, too. But back where I come from, people don't take to such comments very well."

"I meant no offense," Stern said. "But in my few years as a studio guy, I've seen it happen again and again. These guys can put all kinds of pressure on the rest of us. They're part of the in-group that runs the music business. They always get what they want, one way or the other. Neither you or Jack would stand a chance against them, at least not right now. Maybe in a few years. Neither of you needs to stick around right now. You've spoken with your music."

"You're thinking they can make me turn my back on Jack, after all he's done for me? I could never show my face again back in Marvin if my townsfolk knew I treated a brother that way." Eddie shook his head to emphasize his rejection of such an idea. "And listen, friends, we'll never get along if everyone is suspicious of each other."

"He's right," Bernstein said. "Let's go. I'll leave the key under the mat," he said to Tennessee Eddie.

"I won't wake you up," Eddie said. He smiled as Bernstein and Stern left the stage. Stern was not smiling.

"You weren't very diplomatic," Bernstein said as they drove over what Manhattan called the 59th Street Bridge, but in Queens was the Queensboro Bridge. The lights of Manhattan twinkled in the Volvo's rearview mirror. The news was on the radio, and the reporter was discussing the police strike, which had started with the swing shift. The city expected up to 85 percent of the officers to call in sick. They would be replaced by other officers, retired cops, and desk-bound career cops who hadn't seen the streets or handled a gun since before the Korean War. It would probably be a good day to be a criminal.

"I'm a studio musician, not a diplomat," Stern replied. "I'm your friend, among the few you have in the industry. So that makes me the one to tell you how it is. And I'm telling you that in this business, there are no friends, no families, no honor, nothing but an endless search for money and power."

"So, what are you saying, Ed? Just say it."

Stern turned down the radio.

"Tennessee Eddie is the kind of talent that doesn't come along very often. If people didn't know it before tonight, they know it now. Those sharks don't earn the money to buy expensive suits by being nice guys. Same with artists. Eddie is a nice guy, but he wants to succeed, and sooner or later he's going to figure out that being a nice guy isn't going to do it. Otherwise, he would've made it by now. Don't think for a minute that you're being so kind and generous to him will matter when it's to his advantage to toss you away like yesterday's newspaper."

Bernstein laughed nervously. "Come on, Ed. The guy knows what I'm doing for him, going above and beyond just being a manager."

"Do you really think that will matter to him if it suits him to think and act otherwise?"

"Ed, I know you're in the business, and you've seen a lot. I've relied on my gut feeling with Eddie since the day we met, and so far, it's working out fine. If I were to cause him to think I don't trust him, then your fears would definitely come true. Can't insult a guy like Tennessee Eddie and not expect him to take it hard. If I were to do that after all we've gone through the past six months, he would be right to be pissed at me. That's why I left."

Stern shook his head while staring straight ahead at the road.

"You gave him his best offer when he was a fresh face trying to break in, playing for free. Now that you've developed him and people know who he is, other offers will come his way."

"I've got a contract," Bernstein said.

"There are music industry lawyers who do nothing all day except shred contracts like yours. The Big Boys spend what it takes and send in as many lawyers as they need. You and Walter would be buried alive in paper."

"It's not something I'm worried about," Bernstein said. He turned up the volume on the radio.

~

BERNSTEIN LAY IN HIS BED, Bob Dylan's *Planet Waves* album on the turntable. "On a Night Like This" flowed through the speakers, soft enough to not be heard beyond the basement. A half-smoked joint sat in the jar-lid ashtray on his nightstand. The clock on his radio said three fifteen in the morning. He'd left the key under the mat, but Eddie hadn't returned yet. He thought about Stern's unadorned assessment, which made him uncomfortable. He allowed himself to be absorbed by the music, which slowly relaxed him until he drifted asleep.

Chapter 6
The Morning After Max's Kansas City

Bernstein's phone rang. He rubbed the sleepiness from his eyes. The clock radio read eight thirty. He grabbed the heavy black receiver, cursing himself for not following through on his promise to get one of those new light and easily movable Princess phones. It was Stern inviting him to breakfast at the Island Diner.

A half hour later, showered, shaved, and gripping a cup of coffee as if it were a life jacket on the high seas, Bernstein sat across a table from Stern. Bob, the short order cook, stood at his station by the griddle, managing the orders like a battlefield general moving troops. It seemed whatever time Bernstein arrived at the diner, Bob was on duty. Did he work around the clock, or was he constantly changing shifts? It was one of many Island Diner mysteries.

Denise, the morning waitress, brought their coffee and took their orders. She was prettier and younger than Marnie, but she was also married. Bernstein dithered for moment and then settled on a bagel with a schmear. A counterman like Bob knew the mystical quantity of cream cheese constituting a schmear. Bernstein described it as a cross between a spoonful, a smear, and a splotch.

"Did he come home?" Stern asked.

"Not as of the time I left," Bernstein replied.

Stern played with his cup. He raised his eyes to meet Bernstein's.

"Get used to the fact he's not coming back other than to pick up whatever he's got at your place. Expect a letter from the shark that nabbed him, telling you he's now in charge of Tennessee Eddie's career."

Bernstein wished he hadn't ordered the bagel. His stomach wanted no visitors at the moment.

"Maybe he met some chick and went back to her place."

Stern laughed. "And maybe the Airplane will decide they don't want Jorma anymore and I get the call."

Bernstein knew Stern idolized Jefferson Airplane guitarist Jorma Kaukonen. Stern also loved that Jorma played in Hot Tuna with Airplane bassist Jack Casady. They didn't limit the sets to only their own numbers, but played all the blues classics, including from old-timers like Jelly Roll Morton, Jimmy Cox, and Blind Willie Johnson. Those were the artists Stern's parents played. Stern embraced their affection as a child and later passed it on to his friend Jack Bernstein.

"So, tell me what to do," Bernstein said. "Obviously I don't have any idea what's going on."

"Have Walter get whatever he can for you out of the sharks," Stern replied. "And don't make the same mistake again."

"How do I do that?"

"Next time you have someone playing in the city, bring along one of those greaser hoods that hang around the clubs to act as your bodyguard. Then the sharks will stay away. They'll be afraid if they mess with you their legs get broken. That's the way half of them operate."

"You really think that would work?" Bernstein asked.

"No," Stern said. "But it would be a hell of a lot of fun."

AFTER BREAKFAST, Stern and Bernstein retreated to the Volvo, where they fired up a joint while listening to the news on WBAI, the leftwing, listener-supported FM Station. They both liked the station because it played real blues, and it had several amazing characters as hosts. He especially liked Bob Fass, who was on air in the early hours of the morning when Bernstein was finishing his workday and driving home. Bernstein hated the Vietnam War, Richard Nixon, and George Wallace, and he felt WBAI was the only media outlet that sufficiently shared his views. This time, Larry Josephson was delivering the morning news, and his leadoff story was about a twenty-seven-year-old army colonel who just seized power in Libya, overthrowing King Idris. Neither Bernstein nor Stern had ever heard of King Idris or the colonel named Gaddafi. They were more interested in Josephson's attack on the ten-cent rise for a subway token to thirty cents. "It should be free!" Josephson railed. Neither Stern nor Bernstein took the subway more than a handful of times a year, but they agreed it was unfair to charge working people more while the subways were growing dirtier, more dangerous, and less reliable. In the summer heat, the cars, lacking air-conditioning, were stroke-inducing.

Mrs. Bardoni eyed Bernstein suspiciously when he passed her in the vestibule. He felt her eyes burrowing into his back as he descended the steps, even after he closed the door behind him. The second he looked over his room, he saw that Eddie's duffel bag was gone as were the few items he had hanging in the one closet.

Bernstein put Van Morrison's *Moondance* album on the turntable and listened to the jazz-oriented fusion sounds as he tried to sort out all that happened to him in less than ten hours. His thoughts were interrupted by his phone. It was Barry.

"Tennessee Eddie just came by and picked up Fred. He said he wouldn't be bringing him back, that he found his own place. So, you have your castle back to yourself?"

Bernstein told him it was a long story and he'd get back to him later on, but right now he had a few things that needed his attention. After hanging up, Bernstein banged his fist on the nightstand so hard it swelled up and he needed to wrap a towel with ice around it for half an hour. While he was icing his hand, he heard a loud knocking on the front door of the house. He heard Mrs. Bardoni ask who it was, and then the front door opened. He made out some conversation, and then came a knock on his own door.

"It's unlocked!" Bernstein yelled. "Come on down!"

The clicking sound of smooth dress shoes filled Bernstein's room as the feet wearing them worked their way down the stairs. They were attached to a man a few years older than Bernstein, dressed in a gray wool suit showing through a flannel-lined, black London Fog raincoat. He carried a thin attaché case.

"You're either a cop or a lawyer," Bernstein said.

"Lawyer," the man replied, handing Bernstein a card. His name was Harold Levine, and he was with a firm with at least six names, none Levine.

"I suppose Tennessee Eddie told you where I live."

"It was my client, Mr. Wayburn's manager, who provided the information," the lawyer said in a flat monotone.

"Can you speak like a normal human being?" Bernstein asked. "You sound like Robbie the Robot." A puzzled look crossed the lawyer's face. *Maybe a few years older than me*, Bernstein thought. *Missed that toy.* Levine didn't respond to the question. "Besides, *I* happen to be Tennessee Eddie's manager."

"Mr. Wayburn has decided upon a change of management," he told Bernstein. "Our law firm has been retained by new management. We've reviewed the contract you had him sign. Our firm has no doubt it would not stand up in court. It's one-sided, unfair, and will not be enforceable. Nevertheless, Mr. Wayburn, as you know, is a man of honor, and in view of the acts of friendship and charity you have afforded him, he would like you to feel well-treated. I have here a settlement agreement and a release for you to review. Get back to me as soon as you can. We can have your check delivered the same day you sign, but our client's generosity will not extend very long. We must move on."

Bernstein stared at the lawyer. He held up the hand wrapped in ice and waved it furiously. "You can shove it up your ass, shyster."

Levine stepped back.

"I'll leave it with you," he said, reaching into his case and taking out a manila envelope.

Bernstein took a step toward him. "If I don't see your ass moving up those steps at the count of three, I'm cutting it off with a butcher knife and feeding it to Fred next time I see him."

Levine snapped his case shut, turned around, and walked up the steps. When he reached the top, he dropped the manila envelope.

"Go over it with your lawyer and get back to me no later than tomorrow night. Otherwise, you get nothing."

Bernstein moved toward the stairs. The lawyer moved quickly through the door, past the vestibule, and into the street. Bernstein saw him run to a cab that must have been waiting for him. Levine looked out the window at Bernstein, who gave him his middle finger.

Chapter Seven

Walter didn't have a secretary, but he had an answering service that always knew his whereabouts. When the service informed Bernstein that Walter was expected back from court no later than eleven, he grabbed the envelope from the floor where Levine had dropped it. A minute later, he was fiddling with the choke of the Volvo, which was in a bad mood. Finally, he found the sweet spot where the mixture of air and gasoline was just right, and the Volvo's engine came alive.

WBAI was playing the latest Peter, Paul and Mary hit, "Leaving on a Jet Plane," and when the song ended, they pitched a free record to the next hundred listeners who donated five dollars or more, courtesy of a wealthy Peter, Paul and Mary fan. Bernstein loved folk music, but the smooth, well-arranged Peter, Paul and Mary style was his least favorite. He was partial to Bob Dylan, Jack Elliot, Judy Collins, Tim Hardin, Joan Baez, Tom Paxton, and Phil Ochs. Just a folksinger and a guitar and maybe a rawer message then from Peter, Paul and Mary. These days, there was less and less folk music, so he satisfied his craving for authentic music by listening to the blues. He shared Stern's adoration of Hot Tuna, who kept alive folk and blues traditions.

But he wasn't driving to Walter Blickner's law office to discuss his music preferences.

~

WALTER SAT HUNCHED over a Smith Corona electric typewriter when Bernstein walked into the office. Walter's wife did most of the typing at home, but if something was urgent Walter did it himself. Bernstein saw Picarelli through the open door of his office. He was talking on the phone and waved to Bernstein.

Walter looked up when he saw Bernstein and asked him to have a seat in the waiting area for five minutes while he finished what he was doing. Picarelli stuck his head through his office door and invited Bernstein in while he waited for Walter. *Why not?* Bernstein figured. *He can only make today better.* Picarelli greeted him warmly, squeezing his shoulders and directing him to sit in a client chair.

"So, how's the music business coming along, Jack? Get to hang out with the Rolling Stones yet? By the way, did I ever tell you my cousin knew Eddie Brigati of the Rascals? Maybe he can talk to Eddie about helping you out some time. You're a good guy. Walter loves you."

"Hey man, if Eddie Brigati wants to know me, give him my card," Bernstein said, handing one to Picarelli.

"Sure will," Picarelli said, putting the card in his desk drawer. "And you know, being in the music business and all, you must run into a lot of guys who get in trouble. Drugs, sex, guns, drunk driving. How about you take one of my cards, and anything like that comes along, you call me. I give little presents to people who do that for me."

"Same here," Bernstein said.

"And you know, Jack, Walter doesn't take criminal cases anymore. Takes just about everything else. You're not screwing a buddy if you send me a criminal case. I'd never expect a guy to do something like that."

Walter called out that he was ready for Bernstein. Moments later, Bernstein was sitting across the desk from Walter, explaining everything that had occurred, from the gig at Max's through the visit by Levine. He handed Walter the envelope, which he himself had not yet opened.

"Go around the corner to the donut shop and have a cup of coffee with Picarelli," he said. "Then when we start talking about this problem, you'll feel like things are getting better."

Picarelli accepted Bernstein's offer to buy him a coffee and tacked a chocolate glazed donut on his order. Bernstein didn't mind. He was worried and angry and needed companionship, even in the form of Picarelli.

"You've got that look of a man in a world of trouble," Picarelli said. "A criminal lawyer knows that look well. Everyone coming into our offices has one. And if you want to tell me, go right ahead. It stays within the attorney-client privilege. I know Walter's your lawyer, and he's a good one. I'm just saying you can talk to me if you need someone, and I'll never say a word to anyone."

Bernstein surprised himself by opening up to Picarelli. He told him exactly what he told Walter.

"Big mistake to trust one of these Southern Protestants," Picarelli declared when Bernstein was finished. "They don't have the kind of honor like Jews and Italians have. Or colored people. My South Jamaican clients are better than any of those redneck assholes."

Which is the act? Bernstein wondered. *This, or the "yom" remark from last time? Can it be both? Is that possible?*

"Whatever it is, I'm in a tough spot. I've spent most of my time working up this one guy, not really building up my artist list because I figured Tennessee Eddie and I were on a fast elevator to the top. Looks like Eddie will be taking the ride with someone else."

The two men sipped their coffees, and Picarelli chewed on his donut while they sat in silence for a half a minute.

"If there's any way to take down these jerks, Walter's the man," Picarelli said. "Don't be fooled by his little office over a pizzeria. A few years from now, he's going to be the top business lawyer in Queens. Big office near the courthouse, or maybe in one of those office buildings in Flushing, on Main Street."

"Maybe he'll rent me some space at a good rate," he said with a smile.

"Good for Walter," Bernstein said.

Picarelli's face flushed slightly red.

"Hey Jack, I didn't mean just Walter and maybe me. You too. You're a real good guy. You and me and Walter, we're all in the same boat. Starting out, taking some lumps…you learn from the mistakes or there's no future. Guys like us learn, so we have futures. When you're done with Walter, you get off your ass and find someone better than Tennessee Eddie. Just no Southerners, no Protestants. Unless they're colored Protestants, of course."

They finished their coffees and walked back to the law offices. Picarelli explained he would grab his briefcase and head off to court for an afternoon hearing, and he wished Bernstein the best.

"Come on by and visit any time you like," he said. "And remember, you run into anyone needing a good criminal lawyer, you call me. I hear of any musicians needing a manager, I give them your number. And I'm asking my cousin to talk to Eddie Brigati." Picarelli went to his office, Bernstein to Walter's.

WALTER EXPLAINED that Eddie's new manager's law firm represented music industry sharks and were known more for intimidation and threats than courtroom litigation.

"So, if we have to go to trial against them, I'm not worried. Trial would be in Queens Supreme Court. I'm a known quantity there. I'm willing to bet no one in that firm ever set foot in the building. We ever get in front of a jury, who you think they're going to like? A sleazy shark in a fancy suit and a Tennessee redneck or a local Queens guy?"

Bernstein leaned forward. "I don't like the sound of this. What do you mean 'if we have to go to court?' What are they saying?"

Walter sighed and tapped a document sitting before him.

"They say that our contract is worthless, which is bullshit. They say the five grand is an unfair penalty for someone who decides to change managers because he can better his career. They're going to argue that tying Eddie up and making him pay to leave early is illegal. They claim five grand to get out is extortion, but in the interests of putting everything behind us, they offer five hundred. They included a release, and they'll send a check by messenger later today once they get the signed release."

Bernstein felt a wave of heat run up his spine into his face.

"You look awfully red, Jack," Walter said. "Everything okay?"

Bernstein managed to croak a reply. "It's just that at worst I was figuring on getting the five grand. I put a lot of time and money into Eddie and have no way to replace it anytime soon."

Walter looked Bernstein in the eye and spoke slowly. "Listen, Jack, you're going to get a lot more than five grand when this is over."

"How are we going to do that?"

Walter picked up the packet from the law firm and waved it. "First thing I'm doing is sending this back to these assholes with a reminder to do as you told that punk and shove it up their asses. Right after that we're suing Eddie for breach of contract and this new manager for tortious interference with business."

"What does that mean?" Bernstein asked.

Walter twice rapped the papers on his desk. "It means they screwed with the wrong people."

BERNSTEIN DROVE to Barry Tarpol's home and pounded on the basement door. The instant Bernstein was settled on Barry's couch, he told Barry everything that happened, from the gig at Max's to his meeting with Walter, even his coffee with Picarelli.

"Keep the Italian's card," Barry said. "He's right. You never know when he might be needed. Rock stars are always getting busted for drugs or destroying hotel rooms. And take a deep breath, my friend."

Bernstein breathed in and out and shook his head a few times. "I didn't come here to talk about Picarelli. I want to know what you think. Should I call Walter and tell him I decided to take the five hundred? Isn't it better than nothing?"

Barry gaped at his friend, his mouth forming an O. "What, are you out of your mind? Walter's a tough guy. He was a DA. He put away gangsters and murderers. Did I tell you my father used him to collect a debt someone owed him? My dad says if he ever has a business problem again, he's calling Walter."

The Tarpol family endorsement of Walter's skills calmed Bernstein.

"Yeah, I shouldn't doubt him. It's just, you know, I got rattled when I saw this big time Manhattan firm coming after me, and Walter's got a little office over a pizzeria. With that idiot Picarelli as his sounding board."

"Picarelli's no idiot," Barry said. He explained how his father called Walter when his business partner's son was arrested for possession for sale of a pound of high-grade Columbian weed.

"Convinced some hardass judge over at the courthouse that the search of the kid's car was so bad it couldn't possibly be legal. Got the whole case tossed out."

How can I be so wrong about everything? Bernstein thought. *Such a poor judge of people?*

Barry reminded Bernstein that Walter was taking the case on a contingency and would take a third of whatever he recovered for Bernstein.

"So, he thinks it's worth his time and money," Barry said. "That ought to tell you something."

"Isn't that what we said about me and Eddie?" Bernstein asked.

"I TOLD you not to stop for him that night on Queens Boulevard," Jennifer said. "You never listen to me. Now look where it's gotten you." When she arrived at Bernstein's basement, she promptly changed the radio from FM to WABC, home of the Top Forty.

They had dinner at the Italian restaurant down the road, and when they arrived at Bernstein's basement, they were both a bit tipsy from the red wine they drank. The lights were low, the music was soft, which pleased Bernstein, and despite tension caused by Eddie, neither had fully become unshackled from their mutual attraction. They sat on the edge of Bernstein's bed.

"Let's not talk about that tonight," Bernstein said.

"Then what do you want to talk about?" Jennifer asked.

He didn't answer. He put an arm around her shoulder, pulling her against him, and then the two of them laid down on the bed, arms around each other and lips pressed as their tongues became entwined. They were soon helping each other undress.

It was over too soon, at least in Bernstein's mind. The lovemaking was hurried and without the emotions he usually felt during sex with Jenn. They dressed themselves silently. When Jennifer was fully dressed, she turned up the volume on the radio and returned to the subject of Bernstein's future.

Bernstein preferred even the bubblegum sound to Jennifer's hectoring him over his dismal situation. They sat up in his bed, their backs propped against the headboard, Jennifer's hand resting on his shoulder. Bernstein felt relaxed for the first time that day when Jennifer brought up Tennessee Eddie.

"You put all your eggs in one basket, and now you're out on the street," she said. "Have you ever thought about getting a real job?"

"I love music, and if I have to work, it should be doing something I like," he replied.

Jennifer scowled. "In that case, start knocking on doors in the city. You have a much better chance of landing a good job than finding a star. That's just reality, Jack. You have a college degree, and you have experience and know a lot."

Bernstein rose from the bed and looked at Jennifer. "I don't want to put on a suit, especially after I've seen what it does to a man. I don't want to have some boss telling me what to do. I want to decide what music to work with, not have someone else tell me."

"I'd like to have a future with you, Jack," Jennifer said. "Get married and have a family. You can stay in music and do it. Look at your friend Ed Stern. He has a house and a wife and a child, and he's making a good living."

Bernstein laughed. "No one's going to pay me to play guitar on their albums. I wasn't born with that talent. I've got to do it this way."

"But you're not!" Jennifer screamed. Bernstein placed his fingers on his lips as a warning not to awaken Mrs. Bardoni. Then he opened the drawer of his nightstand and withdrew a joint he had rolled earlier.

"I'm going to my car to smoke this," he said. He often did so when Jennifer was at his place since she despised the smell of grass. Jennifer said nothing as he pulled on his pants and a sweatshirt and went up the stairs.

Bernstein passed Jennifer's Mustang as he walked around the corner to where he was parked. *Funny how I live here, but she always gets the spot in front of my house.*

It was too cold to be out at night without a coat, so Bernstein hurried, and when he got in the Volvo, he muttered a prayer that the choke would work. It did, and he turned up the heater and turned on the radio. His favorite deejay, who had taken to calling herself "the Nightbird," held the all-night shift on WNEW FM. Bernstein tuned in during the middle of a slew of psychedelic rock classics the Nightbird was playing in appreciation of the music form that was slowly slipping away. She announced the next song, "It's a Happening Thing" by The Peanut Butter Conspiracy. Bernstein found it hard to believe the song was released only three years ago; it seemed like ancient history already. *Too bad*, Bernstein thought. *I really liked this sound.*

Bernstein used the Volvo's lighter to fire up the joint. He wasn't worried about the likelihood of a patrol car ambling by this quiet street in Bayside. He allowed himself the luxury of being enveloped by the smoke and the sound, pushing all other thoughts from his mind.

When Bernstein recognized the music coming from the Volvo's speakers was the sound of "I Had Too Much to Dream Last Night" by the Electric Prunes, he knew he had been sitting behind the wheel longer than he expected. He saw the open ashtray, and sticking his finger in amidst the darkness, felt the small roach that was left of the joint. He didn't have his watch on, and the car had no clock. He had no idea what time it was or how long he'd been there. The gas gauge hadn't moved, and the engine hadn't stalled or overheated, so it couldn't have been all that long. He turned off the engine, grabbed the roach from the ashtray, and swallowed it, grimacing as it went down. He locked the car and walked back home. He noticed it as soon as he reached the house.

Jennifer's car was gone.

Chapter Eight

"I wouldn't bother to call her," Barry Tarpol told Bernstein over tuna fish sandwiches at the Island Diner. "You're in the midst of this big crisis and she starts giving you a hard time and running you down? Let her go, Jack."

"Easier said than done," Bernstein replied.

"Well, it shouldn't be," Barry snapped. "The bitch gets on your case when you need a little love, then she runs off behind your back because you wouldn't change your whole life on the spot when she demanded it? Good riddance to her. She was just a JAP anyway." Every male in the greater New York area knew those initials stood for "Jewish American Princess." Barry and Bernstein shared the view that they, as Jewish men, could use the term objectively, but any non-Jew who used it was clearly an anti-Semite.

"We've been together almost three years," Bernstein said. "She was a freshman, and I was just starting to cut loose. I only started smoking grass a few months before I met her."

"You didn't tell her that for a year," Barry said. "You knew how she'd react, and you were right. Bad sign. You should've seen it then."

"I think it's really a moot point," Bernstein said. "My gut tells me she's had it with this relationship."

"I'm glad somebody has," Barry replied.

ED STERN WAS NO MORE sympathetic than Barry.

"This is when she decides to give you a hard time?" he asked. "And she uses me as some sort of role model? That just opens rifts between guys. I have to tell you, Jack—I'm with Barry. Let her go. Don't call her. If she calls you, tell her you need time to think about it, and you'll get back to her. Of course, you never will."

"You are a cold man, Ed Stern."

"You know how Leo Durocher said 'nice guys finish last'?"

Bernstein nodded. His father was a lifelong Dodgers fan, even sticking with them when they moved to Los Angeles. Durocher managed the team for a long time. Bernstein grew up hearing about him.

"Jack," Stern said, "that was baseball. In the business of music, nice guys don't even get to finish."

"I get the picture. My best friends think it's time to end it with Jenn. Probably right for both of us. But I have bigger problems. Jenn happens to be right about one thing. At the moment I've got no business, no clients, and the only person who's going be calling my answering service is me."

They were in Stern's home studio. Miles Davis poured out of the KLH Solid State speaker-FM radio perched on a shelf. Bernstein remained quiet, allowing the jazz to envelop him and drive away the fear and anxiety. He was much more relaxed when Stern spoke.

"Jack, you found people before you found Tennessee Eddie, and you'll find them after Tennessee Eddie. I have a feeling you're going to find the next one real soon. And hang on to them this time!"

BERNSTEIN STOPPED by Walter's office a few days after his break with Jenn. There were some papers to review and sign. One was the agreement with the lawyer, who would receive nothing up front but one-third of anything he won for Bernstein after deducting expenses. *He must be pretty confident*, Bernstein reasoned.

Walter explained the lawsuit charged the shark with inducing Eddie to breach his contract with Bernstein. The new manager's lawyers refused to pay Bernstein the five-thousand-dollar termination fee for a breach, a second breach. That left Bernstein free to sue for actual damages, which were far more than five thousand dollars.

"You dragged Eddie all over Queens and Nassau until he really honed his talent. By the time he played a real gig at Max's, he was ready for the studio and the concert trail. If a guy like that gets a recording contract, sells a bit of records, gets on some good tour bills with some decent fees, gets lots of radio play, hey, we're talking some serious dough. I'm thinking hundreds of thousands over the remaining four and a half years on that contract. Maybe more."

Bernstein sat frozen in the client chair. He spoke when his vocal cords thawed. "Why would a big-time law firm risk all that over five grand? That's peanuts to them."

"They figured you'd be intimidated and needed every penny. These lawyers are representing sharks who expect their attorneys to be just like them. It usually works. Nine out of ten guys in your situation would take the five hundred and slink away."

"We didn't take their lousy five hundred," Bernstein said. "And we are not slinking away."

Walter slapped the top of his desk. "No, we are definitely not slinking away, Jack."

If only I had his confidence in what I do, Bernstein thought.

After Bernstein signed everything and was given copies, Walter treated him to a slice of pizza and a cola at the pizzeria downstairs. When they parted ways, Walter told Bernstein that when they won the lawsuit, it would be Jack's turn to treat, but at Delmonico's.

Chapter 9
Mid-February, 1970

T he first time Bernstein heard Galahad's music was at his friend Willie's house. Bernstein met Willie in a poetry class his junior year at Queens College. They shared several joints after class that semester and remained in touch after graduation. Immediately upon receiving his degree in anthropology, Willie joined the family business, selling plastic slipcovers to working-class Queens at an enormous and obscene profit. Based on the quality of his stereo equipment, Bernstein knew Willie was making very good money. Whenever Bernstein entered a home for the first time, he immediately checked out the sound system. Willie owned a McIntosh amp and preamp, Bose speakers, a Fisher turntable, and a Pioneer reel-to-reel tape player, all rated among the very best. *In Queens, plastic slipcovers definitely pays better than rock and roll*, he thought.

Willie had a tape he wanted Bernstein to hear.

"Old buddy of mine, just back from the West Coast," Willie explained. "Biggest acid head in Queens till he split for California, got into Eastern religion, changed his name from Don Scribiner to Galahad."

"A really heavy dude," Willie added. "You may have run into him on campus when we were there. He was around until sometime in our junior year."

Bernstein had neither met nor heard of Galahad, not surprising on a campus of over twenty-thousand students. It wasn't possible to know every musician on campus; at any given moment there were scores of guitar-strumming students filling the stage at the College Memorial Center, where the hippies congregated, or scattered about the broad expanses of lawn.

Bernstein expected another poor-quality tape that captivated the party playing it but bored him. He accepted this as an occupational hazard of the music business. There were hundreds of thousands, if not millions, eager to join the giants of the industry, hoping to be the next Beatles, Dylan, or Hendrix. Bernstein met several each day. Every aspiring star and their supporters see someone like Bernstein as their gateway to fame and fortune. Everyone knew someone, often themselves, that Bernstein simply *must* hear. He would fall in love, of course, they assured him, and would want to devote himself totally to advancing the artist's career. *If only they knew the truth*, Bernstein thought.

Whatever his feelings, Bernstein always relented and listened. His modest status required continually sifting through wastelands in search of the gem the big boys missed. The big boys focused on Manhattan, where the high-status offices and choice venues were found, the playground of anyone in the business who managed to make that first breakthrough.

Bernstein was still trying to figure out a means of entry. Queens and the eastern Long Island counties, Nassau and Suffolk, were the minor leagues, barely an afterthought, and artists who hadn't broken through to the lowest level of Manhattan were deemed not worth the long ride. Until something changed, that was Bernstein's territory.

Willie was rock music obsessed and enthusiastically delivered a soliloquy of praise for Galahad.

"Galahad sings tenor, but he can stretch slightly in either direction as needed. He figured out John Lennon's trick, moving away from the microphone to get that sense the voice is coming from a special world, or he's singing directly to you, only he does it better. He makes you feel the song is meant specially for you. When he sings about sad things like breaking up, or losing someone you love, it's him telling us, 'We've all been there.' I'm telling you, Bernstein, you have to hear him, and you have to sign him up. He's going to be big, real big. Really best if you can see him live, of course…"

"Tell you what, Willie," Bernstein said. "I've been looking for an excuse to hear that Pioneer reel-to-reel." *And you'll never leave me alone until I hear this tape.*

Bernstein felt Willie deserved his attention. When Eddie deserted Bernstein, Willie had been a great comfort, getting his college buddy through the crisis with kindness and weed, and distracting him from Eddie by engaging in long and knowledgeable discussions of rock and roll. Willie lived a different life than Bernstein in many ways, starting with a job requiring him to keep his hair short and wear a suit and tie, whether in a business meeting or making a pitch to an Italian-American family in Bayside. But his understanding of rock music was as deep as any professional Bernstein knew, and he was a far better person than any of them.

"A mere flesh wound, my friend," Willie told Bernstein when informed of Tennessee Eddie's betrayal. "You'll be sure it never happens again. There are plenty of great artists out there waiting for you to discover them. You know I've always got my antennas out looking for you." Willie spent a great deal of time listening to music in small clubs throughout the Greater New York area. He had connected Bernstein with a half dozen bands, and while none went beyond the bottom end—playing for tips in burger and pizza joints—Bernstein knew many bands selling platinum records were discovered that way.

Bernstein agreed to hear the tape, prepared for disappointment. Instead, he heard an artist who married lyrics to melody and drew the listener into his music with both.

It was only one song, "I'll Dream Tonight," which Willie considered Galahad's masterpiece. A minute into the number, Bernstein knew Willie had done him well. Galahad's voice was exactly as Willie described. A professional backing band with Stern doing the heavy lifting on guitar would create a seriously professional demo tape. Tapes were expensive, but he would come up with the money, and at last, his long slog through the musical hinterlands would pay off. That was exactly how he felt the first time he heard Tennessee Eddie. He knew he had that something special, and he was right about that part at least. He felt the same upon hearing Galahad's song, and he hadn't even heard him live.

Galahad was not like the ubiquitous copycat versions of Crosby, Stills, Nash & Young, the Eagles, Loggins and Messina, or whoever was the flavor of the month. He wasn't George Harrison or Carlos Santana, but he was a highly competent rhythm guitarist who could also fingerpick and even play short riffs. Bernstein wondered why the poseurs never grasped that if someone wanted to hear the music of famous bands, they could buy their records or turn on the radio.

Bernstein's own tastes trended toward blues, soul, and jazz, but he could work with artists who blended rock with any of these genres, or even with folk. Bands could earn a living, often a good one, on music's B level—lounge acts, weddings and bar mitzvahs, sweet sixteens, proms. The cream of the crop won record contracts, or like Ed, preferred the studio to the wild life of touring. Others lived for the opportunity to tour. Bernstein wanted recording contracts and tours for his artists. Concerts promoted record sales, created a brand with followers, and made money hand over fist. They also made musicians grow and become better.

Willie mentioned that Galahad was serious about his yoga and, over the last year, had dived deeper into Eastern religion, which for Willie was creeping into the songs he didn't like. He told Bernstein how he had tried to talk Galahad out of recording such music, but the artist was insistent they were to be part of his oeuvre, and the world would embrace those songs.

"I've tried to explain to him that rock and roll is the name of the game," Willie said. "Who knows how long this yoga thing will last? I mean, Ben-Gurion stood on his head all the time, and I didn't see anyone start doing yoga."

Bernstein was not at all surprised to hear this. He knew it was a manager's job to disabuse the artist of incorrect notions of what would sell. He had no doubt he would disabuse Galahad of many notions.

First things first, though—he had to hear Galahad live, like Willie said. He had to get to know the artist as well as the music and decide if they could work together. Talent will go places with the right management, but only if the chemistry works. Artists and managers can be difficult people, especially with each other. Bernstein didn't expect Galahad to be especially difficult, but one could never be certain.

Willie's reel-to-reel was of such high quality that even on a raw, unfinished amateur tape, the power of Galahad's voice gripped Bernstein the moment he heard the first notes. The guitar accompaniment was more than competent, if nothing special; a session guitarist was needed in the studio. He caught himself; it was too soon to be thinking of studios. Record labels didn't want to waste their time, money, or good name on bands that would embarrass them. They wanted the opposite—acts that earn money. Club owners wanted bands that sounded like the top-forty AM hits. The big venues wanted only proven winners, or those just about to be.

The only music record labels wanted to hear was the rhythm of coin dropping into palaver. Their A&R men followed whatever latest rage induced the record-buying public to drop that coin. Today, outside of Duke Schwartz's bubblegum stars, that meant bands who wrote their own songs and played their own instruments. The era of singers accompanying themselves on acoustic guitar, the folk days of one guitar and one voice, were long over. Even Dylan was backed by rock musicians. A third-rate hack who sold records by the million to teenage girls or drunken rednecks was of far greater interest than the most accomplished musician with little market appeal. Bernstein's problem with the major record labels was his inability to internalize their values. He was still in love with the music and wanted to offer the very best he could find. Hopefully, that was also what would sell.

If a band wasn't particularly accomplished on their instruments, Bernstein expected they should at least be able to play them in public. With all the noise and distortion, and the stoned state of most audiences, a band could get away with a lot of mistakes and even poor playing at concert. In the studio, of course, top quality musicians like Ed Stern in New York or the Wrecking Crew in L.A. made those bands' records sound better than the bands ever could themselves.

Stephen Shaiken

When a manager signs an artist, both face a long and difficult road ahead with an extremely high failure rate. The cream of the agent crop worked out of offices in Manhattan's Music District with expense accounts and, most importantly, backstage concert passes affording access to the record company executives as well as producers, rock writers, and concert promoters who guarded the gates of fame. A regular backstage presence elevated an up-and-coming manager, eventually generating the business that goes with such cachet. It was a club of which one had to be a member to advance, and Bernstein didn't have a clue how to join. He was essentially unknown in Manhattan and could count on the fingers of one hand the times he'd been backstage in any important venue in the city. He was backstage all the time in Queens and Nassau, decidedly unimpressive to anyone on the other side of the bridges and tunnel.

Bernstein had Queens and Long Island to himself—mostly to himself—because no established managers wanted it. He eked out a living, but not enough to alleviate fears he might be unable to afford the next repair on his eight-year-old Volvo. Bernstein had to meet Galahad, size up the man, and hear him live. Galahad was back in Queens and moving in the same circles as Bernstein, so that wouldn't be difficult.

Chapter 10
Early March, 1970

Over the following days, Bernstein reached out to his Queens College network. A few people recalled Don Scribiner from his student days when he played guitar and sang on the stage at the CMC or in the vast open space surrounding the gym. One contact explained that since returning from the West Coast with a new name and greatly improved musical skills, Galahad was being treated like a prophet by some. Recently, he dressed mostly in white, practiced yoga, meditated, and followed a strict vegetarian diet. He was most eager to share his insights with the world through his music.

Enchanted as Bernstein was by Galahad's primitive rendition of "I'll Dream Tonight" on that crude tape, he understood he needed a real studio demo to present him to labels. Those cost a lot of money. The artist had to be ready and committed, and someone had to come up with the money for a studio and a band. That someone was Bernstein. He wasn't about to embark on a project of that magnitude unless he were assured the artist had what it took, and that couldn't be known until he saw and heard him.

The first time Bernstein met Galahad was in someone's basement in Douglaston, a suburban neighborhood in North Queens. Unlike Bernstein, whose abode was nothing but a basement, the hosts, a young couple who had been a year ahead of him at Queens, inhabited a full house. How they afforded such a huge place in an expensive neighborhood was not clear, but Bernstein suspected it was hashish. Many people, in and out of the business, mentioned buying from them. Bernstein knew a lot of dealers, and all made more money than he did.

The word was out about a freestyle jam, the kind the Grateful Dead made famous. Ed Stern was the main attraction. Ed was rock royalty in Queens. A *Rolling Stone* article on session musicians cited him as "a first-rate, versatile lead guitarist." Bernstein thought they should have added he was accomplished at rhythm as well. Lead guitarists get all the press and most of the money and women, but truth be told, 90 percent of guitar work is rhythm. If it were so easy, there would be more good rhythm guitarists, and it wouldn't be seen as a consolation for those not good enough to play lead. Bernstein was forever hectoring his bands to pay more attention to rhythm guitar.

"If you don't have a good rhythm guitarist, you're gonna throw off the bass and drums. You'll screw up the timing and the beat. Then you'll never get work in the clubs, which means no label will ever get to hear you. So, practice those chords, and use a metronome if you have to. Remember, Pete Townsend of the Who is one of the richest and most famous guitarists in the world, and he plays all chords. Do you ever hear any serious leads on Who albums?" The guitarists usually stared blankly as he delivered this lecture. They didn't listen, and the prediction of failure almost always came true.

Ed Stern told Bernstein to be there. Some of the best musicians in Queens would be stopping by throughout the night. Stern mentioned he heard Galahad would be attending.

"I don't remember any Don Scribiner from Queens College, but recently several people I respect are talking up this Galahad, and I want to meet him and play some music with him. Of course I'll tell you what I think."

The bass player was a philosophy major at Columbia who dropped out a few months later to pursue a music career, and Bernstein never heard or saw him again. A shame, as he was really good. The drummer was the host's sister's boyfriend, at best a weekend amateur who managed to keep a beat and was not likely to overpower real musicians like Stern and Galahad. Two pretty women played flutes on several songs. They were quite good and added a different sound to the rock music the group jammed. Competent but uninspiring guitarists filtered in and out, taking turns with what was really Ed Stern and an ad hoc jam band. *Ed and the bass player take this way above a typical basement jam in Queens*, Bernstein thought. *Better than what you'll hear in most local clubs. Such is the state of the music scene in Queens. At least for now.*

The ad hoc band warmed up with the rock standards—Chuck Berry, Rolling Stones, Buffalo Springfield, Beatles, Grateful Dead. An hour later, they had jammed to a half dozen blues standards, which pleased Bernstein.

When the doorbell rang, one of the flautists ran to get it. When she saw who had arrived, she cried out her greetings to the tall man whose face was obscured by his long hair.

"Galahad," Ed Stern explained. "No doubt that's who it is. Now we'll play some original music."

Galahad set his guitar case down before he made his way around the basement, hugging and kissing all. Bernstein felt a tinge of envy at being outside this camaraderie until Galahad stood before him, a wide smile across his face.

"I'm Galahad," he said and embraced Bernstein. Galahad's hair reeked of weed, which comforted Bernstein.

Bernstein always tried to present a confidence and assertiveness to a prospective client, taking care not to appear overly aggressive or scripted and inauthentic. In his experience, sharp artists were on the lookout for such people and avoided them. This time, in Galahad's immediate presence, his body and his mind went their own way, and he was overcome by a calm, pleasant feeling. It felt as if Galahad himself were somehow communicating telepathically, telling him to do nothing and he'd feel just fine. Bernstein was not unnerved or threatened by this message, if it indeed was a message and not just his own mind at work. *Am I just reacting to what Willie told me? Maybe after Tennessee I ought to keep some distance from my artists so I can see them as they really are.*

Bernstein stared at Galahad, but the musician showed no sign that he minded, and to the contrary seemed at ease. Galahad smiled as Bernstein studied him from head to toe.

Dressed exactly like Willie said, and the crowd reaction is as described. So far everyone says the same thing—there's something really special going on here. Bernstein saw Galahad's hair was past shoulder length, even longer than Stern's. He was clean-shaven, and with his hair pushed back, Bernstein noticed Galahad's eyes dominated his face. They were dark brown and shined with enough intensity to call attention, but not so much as to raise concerns. Bernstein's eyes locked with Galahad's for a moment, and Bernstein felt a wave come over him, the feeling he had when he stood naked beneath a waterfall on a camping trip his junior year. This feeling was pleasant, but Bernstein wanted to maintain control of himself. He looked away, seeing Stern sitting across the room, his guitar resting on a thigh, and the under-the-waterfall feeling was gone. When Stern noticed Bernstein, he turned his head slightly to Galahad, smiled, and nodded. Bernstein turned his gaze back to Galahad.

"I'm Bernstein," he said, aware most people in the room were looking in his direction. *It's him they can't take their eyes off. Charisma on charisma. Thank you, Willie.*

"I know who you are," Galahad said. "I've been expecting to meet you." Galahad's demeanor reminded Bernstein of a face-to-face meeting with professors at Queens College, one of a hundred fifty students in the class granted precious time with the master.

Time to stop being a fan and become a manager, Bernstein thought.

"It's karma," Bernstein said. "My number's on this card. I'd love for you to call me so we can get together, and you can tell me all about yourself and your music. I've been hearing about it from everyone else, so why not from you?"

"No reason why not," Galahad said. He looked at the card before sticking it into a pouch on his waist. "We'll talk real soon."

Anyone else would be laughed off as last year's Donovan. Not this guy. He's next year's Donovan.

Bernstein watched Galahad walk back to the other musicians. His white robe stood out among the sea of jeans and colorful skirts.

Bernstein listened as the jam band played one or two blues standards before launching into one of Galahad's songs.

That first night, when Bernstein heard Galahad perform "I'll Dream Tonight" with Ed's tasteful lead, he knew he had found his star. Galahad's voice had grown stronger and his phrasing more pronounced. He was fine on rhythm and some picking. Ed's leads gave the number the professional arrangement Bernstein hoped to hear.

Chapter 11
Mid-April, 1970

Over the next several weeks, Bernstein spent a great deal of time with Galahad, and it didn't take long for him to believe he knew him intimately. Galahad's relaxed and welcoming manner eliminated most of the touch-and-go so common at the start of any relationship. As time passed, Bernstein came to realize that while he may have come to know Galahad better than most people, in many ways he was still a cipher. Bernstein determined Galahad wanted to both like and be liked at all times by all people and avoided saying anything he thought would be controversial.

Bernstein knew his professional relationship with Galahad required an objectivity that ruled out idolization, yet he couldn't deny Galahad was unique in ways beyond his music. Bernstein didn't share Galahad's attraction to Eastern religions and doubted he ever could. From what Bernstein could discern, Galahad espoused an uneven blend of Hinduism and Buddhism—both Thai Forest and Zen—with a dash of Sufism thrown in for good measure. It was unclear how much of this Galahad actually understood, though he certainly sounded knowledgeable enough. Bernstein knew from his studies of comparative religions with Professor Mulvaney how easy it is to memorize a list of rules, principles, or values, but also how much more difficult to understand what they meant. Bernstein thought Hinduism a mishmash of gaudy gods and intricate folklore that collided with his rational mind. The potential deprivations of Buddhism ran contrary to his healthy pursuit of pleasure and success. He didn't mind being Jewish, since he didn't really have to do anything to remain a Jew forever. This felt natural to him, the way it was supposed to be. It seemed a lot easier than chanting, sitting cross-legged, or twisting one's body into a pretzel, but he resisted sharing these thoughts with Galahad.

Galahad was a strict and dedicated vegetarian who abstained from meat, fowl, or fish and did all he could to avoid products made from the death or suffering of animals. Bernstein believed humans were natural carnivores, and vegetarians were ill-informed, superstitious faddists fueled by the self-righteousness of the naive.

Galahad was different, and the strength of his convictions caused Bernstein to respect his beliefs, even if he couldn't share them. Galahad never drew attention to himself in a way that might hurt or insult another, never proselytized beyond a light touch, and if pressed, would offer rational scientific and economic arguments for eating plants instead of animals—it was cheaper, able to feed more people, better for the planet. He preferred to offer these reasons instead of his religious beliefs when he knew the latter would not be well-received.

"Vegetarians suffer less heart attacks, strokes, high blood pressure, and obesity than meat eaters," he explained. "We could feed more people if we didn't waste plants feeding livestock."

He once revealed his real guiding principle to Bernstein at the end of a long evening of working out details in the arrangements of Galahad's songs. He explained all violence was wrong, no matter who it was directed against or why, and that all people should strive to reduce the total amount of violence already in the world. Eating meat, fowl, or fish required an act of violence by someone. Bernstein told him he didn't consider eating animals to be practicing violence.

"Someday you will," Galahad replied.

Galahad insisted his music must not control his life and interfere with his spiritual practice, but for Bernstein, things were drifting dangerously close to the other side of the pendulum. Practices and jams were delayed while Galahad chanted, meditated, or practiced yoga. An increasing portion of his songs was religious and spiritual in content. Bernstein feared this could impede progress on the game plan he was creating.

"Those songs are often musically as good as anything else you write, if a little slow, but the lyrics are only going to appeal to scholars of Sanskrit," Bernstein told him after hearing a recent composition which by his count contained at least fifteen words in that language. "Keep that stuff as something special for yourself and your fellow worshippers and stick with what the audience wants in your songs." Bernstein knew the audience he was talking about was not the audience that listened to top-forty AM radio, but the new FM radio boom around America had opened up a whole new audience that wanted real music, not the top-forty stuff.

"The audience isn't sure what they want," Galahad replied. "Maybe I can help them find out by giving them the spiritual message in my newer songs."

"No one will like it," Bernstein replied. He and Galahad engaged in an ongoing dialogue as to the subject matter of Galahad's work. Galahad would present Bernstein with his most recent songs, usually playing them on the guitar. A few of the songs were always religious in nature, and Bernstein would politely dismiss them in favor of the others.

"It has nothing to do with the quality of those religious songs. They're actually quite good," he told Galahad, though he didn't really feel that way. "There's going to come a time when you can record and perform whatever songs you want. That time is not now. People want to see you established as an artist before they start looking to you as a spiritual adviser. Look at George Harrison or Seals and Croft. They didn't mention their spiritual values until they made it big, and now they have a free hand to say what they want when they want. Work with me on this, Galahad, and we'll both be very happy."

Galahad never argued this point with Bernstein.

"I'm not asking you to record these right now or even to have me perform a whole bunch of them. Just let me slowly release them into the stream, okay?"

"Only slowly," Bernstein said. "Very slowly."

As TIME PASSED Galahad became more forceful in his advocacy for his spiritual music. Bernstein did not yield.

"You have to be patient, Galahad. We've barely been at this for three months. The market is still people who like the melodies and the way you sing them, and of course, the words, so long as they don't think someone is trying to push a religious message they're not ready to hear." *Or that they will ever be ready to hear.*

"I know you have my best interests at heart, and you're very smart, and I trust myself in your hands. That's why I don't wear all white or robes when I perform, and why I've been taking your advice about what to sing. But you have to understand one thing—if I can't use my talents to tell the world what I've learned, then I don't care about being a star."

Bernstein smiled and patted Galahad on the back.

I'll say one thing about this guy. He's got the right attitude to be a star. 'Tell the world what I learned?' I love it.

BERNSTEIN MET ED STERN when the latter was strumming his guitar on the lawn of Queens College in the spring of 1967. Ed was playing "San Francisco Bay Blues," a favorite of Bernstein's. It was written and recorded in the mid-fifties by the blues artist Jesse Fuller and later covered by Dylan; Peter, Paul and Mary, Ramblin' Jack Elliot, and the Jim Kweskin Jug Band. Bernstein liked the folk music revival of the sixties because it rediscovered old-time blues musicians like Jimmy Reed, Son House, and Brownie McGhee and introduced him to new artists. Bob Dylan was the most famous of the fresh faces, and when he went electric in 1965, Bernstein fully embraced the change and saw it as an enhancement.

By the Summer of Love in 1967, there was far less interest in folk, which meant fewer openings for the old-time blues music, but Ed

Stern remained as much an aficionado as Bernstein. Ed's parents filled the Stern home with the sound of the blues, but he never thought of playing guitar until he heard the Beatles over the Christmas school break in 1963. It was Hanukkah, and he cajoled an electric guitar out of his parents. He turned out to have a natural talent.

Ed made most of his money playing rock and pop as a session man, but his heart was with the blues. When he played without pay, it was almost always the blues.

It was Ed who first suggested a studio tape. He offered to play without fee with the understanding that if a label signed Galahad, Bernstein would insist on Stern being his guitarist. "Doubtful they'll complain," Stern explained. "It's not like anyone else is going to be better with Galahad. And I can find us a studio and engineer you can afford."

Stern was right. He knew he was fortunate to have a friend like Ed. Willie was the consummate rock fan, a very astute and knowledgeable one at that, and acting as freelance scout for Bernstein. Stern by contrast was the consummate professional who understood the production side of music down to his bones, muscles, and sinews. When Ed Stern gave Bernstein advice, he listened.

One bit of advice Stern gave was to never call Galahad by his real name.

"I'm always dealing with artists who changed their name for one reason or another. I don't know what they go by with their close friends and family, but in the business, use the professional names only. Start with Galahad."

Bernstein listened. He never once slipped up and called Galahad "Don."

GALAHAD WASN'T the only artist on Bernstein's roster when Bernstein became his manager, but soon he was because he had the greatest potential. After Tennessee Eddie, Bernstein briefly worked with a few local bands, but none of them had any hope of rising above the second-tier coffee shops and working-class bars of Queens. In order to finance Galahad's career and put in the time it required, Bernstein gradually released the lesser talents until his sole client was Galahad.

The tape of Galahad would be Bernstein's first, the sum of all he owned and all he had borrowed. The borrowing included Pete Malden's Stratocaster sitting in a pawnshop in South Jamaica waiting to be redeemed before the clock ran out. Pete left it with Bernstein when he took off for Europe a year ago on a six-month trip. Pete was an experienced guitarist who could always find studio work or be called as a fill-in for bands, but not without his guitar.

Pete sent Bernstein a postcard from India a few months ago. There was no sign of an imminent return, but it could happen any day. Just like Galahad suddenly returned from the West Coast.

Bernstein also borrowed from Mitty the Mole, who operated an unofficial bank out of his green Lincoln Continental. Mitty could be found parked at various locations around Queens, where those who knew him and needed quick cash would be waiting. Anyone who didn't know how to find Mitty had no business borrowing.

Mitty carried a lot of cash. He also reputedly carried a gun. Word was that for every stop he had another armed man watching. Most people thought Mitty alone was enough to scare off any would-be robbers. Mitty wore the kind of blank face that said he could shoot a man dead without thinking about it afterward. Rumor was that he'd done so several times. Mitty never said anything about what might happen if a payment was missed, but that was unlikely to happen. There were rumors, dark ones, whispered in bars and over poker games that Mitty carried a baseball bat in his trunk and used it when persuasion did not result in payment. The one rumor Bernstein absolutely believed was that Mitty paid off the cops. How else could he operate so out in the open? Still, the talk of Mitty's violence could not be ignored, especially if Mitty was buying protection from the law.

Mitty was known to loan to those in need but could never satisfy a bank loan officer, and many were small business people like Bernstein. Despite his reputation and demeanor, Mitty was not what Bernstein had expected of a loan shark. In fact, to Bernstein, Mitty was more like a bank for high-risk borrowers. His interest rate was 3 percent a month, quite low compared to what Bernstein heard from people in the city about real mob loan sharks. Mitty capped loans at two thousand dollars, and the kind of people he loaned to could handle the monthly payment. Like any lender, Mitty ran his own form of credit check. In his case, that ran from an eyeballing to word on the street. There were people to whom he would not lend.

The first time Bernstein negotiated a loan at the window of Mitty's Lincoln, Barry was at his side and made the introduction. Barry's father and Mitty were high school classmates, both still in the neighborhood where they grew up, and that was good enough for Barry's friend to pass muster. He asked how much and nodded his head when Bernstein said a thousand dollars. Mitty was smoking an El Producto cigar as he counted the bills with stubby, stained fingers.

"Usually don't loan a new guy more than three hundred, but if Barry and his old man say you're good, then you're good with me." After that, Bernstein handed over an envelope at the same spot and time every month. Mitty would often engage Bernstein in brief conversation, usually about sports, recommending college and professional teams to bet on.

"You can't do wrong betting against that spread," he sometimes said about an upcoming football or basketball game after sending a plume of cigar smoke in Bernstein's direction. "Always bet on Joe Frazier," he counseled at least twice. "He's going to be champion for a while." Bernstein followed the Jets, Mets, and Rangers, but he never gambled. He suspected Mitty was hinting Bernstein should borrow from him to fund his gambling. *I guess he doesn't know I'm already gambling everything I have and more.*

Bernstein could handle thirty dollars a month, but when the balance of the loan came due in another seven months, he wanted it cleared. He didn't like the idea of dealing with Mitty any longer than he had to, and he definitely didn't want to ask for more time.

I want to pay him off and never see him again. Or smell his cheap cigar.

Chapter Twelve

Bernstein didn't rush into the studio. His primary focus at the start of a relationship with an artist was to learn all he could about them. If he was to plot their careers, he had to know them as people, understand their hopes, fears, and dreams. Galahad struck him as a performer of enormous breadth with the potential to capture an audience in an amphitheater as easily as small crowd in a coffee shop. Galahad preferred acoustic to electric guitar, which would not be a problem in the small clubs. He would have his fix of acoustic and would not object to the occasional electric set where the venue allowed for it. Galahad's insistence on one too many religious songs in his playlist was becoming a problem, though. These numbers were often melodic but burdened with cumbersome lyrics delivered at a snail's pace. Galahad's output of these songs grew with each passing week. Bernstein hoped once Galahad saw that spiritual numbers were not crowd pleasers, he would drop most of them from the playlist.

Bernstein was relieved Galahad accepted the need for electric music. When he and Ed played together, it was always electric-oriented. Good as Ed Stern was on lead, Galahad's rhythm guitar had to be heard, and that meant going electric as Dylan came to realize years ago. Galahad's only concern about switching from his Martin to his Strat was not wanting to "commercialize" his music.

"If you're being paid, you're commercializing, no matter what songs you play," Bernstein told him.

~

THE FIRST FEW gigs were just Galahad on acoustic, and as he moved to larger clubs, Ed Stern played softly on electric through a small amplifier. His promise of only one such appearance was happily forgotten. "If I can help you, I'll do it," he told Bernstein.

Sometimes the clubs had in-house musicians, and Bernstein used their drummers or keyboard players on some songs, and he always used their bass. If the club had no bass player, Bernstein or Stern rounded one up. On a few occasions, when no bass player could be found, Ed brought an old bass he picked up at a flea market and accompanied Galahad's acoustic. When they had a real bass player, at the end of the set, Galahad would sometimes strap on his electric guitar and jam with Ed and the bassist. Galahad strummed power chords while Stern tossed out a string of classy blues-rock riffs. Galahad's voice was as strong in rock as it was sweet in folk as if there were two Galahads who might appear on stage. Bernstein preferred the one who rocked with Stern and could not understand why Galahad didn't want to be that guy. Ed clearly preferred the rocker.

"I'm doing all I can to pull him there," he said.

In some clubs, the stage was so small a drum kit had to be set up off to the side. In several coffee shops, on open mic night the audience literally sat at Galahad's feet. Eventually, Galahad didn't need to ply the open mic circuit because he always drew enough audience to make booking him attractive to the owners. Whether pizza, burgers, beer, booze, or coffee, Galahad sold more for the club owners than any other up-and-coming or down-and-out performers traveling the same circuit.

Bernstein had Galahad play three times a week, aiming for paid gigs Fridays and Saturdays, where the exposure and the money were better. Tuesdays were for open mic nights, the slightly more lucrative "pass-the-hat" gigs, or sitting in for a song or two with other artists. As Galahad became better known in the insular world of Long Island rock clubs, more people wanted his light shining on them.

Bernstein grew concerned that Galahad was becoming more interested in shining that light than in developing his musical career. The man had a natural talent—clear to Bernstein, Stern, and Willie—but natural talent was only the entry point. Guitar playing and vocal skills had to continually improve, and the artist had to constantly experiment with new material and variations on existing songs. Most of all, an emerging artist had to cast the widest possible net. Pure folk and blues gave way to rock infused versions, and those who could not make the change disappeared from the scene.

"You've got to practice more," Bernstein found himself telling Galahad with increasing frequency. "I understand you have your yoga and your meditation, and you've started having these little sessions once a week where you talk about your religion, or your diet, or whatever. That's all fine and good, but it's coming out of your practice. I've seen you flub a chord or two on some nights, and you've mixed up lyrics more than once. You shouldn't just write a song and it throw at the audience. You need to practice it for a while."

Galahad smiled and told Bernstein not to worry.

"It all comes from the soul. It's all karma. If mine is to be a rock star, I will be a rock star. If it is to be a yogi, that's what I'll be. Hopefully I can be both."

"Okay, but for the time being, how about if we stick with the rock star path? That means cutting down on writing new songs that keep going over the same religious stuff. Get back to all those earlier songs about broken hearts and betrayal by friends, or your cross-country trips. Things that people want to hear."

"And practice more. Being the best in the Queens coffee shop circle isn't close to what they expect at the top."

Galahad thought for half a minute. Bernstein waited patiently as he learned to do when waiting for Galahad to make an important pronouncement.

"I love you, Bernstein. I really do. I know how hard you are trying to help me, and yes, you are right, if I become a star, I can start saying and singing more of what I want. That takes a lot of work. So I'm going to give very serious thought to everything you tell me. But I am not making any promises. I can do it my way. I know I can. But let's see if I can do it your way as well."

STERN APPROVED of the way Bernstein was grooming Galahad.

"Unlikely an unknown guy with a guitar gets this much play time over the bridge," he said. "This is our version of the Beatles playing Hamburg for a year. Just getting better and better."

"The Beatles played eight hours a day, seven days a week for that full year," Bernstein reminded him.

Stern reflected for a moment, then replied, "Well, those guys wanted it more than he does."

It's my job to change that, Bernstein thought, *because I don't want to be doing this in five years. In five years, I want to be either rich and famous in this business, or maybe Willie has a place for me in the plastic slipcover business. In five years, it's either up or out.*

SMALL CLUBS, bars, and coffee shops featuring live music to draw customers were scattered throughout Queens and Nassau. Most were unknown beyond their neighborhoods. Those were the fields in which Bernstein toiled, seeking the band that would carry him away. Managers didn't book acts into these places; the acts played for free with little or no vetting, hoping to be discovered. Few of the bands he saw would realize their dreams, but working the club circuit improved their chances because they practiced and played. Bernstein first had Galahad play in several of these dives. He wanted him on stages playing in front of real people who didn't know him. Bernstein used the instant feedback—applause or catcalls, tip level, encore calls, and future dates—the same way a football coach used films of games and practices.

Those audiences loved Galahad, and not for the spiritual numbers; 90 percent of the listeners showed enthusiasm for the melodic folk-rock ballads telling stories of love, rejection, hard times, and good times. When Galahad slipped in a song about the meaning of life or the benefits of losing one's ego, most in the audience politely waited for the next number. *Sometimes not so politely*, Bernstein recalled.

After each performance, Bernstein and Galahad discussed what worked and what didn't. In most cases, Bernstein insisted it all worked except for the spiritual songs, which slowed down the performance. Galahad eventually agreed to limit the spiritual songs to two or three per night, and whatever the artist thought of the restriction, to Bernstein's relief he abided by it. He was booking Galahad for paying gigs, and didn't want to drive customers away.

AT THE BEGINNING, Bernstein set his sights to work with Galahad and Stern to put together a backing band for a demo tape and prepare for the recording session. Galahad first needed to reach the point where he was ready.

Bernstein was pleased with the attention he had gotten Galahad. There was a passing reference in the *Village Voice* and two mentions in the *Soho News*. Those were not easy journalistic nuts to crack; they were quite selective about who they mentioned on their pages, unless it was a paid ad. The *Long Island Press* mentioned him in their music column, as did smaller Queens and Nassau publications that covered any event, but all publicity is good when no one knows you.

Still, for the most part his growing popularity was fueled by word of mouth. Bernstein had not anticipated the fruit they would harvest by cultivating existing networks—Queens College, the music lovers who caught him once at a small venue and made it a point to see him again, even the small and tightly knit yoga community. Bernstein appreciated all support, but would have preferred fewer yogis and more pure music lovers. He was just beginning to develop Galahad's image, and a Donovan clone or a would-be swami were not what he wanted. Club owners didn't care where the customers came from, so long as they showed up and spent. Having Galahad on the bill guaranteed a crowd that was willing to spend. Yogis were the smallest component of the crowds.

Chapter 13
Late April, 1970

After working clubs for several months, Bernstein decided the time was right to bring Galahad into the studio. There were two matters to resolve—his legal arrangement with Galahad, as despite months of working together, Bernstein had not entered into any formal agreement with his client, and funding for the studio.

The first was easy. Walter had drawn up previous contracts for Bernstein, and he was quick and cheap. This one was the same. Bernstein would receive 10 percent after recouping any expenses, and the 10 percent included everything and any place.

"Never know when one of your people goes international. You don't want to be negotiating foreign rights then," Walter explained. "None of these folks will be thinking about this when they sign."

The hard part was getting the money. Stern knew of a small studio that didn't usually record rock, but there was no reason they couldn't, and Stern had an engineer in mind, someone he had worked with many times over the years who would love to pick up some extra cash. Stern would of course play lead, and finding a bass and drums wouldn't be much trouble for him. Stern would work for free with the understanding that on any paid album work or live shows, he had the lead guitar spot. Bernstein couldn't imagine anyone arguing with Ed Stern playing lead for Galahad.

Paying for the demo was beyond Bernstein's means. Even with Ed's connections, studio time for recording and mixing and an engineer would cost over a thousand dollars. A backup band, aside from Stern, expected to be paid cash on the barrel. Tape copies were not free, food and drink would have to be supplied, and Bernstein's weed bill for the band and himself was going to be a line in his budget, a budget he could not afford, as his bank account would barely pay for the first hour in the studio. That was how Pete's guitar wound up in a pawnshop, and why Bernstein met Mitty in his green Lincoln the same time and place every month. The clock was running on reclaiming the guitar and the due date for the loan.

Bernstein and Galahad spent a long two-hour lunch in Chinatown settling on a playlist several days before they started recording. It would be four songs, three crowd-pleasing favorites with the full band and a fourth featuring Galahad on acoustic guitar, overdubbing an acoustic melody line. He would be accompanied on that song by only a tabla player from the ashram where he studied yoga and meditation. Bernstein didn't like yielding on that fourth song, but that was the price to be paid for working with Galahad. He hoped to mitigate any damage by persuading Galahad to allow Ed Stern to lay down a slow, tasteful lead, which Bernstein thought would make the song sound more like the others. Galahad reluctantly agreed but made no further concessions on the song.

Bernstein cringed as he calculated the percentage of record labels whose A&R people would instinctively throw out any tape with a slow, acoustic, religious track with lyrics as thick as whole-wheat pizza dough.

Chapter 14
May, 1970

W hen Bernstein paid for the studio time, he imagined the biggest problem he faced was keeping Galahad's admirers at bay during the recording sessions, especially the ladies. This task portended promise; if an unknown Galahad drew crowds to a tiny studio, he could only imagine the audience after a few albums and national tours. As the recording progressed, Bernstein learned how much he had failed to consider, and while he tried to act like he was as at home in a studio as Ed Stern, he knew how fortunate he was to have a good friend who actually understood the process in the studio at all times.

"Don't worry," Ed told Bernstein the day before. "Anything you don't understand, ask me. You can talk to the engineer, too. He's cool, and he's always dealing with managers who haven't set foot in a studio before. He's happy to work with them, hoping they'll be back someday."

~

ED STERN WAS the sessions's musical anchor. He was the most experienced and accomplished musician, as he had spent most of his professional life in studios. He spoke the language of musicians and engineers. More than any other person, he reached the musician in Galahad. Stern's guitar riffs and leads pulled Galahad into the rock numbers, even if Galahad's heart lay in his spiritual balladry. Ed explained to Bernstein that he was saving a great deal of money because, in the typical case, it required several takes before a recording was of the quality a label expected. When musicians hadn't practiced or hadn't played together before, like he and Galahad had, it could require several more costly takes before it sounded right.

"I've played with Galahad for months now, and the bass player and drummer are experienced studio men who are always called upon to play with others for the first time. That's what makes us pros," he said. Bernstein sensed the pride in his words.

Stern had his theories about Galahad's music. "It's easy to pull him in because at heart he's a rock and roll musician, not the heaviest or loudest, but he's a rocker, and he loves jamming. Blues-based rock. He'll even take a few short leads if you notice. Watch him. The rock and the jams come naturally, but if you look closely, you'll see he really has to work at keeping that calm and saintly demeanor. I'm not sure if it's an act or if he's gotten himself dragged into some cult, but I'm telling you—I've been making music with the guy often enough these days, and I know the real musician in him."

When the two played together at Ed's home studio, Stern drew Galahad into rock music and wouldn't let him leave as long as either could keep playing. Bernstein appreciated Stern as teacher, showing Galahad through his electric guitar that rock was as poetic and communicative as folk and as meaningful as religious music. Stern made his Stratocaster cry, wail, weep, whisper, and sigh. Whatever Galahad said with his lyrics, Stern said with his licks. Bernstein also knew Galahad grasped that he needed Stern to infuse his songs with the musical quality they demanded. When Bernstein watched Galahad make music with Stern, he saw two artists who loved playing with each other despite being very different people. Bernstein knew no manager could have that relationship with their musicians, because business and art were like oil and water.

What Bernstein didn't understand was why Galahad would resist his natural instincts and insist on recording spiritual songs that didn't have the audience potential of rock.

~

ON THE DAY of the recording, Bernstein was the first person the engineer admitted into the studio, which was on the third floor of an office building just outside the main music district. He limited admission to Bernstein and the musicians. If any of Galahad's fans showed up, they would have to wait in the lobby of the building. The engineer, named Rick, had hair as long as Stern's and a nicely trimmed beard and mustache. He wore a long-sleeved denim shirt. Stern had warned Bernstein that the studio could be chilly, as working musicians appreciated not sweating themselves into exhaustion. He too wore long sleeves despite the short-sleeved weather common in early May in New York.

Rick said he was a transplant from Los Angeles who combined his obsession with machinery with music appreciation.

"I came to New York through some connections in soul music back in the mid-fifties, and when that dried up, I knew enough people to start freelancing. Music is a much bigger business these days, and listeners demand the best. That's why studios became more important than ever, and why we have studio musicians like Ed Stern. You ever hear some of these top forty bands play live? Tell me if they sound anything like the records. It's the studio pros on the albums. You don't want some kid playing through a half million dollars of equipment when they don't know what they're doing."

He gave Bernstein a brief tour of the floor where the musicians would play and be recorded, the glass-enclosed booth where the recording engineers operated their controls, and the adjacent separate enclosed section for observers. Inside the engineer's booth, Rick fiddled with various dials and flipped several switches before leaving the little room.

"Setting it up for the sound check," he explained.

Bernstein could see from Rick's breezy confidence and his ease at the control board that he and Galahad were in good hands. Rick played the studio as well as Stern played lead guitar. His rates were reasonable and well worth it, but still high for Bernstein, who was most appreciative of the break in the fee Stern negotiated.

"Managers and producers can come into my booth any time they want so long as they don't disturb me," he said after the tour.

"There's no producer here," Bernstein said. "Just me."

Rick arched his eyebrows and chuckled.

"You're the producer, Jack. You paid for everything, you assembled the band, you will be the one I turn to if there's an important decision to be made."

Stern's prediction proved right—not one of the four songs needed more than three takes.

"Anyone can miss a note or be off on the rhythm," he told Bernstein. "But when you've practiced these numbers as much as me and Galahad with two smart studio guys like we have, we get it down pretty quick."

The recording took one full day, the majority of the time spent on matters other than recording—setting up, sound test, jamming, rehearsing each song once and then a complete dry run. Stern had recorded some of the practice sessions from his home studio and shared them with the two studio musicians so they were familiar with the songs.

"That's actually more of a heads up than most session guys get," he told Bernstein.

A fair amount of time was expended smoking the strong weed Bernstein brought. Between songs, he broke it out, and he and Ed rolled joints. Two or three went around at the same time and the glass-enclosed viewing room quickly filled with smoke. The odor of marijuana lingered throughout the day. Fortunately, it was a sativa strain, which the assembled potheads considered an "up" as opposed to indica, which they all knew to be a "down."

"It wouldn't really matter anyway," Stern admitted. "We studio musicians are pretty experienced at playing stoned out of our minds. A lot of guys actually prefer to play that way."

Galahad didn't join everyone else on the smoke breaks. He stopped smoking shortly after Bernstein met him. He went into the engineering booth and meditated while Rick was smoking with Bernstein and the band.

BERNSTEIN WATCHED all four numbers with full attention. He knew Ed Stern would play his parts perfectly, and he had no doubt as to the drummer or bass player's abilities. He kept his eyes on Galahad the entire time. When Galahad missed a note on the first song, he saw the confusion in his artist's face and winced. He held his breath after Rick announced "Take two" through the studio sound system and exhaled only after he saw a new look of confidence come across Galahad's face when he made it through the song without a mistake. After that, neither Bernstein nor Galahad panicked when another take was needed. When the recording session ended, the two camps reconvened —Galahad meditating in Rick's booth while everyone else got stoned in the observation area.

Stern told Bernstein this was one of the most efficient sessions he'd ever participated in.

"We got four really nice songs, even that stupid song with the Indian bongo player," Stern said, referring to the tabla player accompanying Galahad on the lone spiritual song. "Usually takes two or three days of studio time to get something this good."

Couldn't have afforded another day, Bernstein thought. *Sounds like we got what I need. If not, I'm screwed.*

Chapter 15
Last week of May, 1970

A week after recording, Bernstein, Galahad, and Stern met with Rick to mix the tape. Bernstein was happy to step back and allow the musicians and engineer the first go at mixing, and he would only weigh in on commercial appeal. Mixing required balancing and fine-tuning the various music components of the song —vocals, lead and harmonies, and each instrument. Bernstein believed a smart producer—as Rick designated him—needed a good engineer and should rely on them.

During the mixing, Rick not only allowed smoking in his booth, he encouraged it. Stern insisted that Rick and Bernstein save their own stashes and enjoy smoking the Panama Red a grateful band had given him when he stepped in to play leads their own guitarist could not. That was due to the cocaine adulterated with speed that had given him heart arrhythmia and caused his physician to bar him from leaving bed for at least a week. Galahad left the booth when they smoked and sat quietly in the viewing room.

"Couldn't afford to blow the studio money and couldn't afford not having a new album released before fans forgot them," Stern told the others. "Obviously, I can't get any album credits because everyone is supposed to think it's their guy doing the leads. I did get double pay and an ounce of this mind-blowing weed."

Rick suggested several places in the songs where a bass or treble adjustment would improve the sound, and Stern persuaded Galahad to allow a more prominent bass line in the rock numbers. It took several attempts because Galahad believed too much bass ruined a song, while Stern held just the opposite view.

"I don't want people to think I'm heavy metal," Galahad said as he, Stern, and Bernstein stood in the control booth and Rick sat hunched over the controls.

"No chance you're gonna be mixed up with Led Zeppelin," Stern replied. "Remember, every song needs a good bass line, and if it's good it should be heard. The bass sets down the beat as much as the drummer. They go together. No one says to keep down the drums, do they?"

"If you say so," Galahad said.

Bernstein saw Rick look quickly at Stern. Stern didn't react. Later, when Rick took a coffee break and Galahad meditated while seated in the recording area, Stern told Bernstein what he felt.

"Didn't like being shown up by a professional in front of professionals. Well, maybe that's a good sign. The big stars hate being told they're wrong, even if the advice helps them. But he did agree, which is what matters."

"You said he doesn't like being shown up in front of professionals," Bernstein said. "First, thanks for the compliment. Second, isn't Galahad a professional too?" he asked.

"That's what we're here to find out," Stern said.

When they were done mixing, Stern and Galahad went back to Queens in Ed's car. After Galahad and Stern departed, Rick invited Bernstein back into the recording booth for one more celebratory joint.

"A pleasure working with you," he said. "This guy has that special something you need to stand out from the crowd. And I don't say that to everyone."

"Hope we work again on the album," Bernstein replied, assuring Rick there would be an album. "I mean, like, there has to be one. Otherwise, what's the point?"

"None," Rick said. "That means no reason this Galahad doesn't become a star sooner rather than later. I would, however, suggest dumping the religious stuff. No market for it."

Bernstein had no doubt Rick, a pro with a sterling reputation, was being candid. He was not likely to undermine confidence in his judgment with false promises. There were enormous fees to be earned engineering an album from a major label. Whoever signed Galahad would know Rick and would probably agree to hire him.

"I can make a call to the head A&R guy over at Luna Records," he said. "I've done a lot of work in their studio and sent a few bands their way."

Luna had the money and pull to make their artists stars, and the best studio in the world. They made their fortune promoting the music he hated—bubblegum, loud and obnoxious glitter rock, and middle-of-the-road soul listened to mainly by White people. Bernstein never knew Luna to handle anything like Galahad, but he saw no downside to pursuing Rick's offer, nor did he discount the possibility the engineer, having worked at Luna's studio, saw something he thought would appeal to Luna.

"I can't thank you enough," Bernstein replied. "Luna would be wonderful, just fantastic. Be an honor to be associated with Luna."

But only when they write a check.

Chapter 16
Late January, 1971

Bernstein waited a full three months after the tape was completed to call Luna. He appreciated Rick's connection, but in his heart, Luna was the last resort, not his starting point. By the time Bernstein broke down and decided to contact them, Columbia/Epic, Capitol, Warner Bros, RCA, and even Polydor had passed on Galahad. Each label said the same—drop the religion, get a permanent backup band, add more rock, and then they might talk album and tour. A couple of the labels offered to purchase the songs, thinking they would be perfect for their own artists. Bernstein declined, as he and Galahad agreed ownership would always remain with the artist. Galahad insisted upon complete artistic control of his work, which Bernstein found admirable. He would not change this to suit the labels, and if they wouldn't take him as he wanted, they wouldn't be able to play his music their way.

"The labels see this as being too rigid," Bernstein explained to Galahad, "but if you're a performing artist, that's how it has to be. If you were only a songwriter, that's different. You sell the song, you license it, whatever…that party can arrange it and sing it any way they like, unless it hurts you somehow. You have the right to say 'play it as I meant it to be played, or don't play it at all.'"

"That's why I like you as my manager," Galahad said.

~

BERNSTEIN KEPT GALAHAD BUSY. He got him gigs at Queens College and Queensborough Community College opening for folk-rock acts Bernstein never heard of, groups whose careers were just a few months ahead of Galahad. *But he'll pass them soon.* These gigs placed Galahad before audiences of several hundred—much larger than before. He easily adjusted and was well-received, more so on the nonspiritual numbers.

~

BERNSTEIN WAS SITTING at his desk, which also served as his dining table, coffee table, and on rare occasions, his ironing board.

Bernstein knew well a basement apartment in Bayside, Queens was hardly a prestige address for an up-and-coming figure in the music industry. This condescension was brought home to Bernstein when he tried to gain the interest of a young woman who worked as an entry-level public relations position with one of the labels. "Queens?" she scoffed when he answered where he lived. "Wouldn't you even be better off in Brooklyn? At least they've got the Brooklyn Museum and Prospect Park."

~

BERNSTEIN WAS PERUSING a new form contract sent to him by Walter. Bernstein required his artists to sign a contract with a five-year commitment, which could only be terminated for good cause, like criminal behavior or inability to honor the contract. If the artist changed managers within that five-year period, they had to pay Bernstein a fixed amount of liquidated damages as his lawyer called them. Walter Blickner assured him this was legal. Since Tennessee Eddie betrayed him and was attempting to breach the written contract's terms for damages, Walter had tightened up the language and added new conditions. From now on, if an artist under contract wished to terminate for cause that would justify nonpayment of the liquidated damages, the artist had to state specific reasons in writing and allow Bernstein seventy-two hours to offer a written response.

"Why would you put in all your time and money, share your expertise, only to let someone else reap the rewards?" Walter asked. "We can't really stop someone from walking away from a contract, but we can make it easier to collect on the damage clause if there's no justifiable reason."

In other words, no more Tennessee Eddie hiring shark lawyers to intimidate. They messed with the wrong guys this time.

The ringing telephone shook Bernstein from his thoughts on contracts, shysters, and traitorous singers. He walked to the night table next to his bed and picked up the black receiver. It was Luna Records, and a voice Bernstein strongly suspected to be the receptionist who treated him so dismissively. She told him Mr. Krumpert had his tape and wanted to see him at six o'clock.

Bernstein's fingers tightened around the receiver's grip. It was four thirty. When Bill Krumpert of Luna Records wants to see someone, that someone drops whatever they're doing and goes to see Bill Krumpert. Bernstein would be going against traffic heading into the city. He could do it in about an hour. Bernstein liked driving. That was something that separated Queens people from city people. Bernstein not only needed a car for work, he couldn't imagine not having one. He loved driving on the highways or on Queens Boulevard when they were light on traffic, the FM radio or tape deck he installed blasting his favorite music. Bernstein didn't think he could ever be a straphanger, and he rode the subway as infrequently as possible.

He was soon cruising on the Long Island Expressway, heading for the Midtown Tunnel. For Bill Krumpert, he'd pay the toll. He passed a spot where he could make out the towering buildings of Lefrak Tower in Rego Park, where an old girlfriend lived, or at least lived there with her parents when they were going out, some five years ago. Bernstein never really liked her but felt compelled to stay with her for a while, principally because Lenny, one of the bigmouths from his old neighborhood, had told him, "Bernstein, you couldn't get near a girl in

Lefrak." He enjoyed having a girlfriend from Lefrak, especially since Lenny had no girlfriend at all. Bernstein kept the relationship going just so he could rub it in, until he had his fill of both revenge and the girlfriend. He hadn't seen either in years.

BERNSTEIN HATED TO pay for parking. Free space was one benefit of living in Queens, but he couldn't expect Bill Krumpert to wait while he trudged his way from the free parking available by the West Side Highway. He forked two singles over to the surly attendant at the lot a few blocks from Luna and left his keys in the car.

Inside, he found the same receptionist on duty.

"Mr. Krumpert is expecting you. Fifth office on the right. You're three minutes late."

Bernstein passed Duke Schwartz's office, and the door was open. The little man was seated behind his desk, and when he spotted Bernstein, he held up his hand. Bernstein stopped, and Schwartz beckoned him in.

"I told Bill good things about you," Schwartz said when Bernstein was within earshot. "Make me look good."

"Thank you," Bernstein said. "Any feedback on the tape?"

"Don't worry about the tape," Schwartz replied. "Bill already heard the tape. It's you he's checking out. Good luck."

Schwartz reached for a tape buried under the mess on his desk. "We both have work to do," he said. Bernstein nodded and left the office.

THE DOOR to Krumpert's office was slightly ajar, and Bernstein announced his arrival from outside.

"Come on in," Bill Krumpert's deep voice announced. Bernstein walked through the door and was greeted by one of the tallest men he had ever seen. Krumpert stood six foot seven if he were an inch, and his body was half again as broad as Bernstein's. He wore a dark suit and tie, and his short hair was more typical of a Wall Street lawyer than one of the most important people in the music industry. Krumpert pointed to a round table against a window looking out on Broadway, gesturing for Bernstein to take a seat.

"Duke's quite impressed with you," he said when they were settled. "Don't be fooled by that ridiculous wardrobe and the way he can act like a ten-year-old. Mrs. Schwartz didn't raise her son to be a dummy, I can assure you of that."

"Forty-five ears," Bernstein said.

"Not bad ears to have," Krumpert replied. "Those ears are Luna's bread and butter. How long you think we'd stay in business if we only recorded bands who could play their instruments well and write songs that appealed to people with a maturity level above age twelve?"

"Galahad can play his instrument and writes serious lyrics. Not everyone wants bubblegum. You heard that tape. Everything about it says class. We have Ed Stern playing."

"I know Stern. Good man. Used him many times," Krumpert said. "And you're right—that tape, on every level of musicianship, is light years ahead of the kind of music Duke handles. That's why he gave it to me, because my tastes are a bit more eclectic. The problem's that there's a hundred fans of Duke's music for every one of Galahad's. You see that I'm recording some groups that don't make us a whole lot of money, but there's a limit to how often I can do this. And to be blunt with you, that religious stuff could drag us into a real problem. There's no market for it. No one wants to hear it."

"Maybe we can tell that to Galahad and record the rest," Bernstein said.

Krumpert sat in thought for a moment.

"Jack, if it's okay for me to call you that," he began.

"No problem," Bernstein replied.

"And you can call me Bill," Krumpert continued. "Jack, what I like is your energy. You remind me a little of how I started out. Roaming New Jersey, looking for any band or solo artist we could book, and as soon as we got them some following, we dragged those record label A&R guys out to the clubs to hear them. Then Duke figured out they were basically using us as free talent scouts, signing up the good ones and making money while me and Duke didn't have a pot to piss in. So, we started doing our own recording, just like you. When we still couldn't get anyone to sign our talent, we just cut our own albums. I mean, once you have a studio master tape, it's not really that hard."

"I'm not interested in running a record company," Bernstein said. "I want to work with the artist every step of the way. Find them, guide them, record them, get them a contract and tours. I'll leave the record making and marketing to guys like you."

"Just find them and we'll take care of the rest," Krumpert replied.

In other words, come work for him, doing what Willie does for me, except Willie looks for good music. Bernstein hesitated before speaking his piece. He knew the consequences of saying the wrong thing to a man like Bill Krumpert.

"I appreciate the offer, but I'm really not interested in the kind of music you're talking about. I wouldn't even be good at trying to fake it. None of it would ever get past Duke."

Krumpert let forth a long laugh. He stood, raised Bernstein off his chair with a palm under his elbow, and led him to one of the walls.

"See these two photos over here?" he asked, pointing to the center of the top of three rows of glossy black-and-white photographs in gold frames. "Those are the two groups I really care about, the ones I really love, whose music sends shivers up my spine. It's just that good. The rest? They make all the money."

They stood there in silence while Bernstein scanned the photos. He knew every name on the wall but rarely heard their music on FM, which was the only radio band Bernstein liked. The two Krumpert loved were standards on those FM stations, if not superstars.

Krumpert broke the silence. "Get yourself set up, make them take you seriously, make a lot of people rich, and then they let you get away with all the vanity projects you want."

Bernstein wanted to tell Krumpert he hadn't come there to interview for a job as an A&R guy stuck out on the Island, rooting around for hidden truffles amidst the musical bog fields, finding bubblegum to bring to Duke Schwartz in exchange for a pat on the head and a wad of dough that was just walking-around money for

Krumpert and Schwartz. He knew he couldn't say such a thing to Bill Krumpert, not if he wanted to work in the business.

"I'm pretty committed to my music and my artists," he squeaked.

Krumpert patted him on the back. "That's what I see in you that I like. I see a lot of myself in you. I do. That's why I'm sharing with you a little about my background. I don't talk like this with everyone. But here, I know exactly what's going on. I was there myself. You think if you make a lot of money with music that isn't really what you listen to, there's something wrong. Nothing at all wrong with making people happy by giving them music they want to hear. As you can see, I still have time to produce the music I want to hear. It took me and Duke a few years to figure out the secret was not finding artists we like, but artists everyone else likes. You have some street smarts and a lot of good energy. You come and work with me and Duke, we'll make you rich and happy."

Bernstein felt a slight lightheadedness. He hadn't felt that way since the day he received two college acceptances in the mail—one to Queens College, competitive and free, the other a lesser-known state school hundreds of miles away. The latter might have been more enticing to a young man who shared a bedroom with two brothers and had never been far from home. A quick calculation informed him it was far beyond his family's resources, and that would mean becoming an indentured servant after graduation, struggling for years to pay off college loans.

Bernstein had read in the *Long Island Press* that a four-year education at a state school could cost the student over ten thousand dollars, and that included Bernstein working a part-time job every semester. Bernstein's father was working at the same place he'd toiled at for over twenty years, and he dreamed of making ten thousand dollars in an entire year.

Standing in front of his door, a letter in each hand, Bernstein made his choice—Queens College and no debt. A wise move because, had he gone upstate, he would never have tried his luck in the music world and Bill Krumpert wouldn't be offering him a job with Luna Records. Being an A&R man for Luna was a prize for any ambitious young man seeking upward mobility. That made it even harder to say no.

To Bernstein's relief, Krumpert took the rejection without any anger or even disapproval.

"Sort of expected it. Exactly what I would have done when I was where you are. No hard feelings, I promise. Any time you change your mind, give us a call." They shook hands, and all the while as Bernstein walked past the album-lined hallway, past the supercilious receptionist, all the way to the Volvo under the West Side Highway, he kept asking himself if he had made the right choice.

Chapter Seventeen

E d Stern wasn't exactly supportive of Bernstein's decision. When he was told, he shook his head with such vigor that his long hair obscured his face as it moved in cadence.

"You turned down a job offer from Bill Krumpert? Do you have any idea how many guys in your shoes would give their eyeteeth to work at Luna? What's happening to you, man?"

Bernstein had expected this response and was resigned to the reality that it made little sense to the other, but he knew he owed Stern an explanation.

"To me, being an A&R guy at a label is something you do when it's clear you can't do anything else. You're running around like a pig with its snout in a pile of garbage, hoping you'll find some treasure for the boss. It's not going to be the music I'd ever listen to. Bill Krumpert made that clear."

"He told you how he had to record music he didn't like much because it made money, and some point he was able to record what he really loved. He was suggesting rather strongly that if you worked with him, you could be doing the same someday. You could then do whatever you want in the studio. Including hiring me," Stern responded.

When Bernstein heard these words, he felt an unpleasant sensation in his stomach, just like when he felt acid indigestion just around the corner.

Maybe I played it all wrong with Bill Krumpert. Did he write me off as an idiot, and if my name ever comes up in his world, is that what he'll call me?

"Are you telling me I blew it?" Bernstein asked Ed. "I made a wrong turn into a dead end?"

Ed must have seen disappointment and confusion on his good friend's face, and he qualified his statement.

"There's also another possibility," Stern said. "Krumpert thinks the bubblegum, in some form, is going to be around for a long time, but that's a fallacy. All styles run their course, every one of them. No one knows how many years Krumpert's music has ahead, or if its audience will exist for as long as he expects. A couple of years ago, we would have bet the farm on psychedelic rock. It was everywhere. I was getting called in twice a week to play on those albums. Most of the psychedelic band guitarists couldn't play anything beyond a basic chord progression or a simple pentatonic scale. No one cares at a concert since there was too much noise and drugs to even know. On an album, people listen. That was good for me. Then one day, I woke up, turned on the radio, and discovered the golden age of psychedelic rock was over. Have you noticed we aren't hearing a lot of the 13th Floor Elevators, Ultimate Spinach, or the Electric Prunes? The Beatles moved on, and the Dead are more blues jam band than psychedelic."

"If they ever teach rock and roll in college, you're going to make full professor," Bernstein said. "You're right. Music changes, and so do the memories of record label owners. I'll bet he wouldn't put that promise down in writing."

"And you'd be a damn fool to even ask," Stern replied. "There will be other tapes. So, what are your plans now?"

Bernstein spat them out as he thought them up.

"I've got to come up with the money to pay back what I borrowed and get that guitar out of hock. It would be nice if I had a little to live on."

"That's not a plan," Stern admonished.

"I do have one," Bernstein said. "I'm going to get back to basics. I'm the guy who can book a good band anywhere on the Island. Problem is I don't have any bands. I spent most of the last two years on two men, and right now, I have nothing to show for it. I'm going to keep doing everything I can to land a contract for Galahad, but it's not looking promising. I need to have other acts bringing in something so I can make ends meet. So, I'm off to sign up some more. I know just where to go."

"I'll bet you do," Stern said.

THE TALK of psychedelic rock and great bands of the past (in the music business, two years was the past) triggered thoughts of Bernstein's single psychedelic experience. He had never been a serious drug user and rarely went beyond grass but reading Tom Wolfe's *The Electric Kool-Aid Acid Test* and Aldous Huxley's *The Doors of Perception* made him curious, not to mention a very beautiful blonde in his Communications Science class told him she had tried LSD and it was nothing to worry about.

It happened in the fall of '68. He was certain of that because he remembered talking about the Democratic Convention and how the Chicago police took off their badges to avoid identification and started beating up and tear-gassing protesters. More than two years later, both the Convention and the acid trip still held some sway over him. The Convention assured he trusted no politician not named George McGovern or John Lindsay. The acid trip allowed him to speak with authority on a subject of some interest in the music world, and the psychedelic experience gave him a lasting and healthy respect for drugs. *Weed isn't even really a drug*, he reasoned.

They were gathered in Barry Tarpol's basement. The occasion was the first listen to the latest Hendrix album, *Electric Ladyland*. Bernstein managed to snatch a copy, but not through any connections; the few he had were on the short end of the stick when a new Hendrix album was released. Bernstein scoured every record store in Queens; he'd been to all of them to post fliers for his bands' performances. Every one he visited that day had sold out the album. He was out of luck until he stumbled upon Macbeth Heights Melodies, a cramped local dealer on the main street of a dingy, off-the-beaten-path, working-class section of Queens whose customer base was more likely to buy *The Four Seasons' Greatest Hits*. The salesman, also the owner, was relieved when Bernstein bought a copy.

"It's four o'clock, and you're the first sale on this one," he said, shaking his head. "When Jimi releases an album, people should be lining up before dawn."

"I guess not in Macbeth Heights," Bernstein said, grabbing his album and happy to be leaving the area.

When Bernstein arrived at Barry's basement, Henry Marble and Howie Felter were smoking a joint on the beat-up couch Bernstein knew well, having fallen asleep and spent many a night on it. He was familiar with every lump.

Henry and Howie were dressed in their usual uniforms—worn Levi jeans and blue work shirts intended for people who actually worked. Their long hair and trimmed beards were almost identical. Neither stood an inch over five foot five. Fortunately, Howie was thirty pounds heavier, so it was never difficult to tell them apart. Barry wore his hair shorter and was clean-shaven like Bernstein. He dressed in chinos and dress shirts. This fit his parents' conception of how a pharmacy student ought to look and kept from them his secret life as a hedonist.

"I got *Electric Ladyland*," Bernstein announced. "Let me peel off the plastic and drop it on the table," he said, pointing to Barry's fancy turntable.

Barry told him to hold off playing. "We're waiting for Stanley Gordon to stop by."

"Did you say Stanley Gordon?" Bernstein asked. His last sighting of Stanley was at his own bar mitzvah almost eight years before. When the service ended, and Bernstein was free to depart the *bimah* (the raised platform where the rabbi, celebrants, and the Torah were found), Stanley was waiting for him. As was his custom, Stanley informed Bernstein of the number of mistakes he had committed during the rendition of his *haftorah*, a selection from the Book of

Prophets rendered in Hebrew. Bernstein neither knew nor cared what the Hebrew words meant, but he did care about Stanley Gordon trying to disrupt the relief he felt now that it was all over. He punched Stanley in the face, causing his glasses to fall to the ground, followed by a spurt of blood trickling down the lower part of Stanley's face.

The following week, Bernstein's parents received a call from the rabbi informing them their son was *persona non grata* at the temple. Stanley may have been the bane of every bar mitzvah boy and their families, but he was a permanent member of the daily *minyan* needed for prayer, so he pulled rank to have Bernstein banned. Bernstein didn't care at all, as he had decided at age twelve that he was an atheist, and he remained one. *A Jewish atheist*, he explained to himself. His parents were not especially troubled, concluding they could use it as an excuse to lower their annual donation. "What, you ban my son and I give you more money?" his father asked when solicited.

"Stanley's coming by to deliver some acid," Barry said. "Supposedly it's the stuff Owsley made before he got busted."

"Well, that would have been over a year ago," Bernstein said. "Does the stuff hold up that long? Is it on a sugar cube or something like that?"

Barry laughed. He had told Bernstein of his three prior trips and was the only person Bernstein knew beside the young lady who had taken LSD. He was also a first-year pharmacy student, which to Bernstein meant he knew what he was talking about.

"Don't be an idiot," Barry said. "Owsley came along and did it just like Bayer Aspirin. He made them in little tablets. Millions of them. Some of them came into Stanley's hands."

The notion of Stanley Gordon as LSD dealer was not one Bernstein could easily absorb. He explained this to Barry.

Bernstein didn't tell Barry, but he was disappointed his friend knew Owsley as a drug manufacturer and LSD apostle. Not that Bernstein had any issue with either, but as far as he was concerned, Owsley's place in history was cemented by his work as sound engineer for the Grateful Dead and for his insistence on taping every concert and keeping it available for Deadheads to enjoy many years down the road.

"What can I tell you?" Barry replied. "People change after high school. Stanley went off to City College, met some people, and next thing you know, boom, he's selling tabs of Owsley's White Lightning. That's why these guys are here," he added, pointing to Henry and Howie, who were passing the end of their joint, down to a roach, and dangerously close to singeing fingers and lips. After one deep drag, Henry dropped it into the jar lid serving as an ashtray.

"I didn't come here to trip on any LSD," Howie called out. "I came to hear the new Hendrix album. One of us has to be able to drive."

It would have to be Howie who drove, Bernstein figured. Henry Marble became obsessed with the Aston Martin the first time he saw James Bond at nineteen. He dreamed of owning one, but they were clearly out of his range. As he grew, so did the obsession. Henry dropped out of Queens College his junior year to work delivering pizzas with the goal of saving enough to buy the car of his dreams. A year later, he had barely enough to purchase a twenty-year-old Aston whose dents and scratches told a history of abuse. Regardless, he paid the elderly owner and drove off. Twenty minutes later, while exiting the Long Island Expressway, the front right wheel came loose and separated, sending the car skidding to a halt on the grassy shoulder, inches from the guardrail. So far as Bernstein knew, it was still sitting there. He doubted Henry had the money for towing, storage, or repair.

"I hope he's still not mad at me for punching him in the nose," Bernstein said, "and for not buying any of what he's selling."

"Come on, Jack," Barry said. "Don't be afraid. Don't believe all this stuff you read in the papers."

Bernstein explained it had nothing to do with LSD. He just didn't want to deal with Stanley after all these years.

"Well, he'll be here any minute, so you're going to have to deal with him," Barry explained.

"And you don't condemn a drug just because the dealer is a putz," Henry chimed in. Suddenly, there was a loud knocking on the door to the backyard. Barry's friends routinely walked to the rear of the house when they visited. Barry opened the door, and Stanley Gordon walked into the basement.

He was six inches taller and fifty pounds heavier than the last time Bernstein laid eyes—and fists—on him. The thirteen-year-old boy was now a twenty-one-year-old man with a scraggly, unkempt beard and a mess of curly ringlets piled high on his head and falling over the sides. He gaped when he saw Bernstein, and Bernstein gaped back. Stanley's wild beard and hair and the fiery look in his eyes reminded Bernstein of the pictures of Rasputin he saw in his Russian history class.

"You're not planning to assault me again, are you?" he asked. Bernstein couldn't tell if Gordon was serious.

"I'm over it," Bernstein replied. "Sit down and listen to Jimi." Bernstein used his teeth to tear the cellophane wrapping from the album. He tilted the cardboard and the edge of the album peered out.

"Some other time," Gordon said. "I've got a few more stops to make. What is it, two tabs today?"

"That's right," Barry said. "Henry and me. Unless you want in, Jack."

"You guys aren't worried?" he asked Barry and Henry.

Stanley Gordon responded. "It's the worry and the fear that causes the bad trips," he said. "If you're in a comfortable place surrounded by friends…even if things get out of hand, they'll pull you back."

Bernstein didn't like "pull you back."

"Pull me back from where?" he asked.

"From whatever place you might slip into," Stanley explained. "That's part of the experience. Think of yourself as an explorer, discovering your own mind. I've taken over twenty-five trips and look at me."

Bernstein looked at Barry, who nodded and gave Bernstein a wink.

"So, what would I have to do if I were interested," Bernstein asked.

"Give me five dollars," Stanley replied.

Barry and Henry reached into their jeans pockets and handed the bills to Stanley. So did Howie Felter, abandoning his role as designated driver.

"So, you're going to be the odd man out?" Stanley asked as he carefully handed out three small white tablets not even the size of aspirins. Barry, Henry, and Howie each grabbed one.

Not if it would make you feel good, Bernstein thought. "Sure, I'm game," he said. "I'll take one."

"Five dollars," Stanley said, palm outstretched.

Bernstein thought for perhaps ten-seconds before slapping the five on Stanley's palm.

"Is this going to affect me tomorrow?" he asked. He thought of the audition he had arranged the next afternoon for his one band, the first and only client he had since starting to manage a few months before. The audition would be held at a fraternity house, the biggest on campus. Bernstein had already checked it out to make certain there was room for a full band, drums included.

"I wouldn't want to judge colors," Stanley said. "Other than that, you should be fine. Have fun." He headed for the door.

"Wait a minute," Howie called out. "I have questions."

"What is it?" Stanley asked, turning to face Howie. His scowl showed his annoyance.

"Now that I've paid you, can I just swallow my tab?"

Stanley glared at Howie. "As far as I'm concerned," he said loudly, "now that you've paid me, you can swallow it, snort it, shoot it, shove it up your ass with a bicycle pump for all I care." He stormed out, the door slamming behind him.

"Nice guy, huh?" Howie asked the others.

"Must have been some piece of work to get Jack here to punch him out. At his bar mitzvah, no less." Henry had witnessed the punch, and once or twice told Bernstein he wished he were the one who had delivered it.

"But then they wouldn't have banned me from the place," Bernstein countered.

"I don't feel anything," Howie said fifteen minutes after they downed their White Lightning with swigs of sangria from a bottle they passed around.

"Me either," Bernstein added.

"Give it another ten minutes," said Barry, the only LSD veteran among them. "In the meantime, listen to Jimi."

Side one of disc one ended with the fifteen-minute "Voodoo Chile." So far, the music was definitely psychedelic. Bernstein got up and turned the record over, glancing down at the label as it spun around the turntable. *It was a really bright red*, he thought. *No, it's actually blue. Now it's not a turntable anymore. It's someone's face. Whose face? It keeps changing.*

"Sit down," a voice called out. Since Bernstein was the only one standing, it had to be directed at him. Whose voice? Bernstein couldn't tell because the voice seeped through a sound between ice cracking and glass splintering. He sat on the floor.

Music filled the room. It wasn't Jimi Hendrix anymore. It sounded like the Beatles, one of the songs from *Sgt. Pepper's*, except it was being played at a speed so slow the words couldn't be understood.

"What happened to the record?" someone said in a voice that kept fading out. Bernstein heard another voice say it was the radio. The voices were drowned out by the sound of cymbals and then trumpets. Bernstein felt his body shaking, or was throbbing more correct? He thought he was watching himself from the ceiling, but he couldn't be certain who or even what he was seeing. He tipped over and lay on the floor. He was frightened, wanted to cry for help, but his vocal cords ignored his commands.

Sounds were distorted and constantly changing. He heard the fierce pounding of drums, then the clanging of the machinery at the 7 Up bottling plant where he had worked one summer. Then it was a broken muffler, a jackhammer breaking up concrete, and finally the distant pounding of the surf at Rockaway Beach.

Bernstein felt heat on his shoulder. It quickly spread throughout his body. Someone told him to sit up. He turned to see who, but all he could make out was a red mist with amber lights glowing from within. He started to fall back and felt something stop the fall. He detected distant sounds that resembled human speech but lacked the clarity of any language and sounded like a series of grunts and hoots. After a while, Bernstein realized that those sounds were words in his own language.

"Sit up and open your eyes. Keep them focused on me." Bernstein struggled to follow the instructions but recognized Barry. "Remember at all times that what you see and hear is not always real, and good or bad, it all comes to an end."

"Nothing is real?" Bernstein croaked.

"Only what you want to be real," Barry said. "That's not the same."

Barry sat next to him, and when Bernstein looked, his friend was the same as always.

Only what you want to be real.

The heat and the fright left Bernstein. He and Barry sat in silence, the radio playing the very same Hendrix album he had brought to Barry's, and they sat and listened to the man they considered their guitar god. Every now and then, images like Rorschach test blots flashed before him, and he reminded himself they weren't real. Gordon appeared twice, once pressing a handkerchief against a bloody nose, then later holding a bicycle pump and laughing maniacally. Bernstein learned he could make these apparitions disappear just by willing it so.

Emotions were a different story. After the fear washed away, and Bernstein mastered the skill of willing away unwanted hallucinations. Flushes of euphoria teased him, alternating with flat calmness. A few times, the euphoric bursts simulated orgasms with Jennifer. When he thought of her, a moment of panic gripped him, but he pushed the image out of his head. He waited for the emotion to leave on its own, and when it did, his mind went blank.

Barry shook Bernstein awake.

"Let's watch the sun come up," he said. "Henry and Howie are already outside. There's a pot of coffee if you want."

It took Bernstein a minute to stand up and stretch every part of his body. He blinked several times. Barry's basement looked normal, and he felt fine except for a worrisome concern that whatever force possessed him the night before still lurked inside.

THE YARD behind Barry's house was large and protected from the rest of the world by fences and trees. The neighborhood was still asleep, all lights out and no sounds coming from anywhere. A pale sliver of moon faded as the beginnings of daylight peeked through the dissipating darkness, the sun's red glow tingeing the edges.

Henry and Howie were lying on their backs on the grass. Barry sat cross-legged, and Bernstein did the same.

"How was your first trip, guys?" Barry asked.

Howie was the first to answer. "Nothing like I expected. No urge to jump off a roof or anything like that."

"We were in a basement," Barry said.

"I never felt afraid," Howie continued. "Not for one-second. I loved every bit. It felt like I was dreaming but knew it and could change the dream any time I wanted."

"Did you?" Barry asked.

"A few times," Howie replied. "I was seeing myself on a cloud, floating around. I was feeling bored and kept wishing something would happen. Next thing you know, I'm back in summer camp when I was like twelve years old. There was a whole story that played out, but I don't remember any of it. Last thing I recall was hearing music with lyrics in some foreign language I couldn't understand. Then Henry here is shaking me, telling me to stop yelling out French words."

"You speak French?" Bernstein asked.

"No, but they tried to teach us some in camp that summer. Not what I wanted."

Barry asked the other two to describe their experiences. Bernstein recounted all he could remember. "It was an interesting experience, not one I'd repeat."

"Why's that?" Barry asked.

"Because I had this feeling the whole time that something could go really wrong at any moment. Like I might totally freak out and be brought to the emergency room. Or slip into some place I can't get out of. I think I'll stick with pot."

When asked how his trip went, Henry said he would let them know when it was over and a few minutes later fell asleep.

"He was up all night, from what I gather. Grooving on the music, watching whatever the hell was playing in his head."

Bernstein asked Barry how things had gone for him.

"I read part of a book, wrote a letter to this chick in Boston, went upstairs, and made myself a snack. Then, at about one in the morning,

I fell asleep. Set the alarm so we could watch the sunrise. By the way, it's happening right now."

"That's what four trips does for a man," Howie said. Bernstein swore he'd never find out if that were true.

~

BERNSTEIN FELT the need to tell someone about the experience, someone who wasn't there. He tried Ed Stern, but there was no answer. Ed was probably earning money in a downtown studio. He considered calling his childhood friend, Phil Blickner, with whom he remained in regular contact, getting together every couple of months. Then he remembered Phil had a brother, Walter, who was a lawyer and had recently left the Queens District Attorney's office to set up his own practice. The brothers were very close and spoke daily. Bernstein's trip was a likely topic. Walter had offered to help Bernstein with any contracts or business issues that might arise, although at this stage in his career, Bernstein couldn't afford a lawyer. He expected to in the near future, and he didn't think it was a good idea to have his lawyer know he was experimenting with LSD. If nothing else, the lawyer would want all money up front. Suddenly, Bernstein pictured Walter sitting at a desk, wearing a suit, and belting out a version of "White Rabbit," originally sung by Grace Slick of Jefferson Airplane.

Wait a minute, Bernstein thought. *Walter Blickner can't sing a note, and if he could, he would definitely not sing a Jefferson Airplane song about drugs. The guy is a former prosecutor, straight as an arrow, a man destined to be president of his synagogue, the very model of all my mother wanted me to become.*

Now Bernstein understood why Stanley had warned him not to do anything too complicated the day after the trip.

The clicking of the rotary dial was much louder than it should have been each time he released it upon dialing a digit.

Definitely never again, he promised himself.

~

JENNIFER WAS PLEASED to hear from him, but not happy about his taking LSD. She still didn't even smoke grass. Over the year she had been Bernstein's girlfriend, it hadn't been much of an issue because he never smoked when she was around. Acid was different.

"Are you crazy?" she asked. "Have you forgotten what happened to Blue Boy on that episode of *Dragnet '67*?"

Bernstein faithfully watched the show because it reminded him of the original he had loved so much as young boy. Jack Webb still played the laconic Sergeant Joe Friday ("Just the facts, ma'am"). Webb was older and beefier, and he had changed partners for the new show. He also allowed his ultra-conservative views to seep into the stories. The "Blue Boy" episode told the tale of a crazed young man who mumbled non sequiturs, subsisted on LSD, and painted half his face blue like pre-Roman British tribes. Of course, in the end, Blue Boy was found dead, though it was never explained if acid killed him and how. It bothered Bernstein that this was supposed to be a crime show, and at the time, LSD was perfectly legal. Where was the crime? Bernstein didn't like LSD, but he despised anti-drug warriors with a passion. They couldn't see the difference between grass, cocaine, heroin, and LSD.

"That was a ridiculous story," he told Jennifer. "Crap like that probably encourages more acid dropping because their warnings are so ridiculous no one believes it. Webb wasn't giving us *Dragnet*, he was just doing *Reefer Madness* all over again."

He told her everything he could recall about the night before, from the moment Stanley walked into Barry's basement until he drove home the next morning, fueled by several cups of strong, bitter, black coffee brewed on the electric percolator in the kitchen upstairs from Barry's basement.

"So in this whole thing, I was only there for like a minute?" Jennifer asked when he was done. "I think I deserve a little more than that."

"Jenn, I was tripping on acid. What pops into someone's mind when they're tripping has nothing to do with reality. Or let me say it a different way—when someone's tripping, reality gets distorted. What you're seeing and hearing and feeling could be something really different from how it appears. So, you were surely in every thought I had during that whole acid trip. Just like you're in all of my thoughts when I'm not tripping."

"I love you, Jack Bernstein," she said. "But I still think you're full of crap."

THAT WAS A LONG TIME AGO, *and this is 1971, not 1968.*

Chapter 18
Second week of January, 1971

Bernstein hesitated a few minutes before dialing Jennifer's number. They stayed together for years after the acid trip in Barry's basement and didn't part on bad terms. Bernstein recalled how during his psychedelic experience, he was afraid he might be pulled into something he couldn't get out of, something that would only grow worse. His relationship with Jennifer shouldn't have ever started, and ending it was putting it out of its misery. She wanted a house in the suburbs, two children whose names she had already settled upon, and at least three weeks in the Catskills when the summer heat and humidity made New York City a soggy mess. All of this required a husband who worked hard, which Bernstein did, and made a lot of money, which he did not. Whether or not his acid experience was the catalyst, ever since that night in Barry's basement, these thoughts became increasingly more frequent in both their minds.

"You're a very nice guy," she told Bernstein when she ended it. "Great lover, too. But we're just not meant for each other." He took that to mean she knew he wouldn't do a 180-degree turnaround on his career trajectory. She made it clear over the course of their relationship that he was the one expected to change.

At least she said I was a good lover, Bernstein thought. He expected the breakup, as they no longer spoke about much beside her displeasure with him. Bernstein had no interest in what he called "her vaporous future," and she found his status in the music business an embarrassment.

"I tell my friends and family that you're an agent and a manager," she explained after a dinner with her parents, where the atmosphere was chillier than the air conditioning at the Fox Theatre. "But no one's ever heard of any of the people you manage."

"They will," he replied.

THEY ENCOUNTERED each other a few times in the six months after the breakup. It was always pleasant, as they both accepted their being very good but very different people. At least Bernstein *hoped* she thought he was good, aside from as a lover.

Jennifer picked up on the third ring. She was friendly, but a slight inflection in her speech betrayed her suspicion.

"Don't worry," he said. "I'm not trying to get us back together. I gave up on that, and we know it's best for both of us. I need a favor."

"What kind of favor?" she asked, suspicion in her voice.

Bernstein told her how things had gone wrong with Galahad's tape, and he himself was dealing with some pressing bills. Business was bad, and he needed to expand his source of talent. Queens and Nassau were relatively slim pickings compared to the city, even to New Jersey, but there were hidden gems throughout Long Island. One such untapped jewel was the homosexual club scene, under the radar for most straight people. Bernstein read the *Village Voice*, which now used the term "gay" instead of homosexual, but he didn't know if Jennifer read the *Voice*, so he used the latter term at first. He preferred "gay" because "homosexual" was longer and harder to say, especially when stoned.

"No doubt there are great bands playing all over Queens and Nassau that don't get discovered, because most people in the business don't go there. Even more true with bands playing gay clubs. The band makes money but doesn't get much publicity. The only reason someone goes to a gay bar in Queens is because they don't want to be seen or noticed. That's the exact opposite of how to get business. If someone did discover talent at a gay club, the gossip machine would wonder what the hell he was doing there. So most professionals stay away. If we show up together, it's just a couple making a mistake or having an adventurous night out. I just happen to be an agent and manager lucky enough to be there when a great band is playing. I'd sign them on the spot if they're good enough."

There was a brief pause on Jennifer's end. "And you can't think of anyone else to ask?"

"Not anyone who would accept," Bernstein replied.

She agreed to go with him. Bernstein felt warm inside, not just because he needed a female to announce to the crowd that he was not homosexual or gay (he'd have to settle on a term later). He was most pleased Jennifer retained enough good feelings from their relationship to be willing to help. Bernstein wasn't one who believed exes had to remain friends, but he was glad he and Jennifer remained friendly after their breakup.

Bernstein pulled his Volvo into the driveway of Jennifer's family home. She still lived with her parents, but their house in Jamaica Estates was large enough that she saw them only when she wanted. Jennifer was waiting outside the front door, and as she walked over to the Volvo, her tight-fitting jeans and blouse showed off her curves and breasts, which first attracted Bernstein to her several years ago on the campus of Queens College. Her black hair was cut just above her neck.

"No Mercedes yet?" she asked as she buckled herself in.

"It's only been a half year, Jenn. Give me some time."

IN DEFERENCE TO JENNIFER, Bernstein didn't turn his car radio to WPLJ, brand new to the airwaves but already his favorite FM station because it played the kind of music that couldn't be shoehorned into a top-forty playlist with a three-minute limit. John Zacherle, using only his last name, was one of WPLJ's disc jockeys. Zacherle once hosted a weekly horror movie show on television, entertaining Bernstein throughout elementary and junior high school. These days, Zacherle introduced songs in the same soothing, melodious voice that once introduced Frankenstein and Dracula. The new station also had this sharp and funny new kid, not much older than Bernstein, named Alex Bennett, a Jewish guy from San Francisco, like Marty Balin of the Airplane. It would be interesting to see if he stuck around. Bernstein gritted his teeth as Jennifer set the AM dial to WMCA, the worst offender in his eyes. *Duke Schwartz music*, he thought as the soprano sounds of AM bubblegum filled the cabin of the Volvo.

"I see you got the choke fixed," Jennifer said as they passed the Lemon Ice King of Corona. Actually, he hadn't, but it showed she knew the car well. He turned his head just in time to catch sight of the Queens icon. The lines were always long but worth it. Many were the nights he and Jenn had stopped off for a freezing cold scoop or two of flavored ice, and afterward, as they lay in each other's arms, he could swear when they kissed he tasted the flavors of the fruit in her mouth.

The place he wanted was in the least likely neighborhood for a gay dance club—an old-time Italian Catholic stronghold where the Church came first, the labor union second, and until Nixon came along, the Democratic Party third. Bernstein knew the club was owned by Vinnie Calamato, rumored to be a Connected Guy who had a half-dozen clubs between Corona and the Hamptons. This was his only gay place. Word on the street was it was his biggest moneymaker, as he could charge what he wanted for drinks and no one would complain, even add a cover charge if the band were any good. Bernstein presumed the police were paid well to stay away. Or maybe after seeing some of their comrades getting their asses whipped at Stonewall, they were no longer so eager to fight.

Bernstein found a parking spot around the corner. He and Jennifer walked to a nondescript squat brick building whose sign simply said "Drinks." Three beefy, scowling men dressed in black kept away potential troublemakers.

One of the tough guys nodded at Bernstein when he neared the door. Bernstein recognized him as a bouncer at a rock club out in Hempstead where Bernstein once booked promising local bands—until the son of a big-name record producer decided he wanted to drop out of Hofstra and manage. From then on, word was if you wanted a shot at the big leagues, better hire that kid, and his band did. If the tough guy was surprised to see Bernstein show up, with a female date no less, it didn't show in his blank face as he opened the door.

Inside, the club was bathed in a soft red light, enough for Bernstein to scan the room, though it became blurry at the far ends. A five-piece band played on the big stage to the left. The drummer's skill caught his immediate attention. A band needed a good drummer to keep the beat or they get nowhere. Bernstein recognized the bass player and the singer. Both were clients when they played with a different band. The bass player was very good, but the singer wasn't good at all. In fact, he was so bad the band fired him. The band itself fell apart a few weeks later, but Bernstein was glad to see the bass player was still working, even if he couldn't understand how he wound up backing that horrible singer again. Bernstein began to run through available singers he could bring in to make this band work and earn money. Then again, Vinnie Calamato might not like the idea if the crowd was already happy. *Doesn't matter anyway, because right now I don't have any talent to work with. Isn't that why I'm here looking?*

Bernstein had never set foot in a gay bar, nor did he know anyone who admitted to doing so. Bernstein believed two things—one, any club owned by Vinnie Calamato was safe from violence except if initiated by Vinnie, and two, with Jennifer at his side, everyone knew Bernstein wasn't gay. Not that someone's sexual orientation mattered to him all that much, but he knew it would be a hard sell to rock bands on Long Island. Those guys, and they were mostly guys, were quite macho, especially the Italians who made up a big part of the talent pool in Bernstein's territory.

Jennifer tugged his sleeve. "The last time I saw men dancing with men was when my cousin Sheila married this super-Orthodox Jew in Brooklyn," she whispered.

"I don't think these guys are Orthodox Jews," Bernstein replied. "And don't gawk. It's not polite." Bernstein's attention was then drawn to a small rotund man dancing in a close embrace with a tall, thin fellow. Jennifer told him she was reminded of the *Mutt and Jeff* comic.

"Do you know who that is?" Bernstein asked her.

"Which one?"

"The small guy. That's Winston Crane. British manager. Comes to New York all the time to promote his English groups and find Americans to book in the UK. Wonder what the hell he's doing out in Queens. All his business is in the city. Didn't think he knew about us."

Jennifer looked at Bernstein and shook her head. Her hair briefly covered her face.

"Maybe he doesn't want people in the city to know he's gay. Not likely to run into anyone he knows from Manhattan."

Bernstein chewed on the comment for a moment. "So you think he's afraid of what might happen if people found out?" *I sure would be,* he thought.

Jennifer told him that was exactly what Winston feared.

"It didn't hurt Brian Epstein," Bernstein said.

"Yeah, well this guy may be big, but he doesn't manage the Beatles," Jennifer countered. "He's right to be worried. Look at the way you guys talk about gay men."

So, she does know the new term, Bernstein thought.

"Not me," Bernstein replied. "Let's dance."

"I don't remember you being all that big on dancing," Jennifer said. "What's changed?"

"How often do I find myself on a dance floor with a beautiful woman? Especially in a place like this?"

Jennifer took his hand and pulled him to the center of the dance floor. He looked for Winston Crane on the crowded floor.

It feels really good to be holding her again, Bernstein thought as he glided around in circles, Jennifer wrapped in his arms and pressed tightly against him. *But right now, I've got to focus on business,* he reminded himself.

Jennifer led him around, choosing every twist, turn, and step, finally navigating to within three feet of Winston Crane and his elongated dancing partner. Jennifer pushed Bernstein a foot closer to them. "We're here," she whispered into Bernstein's ear.

How did she know? he wondered.

"My lord, is this Mr. Winston Crane?" Bernstein called out to the little man. "Just fly in on the Concorde?"

Crane looked up; his eyes focused on Bernstein's face bathed in the blue light.

"Do I know you?" he asked in his thick accent. Bernstein read in *Rolling Stone* that while Crane presented himself as upper class, he was in fact the son of a pipe-fitter and a seamstress who raised him in the British version of public housing. His education crested when he earned the British version of a high school equivalency diploma.

"Sure you do," Bernstein replied. "We met backstage at a Joplin concert at Queens College. February of '69." Bernstein really had seen Crane backstage at the concert, if only briefly, because Bernstein worked part time at Colden Auditorium, where the concert was held. As a graduating senior, he was awarded the plum assignment of shepherding VIPs backstage to the rooms where the band and their hangers-on gathered when Janis wasn't on stage. He hadn't escorted Crane, but he passed within a few feet of him later on. Crane's small, beach-ball physique and uncommon shaved head made him an easily identifiable figure. Bernstein had managed bands since the end of his sophomore year and made it a point to read all the trade journals. He knew about Winston Crane, who could turn an ordinary British pub band into an overnight success, sometimes scoring just one or two hits before they disappeared. Other groups of his released one hit album after another and packed crowded stadiums on tour. Winston Crane became a very wealthy and powerful person. Now he stood in front of Jack Bernstein, who danced with a woman while Winston danced with a man.

Crane looked at his shoes, lips pursed. A moment later, his eyes met Bernstein's.

"I recall the event," he said, barely audible over the music.

"Let's grab a quick drink," Bernstein said, and the two walked toward the bar. Jennifer nodded, telegraphing to Bernstein he would find her at the same place when he was done with his business.

"I don't drink," Crane said when they were out of earshot of their dance partners.

"Neither do I," said Bernstein.

"What is it you want?" Crane asked. He struck Bernstein as being annoyed and impatient but not afraid. Bernstein knew he had to frighten Crane to get what he wanted.

"Do you come here often?" Bernstein asked. "Or were you like me, didn't know this place was for…well, you know, those kind of people." He looked at Crane, certain he saw his confidence and impatience giving way to concern.

"Not that I mind at all," Bernstein added. "Far as I'm concerned, what a man does in bed is his own business, be it with woman, man, or beast. You know, like Mrs. Patrick Campbell said, 'So long as they don't do it in the street and frighten the horses.' Of course, not everyone feels the same."

Bernstein was confident he had Crane's full attention.

"Again, what is it you want?" Crane asked. This time, Bernstein detected a plea, not an arrogant dismissal.

"Three opening acts, anywhere within driving distance," was his reply.

The little man stopped walking as did Bernstein.

"Two," he said softly.

"I need three. I'm in a jam and need the bookings," Bernstein explained.

Crane tapped Bernstein lightly on the forearm. Bernstein withdrew his arm. Crane continued speaking.

"Vinnie owes me some favors. He can find something for the third gig. Give me your card, and we'll let you know when and where for our two. Go see Vinnie later this week. Give it a day. I'll let him know who to call for mine and give you a number to reach Vinnie."

Bernstein handed Crane his card. Crane took it but did not offer his own. He turned and walked back toward where Bernstein had left Jennifer. Bernstein saw that she was deep in conversation with Crane's tall dancing partner. He walked to her, his longer strides pulling ahead of Crane.

"I'd like you to meet my new friend, Marvin," she said as the tall man extended a hand, which Bernstein shook, surprised at the powerful grip.

"He's known Mr. Crane for many years," Jennifer said. "Can you believe they met at that same Joplin concert where you met Mr. Crane? What a coincidence."

"My psychology professor was a Jungian," Bernstein said. "He taught us there are no coincidences."

Marvin laughed.

"And I suppose Winston stole you away from this delightful young lady because of pressing business? We supposedly come here because he wants to avoid this and just enjoy ourselves, but I suppose it's inevitable." Marvin spoke in the slightly clipped accent of a New Yorker trying to sound British.

"Sorry to have cut into your enjoyment," Bernstein said. "I've been trying to get his ear for a long time, and this is one of the busiest guys on either side of the Atlantic."

Marvin nodded in agreement.

"If you think he's running himself ragged over here, you ought to see him across the Pond."

"I can just imagine," Bernstein replied, hoping Marvin didn't plumb for details of his knowledge of London, which was nonexistent. It wasn't a good thing for a rock manager in New York to exhibit such ignorance. The producers, agents, and managers in Manhattan spent almost as much time over there as in the States. Bernstein's rumination ended upon seeing the small, rotund figure of Winston Crane rejoining them.

"Mr. Crane has graciously agreed to use some of my bands as opening acts," he said.

"I hope we can meet up again at those events, if not in London," Jennifer interjected.

"It would be a high honor and distinct pleasure to entertain you there," Marvin replied, handing Jennifer a business card. "Stay in touch. I insist." Jennifer assured him she would.

Everyone has a business card these days, Bernstein thought. *Even people who don't really have a business.*

A half minute later, Marvin and Winston were dancing to a disappointing cover of *Black Magic Woman*, clumsily moving in what appeared a combination of the cha-cha and Deadhead-style freeform dancing. Bernstein and Jennifer, meanwhile, were back on the street. He disclosed his conversation as soon as they were inside the Volvo.

~

"So, you're really going to see this mobster?" Jennifer asked as she turned on the radio, still set to her favorite AM station, which blared out the 1910 Fruitgum Company as Bernstein grimaced.

"Duke Schwartz music," he mumbled.

"What was that?" Jennifer asked.

"Oh, nothing," Bernstein replied. "I was just trying to come up with the words to thank you for coming with me. And for sucking up to that queen so you could help me."

"Marvin is a lovely man," Jennifer said. "Don't look down on him."

"I don't," Bernstein replied. "I really don't care if someone's a homosexual. But I have to tell you, Jenn, there's an awful lot of people who do."

"So what?" she asked as the music ended and the disc jockey launched into a commercial. "Those are the same people who don't like us."

"You're right," he said softly. Jennifer patted his arm.

"You didn't have to blackmail poor Winston into helping you," Jennifer continued. "Like you saw, I can charm Marvin."

Bernstein killed the engine when they were in front of her house, but as Jennifer opened the door, she signaled to Bernstein she would make her own way into the house.

"It was great seeing you," Bernstein said. "I don't know how I can ever thank you for what you did for me."

"Try calling," she said and closed the car door.

Fortunately, the Volvo started again without any choke problems.

Why would she tell me not to see her to the door, Bernstein thought as he drove home, *but then want me to call her?*

～

BEFORE CALLING JENNIFER, there were two more pressing ones to make—Winston Crane and Vinnie Calamato. *Hold on*, he reminded himself. *Before you call these guys, make sure you have the talent lined up.*

There was Galahad, of course, especially if Stern would join him (Bernstein couldn't imagine otherwise). Maybe after some more serious gigs, the tape could be passed around again. Or maybe he'd eventually be discovered. Everyone who heard Galahad liked him. *Everyone except the record labels.*

Galahad still offered the best chance of breaking through, but the odds had dropped significantly. Putting all his eggs in one basket wasn't working. Bernstein needed real talent, and needed it immediately.

He checked out an act in a tiny club on the northern Queens-Nassau border. The band had potential but was nowhere nearly as talented as Galahad. They were a competent cover band but didn't show Bernstein any unique style, and their own songs were dull and leaden. Bernstein was done with such groups. After discovering Tennessee Eddie and bringing Galahad into the studio, Bernstein was not taking several steps backward.

If only Tennessee Eddie hadn't jumped and signed with that agent from the city right after I booked him at Max's. It was the first time any of his artists played Manhattan, and the next step is usually a recording contract. In fact, that's exactly what happened, and it was that slick city guy whose name was in all the trade papers, not to mention on the checks for 10 percent that would flow from record sales and concerts. *It should have been mine. I literally picked him up off the streets, supported him, and made his career. When success knocks, he sends someone else to open the door. Now I know how Pete Best must have felt when he saw Ringo sitting where he thought his ass belonged.*

Bernstein had a few other people he needed to speak with while waiting for Crane's call with the contact numbers. He pulled his little red phone book from his pocket and looked up a number he hadn't called in many months. It took a while to find it because there were so many cross-outs, changes, and notations that many entries were nearly illegible. The little phone book told the history of rock music in Queens. He found the number he was looking for, took a breath, muttered another of his silent, nonbeliever prayers for luck, and dialed.

Chapter Nineteen

Bernstein slowed the Volvo as he crept along Jamaica Boulevard, searching for the street where he had to turn right. He hadn't been here in well over six months. He knew he had to turn at a corner luncheonette, but he had already passed several that looked the same. He didn't want to turn down the wrong street in South Jamaica. He was embarrassed to feel that way, but he couldn't help it. He was no racist, just someone with legitimate concerns. He pulled into the parking lot of a Grand Union grocery store and found the telephone. Bernstein always carried coins for phone calls, the first thing he learned when he started out in the music business. Deals fell through for lack of a dime. He called Sonny, who gave him the directions. As it turned out, the luncheonette he wanted was a mere block from the Grand Union.

Thirty-seconds and two blocks later, Bernstein spied a parking space a stone's throw from a cinderblock building set between a seltzer delivery service and a monument maker. There was no sign over the door, just a neon musical note, and the picture window facing the street had one-way visibility from the inside. The club wouldn't open for another four hours, so Bernstein knocked.

Everyone who knew the place called it "Sonny's," after the large

Black man who opened the door. Sonny wore a white t-shirt stretched tightly across his large, well-developed biceps and chest. At six-three, he towered over the five-foot-eight Bernstein. His head was shaved, and he sported a Fu Manchu mustache. Bernstein followed him to the far end of the room, where Sonny went behind the bar. Bernstein sat on the stool across him.

"Before I ask what you'd like to drink, let me ask what brings you out here, Mr. Jack Bernstein. Been a while since we've seen your pretty face."

Bernstein nodded. Before Tennessee Eddie and Galahad, he relied on Sonny to find him a musician whenever he needed one. Managing bands meant regularly being a musician short. Bands fought, members quit or were fired, musicians fell prey to alcohol and drugs, and some were even legitimately ill or injured. Sonny's offered live music every day of the year except Easter Sunday, and he had a stable of hundreds of musicians, every one capable of stepping in on a moment's notice and playing at a local club. Most were Black, but some were Puerto Rican, and there was even an occasional White man. All were affordable and far less expensive than the studio musicians Ed Stern knew. The music ran the gamut from R&B and soul to blues-rock to sometimes pure blues. There was even a smooth balladeer every once in a while, a Johnny Mathis clone who was fine when the audience was in the mood for slow dancing until the main act took the stage. But every last act at Sonny's put on a show, exactly what was needed for the spots Winston and Vinnie had waiting. Real bands were expected to be ready to play anywhere on demand, so long as it paid. They were the live music version of session musicians like Stern, except session work was a lot steadier.

"Thanks to me, it's Christmas for them every month." Sonny once told Bernstein as they shared a joint in the back office after a night of listening to two passable and entertaining Hendrix clones, a fairly impressive Chambers Brothers tribute band, and a young lady who looked like Diana Ross but sang like Big Mama Thornton. Both men applauded the loudest for her. Bernstein was a lot busier back then and constantly called on his old friend to fill in the missing piece of a band.

"Sorry to say, I haven't had enough business lately to be worrying about filling up a band," Bernstein said. "You should have figured that out." Bernstein explained how the time and money put into Galahad's tape and the loss of Tennessee Eddie had set him back to practically where he had started out a few years back.

"I figured so," Sonny replied. "What I can't figure out is why you never came by to see your old friend and have a drink. I thought we were more than just two guys doing business."

Or maybe drop into the back office for a quick joint, Bernstein thought. He much preferred that to booze. Sonny, the perfect host, always had one ready. Bernstein felt embarrassment burning within him. Bernstein told Sonny he was right and apologized. Then he got to the point of his visit.

"I may have been a terrible friend, but I wasn't a bad business partner. So, I have a business proposal."

Sonny walked around the bar and sat on the stool next to Bernstein.

"From a businessman who happens to be down on his luck?" Sonny asked.

"Sometimes that's when we get the best ideas," Bernstein replied.

The big man reflected for the length of time it took to pour a drink.

"Let's duck into my office and talk," he said.

SONNY PALMER MADE it to the semifinal tryouts for the 1952 Olympics after dropping out of his sophomore year at Queens College to devote himself to the effort. He was a light heavyweight then, but almost twenty years later was a heavyweight.

After the Olympics, Sonny's grandmother persuaded him that being punched in the head for a living was not the wisest career path. "Get your ass back to Queens College and find yourself a job that uses your head for something other than a punching bag," she commanded, and Sonny listened. Both of Sonny's parents died when he was young, and his grandmother raised him. He feared no opponent in or out of the ring, save his five-foot-tall, ninety-pound grandmother, whom he revered as the strongest person he'd ever encountered. Sonny shared with Bernstein that he said many silent prayers for his late grandmother and visited her grave weekly. She'd passed away a year after he earned his doctorate. Without her no-nonsense approach to life, Sonny would have never gotten a bachelor's degree in education, let alone a masters or a PhD, nor would he would have recently been made a tenured professor at Queens College. Sonny was especially proud of this achievement, and like Bernstein, he was also proud to be born and raised in Queens and had no interest in leaving. He lived in his grandmother's house, bequeathed to him upon her death.

IF SONNY CARRIED anger or resentment over even one of the cards life dealt him, Bernstein never detected any. Sonny was the most even-tempered, unexcitable man Bernstein ever met. Bernstein took a course in comparative religion at Queens College and learned that all the world's religions had some version of people enlightened to such an extent they could remain calm and centered no matter what goes on around them. Sonny was that kind of person.

Destiny brought the two Queens County lifers together in a poorly lit Remsen Hall classroom in the tumultuous year of 1968. Sonny was a newly minted associate professor, working his way up from lecturer, and Bernstein took his Education I class with the expectation it would keep him from the draft. Despite his absolute disinterest in teaching or the field of education, Bernstein came to recognize Sonny as the best professor he ever had, and that included a bevy of Ivy League PhDs.

Bernstein felt good to be back at Sonny's club. He sat on one of the big, cushioned chairs facing Sonny's cluttered desk. There wasn't much room in the little office for anything else except a mimeograph machine on a stand and a small television perched on a shelf.

No one knew if the place had any necessary legal permits to sell alcohol, nor did anyone ever ask. The police certainly didn't seem to mind, and Bernstein had been in the business long enough to know Sonny regularly handed cash-filled envelopes to policemen who sat right where Bernstein was at that moment. Bernstein also gathered that more than a few fire marshals had sat on that chair. The place was usually packed far beyond the legal capacity listed on the aging wall sticker off to the side of the front door.

"I've gotten myself in a bit of a jam," he explained again. "I produced this tape, spending everything I had and everything I could borrow. So far, it's going nowhere, and I need to pay off those debts. Not to mention I have to live and grow my business."

Sonny rubbed his chin slowly and looked at Bernstein for a few seconds. "And how am I supposed to be of help?"

Bernstein explained he had commitments for second or third acts at big venues, but he lacked the acts to place. When Bernstein listed the venues, Sonny let out a long whistle.

"With all the talent passing through this place, you should be able to come up with some names," Bernstein said.

"Any time I can help you, I'd love to," Sonny replied. "So long as you explain what's in it for me."

"I'll give you a promise that they play here a set number of times a year and you get extra from the cover charges and I'll make sure the band announces when they're next playing here."

Sonny laughed. "After they get a taste of the big time, you think they're coming back here?"

"Get a written contract. In exchange for the honor of playing here, and I do mean an honor, they have to commit to whatever number of appearances you want. I'll give my lawyer a call, and he'll draw up whatever you need. All on me." It made Bernstein feel confident to refer to his lawyer. It made him sound bigger than he was, even if Sonny knew the truth.

The two men sat in silence for a half minute before Sonny broke the silence. "You think the Black artists playing here will go over with White audiences?"

"Otis went over quite well at Monterey, Jimi at Woodstock. Chambers Brothers, Sly and the Family, just about anything out of Motown…White audiences can't get enough of them. Just give me someone good. Some groups change their style to get cross appeal, but others don't have to do that. Either way works for me."

Sonny nodded and told Bernstein he was interested and would get back to him in a few days with some names and phone numbers. Then the conversation shifted from business to personal. Sonny confided that in seven years he would be fully vested in his pension.

"I'm going to retire from teaching and give full time to music. We'll be working together."

"Fantastic," Bernstein said. "We can be partners."

"Not what I mean," Sonny said and pointed to the big Fender bass hanging on the wall. "I mean you can manage my career."

Chapter 20
Third Week of January, 1971

Winston Crane was a man of his word. He called three days after their encounter and left the numbers for his two venue dates and also Vinnie Calamato's number. Crane had two spots set aside for Bernstein's acts as openers for big names, one at Westbury Music Fair, the other at Stony Brook, in the State University's auditorium. Each venue seated close to three thousand people. Both were available for any concert in the spring. He would call and find out the headliners and decide which of his stable was the best fit. He would do so the minute he had that stable. Booking bands into those two venues would put Jack Bernstein on the map.

The message was not delivered to Bernstein through his answering service. Instead, it was relayed to him by Jennifer, who heard it from her new friend, Marvin, two days after the visit to Vinnie Calamato's gay club.

"Such a delightful man," she told Bernstein when she called. "He mentioned again that we just *have* to visit him in London."

"This is great news, Jenn. I really can't thank you enough for all the support you've given me." *It would still be a much better sign if he called me, instead of having his boyfriend call Jenn,* he thought.

He realized Winston Crane intended their meeting at Vinnie's club to be their only encounter. Crane was treating Bernstein as if he were something unpleasant he had stepped on, to be wiped off the sole of his shoe.

"I guess with Crane it's secretary to secretary," Bernstein said. "Or perhaps Jack Bernstein is someone Mr. Crane would like to forget he met."

Jennifer laughed. "You can have that effect on people. But look at the good side—two really big bookings and a third on the way. Check out the main acts, find your own, and call these places as soon as possible. Oh, and by the way, this is one relationship you definitely do not want to screw up."

Bernstein knew she was right. No matter how Crane treated him, Bernstein had gotten what he wanted and needed.

"I think we can agree I have no relationship with that little man," he said.

"I wasn't talking about Winston Crane," she said.

"I can't get rid of you until after those dates. I might need you to deliver a message to Marvin if anything goes wrong." Bernstein heard a kiss before the call ended with a click.

Bernstein called Vinnie Calamato from a payphone a mile from his home, a weather-beaten booth along Horace Harding Boulevard in front of the Island Diner. He had never called a mobster before, and he had spent the past day nervously running his opening lines through his mind. While having breakfast at the Island, he recognized it was time to call. No more delays. He held the handset between his shoulder and his ear, his fingers close enough to the rotary dial to make the call as he read the phone number from a piece of paper in his other hand.

Bernstein accepted Vinnie was involved with organized crime. The unrebutted music industry talk had him a made man in the Mafia. The good news was that despite rumors, Vinnie wasn't known for violence or thuggery. Everyone in the business knew Vinnie's clubs made money for the mob and provided a legitimate source of income for those who needed one. Vinnie was left to operate the clubs as he saw fit, but no doubt he had some silent partners, the kind Bernstein hoped never to meet. Organized crime was present everywhere in the business, but so long as they didn't threaten him, Bernstein was unconcerned.

This reputed mobster was hardly threatening over the phone. "Oh yeah, the English homo mentioned you'd be calling." Vinnie's voice was a bit gravelly, but friendly. "You need some booking dates in my places? Hey, kid, you must be doing something right because we're having this conversation. I'm sure we can work something out."

Vinnie told Bernstein to meet him the following evening at an Italian restaurant in Middle Village. Dinner would be on him. Bernstein jotted the address on the small notepad he kept in the Volvo. As soon as he was back home, he called Jennifer.

"So how to I dress to meet a mobster?" he asked.

"Lots of gold chains and a silk shirt open almost to the navel," she said. "If only you had gold chains and a silk shirt."

"What about the chest?" he asked. "Surely I've got that."

"Barely," she said.

Bernstein smoked the remainder of a joint, then called Ed Stern. Ed must have met enough mobbed-up guys to give some advice.

"Don't worry about any of that stuff," Ed advised, dismissing Bernstein's sartorial concerns. "Way I see it, these guys are basically businessmen, and he's going to want to know what he can get out of you. Obviously, he owes something to Crane, like half the people in the business, so helping you clears that debt. For sure he's going to try to get something out of you."

Bernstein felt a stream of cold run up his spine.

"What do you mean, 'get something out of me'?"

"Lighten up," Stern said. "Vinnie's not sending you out to whack someone or break a few legs. He wants muscle, he's got all he needs." Bernstein recalled the beefy security men at the gay club. "You're in the music business, and somehow he'll figure out a way to use that to his advantage."

Stern sensed the worry in his friend's voice.

"Relax, Jack. One thing anyone in the business will tell you—if it's to Vinnie Calamato's advantage, it's probably to yours as well. He doesn't like to waste time or money, especially his own. If he asks you for something, almost a sure thing it will pay off one way or the other. Make sure you keep that in mind."

"How could I forget?" Bernstein said. As soon as he hung up the phone, he rolled a fresh joint.

❧

IN THE END, Bernstein decided not to dress any differently than he would on any other winter day. He wore his best Levi's and a black wool sweater that saw a lot of duty on these cold late January days. He pulled on his Frye boots, which he remembered to give a quick polish after he smoked the second joint. Then he put on the beat-up leather bomber jacket Jennifer had gotten him at a secondhand clothing store. He was halfway up the steps to the main level and front door when he heard his landlady, Mrs. Bardoni, speaking loudly to her daughter Anna.

"He keeps all kinds of hours, coming and going in the middle of the night, the early morning. He doesn't have any sort of job. He says he's in the music business, but he don't play any instrument. I'm afraid he's one of those guys that's up to no good. Maybe he's a drug dealer. I don't want any of that in my house. Your father, may he rest in peace, would turn over in his grave if he knew we had a drug dealer living in the house."

"Take it easy, Mom, or you'll give yourself a heart attack, just like Daddy. I don't want to lose both my parents," Anna replied. Bernstein pictured her, a few years younger than him, and from what snatches of conversation he had overheard the year he'd been a tenant in this second illegal in-law unit, knew her name was Anna, she worked at a department store in the city, was a part-time student somewhere, and her current boyfriend's car needed a new muffler. It wasn't the same guy he'd caught her screwing in his bed, because he'd once caught a glimpse of the new fellow. He and Anna never exchanged words before or after that embarrassing incident, rarely saw each other in the house, and only traded mild nods on the infrequent times they passed each other on the street or in the vestibule.

"Maybe I'll just raise his rent to fifty dollars a week," he heard Mrs. Bardoni say. "If he's a drug dealer, he can afford it."

Bernstein calculated this to mean an additional eighty dollars a month. Almost a thousand a year. He was finding it increasingly difficult to make the thirty-dollar-a-week payment.

"Mom, if he were a drug dealer, he wouldn't live in a crummy little paneled basement with no windows, a cheap rug, and a bathroom he can barely fit into. Remember, you offered it to me in high school, asked if I wanted to feel like I had my own place, and I said no? I liked my room better. Still do, which is why you can rent to him. Be thankful this fool's willing to pay thirty. It's not even legal. If the city finds out, you're in trouble."

After a brief silence, Mrs. Bardoni spoke. "Okay, my daughter. I'll listen to you. You know what you're talking about. You go to community college."

"And I'm off to class now," Anna said.

She called me a fool, but she just saved me a lot of money; money I don't have, Bernstein thought. *Better than being a drug dealer. Or maybe Galahad's right, and this is what good karma looks like.*

He didn't leave the basement until he first heard the front door close and then the muffled sound of a car driving away. The Volvo was parked up the block, but the walk seemed like a mile, and every second he felt people peeking at him from behind closed curtains.

Willie wasn't kidding when he said this stuff is super, Bernstein thought as he felt for his key in his pocket. *Pressed Colombian buds. They call it "wacky weed," and now I know why. I hope it's only the weed that's making me so paranoid.*

Willie always had the best since he could afford it. Willie sold him half the ounce he managed to get his hands on, and Bernstein suspected he charged him less than the true value. Willie was generous with Bernstein without making him uncomfortable.

~

THE RESTAURANT WAS SMALL, dark, and smelled of Italian food Bernstein knew would be red—the only way he thought Italian food should be cooked. As soon as Bernstein entered the building, a squat man in a well-worn tuxedo asked if he was Jack Bernstein. As Bernstein's eyes adjusted to the low-wattage lighting, he caught the mole on the man's cheek and the cheap toupee atop his head.

"Guilty," he replied.

He followed the man to a table in the rear, where Vinnie Calamato sat with his back against the wall. Vinnie rose slightly to greet his guest. He was almost the same size and build as Bernstein. He wore a suit and light blue shirt that fit him perfectly, unlike the rumpled style of Bill Krumpert, and his dark blue silk tie was expertly knotted. His hair was black and slicked back. A big smile crossed his round face as his brown eyes studied Bernstein.

Hope I didn't dress wrong for this guy, Bernstein worried, but if his hippie style bothered Vinnie, it didn't show.

"Welcome to my favorite little hideaway," Vinnie said as the man with the funny toupee pulled a chair behind Bernstein and motioned for him to sit down. When he did, the man asked if he could get him anything to drink.

"I'd recommend a glass of Sangiovese," Vinnie said. "Great for starters. I've got us a really fine bottle to go with dinner."

"I'll take that recommendation," Bernstein told the squat man. He couldn't pronounce the name of the wine.

"How did he know who I was?" Bernstein asked Vinnie.

"My people are good," Vinnie replied. "Albert's been here since the war."

Bernstein understood the reference to the Second World War. In Queens, the war in Vietnam was referred to simply as "Vietnam," just as the Korean War was known as "Korea."

Vinnie explained there was no need to order. He had arranged it all, the antipasto and salad, the main course of veal, and tiramisu and espresso for dessert. Bernstein didn't feel dominated or disregarded. He was quite certain Vinnie was proud of his restaurant—it must surely be his—and wanted his guest to have the very finest cuisine on the menu. Bernstein prided himself on being able to size people up. He knew it wasn't sheer luck he had lifelong friends like Ed and Barry but punched out Stanley Gordon. This radar told him Vinnie had some admirable traits, and playing the host was one.

Another was directness.

"Okay, kid, and don't take offense. I'm fifty-one and so I get to call any youngster like you a kid. I wouldn't mind if you called me kid, but then you'd be lying, and nobody lies to Vinnie Calamato, do they?"

"Not if they want to see the sun the next morning," Bernstein said, thinking at once he had made a serious error.

Not the case. Vinnie let out a loud laugh and slapped the back of the empty chair next to him.

"That's good, kid," he said. "I gotta remember that. You're funny, but smart funny."

"If I'm to be funny, that's the only way to do it," Bernstein answered.

Vinnie studied Bernstein's face. His dark eyes focused in the dim light.

"Of course you're smart," he said. "Like your name wasn't a tipoff. Of course you're gonna be smart."

Albert slipped in next to Bernstein and set down a glass of wine before scurrying off.

"I mean this as a compliment," Vinnie explained. "I hold your people in the very highest regard. My grandfather, he knew Meyer Lansky."

"Yeah, well, my grandfather, he knew Mussolini," Bernstein said.

Vinnie laughed again.

"Kid, you crack me up. I know none of your grandparents ever got near Italy. Anyway, my family hated that prick Mussolini. He was an embarrassment to the Italian race."

A skinny waiter came toward their table balancing a tray laden with covered dishes in each hand. Vinnie told Bernstein to enjoy the meal. They would talk business during dessert. That was fine with

Bernstein. Willie's weed calmed his nerves for the meeting, but made him very hungry. Vinnie delivered a running commentary on the ingredients and preparation of each dish, and a long soliloquy on the imported Sangiovese, explaining how in Tuscany it had a strong black cherry taste and in the south of Italy was lighter and tasted of strawberries and roses.

"You're quite the gourmet and wine connoisseur," Bernstein said as they rested between the veal and the pasta courses. He meant every word.

Vinnie beamed with pride. "Of course I am," he said. "Besides loving to eat, I own restaurants. I own clubs. I entertain. I got to know this stuff, just like you got to know music."

This guy may seem like a buffoon, Bernstein thought, *but he's not.*

After dinner came espresso and a tiramisu Bernstein described to Vinnie as coming from heaven. Then Vinnie came around to business. Stern had advised Bernstein to wait for Vinnie to start such talk. "That's the way they like it," Ed advised. Bernstein knew whom Ed meant by "they."

"Whatever you did to that little fairy, if you charmed him or scared him, he called in a bunch of favors to get me to help you. I just want you to know this."

"Consider it known," Bernstein said.

Vinnie explained he couldn't book Bernstein's acts into the same size venues as Crane. "Huge places like Westbury and Stony Brook are outside my territory," he said without elaborating on who established territorial limits or the consequences of illegal border-crossings.

"But I guarantee you that you will be booked at The Action House or that club that just opened up on the North Shore, up in Roslyn, called My Father's Place."

Bernstein had read about the new place, and it was supposed to be set up well.

"It's a really big break for any act you book at The Action House. Big break for you too, kid."

Everyone in the business knew about The Action House, and that included the sharks of Manhattan. Every local band of note played there as did some of the biggest names in music. For quite some time, the house band was The Vagrants, whose guitarist later joined Mountain and became internationally famous as a virtuoso lead guitarist after playing at Woodstock. The guitarist was known to the world as Leslie West, but to Bernstein, he was Leslie Weinstein from Forest Hills; another Jewish kid from Queens and only two years older than him. The only difference was Leslie had succeeded beyond his wildest dreams. Bernstein knew there had to be other Leslie Weinsteins out there, just as there had to be other Rascals, Jay and the Americans, Simon and Garfunkels, Shangri-La's, and other talents buried in the monotonous landscape of Queens, waiting to be discovered by Bernstein before the Manhattan sharks started to swim in those waters. Even when he found one, though, disappointment was a distinct possibility. Tennessee Eddie, of course, was a betrayal as well as a disappointment.

The Action House was not limited to local bands. The biggest names played there all the time. Vanilla Fudge, The Who, Mitch Ryder & the Detroit Wheels, Procol Harum, Sly and the Family Stone. Tennessee Eddie played there after he had dispensed with Bernstein's services.

Vinnie waxed on about the time he went to The Action House, maybe three or four years ago, and The Doors were playing. Part of the performance included Jim Morrison coming on stage roaring, out of control drunk, and peeling off his clothing. Morrison found himself in real trouble not long afterward when he was arrested in Miami for indecent exposure and then convicted and sentenced to six months in jail. Morrison was currently appealing his conviction, which didn't prevent him from recording an album in Los Angeles that was going to be released in a matter of weeks. Bernstein looked forward to this, being an ardent fan of Morrison and The Doors, especially their psychedelic numbers like *Light My Fire*, *The Crystal Ship*, and *People Are Strange*. With psychedelic music no longer in fashion, their music would be different this time.

"If it were me," Vinnie said, "I'd take The Action House. That's where the crowds are bigger and anybody who's anybody drops by.

They even got pictures of me somewhere on a wall. Hey, you know, kid—someday it could be yours up there, too."

"What about doing one at that new place up in Roslyn," Bernstein asked. "Maybe get some exposure on the North Shore."

Vinnie shook his head. "It's good thinking, kid, but won't work. You'll never get the crowds, and let's wait and see if people are willing to go up to Roslyn to hear music."

Bernstein knew he was right. As he figured, the mob would not trust a fool. They agreed that Bernstein would call Vinnie and let him know which groups and when. Bernstein wondered why Crane told him to call the venues directly, but Vinnie wanted to handle his booking part himself. It was easy to understand. As Crane was concerned, the less he had to do with Bernstein, the better.

Bernstein sensed the meeting was over, and he told Vinnie how much he appreciated his help and enjoyed his hospitality.

"Just one thing before you leave," Vinnie said. "Just a little favor I ask of you."

Bernstein felt his neck tightening as if he were being garroted. He struggled for words and air. The sensation passed as quickly as it arrived.

"You okay, kid?" Vinnie asked.

"Never been better," Bernstein replied. "Just thinking how happy I am to be able to do a favor for you." With most of the fear out of his system, Bernstein understood Vinnie Calamato wasn't looking to use him to whack a gangland rival or shake down an honest businessman unwilling to pay protection. *None of that was probably true anyway,* he assured himself.

Vinnie explained that the favor required Bernstein to do what he already did—manage a band. The band at issue called themselves the Plateaus, because their leader lived in a building at the top of the highest hill in Macbeth Heights, one of the less desirable "good" areas of Queens. Bernstein understood "good" to mean "White," and among White people in Queens, Macbeth Heights was scraping the bottom of the barrel.

"Macbeth Heights?" Bernstein asked, loud enough to surprise

himself. "They have bands there? If they were any good at all, wouldn't they get out?"

Vinnie laughed, paused, then laughed again.

"Kid, you don't know the half of it. My sister Anita married this total loser, and that's the best he can do for his son, let him rot in that dump. He's too damn proud to take any help, and my nephew's too dumb. My sister thinks their kid's the next Bobby Darin. We're talking about my nephew here, but to be perfectly honest, he's a little shit. If he weren't my own blood…no, make that my sister's son, I wouldn't lift a finger. But you know, it's family."

Bernstein told Vinnie he would jump on in right away. Vinnie handed him a paper with the nephew's phone number.

"His name is Flugel. Max Flugel. Ugly little runt. Nasty, too. Never heard him play or sing, but Anita swears he's got what it takes."

Everyone's an expert these days, Bernstein thought.

"Here's the deal," Vinnie said as he walked Bernstein to the door. "You whip the Plateaus into shape. You get them whatever gigs you can, anywhere except one of my places. If my nephew thinks he can start off with hard-to-get gigs like that, he'll never be any good, and I only allow good music in my clubs. When the Plateaus are that good, I'll put them on stage and pay them. Don't worry about them making money in the meantime, and if you're out of pocket, let me know. When they're ready to open some bigger place, you're their manager. And listen—if they make it, congratulations. If they fall on their face like almost everyone else, hey, you tried. I'm good with Anita, and we're good. In fact, you do this for me, we're so good, any time you're having trouble booking an act, a good act, you come see me. We'll find a place for them. *Capice?*"

"Perfectly," Bernstein said.

"He's a really nice guy, once you get past the image," Bernstein told Barry as they drank coffee in Bernstein's apartment. Bernstein had been a coffee aficionado since the day a friend explained coffee included brews far above the quality of bitter instant or percolated jet fuel. Bernstein bought Bohack's Special Blend, ground it fine right there at the supermarket, and drip-filtered one cup at a time.

Barry almost spit out a mouthful of coffee.

"Jack, he's a mobster. Part of organized crime. Those guys who get shot in barber chairs."

"Barry, this guy manages rock clubs. Even gay ones. And he obviously loves his sister. How bad can he be?"

"I hope we never find out," Barry said.

Chapter Twenty-One
First week of February, 1971

Bernstein loathed Macbeth Heights, but a visit was well worth two extra bookings, bands of Bernstein's choice at any of Vinnie Calamato's clubs.

It was just after rush hour, and the mid-winter twilight cast its glow over the streets of northwest Queens. Nothing had changed since the last time Bernstein visited Macbeth Heights. The Volvo glided past seedy fast-food joints and corrugated steel gates pulled over businesses closed for the day. Working people, back from their wearying jobs, scurried into apartment buildings with broken steps and bars on their windows. Most street corners sported overstuffed garbage cans. Broken cars sat on blocks along the side streets.

Bernstein turned right onto Macbeth Heights Road. It elevated gradually, climbing steeply to a plateau at the top where on a clear day one could see gas tanks and smokestacks on a municipal facility whose function was a mystery. This spot was considered top-of-the-market in Macbeth Heights. He parked in front of a grocery store across the street from where he was to meet the band, a relatively new eight-story apartment building, at fifteen years old the latest development in the neighborhood. There were no bright lights or fancy displays in the grocery store windows, only handwritten signs on butcher block paper. Metal shopping carts stood scattered about the sidewalk. Bernstein spotted a luncheonette a few doors down. Outside, a cluster of young men wearing black leather jackets, cigarettes dangling from their lips, posed and strutted for their girlfriends, several of whom were peroxide blondes. Bernstein wondered if any of them knew James Dean died fifteen years ago. *Definitely not Galahad's audience,* he thought.

The audition was in the building's community room. As instructed, he walked toward the front door, and just before he reached it, he saw the ramp he had to walk down.

As he passed by the vestibule, Bernstein saw its walls were stained, and the floor was a slab of cracked and unevenly colored concrete. He walked down the ramp, into the basement, and through the open door of the community room.

The band was set up in the middle of the large, cinderblock-walled room. Light trickled through a dirty window protected by a wire grating. A damp, musty odor filled the room. A small drum kit was behind a line of two guitars on stands, one a bass. A beat-up piano stood against the wall on the left. The drums were a Zim Gar set, the cheap alternative to professional quality drums like Ludwig, Gretsch, or Rogers. The electric guitar was a Silvertone, a respectable if inexpensive brand sold by Sears. The bass was actually a real Fender, which impressed Bernstein, but that didn't mean the owner knew how to play.

"Jack Bernstein, I presume," a voice called from behind.

The voice belonged to a young man, several inches shorter and twenty pounds lighter than Bernstein. A pile of tight black curls sat atop his thin head, and gleaming white buck teeth contrasted his olive skin. When he smiled, his incisors showed, reminding Bernstein of a rat.

"Guilty," Bernstein replied. "And you are…?"

"Max Flugel," the small man said. "My friends call me Weasel. I'm the leader of the band. Let me introduce you to the others." He motioned for Bernstein to follow him to the piano, where a plump fellow sat on the stool and studied the piano keys as if it were the first time he'd seen any.

"This is our keyboard player, Albert Robinson. We call him Brooks."

"After the Orioles' third baseman?"

"He'd like you to think so," Max replied. "But really it's because Brooks sounds better than Stinky."

Max wasn't joking. Bernstein moved toward Brooks to shake hands but drew back when he smelled a noxious blend of body odor, bad breath, and flatulence filling the air around the band's pianist.

"Yeah, Brooks takes some getting used to," Max said. "He'll need to get some manners if we're going to make it, but at least he has an electric piano we can take on gigs. We don't need it today."

A squat, angry looking man sat behind the drums glaring at Bernstein. *What did I ever do to him?* Bernstein thought. *Never laid eyes on him before.* Then the drummer flung his head up and down several times. When he was done, he bit his left forearm two or three times before settling calmly on the stool.

"Is he all right?" Bernstein asked Max.

The short man flashed a bucktoothed smile. "That's just Kenny Pelko being Kenny Pelko. Tell you about him later. Right now, we figure it's better he beats on drums, not people, especially people he doesn't like, which is just about everyone. He owns a drum set. Know anyone else who does?" The incisors flashed.

Max explained that he played guitar and sang, and again reminded Bernstein he was the leader.

"I choose the venues and playlists," he said. Bernstein didn't ask for details. If Max the Weasel were having any success with finding venues, Vinnie Calamato wouldn't be giving Bernstein a great spot for his other bands while insisting on other venues for the Plateaus before he would showcase them at his clubs.

Bernstein watched the bass player strap on his instrument and loosen up his fingers by running them up and down the frets, and Bernstein saw he didn't use a pick. Paul McCartney played bass with a pick, but as far as Bernstein knew, no other serious bass players did. He suspected the bassist was the only real musician in the band. He would find out soon enough.

"Did you work up a playlist for me?" Bernstein asked.

"Of course," Max replied, pulling a paper from his back pocket. "We can play almost anything. You'll see. Here, we've got "House of the Rising Sun" the way the Animals did it, not the folkie version. Then we can do "It Ain't Me Babe" just like the Turtles. And we got "Denise," you know, by Randy and the Rainbows. I mean come on… these guys are locals. Oh yeah, we do all the 1910 Fruitgum Company and Ohio Express hits. People love them."

Bernstein stiffened at the mention of the bubblegum groups he loathed, whose songs left a taste in his mouth more unpleasant than the Dr. Brown's Cel-Ray his grandfather drank when they visited his neighborhood delicatessen in the Bronx.

"I'll sit down over here while you guys go through your numbers," Bernstein said, making himself comfortable on a couch against a wall facing the band.

The Plateaus played "Yummy, Yummy, Yummy," a bubble gum song released a few years before by the Ohio Express. Bernstein despised the group and the song, but he was not prepared for the low level of musicianship he heard from the Plateaus. He was accustomed to hearing everything from diamonds in the rough to bands almost ready for the studio. He encountered rank amateurs, semi-professionals, and Ed Stern, the real deal, the working studio musician. Even in his earliest days as a Queens College student dabbling in managing local bands, he never heard such poor musicians.

Max possessed some talent as a singer, but it was obvious to Bernstein that he had done little to develop that talent; there was no sign that he had ever taken a singing lesson or picked up tips from other singers and musicians. Still, Bernstein detected something he could work with and improve through practice and performing. His guitar playing, on the other hand, was beyond redemption. Bernstein couldn't recall seeing anyone who played so badly call themselves a member of a band, let alone the leader.

Max kept messing up the chords, placing his fingers on the wrong notes. Even if his electric guitar were properly tuned, the misfingering assured a discordant and irritating sound. Max had no sense of rhythm, and when he attempted to play lead guitar, none of his notes went together.

At least Max could sing. Brooks Robinson never joined in on vocals, only banging out the same loud piano chords that were not synchronized to match the chords Max attempted to play on guitar. Brooks pounded away, oblivious to his bandmates or the song.

Next Bernstein watched Kenny Pelko on drums. Pelko wasn't actually playing drums. He was banging the drum kit haphazardly with no beat as he whipped his head furiously in all directions, regularly bending over and biting his arm.

He's a madman, Bernstein thought. *He needs a padded cell, not a drum kit.*

The bass player was the only Plateau conversant with his musical instrument. Bernstein thought him to be quite good. He occasionally harmonized with Max.

What's he doing with these clowns?

As soon as the Plateaus played the last wrong chords and notes of the Ohio Express song they launched into "House of the Rising Sun."

Max should not be singing this kind of music, Bernstein observed. *At least not until he figures out we're talking blues, not doo-wop or bubblegum.*

To Bernstein's surprise, the cover of Randy and the Rainbow's "Denise" was more than just salvageable. Max sang it just right, exactly like the record. Bernstein envisioned how it would sound with real musicians augmenting the bass player and Max's voice.

When the band took a brief break between "Denise" and the last song, Max called out to Bernstein.

"Do we need to play any spearchucker music, or was "House of the Rising Sun" enough for you?"

"I'm not really sure I know what you mean," Bernstein said. *Even these guys can't be that disgusting.*

"We call them spearchuckers because we're not supposed to say nigger anymore," Kenny Pelko snarled, waving his drumsticks in Bernstein's direction. Brooks Robinson laughed.

"Then don't say it," Bernstein replied. "Drop the other word too." The bass player shook his head when he heard his bandmates.

"Whatever you say, boss," Max said as they began their final number, Max's interpretation of the Turtles' cover of Dylan's "It Ain't

Me Babe." It wasn't as good as "Denise" but stood head and shoulders above the other two numbers.

When they were done playing, the band began packing their instruments. Max sidled up to Bernstein.

"So, I guess now we have a real manager like Uncle Vinnie promised?" he asked in a voice as syrupy as the pancake condiments at the Island Diner.

"Vinnie never lies," Bernstein said. "I'll be in touch to set up a meeting in a few days, once I've decided what direction we're taking and where to start."

"Don't book us in no nigger joints!" Max yelled as Bernstein headed toward the exit.

"You would not believe how bad these guys are," Bernstein told Jennifer as they waited to give their orders at the nearest diner to her parents' home. After the evening at Vinnie's nightclub, where Jennifer went out of her way to help him connect with Crane, Bernstein's thoughts about post-romantic friendships were evolving. He could no longer deny there were benefits. Besides, other than Ed Stern and Barry, there really weren't many people he could talk to about his career. No one else took it seriously. And there were no other women on his horizon. He was also finding it difficult to go so long without sex. When he thought about the times with Jennifer, there was a fifty-fifty chance of an erection.

"I'll say this much for them—the bass player is really good, and Weasel can sing and act like a frontman, even if he can't even play a simple three-chord progression on his guitar. The other two are horrible musicians and not much better as people."

"When you told me they played 'Yummy, Yummy, Yummy,' I knew they were auditioning for the wrong guy," Jennifer said.

"How do you screw up a three-chord piece of crap on the level of a nursery rhyme? These guys managed! And that was masterful compared to the way they butchered 'House of the Rising Sun!'" Bernstein shouted. Jennifer tapped his hand and shifted her head to the side, letting Bernstein know people were staring at him.

"Sorry," he said. "It just drives me crazy that so many good bands can't get anyone to listen to them, and with Vinnie's pull and my managing skills, these have a shot at getting booked at The Action House."

He told Jennifer how Kenny Pelko, the drummer, struck him as a ticking time bomb.

"Good thing he's got the drums to beat on," Bernstein said. "Otherwise, I'd be worried. I didn't like the way he looked at me. He can't play drums at all. Just an angry man banging away mindlessly."

"Get rid of him," Jennifer said. "He's not Vinnie's family. You'll find a drummer who wants to make money playing at real clubs."

Bernstein had to agree. He doubted there would be any objections.

"The band leader, Max Flugel is a runt, smaller than me, and he told me his friends call him Weasel."

"His friends are the ones who call him Weasel?" Jennifer asked.

"That's what he said, and I doubt a guy named Weasel has any qualms about kicking a psycho out of the band if it's in his interest. A drummer can be crazy, but only if they're really good. Think of Keith Moon."

The waitress took their orders. Bernstein was quiet until she left.

"Weasel can't play guitar," he repeated. "Have to admit, though— he can sing, and if someone taught him to be a bit more charming, he's got potential as a frontman. He actually did a pretty good cover of 'Denise,' I think because Randy and the Rainbows came from nearby, he figured he owed it to Queens to at least do that one right. His natural singing voice seems to be between alto and tenor but can hit the falsettos. He could wind up as an American version of Davey Jones of the Monkees, or Peter Noonan of Herman's Hermits. But that's going to take some work. Those two are also nice guys. These guys are not."

"Besides one guy smelling bad, another being psycho, and the bandleader having an uncle in the Mafia, what's wrong with them?" Jennifer asked.

"Plenty. For starters, they're horrible racists. At least three of them, anyway. The bass player never said a word the whole time. He didn't look like he agreed with their racist sentiments. The rest were horrible.

Weasel was the worst. Telling me 'Don't book us in no nigger joints.' I found that surprising, considering how dark he is."

"A Flugel is dark?" Jennifer asked. "How?"

"His mother is Vinnie's sister. They're from wherever dark Italians come from. Weasel got the skin tone from that side."

"But not the brains from our side?" Jennifer asked. Marriage between Jews and Italians were uncommon but not unheard of in Queens.

"Yeah, I think he and I have that side in common," Bernstein replied. "I'm hoping I'm wrong."

Jennifer laughed. "That's reasonable doubt, Jack. He's dumb and a racist. Doesn't sound like he's a Jew. You may be many things, Jack Bernstein, but you're not stupid. Would I have spent time with a stupid man?"

"Only if you were also stupid," Bernstein replied. "But I hope he's not one of us. I really do."

"Well, with that name maybe he's German," Jennifer said.

Bernstein was quiet as the waitress brought their orders and waited until she was gone to continue. "Could be one of those Nazi bastards from Ridgewood. Barry's father grew up near there, and he told us they use to have Nazi rallies there before the war. He says there's still a lot of them around."

"I'm glad you're driving a Volvo and not a Volkswagen," Jennifer said.

Jennifer leaned into Bernstein as they walked to his car.

When she was settled in her seat, she turned on the radio and found her favorite AM Station. "Yummy, Yummy, Yummy," the bubblegum song Weasel's band had played for Bernstein poured from the speakers. Thankfully she kept the volume low.

"At least these guys do it professionally," Bernstein said. "Not that I'd ever listen to this on my own, but if one must hear it, better it's done on key, in tune, in time."

"I thought you said Weasel could sing," Jennifer reminded him.

"He can sing in key okay, but I have to let him realize he doesn't know how to tune a guitar, hold a pick, strum, or play notes," Bernstein said. "If he improves on his singing and learns to sing more than bubblegum and doo-wop, I can probably put him in front of a band and at least not get complaints. And Vinnie will be happy."

"So, if you dump the drummer and the keyboard guys, grab the guitar from Weasel's hands and put it in Ed's or someone almost as good, and keep the bass player, you've got a band."

She's right, Bernstein thought. *It's good to be talking to her about this. She was never interested when we were together. Always trying to talk me into quitting. Wonder what's changed.*

Bernstein stopped in front of Jennifer's house.

"Sounds like you should be in the business, not me," he said.

"Oh, I just want to help you be a big success," she replied. She gave Bernstein a gentle peck on his cheek and patted his arm. He watched her walk into the house and left when she closed the door.

Chapter Twenty-Two

Vinnie had no problem with Bernstein axing Kenny Pelko and Brooks Robinson from the Plateaus.

"If you think they stink, and they're nothing but trouble, that's your call, kid. My only interest is keeping my sister happy. You get that little runt Max in front of a good band, she'll be thrilled. So will I, because that gets one problem out of my way."

Ed Stern had no desire to gig with the Plateaus.

"Sorry, Jack, but I don't want that life. Especially not with that kind of band. Don't worry, you'll have no problem getting talent to back him up. A lot of good out-of-work musicians will jump at the chance to get known on that circuit. You get them a record contract, and I'll be in that studio with you."

"If you know of anyone, send them my way," Bernstein said.

"Of course, I would," Ed replied, "but to be blunt, most of the guitarists I run into are either in bands cutting records or fellow studio musicians like me. They've already been through that stage of their career. Assuming they were available, they'd want some real money. Which you don't have right now."

.   .   .

"YOU'RE GETTING to be a regular around here," Sonny said when he and Bernstein were seated at the empty bar. "Just wish you'd come around sometime when we're open and spend a little money on cover charge and drinks."

"Sonny, I'm being given a really big opportunity. If it works out, you're going to do a lot better than cover charge and drinks from me. You'll pack this place with big names. Big names mean bigger cover charges. We're going make them sign ironclad contracts to play here until you're sick of hearing them."

Bernstein told Sonny everything about his meetings with Vinnie and then the Plateaus. He explained he was going to fire the keyboard player and the drummer and get a real guitarist.

"So, what I actually need this first time is three quarters of a band. I don't need a bass. The one they have is pretty good."

Sonny shook his head. "Won't work, Jack. The group I have in mind is a complete band. Guitar, drums, and yes, bass."

"You'll just have to deliver the news to Mr. Bass that he's not needed," Bernstein said.

Sonny frowned. "No, it doesn't work that way. Two of these guys have been together since they were in grade school, and they're approaching thirty. The bass player's been with them well over a year. We don't sell each other out around here."

"We don't do it where I'm from, either," Bernstein replied.

"Then you know what I mean," Sonny said.

Bernstein looked into the rim of his beer bottle. "I do. It'll tell the bass player it's nothing personal, just getting a new backup band together, and I'll keep him in mind next time I hear someone needs a bass player."

"Then he's in luck," Sonny replied, "because from what I've seen, you're always coming to me looking for one."

THE PLATEAUS' bass player didn't mind at all. When Bernstein returned to the dingy practice spot in the recreation room, he pulled him aside before he spoke to the others and explained why he was being let go.

"Oh, that's okay," he told Bernstein. "I really couldn't take any more of these guys. I'm going to graduate school in business next year. Baruch College. Believe it or not, Max went there as an undergrad. This is a hobby for me. My future is in business. I can make more money that way. But in the meantime, if you ever need a bass, give me a call." He handed Jack a card with his name and phone number, picked up his instrument, and left. Bernstein put the card in his pocket. Bernstein had to agree that, without denying his talent, the bass player wasn't likely to become rich as a musician, but with an MBA he probably would. Something about his cool, clear-eyed detachment…it was like what he saw in Bill Krumpert.

Bernstein assembled the three remaining Plateaus and reminded them he was now the manager of the band. He looked at Max, who nodded, having been told by Vinnie that this was how he was going to break through—with a good young manager who had the time to promote him. That would be good enough for Max the Weasel. "He don't care about nobody but himself," was how Vinnie put it.

Kenny Pelko was set up behind his drums, sulking on his seat. Every now and then he threw his head back and followed it up with a glare in Bernstein's direction. Bernstein had rehearsed his speech but was worried about how Pelko would receive it.

Robinson sat at the battered piano. He was midway through a chocolate ice cream cone, brown droplets falling on the piano keys. *This one will be easy*, Bernstein thought. *A pleasure.*

"Yes, Mr. Bernstein is our new manager," Max announced as soon as Bernstein delivered the news. "We're going to be a lot busier and need a pro to handle the business stuff. So Mr. Bernstein will tell us how it's going to be from now on."

Bernstein threw Max an angry look. He expected to talk to the two fired musicians privately, as he did with the bass player, away from Max to avoid immediate embarrassment. They could tell Max and the rest of the world whatever they wanted, so long as they were gone. Instead, Bernstein faced the three remaining Plateaus, Max grinning and showing his rodent-like smile.

"Guys, I respect anyone giving their all in this crazy business. Believe me, I know it as well as anyone. That's why I was brought in to manage this operation. That means sometimes making some tough decisions, some close calls. That's what I had to do here. I've decided that for the Plateaus to work, Max needs to be up front, singing, and there's got to be a professional band with club experience backing him up. The bass player is gone, on his own, and I'm afraid I have to let go of you, Brooks, and you too, Kenny. Nothing personal, it's just that you don't fit in with the new plan."

Pelko leaped from his seat and charged toward Bernstein, waving a drumstick.

"You kicking me out of my own band?" he screamed, eyes bulging and teeth bared. "You trying to get between me and Max?"

Bernstein took several steps back. Max motioned to Pelko to desist, and Bernstein felt safe enough to speak.

"It's not like that at all, Kenny. Bands change members all the time. Drummers are always in demand. Maybe someday you and Max can play together, just not now, in this band."

Max the Weasel stood to the side, watching events unfold. Brooks stepped next to Pelko. Even from across the room Bernstein could smell the fart Robinson released. The sulfuric stench of rotten eggs filled the air around Bernstein. Rancid body odor and unwashed hair lurked beneath the powerful cloud of putrid gas.

"Can I ask you why we can't be part of the new band?" Brooks asked.

"You guys have no club experience. Never even done a sound check. Never had to deal with someone else playing out of time or tune, or with an angry and drunken crowd. I need guys who have been there and back to be on any stage with Max."

"Plus, to be perfectly honest, you guys just aren't that good. Not good enough for me, not right now."

Pelko took a few steps toward Bernstein, the menacing drumsticks still in hand.

"You think we can't learn?" he screamed. "Max has no more experience than me and Brooks. So why are we out and he's in?"

"That's enough for today, Kenny," Max said. "You and I will discuss this later." He looked at both his former bandmates for a few seconds.

"I think it's best you guys take off right now, and we'll meet up at Grogan's," he said. "I'm buying the beer."

"What about my drums?" Pelko asked.

"Good point," Max said. "Why don't you and Brooks pack them up and take them back to your place while I give Jack here a tour of the Plateau. See you guys later." With that, Max ushered Bernstein out of the room and back to the street.

EVENING WAS FALLING on Macbeth Heights, and from the relatively high elevation of the Plateau, the sinking sun was a darkening red-orange, slowly disappearing as the sky turned black. There weren't many lights in this middle-of-nowhere part of Queens, and stars were scattered across the skies. Bernstein's place was too close to the Long Island Expressway and there were too many streetlights to offer such a view. Bernstein knew no one lived in Macbeth Heights for reasons of astronomy, though. They lived there because they were losers, like Brooks Robinson, Kenny Pelko, and almost certainly Max Flugel. *And no matter how bad things might get for me, I'll never sink that far. Even a basement apartment and a car that runs on hope is better than living in Macbeth Heights,* he thought. Hiding somewhere in the back alleys of Bernstein's mind was a fear he could wind up there.

"Someday we'll look back and wonder how someone from this place made it big," Max said as Bernstein enjoyed the peaceful moment when light succumbs to dark. Bernstein's world was a world of the night, when he always felt most comfortable.

If Max realizes that, maybe he's not such a loser, Bernstein thought.

Bernstein heard the sound of a bus making its way up the steep incline of Macbeth Heights Boulevard, really little more than a wide street. He didn't see any passengers.

"Hope I didn't cause you any problems with your friends," Bernstein said. "Sometimes that's how it goes in this business."

"I know," Weasel replied. "Brian Jones got kicked out of the Rolling Stones, and he founded them. David Crosby got kicked out of the Byrds. Jay and the Americans switched lead singers after their first hit. Brooks and Pelko are just going to have to understand. You just didn't think they were as good as me."

"That's one way of putting it," Bernstein said. "Whatever works for you."

The Weasel laughed. "Actually, I don't give a shit. Those guys are total losers. I can't let them hold me back."

This guy has the mindset you need to make it, Bernstein thought. *I hope he has the talent.*

Max lit a cigarette. Macbeth Heights was still and quiet, aside from the sound of a dog barking and Weasel's exhalations. It was cold, but Max and Bernstein wore warm coats.

"Peaceful out here," Bernstein said.

"Another way of saying boring," Max replied. "That's why I gotta get out of here. A band is my best shot, so I have no problem with you bringing in new blood. The Plateaus needed a transfusion."

Halfway through his smoke, Max offered Bernstein a cigarette, which he politely refused. He had never smoked tobacco, and he vowed he never would.

"Did you grow up around here?" Bernstein asked.

Max laughed. He told Bernstein he grew up in Laurelton, on the southern border with Nassau County. That was where Vinnie and his sister, Max's mother and her husband, were born and raised and still lived. Max wound up in Macbeth Heights when his salary as a junior account executive at a medical supply company wasn't enough to cover rent on his own place and other expenses.

"I ran into Brooks, who I hadn't seen since high school. He had his parents' apartment all to himself. Don't ask me how they wound up here, or why they left. I don't know or care. Brooks offered me my own room, free of charge, until I could get set up on my own. That was six months ago, and it's a miracle I haven't been asphyxiated."

"Yeah, Max, I smelled him. That Brooks is another Hitler. Gassing Jews."

Max threw Bernstein a puzzled look. "Oh, I get it. No, sorry, I'm not Jewish. Not that it's a problem. Actually, I take it as a compliment. I graduated Bernard Baruch College of Business and my boss right now is Jewish. He pays me okay and treats me really well. Like family.

And what's more important than family? You guys are okay in my book."

Does this run in the Calamato genes? Bernstein thought. *Well, better than the alternative.*

"You're thrown off by the name Flugel, aren't you? Well, blame it all on some immigration officer at Ellis Island when my father's father came here in 1912. Bertolo Filageli became Bart Flugel. By the time anyone figured out we could change it back, there were too many places to contact. It would've been a nightmare. Now I sort of like it. With all this bullshit about Uncle Vinnie being mobbed up, no cops are watching a guy named Flugel living in Macbeth Heights with a bag of gas."

Max pulled out another cigarette and lit it with his silver Zippo lighter.

Not such a good idea for a singer, Bernstein thought. "That's a really nice lighter."

Max nodded and told him it was a present from Uncle Vinnie.

"I think it's probably best if you split before Kenny and Brooks come out. Pelko's a real live wire. Stay away from him. Me and Brooks, we can control him, but no one else can."

Chapter Twenty-Three

"I f he wasn't such a sneaky, double-dealing racist, I might grow to like the guy," Bernstein told Ed Stern as they sat on adjoining stools at Creamy Egg Cream.

"By the standards of the music industry, he sounds like a relatively nice guy," Ed declared. "You've been doing this long enough to know that much."

The soda jerk placed two egg creams before them, the top of the glasses filled with the foam that separated a genuine egg cream from a poseur. Bernstein's fascination with the mechanics of food preparation was not limited to Bob the short order cook at the Island Diner. He loved coming to Creamy Egg Cream over on Bell Boulevard for its incomparable namesake beverage, but equally to watch the soda jerks, or countermen as they were now being called, prepare the egg creams. Splash some milk in a tall glass with a flared top, pour in chocolate syrup—Fox's U-Bet and no other—then squirt in the seltzer while vigorously stirring the mixture. The stir creates the head. The guys at Creamy were the Baryshnikovs of egg cream making. The movements of their arms and wrists, the pouring, and the triumphant lifting of the finished product was a balletic performance. *What they could do with a guitar in their hands*, Bernstein thought.

"Does it really make sense?" Bernstein asked. "A guy like Vinnie Calamato needs me to get his moron nephew a gig somewhere?"

Stern took a deep draft of egg cream and grabbed a napkin from the steel holder to wipe the foam from his mustache.

"Vinnie's trying to make his sister happy. The Italians are like that, you know. I see it all the time in the music business. Family is like, really important to them. So yeah, I think it's real that Vinnie wants to at least give this Weasel a chance, just to show his sister he cares."

"Why me?" Bernstein asked.

"My guess is that Vinnie wants to keep family and business separate as much as he can. He doesn't want to go to one of the managers he deals with and drag them into what probably turns out to be a waste of time on a no-talent asshole. Then you drop into his life because you blackmailed Winston Crane, and to get you off his back, Crane called in a favor from Vinnie. So, Vinnie, who's been around the block a few times, sees a perfect opportunity to pay off his favor to Crane and to take care of his sister. And you know what, he's treating you fairly. You're getting some good dates for whoever the hell you find to play them."

"You think a mobbed-up guy like Vinnie Calamato is afraid of a homosexual like Winston Crane?"

Ed stared at Bernstein. "Jack, when a guy like Vinnie Calamato has a debt, he repays it. And when he makes a promise, he keeps it. And he's smart, or he'd be gone long ago. Guaranteed him and Crane have some business relationship, and it's good for both of them. And what the hell, Vinnie owns a gay club, so it can't be too big a deal to work with some of them. Everyone in the music business has to. After a while, you figure out they're just like everybody else, and it's no big deal."

"If you say so," Bernstein said, not certain he completely agreed with Ed about getting used to it. Then again, if Vinnie Calamato could help him, Bernstein would gladly reciprocate.

Bernstein dropped two dollar bills on the counter to cover the egg creams and the two long pretzel sticks Stern pulled from the plastic canister on the counter, handing one to Bernstein. He turned to Stern as they walked out onto Bell Boulevard. Two young people grabbed their stools the minute they were off.

"I didn't blackmail Winston Crane," Bernstein said.

"Of course you didn't," Stern said as he bit off the end of his pretzel stick.

Chapter 24
Last week of February, 1971

Bernstein spent hours over the following weeks mulling over what Ed Stern had advised. Stern was Bernstein's closest friend in the music industry, a thoughtful musician who understood the world he lived in, and Bernstein knew Ed was sincere and concerned. Whenever Bernstein replayed his discussions with Bill Krumpert and Ed Stern, the common thread that weaved through the advice of both men sounded clearly—achieve some commercial success and then you can do what you want.

They're right, and I need to talk with Galahad about this.

He called Galahad's home, then the yoga ashram where he practiced, and when no one picked up at either, he called Ed Stern. The guitarist said he hadn't seen Galahad in a week, and he hadn't shown up for a planned practice the day before. "If I hear from him, I'll have him call you right away," Stern promised.

"I'm starting to worry," Bernstein told Stern. "My experience is that not getting back to someone is sending a message."

"Or artists can just be assholes," Ed replied. "Even Galahad."

After trying home and ashram several times throughout the day, Bernstein was able to leave a message with the latter. "Have a nice day," the receptionist chirped.

Bernstein drove out to Far Rockaway to hear a band as a favor for a drummer he met through Stern, a fellow who came through several times when Bernstein desperately needed a musician. The band wasn't horrible, but their repertoire was limited to uninspired covers of Jay and the Americans, The Association, and The Four Seasons. Even when done well, that was not the music that drew people to the venues where Bernstein worked. For weddings, bar mitzvahs, or sweet sixteens, the band would have been ideal, but Bernstein was a rock manager. If he was to steer Galahad on the path to pleasing a label, there was no time to take on new acts with less promise. *Meanwhile, where is Galahad?*

A DAY later the phone rang while Bernstein was making coffee and listening to the morning news on WBAI. Bernstein managed to pour the boiling water into the one-cup filter just in time to answer. Galahad told him he was just about to hang up.

"I've been going crazy trying to reach you," Bernstein said. He prayed Galahad would not detect the anxiety in his voice. He had given up all other clients to devote all his efforts to Galahad, and he hadn't been able to speak with him for days. Had Galahad lost confidence in Bernstein's abilities to steer his career? Was Galahad being stalked by the sharks Ed Stern warned him about when he lost Tennessee Eddie? He couldn't let this slip away.

"We can't let one label's decision keep us down." Bernstein said. "You're a great artist, and the demo is good. Maybe we do some fine-tuning and keep our eyes on the ball. I've got a few ideas on where we go from here."

"I do too," Galahad replied. "We should talk right away."

Bernstein felt a wave of relief pass over him. Galahad had not gone off the deep end. He was ready to get to work again. He asked Galahad when they could meet, and he felt even more relieved when the musician said lunch at noon would be fine.

"Island Diner?" Bernstein asked. He felt better than any time since Bill Krumpert had taken quick success off the table.

Galahad laughed softly. "I had in mind an Indian vegetarian place down in the East Village." He gave the name and address.

"Want me to pick you up in an hour?" Bernstein asked. Galahad told him it wasn't necessary, as he was already in the city and only a short walk from the restaurant.

Bernstein drank his coffee and thought about the rest of his day. After he finished with Galahad, he would hurry back to Queens, hoping to catch a certain junior high school music teacher as he left work shortly after three. Bernstein had seen the man play guitar one night at a bar in Astoria, and the memory of his slide guitar had not left him. The sound of slide and pedal steel guitar was the rage, and Bernstein hoped to ride its wave. He once negotiated with a country-flavored blues-rock band this slide guitarist would complement. If he referred him, the band's management might reward him somehow, maybe with a little cash, perhaps someday getting one of Bernstein's acts on the same bill. It was worth a trip to the bar. A five-dollar bill slipped to the bartender bought Bernstein the guitarist's name and the junior high school in Elmhurst where he taught music. Bernstein had managed enough bands with teachers in them to know what time a junior high school educator bolted from the building. He had plenty of time to make it there after lunch with Galahad. After those two tasks, he'd be free.

Since he didn't have a girlfriend anymore, Bernstein considered passing the evening at one of the many Queens or Nassau clubs he knew well. Most were unknown in the music business, let alone frequented, especially since the acts were mostly third-rate bands playing standard covers. However, many single women were impressed by a rock and roll manager. Perhaps Barry would join him. Maybe they'd even stop at White Castle, just like in the good old days.

First lunch with my only client.

It was never easy finding a parking spot in Manhattan, and Bernstein considered himself lucky to have found one on 13th Street between First and Avenue A, three blocks from his destination. When he arrived at the restaurant, Galahad was seated at a table with a man on each side. When he saw Bernstein, he rose and with a smile motioned for him to sit in the empty chair across from where he sat.

Bernstein settled in, facing Galahad and his colleagues. All three were dressed in white, Galahad in a gauze blouse, the others in white suits. Both had beards that grew down toward the knots of their white ties, and their heads were wrapped in white turbans. They weren't Indians, just two Caucasians wearing turbans.

"I'd like you to meet Gonesh Ram and Krishna Dal," Galahad said. The two men nodded at Bernstein.

"I didn't realize you were bringing along friends," Bernstein said. "I was thinking this was a business meeting."

"This is a business meeting," said the man identified as Gonesh Ram. "Perhaps just not the meeting you anticipated."

Bernstein looked to Galahad. "Who are these guys, and what the hell are they talking about?"

"Allow me to come straight to the point, Mr. Bernstein," said Krishna Dal. "I am Galahad's new manager, as well as his attorney, and Mr. Ram is the owner of Magic Prana Records, the nation's leading producer of new age and Eastern spiritual music. We have signed a contract with Galahad to record three albums."

"What are you talking about?" Bernstein screamed. Several other diners looked his way. "*I'm* Galahad's manager, and any record deals have to go through me. I've got a contract!"

Krishna Dal shook his head slowly.

"Mr. Bernstein, every contract includes an implied covenant that both parties shall employ their best efforts to achieve the purpose of the agreement, and that neither shall take any steps to impair the other from so doing."

"Well, it sounds like that's exactly what you guys are doing," Bernstein said, glaring at Galahad, whose face revealed no emotion.

"Quite the contrary, Mr. Bernstein." Dal threw Bernstein a glare of the same intensity he had shown Galahad. "You have spent your entire tenure as Galahad's manager undermining him. You have discouraged him from creating and performing the kind of music he was meant for, and you have disparaged such music in public on numerous occasions. You have insisted on forcing Galahad on a path he was not meant to walk, and as a result, you have done nothing for him. We, on the other hand, have allowed Galahad to be Galahad, and the result is a record deal and national tour aimed at yoga and spiritual communities."

"I am entitled to payment for what you're doing," Bernstein said, looking at Galahad. "You signed the contract."

"A worthless piece of paper," Dal replied. "After what you've done to impair Galahad's career, you're lucky we don't sue you for damages."

"What do you have to say about all of this?" Bernstein asked Galahad.

"We've all got to work out our own karma, brother," was the answer.

"THEY'RE RIGHT," Walter said after Bernstein finished his narration. Bernstein didn't take this well.

"What are you talking about, Walter? You're supposed to be my lawyer. You drew up the contract, and now you're telling me it's no good?"

Walter smiled and gently rapped a pencil against his desk. He had gained experience in the art of the client let-down as an assistant district attorney in Queens, where it often fell upon him to explain to indignant police officers why his office was not charging the person they arrested.

"I drew up a good contract that says each party will do their best to facilitate the goals of the contract and for a mutually beneficial outcome. Here's the facts, Jack—Galahad wanted to promote his yoga songs, and you said no, keep them few and far between because they get in the way of a recording contract. He did it your way and got no contract. Now he's doing it his way, cutting an album, and going on tour. Sounds like he has the better case."

"You're telling me I should have thrown away everything I believe in to make a few bucks on music I can't stand?" Bernstein asked.

"I can't tell you how to manage your talent," Walter said. "I can only tell you how the facts of this case play out legally, and they're not in your favor. But as long as you ask for my two cents—yeah, Jack, you should have placed more trust in Galahad's assessment of where his career ought to be heading. Instead of trying to force him to be something he's not, you should have worked with his talent to move him where he belonged. Sounds like these two guys, Dal and whatever the other guy's names is, did just that, and I don't think they're going to pay you for what they see as a really terrible job."

Bernstein sat there, slumping slightly, looking at Walter and shaking his head.

"Don't give me that look," Walter said. "You're still in the beginning stage of your career. Mistakes get made. Just make them one time only."

"So, I'm getting nothing out of this? Not even my costs, or the fees I put right back into his career. Nothing?"

Walter rapped his pencil again.

"I can ask them about that," he told Bernstein. "It's not unreasonable, and you should get that under the contract and under the common law of this state. That's only fair because he would have had to pay those himself. But we're talking peanuts, Jack. My advice would be to not let them know you're so desperate. Learn, forget, move on. Remember, we have our lawsuit against Tennessee Eddie and his manager. You're going get money out of that one sooner or later."

"Any way we can intimidate them, make them fork over some dough?" he asked.

Walter shook his head.

"I knew this guy Dal back in law school. He was Kenny Duberstein back then. He was at Legal Aid when I was with the DA. He was always an asshole, but he's a good lawyer."

"He's a good actor, too," Bernstein said. "He's no yogi."

"Nor a dummy. Go home and take it easy for a few days. I feel like you do right now whenever I lose a case. Or a client. Got to get off the floor to fight again."

Bernstein thanked Walter and left. As he drove away, it struck him —Don "Galahad" Scribiner and Kenny "Krishna Dal" Duberstein— done in by two of his own kind.

WHEN HE LEFT Walter's office, Bernstein drove to the pawn shop. He had to redeem Pete's guitar, but didn't have the money.

The pawnbroker was a wizened old man whose shoulder-length hair and long beard were a mix of white and gray. He wore a threadbare black suit and black tie. Bernstein thought he looked like an undertaker out of a William Faulkner novel. He eyed Bernstein warily.

"I know the look of a man about to ask for a favor. I also know the look of a man coming in to redeem what he pawned. You have the look of the first."

"I just need a little more time," Bernstein said. "Can I pay you something now and come back in a few weeks with the rest? It's okay to charge a little more."

"Why the hell would I do it if I wasn't getting a little extra?" the old man asked. "This is a Fender Stratocaster. Ever since Hendrix, everyone wants one."

"Come on, mister, please. I really need a break." He told the old man about how Tennessee Eddie and Galahad had taken advantage of his good nature and put him in a hole, but a very temporary hole.

"Everyone's got a sob story, kid," the old man said. "Come up with something better."

"How about if I lay a joint on you?" Bernstein asked. *Any old guy who looks like this has probably been smoking since before I was born.*

"Why do I need to get weed from you? I can sell you some when you come up with some money."

In the end, the old pawnbroker relented and accepted thirty dollars to extend the redemption date for ninety days, but it was a one-time favor. The monthly payments to Mitty were becoming more of a strain with no serious income stream. Then there were the small matters of rent, food, and gasoline. Once again, he had invested all his time into one artist. *And what do I have to show for it? That lawsuit better work.*

HE NEVER GOT to meet the slide guitarist.

Chapter Twenty-Five

First Tennessee Eddie, now Galahad. The reasons and motives differed, but the betrayals were the same. Bernstein knew he needed to speak with a friend who would listen and care. He tried reaching Barry from a payphone on the street down the block from the pawnshop. Barry didn't pick up, and he had the same result with Ed Stern. Walter had already weighed in.

He thought of calling Jennifer, but betrayal was something he felt more comfortable discussing with a man.

Home alone won by default. He walked a few blocks to the old-style deli on the corner of Main and Kissena, the one with the big steam table. He ordered a plate of corned beef and cabbage and a Coke and sat by himself.

Walking back to his car, he passed a newsstand where he bought the newest issue of the *Village Voice*. He kept the radio turned off as he drove home. He didn't feel like hearing music.

As he walked past the vestibule and started down the stairs to his basement apartment, a voice called him. He turned to face Anna, the landlady's daughter.

"I hope I didn't scare you," she said.

"After the day I've had, a good scare would be uplifting," he replied.

"You too?" she asked "That's sort of what I came to see you about."

Bernstein walked a few steps up so he could speak softer. He definitely didn't need Mrs. Bardoni on his case, especially if she thought Bernstein was shouting at her daughter.

"You want to ask me about my bad night? Yours isn't enough for you?" He smiled to show he wasn't angry, at least not with her.

Anna momentarily covered her mouth to suppress a laugh.

"No, something else. I was wondering if I could get a little grass off you. I can pay whatever it is. I know you have some because I can smell it sometimes when I come home late at night. Not too hard to figure out you're getting high. My mom would think it was a cigarette, but she's never up that late anyway."

Mrs. Bardoni had a strict no-drug policy. Bernstein skirted it with incense, aerosol fresheners, towels under the doors, and occasionally lighting cigarettes he didn't smoke but allowed to stink up the basement, allowed because Mrs. Bardoni smoked a pack a day of unfiltered Chesterfields. So far there were no problems, and he didn't want to risk any by confessing to the landlady's daughter, even if she already knew. Then again, the last time Anna Bardoni was in his apartment, she wasn't wearing any clothing, and she was engaged in activities her mother would find even more objectionable than smoking marijuana.

"I don't have enough right now to give any away, but if you want to come down, I can stone you. I was just about to roll one myself. I could use some company."

"Me too," Anna said.

~

THE VERY MOMENT Galahad was casting Bernstein adrift, Anna's latest flame, the neighborhood guy from the bed scene, told her he had impregnated a girl from the Bronx, and they were going to be married in two weeks. Anna and Bernstein sat next to each other on the couch. She talked while Bernstein rolled.

"He didn't seem all that broken up because the other girl comes from a rich family and her parents are giving them, get this, a car *and* a house out on the Island. Not bad for a jerk who works in a carwash."

"Maybe his new in-laws will buy him his own," Bernstein said.

"They can have him," she replied. "I might feel a lot worse if he was a lawyer or an accountant or someone like you who's going to be a big shot someday. Someone who can buy us our own house."

"Is that what you want?" Bernstein asked. "Are you really Italian or just another Jewish American Princess?"

"Like your girlfriend?" she asked, smiling in a way that told Bernstein she had given the subject thought.

"Well, yes. Sort of."

"What's sort of?" Anna asked.

Bernstein struggled for a response while he rolled the joint.

"Jenn's really good. She wants the best for me. She just doesn't like the way I'm going about doing it. By the way, she's not really my girlfriend anymore. We broke up a while ago and we're just friends. She's been a big help to me with my business."

As soon as Anna opened her mouth, Bernstein knew his struggle for a good response was a failure.

"Do you guys spend a lot of time talking about business in bed? I saw her come over here one night last week."

"That was a one-time deal," he replied. That was what he intended, and he hoped Jennifer felt the same. He and Jennifer had gotten together a few times because they still felt close enough to share each other's troubles, and Bernstein had plenty to talk about. That night, they met in Bernstein's basement, drank a bottle of red wine, and listened to the Beatles' *White Album*, which was their favorite soundtrack for making love. The wine and the music led them to do just that. Neither had mentioned it since, and Bernstein's thoughts were confused. He knew things could never work out between them, but since the breakup, she had shown him the friendship and understanding that had been absent when they were a couple.

Bernstein lit the joint and after a deep drag passed it to Anna. She inhaled, held it in, and exhaled a large plume of smoke.

"Can you put on some music?" she asked.

Bernstein asked her what she wanted to hear, and after considering the choices offered, Anna chose Fleetwood Mac. "I'm really into British blues, and I just love Peter Green."

Bernstein's eyebrows rose as he scanned the "F" section of his record collection. He would never have guessed Anna was a blues lover. That she knew Peter Green, formerly of Fleetwood Mac, was equally surprising. Bernstein agreed Green was a gifted and unique artist. Unfortunately for Green and his group, not enough people felt the same. Fleetwood Mac should have been more successful. Green left the group right after the release of *English Rose*, the album Bernstein placed on his turntable.

"Wow, that's really cool. Never knew I had another blues lover living upstairs."

"I said *British* blues," Anna snapped. "I don't really care for the American stuff."

Probably because most American bluesmen are Black, and Italians are all racists. "It's all the same. Give the British credit—they own up to borrowing. More than the Americans anyway."

They smoked the joint and talked, and by the time it had burnt down to their fingers, Bernstein understood the woman he had dismissed as nothing more than insurance against eviction was smart, opinionated on almost everything, and except for American blues, her views were not very different from Bernstein's. She didn't like Nixon or the war, and she hated bubblegum music.

"It's nice to have someone to talk to when you need it," he said when Anna paused speaking to catch her breath. "I'm really glad we're finally getting to know each other."

Anna looked into Bernstein's eyes; her face framed by dark brown hair falling to her shoulders. Her own eyes were bright and hazel colored. She was not thin like Jennifer, but she wasn't heavy either. Bernstein and his friends called women with such physiques "well-built."

"Actually, I've been wanting to get to know you for a while. You're in the music business, and you graduated college. You seem like a serious person with a brain. That's why I think you're going places. You work mostly at night and sleep late, so we hardly run across each other.

Sometimes the choke in your Volvo gives you trouble when you're starting up." She leaned slightly against Bernstein, who gently moved his fingers to her waist, barely touching. She leaned into him with the full weight of her body. Bernstein moved his arm from her waist to her shoulder. She took a last drag of the joint and stubbed it out on the jar lid serving as an ashtray.

"I think you probably figured out the guys I go out with are stupid, lazy, and going nowhere." She dropped her head onto his shoulder.

"Maybe our bad nights don't have to be all bad," Bernstein said as he leaned over to kiss her. He felt her tongue meet his as she deftly unbuttoned his shirt. They made their way to his bed just as the second song on the album started.

THE ALARM SOUNDED AT FIVE-THIRTY, and the bleating rings pulled Bernstein from his deep sleep. Three times with Anna had sapped him of all strength. Their third round ended at three, and two and a half hours sleep were nowhere near enough for him. Anna had no such difficulty, and before Bernstein could fully open his eyes, she was dressed.

"I've got to get up to my room," she said. "Mom gets up at six, and she usually peeks in to make sure I'm okay or don't have some guy in there with me." She bent over and kissed Bernstein.

"We'll do this again," she said.

"Anytime," he said. "You always know where to find me." He watched the cadenced movement of her behind as she walked up the stairs.

BARRY SHOOK his head as he handed Bernstein a mug of hot coffee. Before him stood a full thermos, brewed in his parents' kitchen minutes before driving over to his new place. He arrived minutes before Bernstein and had just taken off his coat when Bernstein rang the doorbell.

"Wow, nice view you have," Bernstein said, looking out the living room window that faced the wall of the next building. They sat on the only two chairs in the apartment. Half a dozen boxes and three suitcases were strewn about.

"It's a large one-bedroom on the second floor, and it's only a hundred a month," Barry said. "Never a problem finding parking."

"Yeah, but you have to live in the Bronx," Bernstein countered.

"All boroughs are created equal," Barry said. "This one has the Yankees." He knew Bernstein was a passionate Mets fan who hated Barry's beloved Bronx Bombers.

After they finished their first cup of coffee, Barry reminded Bernstein he had come all the way to the Bronx to seek his friend's advice on women, not neighborhoods.

"I just don't get what the problem is, Jack. For the past six months all I'm hearing from you is how much you miss banging Jenn. You two were together for a long time, so I can understand how much you'd miss her. Now you're back to schtupping her and you have this new babe who sounds like she's impressed by you and just happens to live in the same house as you…what exactly *is* the problem?"

Bernstein gulped down the remainder of his mug and motioned to Barry for a refill.

"The problem is it all happened too fast and too soon. I was getting used to having Jenn as a friend and an advisor and then we're back in bed. I should have figured it was coming. I just have too much going on right now to deal with a relationship that didn't work out last time. Then this hot Italian chick hops into my bed one night and she's been back down three of the past four nights."

"My poor bubbalah," Barry said, gently pinching Bernstein's cheek as their grandmothers would have done, were any still alive. "So many mean women forcing poor Jackie boy to have sex."

"If Jenn finds out about Anna, that's it. No more help and no more sex. If my landlady finds out I'm balling her daughter right under her own roof, out I go. So this isn't all pleasure you know. There's a lot of insecurity involved."

Barry stood, arched his back, and flexed his fingers while pushing his palms forward. Then he sat down again.

"Jack, my old friend, I just got out of my basement, and it was a hell of a lot more tolerable than yours. Have you ever thought about moving? Like maybe to Manhattan, where you belong? Or if you insist on staying in Queens, at least make it Forest Hills or something snazzy like that."

"Too expensive," Bernstein said as Barry placed an album on the turntable. The album was *Anthem of the Sun*, the Grateful Dead's second album, released in 1968. The first song, "That's It for the Other One," was in Barry's opinion the best song in the world to listen to while tripping on acid, but also good any other time. Barry listened to the first few lines before answering his friend.

"Come on, Bernstein baby, that's about the lamest excuse possible. You could find some roommate for a railroad flat walkup over on the far end of the Avenues on the Lower East Side. Alphabet City."

"I wouldn't park my car on those streets. And no cab would ever take me there," Bernstein said.

"Upper West Side, then," Barry countered. "Split one of those nice-size three bedrooms above 96th. You'll be paying less than you pay for that hole in the ground. You ditch the landlady, but maybe the daughter will come across the bridge to service you."

"Not if a new guy moves in," Bernstein replied.

"Would that bother you?" Barry asked. The look on his face told Bernstein he was serious.

Bernstein thought for a moment. "She seems to be a nympho, but she's also really smart. In between screwing and smoking weed, we talk about all sorts of stuff. You know, politics, relationships, parents, school. She wants to follow my footsteps and become a QC grad. She's so impressed by what it's done for me."

"Nympho? You're balling two chicks and no one calls you names. You banged my carhop when Jenn was on the rag. That's loyalty? Come on, Jack, you and her are the same. By the way, does she ever butt into your business like Jenn?"

Bernstein recognized his own surprise upon realizing he hadn't seen it that way.

"Not really. She just argues with me about British blues guys being better than the original Black guys."

"You think she's a racist?" Barry asked.

"Sort of goes with being Italian, doesn't it?" Bernstein replied. They both laughed.

"Actually, that's not fair," Barry said. "We don't like it when they do things like that to us. You ever think maybe she just likes the British blues sound better than the original? You want to know something? I do too. Am I now a racist?"

"Of course not. Just bad musical judgment."

They listened to the third song in its entirety.

"I mean, I don't know what you don't see. One wants you to change, be something you're not and never will be, and if you ask me is getting too involved in your business. It's not like you need her. She's got lame music taste and hates when you smoke grass. The other knows music, loves getting high, leaves the rest of your life alone. And please move so you're not worrying about the landlady knowing you're drilling her daughter."

"I don't agree about not needing Jenn. She was there when I met Tennessee Eddie. She was with me when I met Winston Crane and then Vinnie. She gives me advice all the time."

"And none of it is worth a damn," Barry said. "None of what she did made any difference. You were going to the gay club anyway, and you were the one who spoke to Crane and put the screws to him. Doesn't sound like she gave you any advice about Galahad that made a damn bit of difference. And if I remember what you told me, she didn't want you to get involved with Tennessee."

"Maybe she was right about that," Bernstein replied.

"Even a broken clock is right twice a day," Barry said.

WHEN HE DROVE HOME, every one of Barry's words weighed heavily. They kept him awake as he tossed fitfully in search of sleep, and when he woke in the morning, the hungover feeling told him they had crept into the dreams he couldn't recall.

Chapter 26
First Week of March, 1971

"Where are we going?" Max the Weasel asked Bernstein as the Volvo turned off Macbeth Heights Boulevard onto the freeway. Max was changing the radio from FM to AM and tuned into the same station Jennifer loved.

"To meet your new band," Bernstein replied. The guitarist, bass, and drummer were waiting at Sonny's. "Like I explained, you're going to work up a few sets with these guys, and you'll be playing gigs as soon as I say you're ready."

"What if I don't like these guys?" Max asked.

"It depends on your reason. If it's better for your career, I'll find other musicians. But let's hope we don't have to waste time unless really necessary."

Max glanced at the signs along the expressway. "I see we're heading out to Kennedy. Planning to fly me to London?"

"Not this time, Max," Bernstein said. "Tonight, you'll have to settle for South Jamaica."

"You're not serious."

Bernstein explained that the potential new members of the Plateaus were from the neighborhood, and the club owner was his old friend.

"What is this?" Max asked. "I'm Frank Sinatra, and they're Sammy Davis Jr?"

"Max, stuff it," Bernstein said. "The club owner is a good friend and one of the finest men you're ever going to meet. If he says these guys are good, they're good. It's you I'm worried about. So just sit there, listen to the crap on the radio, and let me drive."

Thirty-seconds later, Max broke the silence.

"Okay if I smoke?"

Bernstein didn't allow smoking of anything but marijuana in the Volvo, but he recognized the ride would be more peaceful if Max were sucking on a Winston instead of talking.

"Go ahead," he told Max. "Just open the window and make sure all the smoke gets blown out. Ashes get flicked out, too."

This time, Bernstein recalled the streets where he had to turn. As they approached the club, the door opened, and Sonny beckoned them in. Bernstein felt a mild churning in his stomach as he realized he had implied the band was Black but said nothing about the club owner. Bernstein introduced him to Max. Sonny and Max looked at each other for a few seconds before Max extended his hand. Bernstein's stomach calmed.

Sonny asked what they wanted to drink. Bernstein asked for a soft drink, and Max took a beer. They walked to the stage area with their drinks, where the band was set up and waiting. The drummer was a jolly man with at least twenty excess pounds, but not fat. The guitarist cultivated the Jimi Hendrix look—orange Moroccan shirt embroidered with white and a frizzy afro three times the size of Bernstein's. It was the bass player who grabbed Bernstein's attention. He was a well-built, light-skinned Black man, smooth-shaven with a beret perched on his head. He scowled at Bernstein and Max. Max scowled back, and Max's scowl seemed more menacing. Sonny seemed to pay neither any notice at all.

"Meet the new Plateaus," Sonny said with a sweep of his arm. "I think you guys are going to hit it off just fine."

"New Plateaus," Max repeated. "I like that name. It's still me and the Plateaus, but my band is new, my manager is new, and this is a new start."

Sonny and Bernstein exchanged glances saying they agreed. The bass player expressed his thoughts unasked.

"Shouldn't this be something we vote on?" he asked in a voice that made no effort to conceal anger. "What, you don't think we Black folks have a right to name ourselves?"

Sonny walked within a foot of the bass player.

"Now Gerald, I expect you to treat a guest in my house with a little more respect. Especially guests who want to pay you money to play music. Let's not forget, Gerald, you're a musician. Your job is to play bass, not to name someone else's band. So let's get this straight— Max here is the leader, and you are his band until he says otherwise."

Actually, until I say otherwise, Bernstein thought.

"That's the story," Max joined in. "I'm here to sing, and you're here to play your instruments and sing some background. Nobody came here to argue. So let's go over my playlist and see how we sound together."

"That's just what I mean," Gerald said. He turned to Clayton and Mickey. "We've been playing together for over a year, and all of a sudden some White boy we never saw before is our leader?"

Let me try reasoning with this guy. He seems quite smart, Bernstein decided.

"Gerald, if I may call you that, and feel free to call me Jack, let's keep things in perspective. In the music business, there are different models for bands. Some are pure partnerships, like the Stones, the Beatles, the Chambers Brothers, the Who, the Grateful Dead. Others have one clear leader, usually with their name as the band's. Think Paul Butterfield, Sly Stone, John Mayall, Jimi Hendrix. In this situation, we're showcasing the singer, who happens to be Max. He was the leader of a band, and he fired everyone else and hired you guys. Now, being the leader doesn't automatically mean Max gets all that much more money than anyone else. One of you musicians might write some songs and get the royalties. We can work all that stuff out later. First let's hear you guys make music."

"Jack's right," Max interjected. "I have some good ideas about what kind of songs I want to sing and how to sing them. Beyond that, it's all up to the musicians. Jack convinced me I couldn't play guitar for shit, and he was gonna get me someone who can, plus drums and guitar to replace the two jokes I had backing me up, and bass because my bass player went off to grad school. I never gave a thought to a person's color and never will. I just want to sing with you guys backing me up. Can't we do that?"

"We sure can," Clayton said, guitar slung around his neck at almost waist height. "Me and Gerald are plugged in, and Mickey's all set up. The man wants to sing, and we're a band, so let's get moving."

Max took his place in front of the microphone.

"We'll leave you artists alone to warm up while I talk business with Bernstein in my office," Sonny said. "We'll be back in a minute."

"I'M IMPRESSED WITH YOUR MAN," Sonny said as he and Bernstein passed a joint across Sonny's desk. "He handled Gerald perfectly. And he seems like he's serious about his music."

Bernstein was relieved. He wanted to hear Max familiarize himself working with his new bandmates. When Sonny suggested otherwise, before he sang a note, Bernstein was certain it was to politely tell him Max was the wrong singer for this band. He had probably given Sonny that impression when he described what he had seen and heard in Macbeth Heights. Now he understood Sonny wanted the new band to get to know each other alone, without the business side looming over them.

"I swear to you, Sonny, this is definitely not the same little prick I told you about. Maybe if you take somebody out of Macbeth Heights they automatically become a better person."

"From what I hear," Sonny replied, "they can't possibly become worse."

Bernstein told Sonny how he feared Max's racism would make it impossible for him to work with Black musicians, and he had not mentioned that fact to Max before they were en route.

"I was expecting him to say something when I told him the club was in South Jamaica and that's where the band lived, but when he saw I was serious, he didn't say a word. It didn't matter to him at all. Did you see how he just took command of the situation?"

"I got two eyes, same as you, Jack," Sonny said. "Now, let me revert to my role as Queens College professor. To survive and prosper in his world, everyone has to play certain roles. Bigot may be one of them, especially among White people, but not just them. Sometimes one can sense that's not really who the person is, and they don't like the role. Soon as they can escape it, they will. I think Max will like working with the New Plateaus, and believe it or not, they with him. I have this feeling he'll turn out to be one of those people I'm talking about. We'll know for sure soon enough."

When the joint was done, they drifted to reminiscing about their mutual time at Queens College. Sonny reported the passing of Professor Karl Munster, Professor Emeritus of Political Science, at age ninety-six.

"Can you believe it, that Old Man Munster cast his first vote for president back in 1896?"

"Who did he vote for?" Bernstein asked.

"McKinley, of course," Sonny said. "Party of Lincoln. Munster was born and raised in Illinois, undergrad and graduate at U of Chicago. Started out at CCNY, then when Queens opened up in the thirties, he was shipped out here to help whip the place into shape. The old bastard never left. Died at his desk grading papers."

"Probably a D," Bernstein said, and they laughed. Bernstein pictured Professor Munster on the first day of his honors elective class—

"A is for God, B is for a full professor, C is for a genius, D is for you."

"Old Man Munster sure gave out his share of Ds," Sonny said. "I was not one. The old bastard gave me a B, but I know I deserved an A."

"Gave me a C. So, I'm a genius. He must have known you were going to be a professor."

"Let's see you use some of that genius on the New Plateaus," Sonny said.

~

MAX WAS deep in animated conversation with the guitarist when they returned. Bernstein sensed the enthusiasm.

"Looks like Max and Clayton hit it off just fine," Sonny said. "And Mickey, your drummer, is Clayton's best friend, so there's two for the price of one. And you, Gerald?" Sonny asked the surly bass player.

"I understand how the music business works," Gerald said. "I don't need a lecture from a White singer. He's just trying to cover up that he gets all the attention and we stay in the background. Why are you going along with this, Sonny?"

Sonny draped an arm over Gerald's shoulder and looked down to stare into the shorter man's face. Then he smiled and turned his gaze toward Bernstein and Max.

"Gerald here goes out of his way to sound like what he thinks a brother ought to sound like, but he comes off sounding like a damn fool. I don't talk like that. Neither do the other brothers here. Am I right?"

Gerald's sneer contracted, and his blazing eyes dimmed.

"Because Gerald here didn't grow up among Black people, and he's never lived among them for one day. Daddy's a real rich doctor. Grew up in Scarsdale. Graduated Columbia University. Isn't that the case, Gerald? School of Engineering, right? You didn't study Black history like my man Jack. You didn't go down to Alabama with me in sixty-six to register voters, did you? Jack did. So how about you keep quiet for a while, play your bass, and get along. Jack and I want to hear you."

"Okay, let's give them a chance," Gerald said, looking at his feet.

"You mean *you* give them a chance," Mickey said, slowly beating his sticks against an imaginary drum. "Me and Clayton already have. Your boy has a voice, and he sure has personality. Just needs a little guidance and a lot of practice. Mr. Bernstein, I'm ready."

"Please, call me Jack," Bernstein said, wondering if he had heard correctly.

~

THE NEW PLATEAUS performed two numbers for Bernstein and Sonny. The first was "The Tracks of My Tears," the soul hit by Smokey Robinson and the Miracles. Bernstein had no idea Max had ever sung it, and he was pleasantly surprised by what he heard. Clayton was correct about needing improvement, but the tools were all there in Max's voice. The second song was "Denise," and this time Bernstein was surprised the band knew it. *That's wrong*, he thought. *If Max knows some soul, they can know some doo-wop with a touch of R&B.*

"We'll all be back in a week for an all-afternoon practice," Sonny said. "Then you play here first, before Jack starts you on the road to the big time."

"You mean this ain't the big time?" Max asked. Everyone but Gerald laughed.

~

BERNSTEIN PICKED up the tab for dinner at the Macbeth Heights Diner, a greasy spoon that made the Island seem like 21 or Sardi's. Max related how he and the band experimented with styles and genre, including the songs Max and the original Plateaus had played so badly.

"They liked the way I sang 'Denise,' even though the way they played it was more like a slow soul number, say something like 'Unchained Melody.' They had me try a few of these Black songs, the kind where the lead is sort of high, maybe even falsetto sometimes. You know, I gotta tell you, I sounded pretty damn good on 'Tracks of My Tears' and 'Stay.'"

He didn't say 'yom,' Bernstein thought.

Max gave his new band two thumbs up.

"Jack, I got to hand it to you—you know your business. How could I ever think I was going anywhere with Brooks and Pelko? I mean, the bass player we had was fine, but those two…whew," he said, pinching the end of his nose. Max went on to explain how Mickey the drummer did things like fills and rolls that Max had never seen from any drummer he played with. "And that guitar player, Clayton…man, no need to hand me a guitar." Max detailed how Clayton could do anything Hendrix did, just not as loud or fast. He didn't mention Gerald.

"I couldn't believe the changes in this guy," Bernstein told Ed Stern. He had stopped by Ed's house on his way home. Ed's wife was out with friends, so they ordered a pizza for dinner, after which they listened to some music, got stoned, and talked about their day. "He went from this no-talent racist jerk to a singer these Black musicians want to work with. Two of them do, anyway."

"Just goes to show what a good manager can do," Stern replied. "And maybe it's time to stop calling him Weasel. Bad for the image."

So Bernstein stopped calling Max "Weasel."

Bernstein arrived home from Ed's around ten p.m. He wasn't in his basement for more than three minutes when he heard a rap on the door. He walked up the stairs and unlocked it.

"Don't you think you should have asked who it was first?" Anna said as she hugged Bernstein.

"No need. It's just you and your mother, and I really wasn't counting on Mom looking for a quickie before going to sleep."

"Don't even joke about that," Anna said.

Bernstein loved sex with Anna. When he was with Jennifer, he also thought he loved it, but he learned that was only because neither knew any better. Before Jennifer, he had sex with a former girlfriend a few times, but didn't learn much to bring into the relationship with Jennifer, whose past contained even less experience than his. She was a virgin when they met. Bernstein always suspected that his two prior partners didn't enjoy sex as much as he did.

With Anna, it was different. She was experienced and enjoyed every minute, which Bernstein took as a compliment. He was the student, and he greatly enjoyed the subject. He looked forward to three or four weekly classes with Anna.

After climax, Bernstein lay back in his bed, actually a foam pad on plywood plank resting on cinder blocks, while Anna played with his member.

"Wow, you know, before you I never did it with a circumcised guy. I hear circumcised men make better lovers. Is it true?"

"I don't know," Bernstein said. "This is the only pecker I've ever had."

"Take good care of it," she said.

They lay in bed listening to music before they dozed off. Anna woke at six and dressed. She kissed Bernstein on the cheek before heading up the stairs.

"One of these days I want to go with you to watch your band," she said.

"Absolutely," he said. He liked being with Anna, and if he showed up at one of Vinnie's clubs with her on his arm, it would only bring him closer to that weird Italian. *He claims he loves Jews, so surely, he wouldn't be upset*, Bernstein thought. *And if he is, screw him.*

Chapter 27
Last Week of March, 1971

Before collecting Max, Bernstein stopped at the Esso Station at the base of Macbeth Heights. An elderly man, potentially a holdover from the Hoover Administration, shuffled to the pump.

"Fill 'er up. High test," Bernstein said through a window he cranked low as the man moved toward him. The old man nodded. Seconds later, he unscrewed the gas cap, inserted the hose, and squeezed the handle.

"See it's gone up to forty-eight cents a gallon," Bernstein said. "What's going on?"

"Beats me," the old man said. "I've owned this place over twenty years, and I never figured out how the oil companies come up with their prices."

"You live in Macbeth Heights?" Bernstein asked.

The old man laughed. "No way! These are the most low-class White people in New York City. I live in Middle Village. Born and raised there."

The old man cleaned the front and rear windows with squirts of liquid and smooth, well-coordinated strokes of a squeegee, its long rubber scraper attached to the handle in the old man's hand. When he was done, Bernstein saw how much more light filled the Volvo.

"That'll be three sixty-eight," The old man said.

Bernstein was told years ago not to tip owners, but he never accepted such a rule. He handed the old man four dollars and told him to keep the change.

The old man smiled for the first time.

"Mighty nice of you, young man. I don't see a lot of Volvos pull up to the pump, and even less tips. It's mostly a rough bunch we see around here, either the folks living in the Heights or the workers from that place just down the road where the city burns garbage. They say it's all special ovens that burn it up in a flash, but I tell you, on a day when the wind blows strong, I can tell not all of it gets burned in that flash."

Sounds like Brooks fits right in with the place, Bernstein thought.

Bernstein was about to roll up his window when the old man asked him what he was doing in Macbeth Heights. Bernstein explained he managed bands and was picking up one of his musicians.

"Well, sounds like that musician is taking the right first step, getting out of Macbeth Heights, even for one night."

"I'm a musician myself," he added.

Bernstein looked the man over from head to work boot when he heard those words. He was thin, gray-haired, and wearing soiled work clothes, spray bottle in one hand, squeegee in the other. When the old man said he was a musician, Bernstein realized that his folksy manner and the way he turned his observations into miniature story about Macbeth Heights was the style employed by performers on stage. Bernstein decided that despite the old man's obvious New York City accent, he would be equally at home in the small towns of the South. Bernstein knew blues well and country well enough to sense that if an instrument were placed in his hands and his clothing changed, he might well be as good as most of his acts. *I am supposed to know these things*, he thought. He asked the old man what instrument he played.

"Keyboards," he replied. "Any kind. Piano, electric piano, synthesizer, electric organ, anything with keys and a stool, that's me.

When I was a kid, I played in a few different bands. None you ever heard of, even you being in the music business, because you weren't born then. We tried really hard, but you know, it's really tough to make it out of Queens. Many try, but few succeed. So when I got back from fighting in the War, Dad passed away, and I took over the business. Here I am, an old man who wanted to be a musician and wound up pumping gas. Funny thing is, I've done really well with this place, probably way better than any of the guys who stuck with music. At least the ones from Queens."

You got that right, old man. "You playing now?" Bernstein asked.

The old man looked down. "Only at home, by myself. My garage is my studio. The wife leaves me alone for an hour every night so I can practice. Mostly blues and rock, but I can play anything."

He lifted his eyes until they found Bernstein's.

"Say, young man, whatever your name is, if you'd like to come by some time and hear me play, shoot the bull, have a beer, whatever, here's my card. Just call me anytime." He pulled a pen from the pocket of his work shirt and scrawled his home number on the back before handing it to Bernstein. The front of the card read:

John "Red" Fleming
Owner
Macbeth Heights Esso

"Only my oldest friends still call me Red," he said. "You can call me John or Red, whatever you like."

"Actually, I like Red," Bernstein said, handing him his own card. "And please call me Jack. Look forward to hearing you play. I'll call you later this week."

Red Fleming smiled for the second time as Bernstein drove off.

As SOON AS Max was seated, he turned the Volvo's radio to WWRL AM, which played strictly R&B. Bernstein didn't mind. It was the only AM station he enjoyed.

"Trying to get a feel for some of this stuff the guys say I can sing," Max said as Marvin Gaye filled the Volvo. Bernstein smiled when Max referred to the New Plateaus as "the guys." He asked Max what he knew about the old man who ran the Esso station.

"Wouldn't know," Max said. "I never had a reason to buy gas."

Bernstein explained that at this practice the band would work on the playlist for the set they were going to perform at one of Vinnie's clubs in a month or so. Bernstein persuaded Vinnie that while he was justified in refusing to present Max when Bernstein took over management, with the new band and Max's noticeable improvement, Bernstein was certain the gig would go over well. Vinnie reluctantly agreed to give the New Plateaus a chance at a small to medium-sized club he owned in Rego Park, provided the band at least played before some crowd first, even impromptu.

"I put my trust in you when I gave you the job," Vinnie told Bernstein. "So I got to go with your judgment, even if I have my doubts."

"You haven't been listening to the New Plateaus like I have," Bernstein replied.

"Just put Max in front of some crowd before mine. Can't be the first time my nephew plays before anyone other than his own band," Vinnie said. "That's a requirement."

Bernstein agreed. *I need to start making some money.*

BERNSTEIN STOPPED by to hear most of their practices. Vinnie's concerns were legitimate. The musicians were ready, but Max needed more polishing. He needed to play before some live crowd, even a small one, to get the feel of what it was like being on stage for real. This was normal with singers who hadn't performed before audiences. Lurking in Bernstein's mind was the fear that Max would not develop fast enough. *It's up to me to change this.*

He started with the playlist. Max didn't object when Bernstein informed him that "Yummy, Yummy, Yummy," and all bubblegum music was out, and that while "House of the Rising Sun" was a great classic, Max was not the right singer. "Denise" would be covered, with the New Plateaus backing him with funkier, more soulful music than on the Rainbows' recording.

"At Mickey's request, 'Tracks of My Tears' is the second song," Bernstein told Max. "He thinks you're perfect for a cover of the Temptations' 'My Girl,' and I agree. Keep practicing with these guys and no reason why you can't improve on David Ruffin's lead vocals." Max sang in an octave closer to the Ruffin version, but the band would play it more in the soul style of Otis Redding.

MAX PUSHED on the Volvo's dashboard lighter, pulled a Winston from his shirt pocket, and held it between his lips while waiting for the lighter to pop up. When it did, he touched its red tip to the unlit end of his cigarette. Seconds later, he blew smoke out the open window. He told Bernstein how Gerald refused to address him directly or even look at him when they played. After several practice sessions, he hadn't softened.

"Guy's got a ten-foot stick up his ass, that's for sure," Max said as he dangled his cigarette out the window. "Maybe he looks down on the rest of us because we're poor."

Bernstein kept his eyes on the road, so Max didn't see the look on his face.

"Max, has it ever dawned on you that maybe it's you and me he doesn't like, and it's because we're White?"

Max brought the cigarette to his lips and blew a cloud out the window.

"What a racist he'd have to be! In this day and age! Jack, let's just leave it at him being an uptight asshole and keep race out of it."

Bernstein gripped the steering wheel tight enough to feel the muscles in his fingers quiver.

"Max, you amaze me. Just totally amaze me."

"Why, Jack? Would you feel better if one of the guys in my band is a racist who hates me and my manager because we're White?"

Bernstein loosed his grip on the wheel. "No, Max, of course not, and I'm not even suggesting Gerald is a racist. A lot of White people who aren't racists have difficulty with Black people in some situations. It's just not knowing what might be right and wrong. Even more the other way. If you know the history, you can see why. Don't feel bad if you don't know this stuff, Max, because if I hadn't taken a year of Black history, I wouldn't either."

"What's it got to do with me?" Max asked.

"Max, you used the term 'yom.' You know how racist that is. I think a Black person can pick up those vibes. I really do."

Max laughed as he flicked his cigarette out the window. Bernstein saw a tiny sparkle of red as the butt faded in the rearview mirror.

"Jack, that's the act I had to put on when around those Macbeth Heights guys. You met Kenny and Brooks. You got to speak their language with them."

"The bass player seemed normal," Bernstein said.

"Yeah, Jack, that's why he left us for graduate school. But don't worry, I don't have any problem with Black people. Tell you the truth, all my life I've been looking for people to recognize my singing, and so far, it's been no one but my mother. Now these guys, the New Plateaus, at least two of them, real musicians, think I can sing. I'm telling you, Jack, they're a hundred percent correct. We're going to make it. You just watch."

The desire to succeed is there. If his bandmates are right, this could be what I've been looking for. Bernstein turned his eyes from the road for a few seconds to look at Max. *Though it's impossible to believe.*

"So, when are you going to have the band play my place?" Sonny asked Bernstein as they drank coffee in Sonny's office. "Have you ever considered that a blue-eyed soul band ought to open in a place where people know soul?"

"Blue-eyed soul" meant Max was White.

"Indeed, I have, Professor," Bernstein replied. "I gave it a great deal of thought. First, let's get one thing straight—this is no blue-eyed soul band. Max does not have blue eyes, and is almost as dark as Mickey. Everyone else in the band is Black. Second, if the New Plateaus are going crossover soul with Max as the frontman, they need to get their act down perfect before they play here. They can get away with mistakes in front of a White audience that they couldn't pull off in this club. Like the folk singer on the stage at the CMC at Queens could get away with stuff that would get him the hook at any folk club in the Village. First I want Max to play before some live audience, I just have to come up with one soon. Then he plays Vinnie's, and if all goes well, the New Plateaus play your club, and play it many times."

"Jack, that's why I want you as my manager someday. I'm starting to feel good about the fact that I couldn't get you to go to grad school in education."

"But I was a history major. Getting into grad school for education would have been really tough."

"Not half as tough as some of the shit I had to go through," Sonny said. "But you have to do this music thing. Who knows what the future holds, but I know you Jack, and you just have to ride this one."

Bernstein took a sip of his coffee and gently rapped his fingers on the desktop.

"If this band doesn't make it, the ride is going to be over soon. I owe a loan shark, I have to take my buddy's guitar out of hock, I have a tank of gas and $275 to my name. Other people are going to be making a fortune off two guys I discovered and brought along. The clock is ticking, as they say."

"Who just released a new album with the song 'Turn Back the Hands of Time'?" Sonny asked.

"Tyrone Davis," Bernstein answered.

"Just checking," Sonny said. "Let's go hear them play."

BERNSTEIN WAS STUCK in traffic on the Van Wyck Expressway, and by the time he reached Sonny's, the New Plateaus were done practicing and were packing up.

Max explained that the band was ready to mount the stage at

Vinnie's with at least four numbers, all covers of real soul or the blue-eyed version. All four songs required a high tenor to low soprano, and Max had that full range. Clayton and Mickey were excited to hear they'd be playing at Sonny's once the new band perfected themselves and after playing at Vinnie's club.

"We don't want to mess up in front of a hometown crowd," Mickey said.

Bernstein explained that before playing at Vinnie's, they would have to play before a live audience of some sort, and he was working on getting one together. *In spirit anyway,* he thought.

Clayton nodded. "I don't want us to mess up in front of any crowd, my friends," he said. "Remember, every crowd is someone's home crowd."

Sonny clapped his hands and the sound echoed through the nearly empty room.

"Before you leave, let Jack hear a sample of your progress."

The New Plateaus broke into "My Girl" just as Max described. The New Plateaus had it figured right, using Ruffin's octave and Otis' funk. When it was over, Bernstein said that whoever arranged the version was a genius. Clayton smiled.

After the band was packed, Sonny lit a large joint and passed it to Bernstein, who in turn passed it to Max, who just passed it on. Mickey reached over and grabbed the joint, took a drag, and it passed to Clayton. The guitarist offered it to Gerald, who declined, so it went back to Sonny.

"The band needs more practice before the real thing, our grand opening," Bernstein said before he and Max left Sonny's. *That includes playing before some audience, even a small one, like I promised Vinnie. I need to see how Max handles a crowd before sending him on stage at Vinnie's and Sonny's clubs.*

As they left, Bernstein heard Clayton talking to the other two musicians.

"I'm impressed," Clayton said. "I've never gotten any of those good-paying gigs at one of Vinnie's clubs, and now after a few weeks in this band we're on the bill."

Just before Bernstein and Max were out of hearing range, they made out Gerald's reply.

"Amazing what adding a White singer and manager can do for a bunch of colored boys."

"Ignore him. He's an idiot," Max said as Bernstein started the Volvo and pulled away from the curb. It was the end of March, and the temperamental choke worked a little better in the warm weather.

"What, are you kidding?" Bernstein asked. "I tried to fool myself, but he's trouble."

"We just heard Gerald admit the band needs you and me," Max said. "So let's leave it at that. Let's not rock the boat. That's what you were telling me not so long ago."

"It's not us who I'm worried about 'leaving it at that,' or 'rocking the boat,'" Bernstein replied.

"Gerald'll be fine," Max said. "I bet he's as excited as Mickey and Clayton about getting a paying gig. He is a musician, after all."

BERNSTEIN MET MITTY on a side street in Woodside, fifteen minutes from Macbeth Heights. He parked his car on the same block as Mitty and walked to the loan shark's green Continental. Mitty sat behind the wheel smoking his usual El Producto cigar while reading a tabloid. When Bernstein approached, Mitty looked up. Bernstein saw he was reading the horse racing section.

"How ya doin', kid?" Mitty said in one of the thickest New York accents Bernstein ever heard. "Can I interest you in a tip on the third race at Yonkers later today? I got a buddy nearby who can take your bet."

"No thanks, Mitty. I'm in a real hurry," Bernstein replied. *He knows if I'm borrowing from him, I don't have money to bet. Probably trying to keep me in debt.*

"I could spot you twenty if you like," Mitty said. "You pay me back twenty-two with your next monthly payment."

Knew it, Bernstein thought.

"Have to pass," he said.

Bernstein passed his payment to Mitty through the open window. A cloud of cigar smoked poured out in salute, shimmering blue in the soft early sunset.

"Thanks," Mitty said. "You know the balance is due next month. You're a good payer, and normally I'd give you a few more months if you need it, but this is a bad time to be asking for extensions. I have my own loans to meet."

"So why did you just offer to loan me another twenty?" Bernstein asked.

"Hey, just checking to see where you're at right now," Mitty said, exhaling a cloud of cigar smoke so thick Bernstein had to turn his head to avoid inhaling it. "I can see you're a smart guy who won't go deeper into the hole." The smoke dissipated, and Bernstein saw the loan shark was not smiling.

"Sure, Mitty. No problem," Bernstein said, managing to squeeze out the words through a throat on fire, and not because of the smoke.

~

WHEN BERNSTEIN RETURNED HOME, he saw mail waiting for him atop the vestibule table on the precise spot assigned him by Mrs. Bardoni. It was a postcard Pete sent from Amsterdam. He would be home next month. *And expecting his guitar.*

He went down the stairs, locking the door behind him. He turned on the radio, content with the music, and sat down at the table that also served as his desk. On a yellow pad he wrote down the sums due the following month. Mitty was due $960. After a year of monthly thirty-dollar payments, Bernstein had barely knocked down the principal. *If I hadn't been carrying Eddie all that time, I'd have no problem paying off Mitty.*

He remembered the $550 he needed for Pete's guitar. He pictured the strange and nasty old pawnbroker.

Aside from the $275 he had to his name, he could look forward to his 10 percent cut from the gig at Vinnie's Club in Rego Park—a hundred if he were lucky. He didn't seek new talent while managing Tennessee Eddie, and the few other acts he managed withered away from lack of attention or talent. When he discovered Galahad, he stopped looking. Since that betrayal, the New Plateaus emerged and monopolized his efforts. Bernstein couldn't help but note the irony in his situation. He possessed the golden opportunity to showcase his talent at major venues, courtesy of Winston Crane and Vinnie Calamato, and all he had to book was Max Flugel and a backup band, a weaselly Italian out of Macbeth Heights singing soul with real soul artists.

Wait a minute. That's exactly the kind of band that could grab attention, if it's done right. I've got the one asset I never enjoyed before— exposure.

"It's all or nothing with the New Plateaus!" he shouted.

Not long after, the phone rang. Bernstein scuttled across the room and grabbed the heavy black receiver. It was Anna. She had a phone with her own line in her bedroom.

"Calling from upstairs? You couldn't walk downstairs?"

"I was afraid there might be an axe murderer on the loose," she said. "If you didn't answer the phone, I was calling the cops. You're lucky Mom's at the store. What's going on?"

"Nothing bad," Bernstein replied. "In fact, it's good. Call it a realization. If you're not so confident, call it a dream. But it's complicated."

"You can explain it to me when I see you tonight," Anna said. "I'll be down as soon as Mom is asleep. Keep the door open."

"I'll be waiting with bells on," Bernstein replied.

"Just make sure there's nothing on but those bells," Anna said.

BERNSTEIN STILL FACED the problem of accumulating $1,500 in a little over a month. He couldn't go to his parents, who had not much more than he, and desperate as he was, Bernstein wouldn't violate his sacred pledge to never borrow or loan money between friends. He had nothing of value to sell; his eight-year-old Volvo, showing its age and wear, combined with his college-days stereo system, wouldn't bring in half of what he needed. Besides, how could he stay in the music business without a car or a turntable?

He was going to need a better plan. Actually, just a plan.

He smoked a joint while listening to a Mothers of Invention album on his stereo. He boiled water, made a cup of coffee, and drank it black. Then he grabbed the pad and pen he kept at his bedside and began computing. When done, he turned the pages of his red pocket phone directory until he found the number he wanted.

Chapter 28
First Week of April, 1971

B ernstein ran into Ronald Hickman at the Allman Brothers concert at the Fillmore East in the middle of March. It was the second night, and while the headliner was supposedly Johnny Winter with Elvin Bishop as the second act and the Allmans the third, the first night crowd ranked them differently. Therefore, the second night, the Allman Brothers with their two guitarists, Duane Allman and Dickie Betts, closed the show. Allman and Betts, both highly accomplished Southern blues rock musicians, traded leads, sometimes playing the melodies at the same time, Allman a great slide guitarist as well, harmonizing as if they were singing voices. Ed Stern considered them the two best guitarists he ever heard.

For a blues aficionado such as Bernstein, the show was a preview of heaven. Johnny Winter with his albino hair and skin, played Texas blues like they'd never been played before, mixing Hendrix-style explosions with blues fingerpicking. Elvin Bishop played Chicago-style blues with a California accent. The Allman Brothers were the forefront of a new Southern blues-rock wave, along with Wet Willie—like the Allmans out of Macon, Georgia—and Texas blues-rockers ZZ Top.

~

BERNSTEIN BROUGHT ANNA to the concert using the ticket he thought would be Jennifer's. It was the first time they had gone anywhere outside his basement. It turned out to be a fine idea because by the end, Anna conceded she might have been wrong about liking only British blues.

They were leaving the lobby of the Fillmore East when someone called out Bernstein's name. It was Ronald.

"Jack Bernstein," Hickman said, embracing his old friend. "I haven't seen you in how long? Two years? Three years?"

Bernstein quickly calculated. He and Ronald met on the stage of the CMC, where they spent most of their freshman days at Queens College. It turned out they were in the same art appreciation class, along with three hundred other students. In the spring, they regularly snuck out to an out-of-sight enclave on the athletic field to smoke a joint or a bowl of hash. Ronald always had plenty of each. After the first few weeks of their sophomore year, Ronald dropped out of sight, and Bernstein hadn't seen him since.

"I figure it's been more than four years," Bernstein said. "You look the same." It was true. Ronald had the same shoulder-length brown hair, scraggly beard, and brushy mustache.

They leaned against a lobby wall and caught up with each other. Bernstein explained he was managing rock bands and would be showcasing his more promising acts at some well-known clubs. He mentioned The Action House, and Ronald nodded with approval.

"That's some heavy shit, man. You'll leave me some comps at the front window, won't you? For old times' sake?"

Anna hung on to every word intently as she held Bernstein's arm. Ronald explained he supported himself by dealing hashish. "Which is what I was doing back in Queens. It's why I dropped out beginning of our sophomore year. I don't see how I could make more money getting a degree than I'm making moving hashish." Ronald spoke softly so that Bernstein and Anna had to crane their necks forward to hear him.

Ronald shifted his gaze toward the front door.

"My friends are waiting," he said. "Listen, Jack—we haven't seen each other for a while, but I'm sure you're the same straight shooter I knew back then. You ever want to make money, you give me a call. I'll front you, because I know you'd never rip me off."

This was true, as Ronald had fronted Bernstein many an ounce of grass and hash while they were fellow students, and Bernstein never failed to pay as agreed. Ronald once fronted him a quarter pound of weed which he split with Barry and Ed at no profit. At the time, Ronald commended Bernstein as someone who looked after his friends. Bernstein thought of Ronald as a friend back then and knew of no reason to feel otherwise upon meeting at the Fillmore. Bernstein sensed the feeling was mutual.

"Sounds good," Bernstein said. He handed Ronald a card. "Call any time. Rock never sleeps. We'll get together real soon."

"I'd like that," Ronald said. "Too many assholes in this business I'm in. Good to see a friendly face again. Peace."

"SO NOW YOU'RE going to become a hashish dealer?" Anna asked as Bernstein drove through the Midtown Tunnel. "If you want to be a criminal, why not speak to Vinnie? I'm sure he can find something for you to do."

"Relax, Anna," Bernstein replied. "I'm thinking if I can get Ronald to front me some hash, I can have my friends sell it for me. I might be able to make enough to cover what I owe Mitty and the pawn shop."

"I have almost six hundred bucks I can give you," Anna said. "I'm sure you can borrow from your friends."

"Goes against my principles, Anna."

Anna smiled. "Your principles allow you to blackmail Winston Crane, cut deals with a mobster like Vinnie, manage a jerk like Max, but borrowing from people who care about you crosses a line?"

Bernstein couldn't help but laugh.

"I guess if you put it like that, it looks bad. I'm impressed how you remember every little thing I tell you! Listen, I got myself into this, and I'll get myself out. My way."

Anna squeezed his thigh.

"But when we get home, we do it my way," she said.

THEY PARKED around the corner from the house, and Bernstein waited in the car for five minutes after Anna left. They realized the difficulties that would ensue should Mrs. Bardoni see them coming home after midnight together. If for any reason the older woman were awake and confronted Anna, a cover story about going out with friends from work would solve the problem. Bernstein's subsequent arrival would be a mere coincidence.

Fortunately, Mrs. Bardoni was sound asleep, and five minutes had barely passed by the time Bernstein and Anna were ripping each other's clothes off in the basement.

TWO AND A HALF weeks after the concert, after Anna snuck back to her room, Bernstein consumed three cups of brewed coffee, listened to the morning news on WBAI, and heard both sides of *Astral Weeks* by Van Morrison. Feeling awake, informed, and inspired, he decided it was time to call Ronald, who had called and left a message a week after their encounter; he left no last name, just his first name and phone number. The number began with the DR exchange, Bell Telephone's abbreviation for Dry Dock, meaning Ronald lived in the East Village, not far from the Fillmore East. Bernstein dialed the two letters and then five digits.

It was almost ten o'clock in the morning, a questionable hour to call a dealer, but Bernstein met Ronald many mornings at the Island Diner to score hash or grass. Ronald picked up the phone on the third ring, cheerful in a morning way, and went straight to business.

"I've got some Magical Moroccan," he said. Bernstein was generally wary of all but Afghan and Nepali hashish, but Magical Moroccan, or MM, as it was known to devotees, held a special place in the pantheon of great hashish.

"What kind of weight can you front me?" Bernstein asked.

There was a brief pause on Ronald's end.

"I can front you two pounds at a grand each. I'm doing you a favor by breaking them into quarter pounds for you. Easier to break into ounces or sell as-is. On the streets out in Queens you can get a hundred an ounce for this stuff, no problem. Don't sell quarter pounds for less than three-fifty. This is one-of-a-kind Moroccan. It won't knock you out or put you to sleep like Afghani or Nepali. Lifts you up. A great head. I love it. I expect to be paid in full no later than thirty days. That's a pretty generous time frame, Jack, because I don't want my people taking any unnecessary risks by cutting corners on safety and security. I highly recommend you start off with your friends, the ones you split weed with at your cost. Wouldn't make money off brothers. I remember that kind of stuff, Jack."

I was right.

Bernstein entered Ronald's address in his pocket phone book, and they agreed to meet that night at Ronald's place on 7th Street between Avenues C and D. Alphabet City was not the safest neighborhood in the city by any stretch of the imagination; on the contrary, it was one of the most dangerous.

Barry told him when he drove a cab his junior year, he would take passengers just about anywhere except Alphabet City.

"The cops won't even go there," Barry told him. "You drive to Alphabet City, you're on your own."

Ed Stern felt the same. He once told Bernstein that while he'd go anywhere in the city to play good music with good musicians, that did not apply to Alphabet City.

"Half the junkies in the city are there at any given time, and those who aren't junkies are there to prey on the junkies and anyone else. Odds are, a musician walks into Alphabet City with their axe, they walk out without it."

Bernstein recalled reading in the *Times* that between 1960 and 1970, the murder rate in the area had more than doubled. The remnants of the old Ukrainian, Russian, and Jewish communities east of First Avenue blamed Mayor John Lindsay. That didn't surprise Bernstein; New Yorkers blamed Lindsay for everything. Bernstein liked Lindsay and voted for him when he ran for reelection in 1969. What Bernstein liked most about him was he was a man without a party. Lindsay didn't fit in with Richard Nixon's Republicans and was too much the aristocratic WASP to be a New York City Democrat. Bernstein never believed anything either political party said, so the fact Lindsay was without a party was a positive factor.

Bernstein was to be at Ronald's at eight. He called Ed Stern and Barry, telling them to meet at Ed's studio at ten. First, he was to meet with Walter that afternoon. Ed had some advice for his friend.

"You may want to tell your lawyer that Tennessee Eddie will be releasing an album real soon, on Epic Records. I got the word from the guy who's been signed to play bass. That's all because of your work, Jack."

~

WALTER HAD LEFT a message with Bernstein's answering service, asking him to come by at two p.m. Bernstein stopped at the donut shop around the corner from Walter's office and bought coffee and donuts for their meeting with extra for Picarelli. If the criminal lawyer were not around, Bernstein would drink his coffee and leave him the donut.

Walter was waiting for him, and he thanked Bernstein for the coffee and donut. He was hungry.

"I've been stuck all day in this deposition in a matrimonial case," he explained. "Nowhere nearly as exciting as your case." Walter bit into a big, glazed cruller, holding it with a piece of wax paper from the bag.

"How are we doing?" Bernstein asked apprehensively.

Walter washed down cruller with coffee and wiped his lips. Bernstein told him about Tennessee Eddie's upcoming album as Walter tossed his napkin into a trash can near his desk.

"I think we're doing great," he told Bernstein. "I sent these goniffs some interrogatories. Those are written questions that have to be answered under penalty of perjury. When it came to the question about why Tennessee Eddie believed he should change managers, they answered with legalese gobbledygook about the question being unintelligible, vague, and ambiguous, assumes facts not in evidence, you name it."

"That's good?" Bernstein asked.

Walter smiled before taking another bite of cruller, followed by another swig of coffee.

"It's great. It means they don't have a reason to prove you weren't doing your job. If they had a legal excuse to break the contract without penalty, they'd be trumpeting it louder than anything Miles ever blew." Walter shared Bernstein's appreciation of Miles Davis.

"Does that mean they admit they screwed me?"

"Not officially, but every lawyer and every judge will see it that way. If they can't explain why they aren't in breach, it's just a question of how much money. That depends on how big a bastard they were. Refusing to pay the relatively small amount of five grand for no reason shows bad intentions. They were trying to put the squeeze on a guy they just impoverished by offering a tenth of what was due. I think we're looking at punitive damages, meaning 'let's stick it to the bad guys.'"

"Anything besides this feeling?" Bernstein hadn't touched his donut or coffee.

"Yeah," Walter said, leaning back in his chair and cradling his head in his hands, fingers interlocked behind his neck. "The fact that they offered to settle this case for $7,500."

Bernstein leaned forward so far that he nearly fell off his chair. He straightened up, as visions of paying off Mitty and the pawnshop danced in his head. Move to a real apartment. Maybe get a better car.

"That's more than they should have paid under the contract, isn't it?" he asked.

"Yes, because the contract says if there's a lawsuit, the winner gets attorney fees. What does that tell us, Jack? They didn't pick the number out of a hat. They know a plaintiff's lawyer takes a cut, and there are filing fees and other costs. They just want us to go away. You read the papers. You see the ads. Tennessee Eddie's going to be playing on a bill at the Fillmore. He's lined up gigs at The Action House and Stony Brook. And you mentioned he will be cutting an album."

"That's what my friend Ed tells me, and he practically lives in studios."

"Even better," Walter explained. "Confirms these fellows have a lot on the line. Maybe stories about how this supposedly simple fellow from the mountains of Tennessee is just an act. Maybe he's really a mean SOB who, with his cutthroat manager, totally screwed the man who discovered and made him. Seventy-five hundred is walking-around money compared to what he's going to make the next few years."

"Did you tell them to have the check here immediately?" Bernstein asked.

"Of course not!" Walter yelled. "I told their lawyers the same thing you did—shove it up their ass!"

"Seventy-five hundred dollars?" Bernstein screamed, louder than Walter. "That's an awful lot of money!"

"They've got an awful lot of ass," Walter replied. "And an awful lot more money. Just be patient. I filed the case a little over a year ago, and we'll be setting a trial date next week."

"I read in the papers it takes years to get to trial." Bernstein said. "Sometimes four or five."

"That's Manhattan," Walter said. "This is Queens. We have plenty of courtrooms."

Bernstein shook his head. "Still, Walter, that's a lot of money. Don't you think you should have at least checked with me?"

"What for?" Walter asked. "I wouldn't let you take such an offer. This so-called deal is no deal at all. It's the very worst you could do in a trial."

"I could use the money," Bernstein said.

"Can't we all?" Walter responded. "That's how they try to squeeze guys like us. They think we're just a bunch of pikers out in Queens who'll fold when the big bad Manhattan lawyers come into court. Well, I have news for them. Out here in Queens County Superior Court on Queens Boulevard, no one knows them, but they all know Walter Blickner."

Bernstein stared at his jelly donut and coffee while he mulled over his lawyer's words.

"You're the man, Walter," he said as he rose from his chair. "Kick their asses."

As he was leaving the office, Bernstein heard Picarelli's voice.

"Thanks for the donut," the criminal lawyer said when Bernstein turned to face him. "I hear you have a new band playing one of Vinnie Calamato's clubs out in Rego Park. Three Saturdays from now, right?" When Bernstein nodded, Picarelli assured him he would be in attendance.

"Maybe after the show, you and me hang out, pick up some chicks," Picarelli said. "What do you say, Brian?"

"My name's Jack," Bernstein said.

Picarelli clapped Bernstein on the back.

"I mean like Brian Epstein," Picarelli explained. "Beatles manager. Jewish guy, too."

"Didn't he wind up killing himself?" Bernstein asked.

BERNSTEIN FOUND a parking spot a block away from Sal's Pizzeria, just one storefront from the corner of Main Street and Roosevelt Avenue. He left his donut untouched at Walter's office and was hungry. When he was a freshman without a car, he took two buses to Queens College, and the second stopped in front of Sal's. He was a slice-a-day man back then, but since he started owning cars, he rarely stopped by. He was greeted by Freddie, the pizza maker and counterman most people thought was Sal. Freddie once revealed to Bernstein that there was no Sal.

"There was a Freddie's Pizza a few blocks away when I opened in fifty-nine, so I used my father's name. I still get checks made out to Sal. My bank takes them anyway."

It had been months since Bernstein last dropped in for a slice, and he and Freddie made small talk while the slice was cut from a freshly baked pizza, placed atop a square sheet of wax paper, then on a paper plate. Freddie poured a soft drink while Bernstein liberally sprinkled oregano and red spice, both in sugar shakers, on his pizza. The pizza maker watched Bernstein as he gently tipped the slice, pointed end down so that any excess oil ran off onto the plate. He handed Bernstein a napkin.

"I ain't gonna insult you by handing you a knife and fork," Freddie said. "You're a real New Yorker, like me." Freddie pronounced the name of the city *Noo Yawk* as any real native would.

"Who eats pizza with a knife and fork?" Bernstein asked.

"You'd be surprised," Freddie said. "If you wasn't born here, maybe it ain't in your blood, and you think it's just like any other food. So, they go for the knife and fork."

"And look like buffoons," Bernstein replied.

"Tell me about it," Freddie said. "The other day I'm sweating away in front of the oven, when in walks this fellow looking like he just stepped out of Wall Street. Fancy looking suit, fit perfectly, beautiful tie, shoes of soft Italian leather. My brother owns the shoe repair half a mile up Kissena, so I know good shoes. I'm wondering what the hell a guy dressed like that is doing in Flushing, let alone my place. Turned out he's a Wall Street guy out here to catch a Mets game in one of them corporate boxes. We start talking, and it turns out he's from Boston. Been living here about five years. Nice, smart guy just like you, maybe a half dozen years older. Loves the city. Says he had this dream he was gonna be mayor someday, so when the game's over, he decides not to take the company limo home. Instead, he walks from Shea Stadium along Roosevelt up to Main and starts checking out what I guess is the part of the city he wants to run. Probably first time he's ever been to Queens."

"Good luck to him," Bernstein said as he studied the landscape of his slice, debating where to bite next.

"I just got this feeling he's really going places. So cocksure of himself. When he said he wanted to be mayor, it was like he thought it was already a done deal. I'll be watching to see if he makes it. Name's Mike Bloomberg. Remember that name."

"Yeah, like a guy who eats pizza with a fork is ever going to get elected in this town," Bernstein said.

Freddie attended to other customers who had patiently waited as he chatted with Bernstein. When his pizza and soda were consumed, Bernstein left a dollar on the counter, including a thirty-cent tip for Freddie. The pizza man waved at Bernstein as he walked out the door. "Come back soon," Freddie called out. "Always nice to see a familiar face."

THE FUEL GAUGE needle was edging toward the red line. Bernstein didn't want to run out of gas later that night, especially when carrying two pounds of hashish. He tried to recall the nearest gas station and realized he was close to Macbeth Heights. He took a left turn off of Roosevelt Avenue, happy to leave the noise, crowded streets, and visual obstructions of the elevated Flushing line. The Avenue on both sides was lined with the kind of inexpensive small businesses working people depend upon. Signs advertising discounts, bargains, and layaway plans filled the windows. It was not a neighborhood Bernstein would choose to live in, but it was a step up from Macbeth Heights.

Red was locking the door when Bernstein pulled up to the pump. The old man recognized him immediately.

"The Music Man," he said. "Slumming again?"

"Not at all," Bernstein replied. "I need a fill-up and was in the area."

"Let me unlock the pump and take care of you," Red said.

"How's the keyboards coming along?" Bernstein asked.

"Just beautiful," Red answered. "Meeting you got me motivated again. I make my money selling gas, but I get my kicks playing music."

"The ideal life," Bernstein said.

"Don't forget to call me sometime," the older man said. "I can come in on a minute's notice and do real good. On the stage or in the studio. Been playing almost fifty years. You can't buy that experience."

Actually, you can, Bernstein thought. *It's just that I can't afford it.*

BERNSTEIN CONSIDERED TAKING a cab to the East Village so he wouldn't have to park his car and walk the streets. The problem was getting a cab on a quiet residential street in Bayside. He decided to drive to downtown Flushing and grab a cab at the hack line. That meant doubling back to the same block as Freddie's Pizza. Too bad there wasn't time for another slice. *I'm a real Queens boy*, he thought and smiled when he realized this real Queens boy was heading off to the East Village for a hashish deal.

Bernstein entered the cab at the front of the hack line and gave Ronald's address. The cabbie wrote it down on his clipboard. He was a young man, probably two or three years younger than Bernstein. His scraggly beard and ponytail were common among drivers the past few years. Bernstein knew many young men who earned money in college by driving a cab part-time. The money was good for a single person with few expenses, and the hours could be tailored to fit any schedule. He knew some men, deemed lost souls, who stuck with it and didn't seem likely to move on with their lives. Barry had driven a cab for a year before giving it up in revulsion.

"It's the Macbeth Heights of jobs," he told Bernstein.

The cabbie asked if the Midtown Tunnel was okay, and Bernstein agreed the fifty-cent toll was well worth it. The tie up on the Manhattan side of the Queensboro Bridge could be daunting at eight o'clock at night.

"Queensboro's usually fine with me," Bernstein said, referring to the bridge by its official name, the one used by all Queens residents. "Just not in rush hour or when in a hurry."

"You mean the 59th Street Bridge, don't you, man?" the driver said. Bernstein couldn't see if the young man was smiling, but the tone of his voice implied so. "I mean, can Simon and Garfunkel be wrong?"

"They sure can," Bernstein replied. "I'm ashamed that two boys from Queens use the Manhattan side's designation."

The cabbie laughed. "Right on, bro. I'm born and raised in Long Island City. But I still love the song. Let's give our Queens brothers a break here. Probably had no choice. I mean, all the record companies are in the city, so I guess they get to call the shots, and we poor Queens folks just have to learn to live with it."

"Unfortunately," Bernstein replied.

The cabbie was soon cruising down Second Avenue. Bernstein looked out in the waning light of early Spring and saw streets lined with broken, crumbling tenants, stoops filled with angry men and women, strung out junkies with hollow eyes and half-open mouths, motorcycle gangs with their gleaming Harleys clustered before them, and a sprinkling of older men and women hurrying along the streets as if to stop would mean to surrender to the ugliness around them.

The cabbie pulled up in front of a building that didn't fit in with the landscape. Its facade was clean and unbroken, a well-lit stoop led into a well-lit lobby, and a uniformed guard stood in front of the door. Bernstein felt secure. He paid the driver, including a 25 percent tip.

"Peace!" the cabbie yelled out the window as he drove away.

Probably can't wait to get out of this shithole, Bernstein thought. *Me either.*

The guard asked Bernstein whom he wished to see, and when he gave Ronald's name and his own the guard pressed a buzzer. Bernstein heard Ronald tell the guard it was fine, and the guard opened the door for Bernstein.

Bernstein found himself in what had to be the finest apartment building lobby east of First Avenue. It was large, bright, and filled with expensive and comfortable looking stuffed armchairs and a couch. He faced an elevator, brass door gleaming. Bernstein pressed the button on the side and watched the dial above the door show the elevator's short journey from the basement to the lobby. The door suddenly opened, and to Bernstein's surprise, a short man in a uniform and red pillbox hat sat on a stool to the left, his hand on a long brass lever. Bernstein told him the floor, the elevator door closed with a *whoosh*, and the car silently glided up.

"You a friend of Mr. Hickman?" the elevator operator asked when the dial passed the third floor. Bernstein said he was. He noticed the operator was Asian and, based on the number of wrinkles creasing his face, he was also very old.

"Mr. Hickman is a nice man," the operator said. "Everyone in this building the same. Best apartment building in East Village."

Bernstein asked the man how long he'd worked for the building. The dial was at the fifth floor. Two more to go.

"Me? I started right after the War," he said.

"So, you've been here how long? Let me see, World War Two ended in 1945, and that's what, twenty-six years?"

"No, no, no!" the man exclaimed. "I started after the First World War! When I got back from the army, no one wanted to hire Chinese.

The owner of this building was a colonel in Army, and he hired me. Been here ever since."

The dial stopped at seven, as did the car, and the door opened with the same *whoosh*.

~

RONALD WAS WAITING for him at the door. His was one of a half-dozen apartments on the seventh floor. Ronald waved Bernstein through his door and they walked down a long hall lined on both sides with framed posters of rock shows at the Fillmore East, and from the famed California music halls—the Fillmore West, Avalon Ballroom, and Family Dog. Bernstein paused to read the acts on several.

"Pretty cool, aren't they?" Ronald asked. "I mean, it's art in its own way."

"Love the bands, but looks like the frames are worth a lot more than the posters," Bernstein replied.

"Maybe today," Ronald said. "Wait a few years."

They sat in the living room facing a huge window. Ronald's apartment was high enough to see over the roofs of most other buildings, but there really wasn't much to see except the dark of night, illuminated by the lights from the hundreds of apartments within view. *4 Way Street*, the double live album by Crosby, Stills, Nash & Young, poured softly through two large speakers. A golfball-sized piece of golden hash sat on the coffee table before them, next to a glass water pipe the size of a small bottle of Coca-Cola.

Ronald pinched a piece of the hash from the ball, rubbed it lightly between his fingers, and stuffed it into the bowl of the water pipe. The pipe was little more than a glass cylinder mounted on a base with a stem on the side, atop of which sat the bowl. He picked up the ball and passed it under Bernstein's nose.

Bernstein first smoked Magical Moroccan a few months before at Ed Stern's house, and this piece smelled exactly as it did then—a powerful musty odor. Ronald drew a lighter from his pocket and lit the bowl. Bernstein watched the cylinder fill with white smoke as Ronald drew in from the top of the cylinder. Ronald coughed, blew a cloud of smoke, and passed the pipe to Bernstein, who followed suit.

Bernstein and Ronald listened to the music and made small talk about people they knew back in college. Ten minutes into this, Ronald asked Bernstein how the hash affected him.

"Sort of like I'm lightly tripping," he replied. "Maybe not so lightly. But not wiped out."

"Yeah, that first big hit off a water pipe will do that to you," Ronald said. "How about I start some coffee and get your bundle ready, wrapped real tight so it doesn't smell. And when you're all set, I'll walk you out to get a cab."

Good thing I didn't drive. He listened to the music for five minutes until Ronald returned with a small bundle wrapped in brown paper and tied with string.

"Triple wrapped in plastic," Ronald said. "Looks like you're from a Chinese laundry."

They drank coffee and listened to the twenty-four-hour AM news station. Bernstein read the *New York Times* daily, listened to the news on WBAI, and watched *The CBS Evening News with Walter Cronkite* whenever he could plant himself in front of a television set at seven o'clock. Ronald obviously absorbed all he felt he needed to know in the twenty-minute roundup.

"Twenty minutes a day, and I know what's going on," he proclaimed.

The two biggest stories remained the release of the Pentagon Papers the week before, and the killing of four students by the Ohio National Guard at Kent State University. Bernstein saw the former as further evidence the government started lying about Vietnam the day they passed the Gulf of Tonkin Resolution in 1964 and hadn't stopped since. The latter demonstrated to him just how far that same government was willing to go to suppress dissent.

"You were really into politics when I knew you back at QC," Ronald said. "Always with the anti-war stuff and civil rights. I admired you for that, just want you to know."

Bernstein suppressed a rush of nostalgia.

"I was, Ronald, and I learned a lot from it. One thing I learned was that sometimes the mountain is just too steep to climb, but maybe a few years later a lot of it has crumbled, and it can be conquered."

"That's what made you stop?" Ronald asked.

Bernstein thought for ten seconds.

"Nothing *made* me stop. It was my choice. After what happened in sixty-eight with Dr. King and Bobby Kennedy getting murdered, Humphrey stealing the nomination, Daley having people beaten up and teargassed, I just thought it was time to take a break. I had started working in music and still am."

"And when you make it to the top, I'm going to those backstage parties with you," Ronald said. "Meanwhile, let's go out and get you into a cab."

THE OLD MAN smiled when he saw Ronald enter the elevator car. They rode to the lobby in silence. The guard outside the front door also smiled at Ronald.

"Everyone here loves you," Bernstein said.

"I'm a good tipper," Ronald replied.

Luck was with Bernstein. At the first corner they came to, 7th Street and Avenue C, a cab was dropping off a fare, and the driver was delighted to be leaving Alphabet City with another.

"See you in a month!" Ronald called out as Bernstein closed the cab's back door.

It was a quarter past nine, and the driver assured Bernstein the 59th Street Bridge, the term he used, would be just as fast as the tunnel and would save the half dollar. He asked Bernstein if the radio disturbed him.

"Not at all," he answered. "That's Traffic they're playing, isn't it?" Bernstein loved listening to music while stoned on good hash; it relaxed him more than grass, and he found it often distorted sound in an interesting way, sometimes sharply focusing on one instrument which Bernstein had not fully appreciated in the past. Ronald's hash was beyond good, and Traffic was superb. *This could be a good ride*, he thought.

"You got it," the driver replied. "The cut is 'Freedom Rider,' off that last album of theirs, *John Barleycorn Must Die.*"

"Yeah man, it was really cool how they got back together last year and cut the album," Bernstein said. "Usually, when a group breaks up, they stay broken up."

"You in the music business or something?" the cabbie asked Bernstein.

After a pause, Bernstein said, "Sort of. I call myself a manager."

"Really? You manage any groups I ever heard of?"

Bernstein looked at the cabbie license prominently displayed below the dashboard. A photo of a young man with a beard and shoulder-length hair looked back at him.

"How about Tennessee Eddie Wayburn?"

"Of course I know him," the cabbie said. "He just played at the Electric Circus last week, and I took a break to hear him. Guy's unbelievable. A happier version of Roy Orbison, or maybe if Neil Young were a hillbilly."

Didn't know the bastard was playing the Circus, Bernstein thought. *Well, the Fillmore is closing in a few weeks. At least that's the word, so maybe the Circus will fold also, and Eddie will crawl back to Marvin, Tennessee.*

He knew that wasn't going to happen. He rode the rest of the way in silence, clutching his bundle and listening to the music.

BERNSTEIN DIRECTED the cabbie to his parked Volvo. He was to meet Barry and Ed Stern at Ed's place, ten minutes away. He could make it there with a minute or two to spare, but at that moment, he was still largely wrapped in the fog of Ronald's powerful hashish. He would drive slowly.

Bernstein placed the package on the passenger's seat while he fiddled with the choke, acting even more temperamental the past few weeks. It didn't catch the first two attempts. *Has to happen when I'm totally wrecked on hash.* When the third try proved the charm, he drove off to meet his friends. He drove as if taking a road test for a license, carefully stopping at every stop sign and red light, eyes glued to the speedometer to insure he wasn't driving even a mile per hour over the limit.

Ed and Barry jumped from their seats when Bernstein entered Ed's studio. They smiled at the bundle in his hands and watched with glee as Bernstein cut the string, using his car key as a saw and then tearing off the brown wrapping paper. He unwrapped the three layers of plastic and stared at the squares of yellow hashish, all the same size.

"Ronald broke the stuff into quarter pounds," he explained. "Break it into ounces or less as needed."

"I came with a scale and a sharp little knife," Barry said.

He cut off a small piece, which he handed to Ed. Stern reached into his pants pocket and produced a small wooden pipe with a screen pushed into its bowl. Barry had a lighter ready, and he held the flame over the bowl as Ed drew on the stem. The bowl glowed red, and the musky-sour smell of the Moroccan hash filled the room.

"Tastes great," Ed said, as he passed the pipe to Barry, who took two hits and passed it to Bernstein.

Barry and Ed each took a pound, less three tasting samples for each.

"This stuff is really nice," Barry said.

"Let's do another bowl," Stern said, and Barry cut off another piece.

As BERNSTEIN DROVE HOME, he wasn't sure if he was floating a few inches above his seat, or if the Volvo was floating a few inches above the ground. *Maybe it's the hydraulic shock*, he thought. *No, those are only on Citroëns, like the bass player in one of my bands drove.*

He managed to parallel park and slowly walk the block and a half home. He had slight difficulty fitting the key into the keyhole, and even more difficulty finding the light switch at the top of the stairs. He walked down the stairs carefully, gripping the railing. When he reached his room, he groped his way in the darkness, guided by the glow-in-the-dark alarm clock on his bedside table. He stripped to his underwear and flopped on top of his bed. He had smoked a lot of Magical Moroccan on his two stops.

The boys will have no trouble selling this, he thought as he drifted into his dream. He saw himself lying on his bed, feeling himself grow erect. He imagined Anna straddling him on top, moving and moaning as he breathed hard and fast. Then he realized he wasn't dreaming. Anna was on top of him, and they were having intercourse.

When they were done, lying next to each other, he asked her how she got into his room.

"It's easy when you leave the door open," she replied.

Bernstein told Anna all that had happened that evening. She stared at him, mouth wide open as he described his journey through the slums of Alphabet City, finding himself in a luxury apartment, and leaving with two pounds of top-grade hashish. He told her how it had nearly overpowered him

"But I was able to muster the strength for you," Bernstein said.

"Barely," Anna replied. "But once you get out of debt we won't need you dealing hashish."

"You wouldn't believe how strong it is," he said.

"You guys are supposed to be selling it, not smoking it."

Bernstein laughed. "Don't worry, we've got it under control."

Chapter 29
Second week of April, 1971

Max had a surprise for Bernstein.

"This will be your last trip to Macbeth Heights," he said as he buckled his seatbelt. "Uncle Vinnie found me a studio apartment in Sunnyside, two blocks from the Court House Square subway stop. Can't wait to get away from Brooks, that stinking pile of garbage."

That's gratitude for you, Bernstein thought. *However bad he smells, he gave you a place to stay for over half a year.* Then it dawned on him that if Max could afford a normal place, perhaps he could as well.

"Would it be okay if I asked what you're paying?"

"No big secret," Max replied. "I'm paying ninety a month. I can cover that with the gigs at Vinnie's club and a share of the cover charges at Sonny's. Just once a month at each will do it. Should be a hundred and a quarter, but the landlord knows Vinnie." Max grinned, the kind of grin Bernstein understood to mean no one says no to Vinnie Calamato.

Holy shit, he's paying less than I'm paying to live in a friggin' basement, even if he were paying full price. I'm getting ripped off by that old bitch. If she knew I was banging her daughter… Then he realized he was talking about Anna.

"I didn't mean it that way," he muttered.

"Mean what, what way?" Max asked.

"I mean, no reason to think your rent would be a secret," Bernstein replied.

"No secrets between us," Max said. "If we can't trust each other, who can we trust?"

That's what I'm trying to figure out, Bernstein thought.

"Well, it sounds great, Max. Sunnyside is nice. Close to the city, easy to get around Queens. You're just moving farther away from me. Maybe I also have to move."

"If I hear of anything, I'll let you know," Max said.

THE REST of the New Plateaus were set up when Max and Bernstein arrived at Sonny's. Clayton and Mickey greeted them warmly, shaking hands and clapping Max on the back. Gerald stood off to the side, scowling.

"Everything okay, Gerald?" Bernstein inquired. Gerald ignored him, and Bernstein shrugged.

I tried.

"You have to forgive our friend," Mickey said loudly from his drum seat. "He's had a bad day. Things are getting so bad back in Westchester, they had to lay off one of the maids."

Gerald stared at Mickey, lips curled. "What, you want to make sure we all know you're on their side?"

Mickey got up and walked toward Gerald, stopping when they were inches apart. The drummer stood a head taller than Gerald, and his thick, muscled arms pressed against the short sleeves of his Mets T-shirt.

"Listen here, Mr. Westchester Gerald. You were born rich, I was born poor. Your mother has all the money she needs, mine has none. I'm a musician. I play drums for money. I can't ask Daddy for money. See these men over there?" he asked, pointing to Max and Bernstein. "They're putting money in my pocket starting when we play that Italian's club later this month, then our hometown crowd at Sonny's.

We have a smart manager. I don't care about his color. All I know is he's gonna get us all the work we need. Am I right, Jack?"

"You've never been so right in your life," Bernstein said.

"One more thing!" Clayton shouted. "Max here's two shades darker than Mr. Gerald!" Sonny and Mickey joined with laughter. Max smiled. Gerald gritted his teeth.

"I get it," Bernstein said. "I have no comment. I came here for the music. Can you guys just get on that stage and play some?"

The band did as ordered. Bernstein and Sonny listened to the musicians jam for a few minutes before trying a new song they hadn't done before, a tune Bernstein didn't recognize. Max sang with confidence, but he was just a little off on the timing, and it seemed as if the band was a beat ahead of him.

"He's getting much better, but he needs a little work with his timing," he told Sonny. "I'll have Mickey work on it with him. Drummers are experts."

"That's why you're the manager," Sonny said as his large hand on Bernstein's shoulder steered him toward the office.

What's on his mind? Bernstein wondered.

~

JOHN COLTRANE's *A Love Supreme* oozed through the speakers in Sonny's office. The professor poured himself a double shot of twelve-year-old Scotch straight up and handed Bernstein an opened and ice-cold can of beer.

"I know you're not much of a drinker, but after all this place is a bar."

"I'll do my best," Bernstein said. He tipped his head back and put the rim of the can to his lips. He tasted foam, then the stream of cold beer. He set the can on Sonny's desk.

"You have to do something about this Gerald," Sonny said. "He's going to be trouble."

"You think it's something I can't handle?" Bernstein asked. "I know you found the band, and they're here because of you, but let's remember I'm the manager."

"Don't get defensive, Jack. I'm sure you can, but why waste your time? I've run across guys like him all my life, and they never do anything but make problems."

Bernstein asked Sonny what he meant.

"The man's got a chip on his shoulder, and the only one that can knock it off is him, and he doesn't seem interested. You see, Jack, Gerald grew up rich but he was still a colored boy in a White world, and all his parents' money couldn't buy him out of that one. When he grows up after his Ivy League education, he decides he's going to come down to South Jamaica and tell the rest of us how it's supposed to be. One day he shows up here with his bass and his attitude. Mickey and Clayton had just lost their bass player when he got drafted, and let's be fair, the man can play. We all figured he'd change once he saw there was no need to act like he does. We were wrong.

"He's telling us how to deal with White people as if we don't know. Problem is he never had to put up with ninety percent of the shit the rest of us put up with every day. His idea of how to deal with White people is to always be a prick because he's a prick, and that's all he knows. But you see, Mickey and Clayton and me, and you too, we don't want to be pricks. We just want to be treated fairly."

Bernstein listened intently as Sonny continued. His old friend was more animated than usual.

"When guys like you and Max come here and treat people like you treat people back in your own places, it gets noticed and you see how folks respond. Except Gerald."

"Well, let's not forget, Max is a racist," Bernstein said.

Sonny slapped his hand on the desk so hard his Scotch glass rattled.

"Max is no racist, and I suspected as much the first time I laid eyes on him," Sonny said. "I don't care what you decided when you saw him in that cesspool Macbeth Heights. Look at the facts, Jack. Max has a White band, lets you fire their asses, and comes down to South Jamaica to join a Black band. They turn him into a soul singer. If Max is a racist, he really stinks at it. You just don't like him, Jack. Don't let it get in the way of your otherwise impeccable judgment."

"If you have to be bad at something, might as well be that,"

Bernstein replied. "I'm not sold on Max not really being a racist, but tell you what, Sonny—so long as Max keeps improving like this, I'll give him the benefit of the doubt." *And you're right about me not liking him*, a thought Bernstein kept to himself.

"Clayton and Mickey tell me they're making him into a singer," Sonny said. "All he needs do is keep practicing with his new band—your idea, as I recall. Everyone agrees it's working. Instead of ragging on Max, congratulate yourself for getting everything right."

They sat in silence for a while and listened to Coltrane. When the album side was over, Sonny turned off the stereo. He asked Bernstein how his other acts were doing, and Bernstein admitted they didn't exist.

"And you have three prime venues available you better use soon. I don't think Vinnie or Mr. Crane want the idea of open dates for you hanging over them forever. I suspect Mr. Crane would like to forget he ever met you."

Bernstein nodded again. Sonny went on.

"So I'm just thinking, Jack, maybe you ought to consider using the New Plateaus for some of them. You know they practice all the time, and they're going to get some really good experience playing at Vinnie's in two weeks and over here the week after. I've been hearing them for weeks, even more than you. I've known Clayton and Mickey for years. If they say Max is fine, I say Max is fine. They say the band is ready, the band is ready."

Bernstein stared at his empty beer can.

"You really think Max is ready to play gigs at The Action House? That's where the heaviest of the heavies play. Leslie West and the Vagrants was their house band before he started Mountain. The Rascals played there. Vanilla Fudge too. You think the New Plateaus are on that level? I want to see them play before some kind of audience before I can say they are. I need to spend some time figuring out how."

Sonny finished the last of his Scotch.

"Tell me, Jack—you've been around music awhile. How often do you come across a guitarist like Clayton or a drummer like Mickey?"

Bernstein realized his focus had been on satisfying Vinnie's desire to see Max promoted and the debts that loomed over him cleared, and he had not fully recognized their talents.

"Sonny, aside from Ed Stern, Clayton is the best guitarist I've ever worked with. He's so good I don't have to do anything. Same with Mickey. He's a drummer's drummer. A real pro. Can't be all that much older than me but sounds like he's got a lifetime of experience. It's Max that worries me. I'm not so sure he's on their level."

"I didn't hear you say anything about how good Gerald is," Sonny said.

"He's okay," Bernstein replied. "To be honest, the bass player in the old Plateaus was better, but he had no interest in playing with us. I might have called him to replace Gerald otherwise."

Sonny clapped his hands loudly just once.

"Fire Gerald's ass and replace him with a White boy? Clayton and Mickey will be rolling on the floor cracking up. They'll say serves him right, and I'd agree. Except he's not interested, right?"

Bernstein felt uncomfortable with the direction of the conversation. *I was thinking maybe we need to read Gerald the rules of the road. I wasn't thinking we have to fire him. He popped off like an ass twice, but if that got musicians fired, we wouldn't have any. No managers either.*

"Correct, he told me he was going off to graduate school. Even if he were available, he'd have to learn the band's style. So, I guess we can't fire Gerald then, can we? So close to our breakout performance at Vinnie's little club in Rego Park? Before we test them in front of some audience ahead of the gig at Vinnie's? No way we find a bass in such short time, one that knows our style and playlist. So, we're stuck with Gerald for the immediate future."

"Not true," Sonny said.

"Oh yeah?" Bernstein retorted. "We're going to come up with a bass player to walk on and replace Gerald in time for the gig? Where are we going to find him?"

"We already did," Sonny replied, pointing to the big Fender bass hanging on his wall. "Now get out there and do your manager thing."

~

THE BAND WAS FINISHING up their practice with "Stay," the soulful version by Maurice and the Zodiacs, not the Four Seasons' version, which Bernstein hated as tinny and whiny. Max's voice, between tenor and soprano, held something for everyone. For Bernstein's review, they ran through a medley of the playlist for the upcoming gig. Bernstein nodded his approval.

Bernstein waited until the musicians were packed and heading for the door. He called for Gerald, who threw an angry look in Bernstein's direction.

"What you want from me?" Gerald asked, his voice dripping with a contempt Bernstein imagined was well rehearsed.

He's trying to sound like he came out of a ghetto. He sounds as fake as I would.

Bernstein invited him into Sonny's vacant office.

"Whatever you got to say to me, you say it right here," Gerald said.

Bernstein stood as straight as he could and stared at Gerald as hard as the bassist stared at him.

"Okay, if that's how you want it. You're fired, Gerald. You're out of the band. Right now."

Gerald was no longer staring. He shook his head and looked around the almost empty club.

"You kidding me?" he asked Bernstein. "You firing me? Me? No way." He looked at Mickey and Clayton, already at the front door. Neither Bernstein nor Gerald saw Sonny gesture in pantomime to the two musicians, pointing to Gerald and throwing the umpire's thumb sign for 'you're out' and then pointing the same thumb at his own chest.

"The White manager just fired me," Gerald called to Mickey and Clayton. "You gonna let him get away with this?"

"You bet your fake Black ass we are," Mickey yelled as he and Clayton passed through the door.

"What about you, Sonny? You telling me you're cool with this?"

"Get out of my house, Gerald. Go home to Scarsdale. Come back here when you learn how to behave around Black people."

227

Gerald cursed as he stormed out to the street. When he was gone, Sonny approached Bernstein.

"Good work, Mr. Manager. I'm already scared of you. What do you want me to do?"

"Start practicing. We have a to get ready for two gigs real soon."

"I'M SO PROUD OF YOU," Anna said as she and Bernstein hugged each other after having sex for the second time since he returned from the band's practice. "It took real guts to fire that bass player a few weeks before the gigs start, but I'm sure this guy Sonny will be fine. He knows the band because they play at his place all the time, right? And he's been listening to the band rehearse. He's going to be fine, probably the best possible replacement for that Gerald guy. By the time the band plays the first gig at Vinnie's, Sonny will be perfect and he'll blow them away when he plays at his own club the following week."

"Who's the manager here?" he asked.

When they were dressed, they smoked several bowls of Magical Moroccan hash, which they'd been doing quite often since Bernstein acquired it. Anna brought up Max's move.

"Even that guy you call an idiot managed to get a real place. Have you ever thought of doing the same?"

Barry's words from the visit to his new place in the Bronx resonated in Bernstein's head: *Jack, my old friend, I just got out of my basement, and it was a hell of a lot more tolerable than yours. Have you ever thought about moving?*

"Too expensive," he said. *Just like I told Barry.*

"That's just real short-term," Anna said. "I know you're going to make it big because you're so smart, and you work so hard. I just have this feeling about your friend Sonny and this new band. I really can't wait to meet them and see if I'm right."

"Well, when that happens, your mother is going to lose her tenant."

"She'll have no problem getting a new one at a higher rent," Anna said. "Around here, there's always some ex-spouse or grown-up kid looking for a place. And if it's too expensive for you to handle on your own, why don't we move in together? We can easily handle one half each."

Bernstein couldn't think of what to say. For years he fended off Jennifer's entreaties to marry. This was different. Anna wanted to live with him. It was a commitment, but not like marriage. *Easier to get out of a lease than a marriage. But there might be a penalty for breaking the lease.*

"That is definitely something to think about seriously," he finally said.

～

"WHAT IS THERE TO THINK ABOUT?" Barry asked Bernstein as they smoked bowl after bowl of Magical Moroccan from a large glass hookah. They laid down a bed of marijuana to ignite the hashish and keep it burning well. Barry's apartment was wreathed in clouds of gray-white smoke. At one point, Barry had to break a new piece off the sales stash. "It's moving like hotcakes," he assured Bernstein. "We should do just fine."

Bernstein's mind was elsewhere.

"What happens if it backfires?" Bernstein asked. "If you're living with someone, it's not like you can just call them to say it's just not working out."

"Can't be any worse than what happened with Tennessee Eddie and Galahad," Barry said. "Maybe you'll get lucky and she'll dump you."

"That's what I love about you, bro," Bernstein said. "You're full of sunny optimism."

Barry was unmoved. "Just get out of that basement any way you can, and if you take the chick with you, that's even better."

"I don't think her mother likes me very much," Bernstein said.

"Won't be your problem once you're out of there," Barry said. "And we won't have to worry about smoking weed or hash in your place."

Bernstein used Barry's newly installed phone to call his answering service. There was a message from Vinnie asking Bernstein to meet him for coffee the following morning. When Vinnie asked for a meeting, it was really a diplomatic order, but Bernstein never minded. Vinnie was the dutiful uncle following up on his nephew's progress. He was a gracious host who always picked up the tab and regaled Bernstein with stories of Queens before Bernstein was born. He never pushed Bernstein about booking other bands in one of his clubs

Bernstein told Barry about his upcoming meeting with Vinnie before he left the new apartment.

"Wow, regularly hanging out with the mob," Barry said. "That's one way to get ahead in music, isn't it?"

"Worked for Sinatra."

"Just be careful. Don't ever get on their bad side."

"No intention of doing so," Bernstein said. *But if I don't pay Mitty, I may wind up on that wrong side.*

Chapter 30
Last Friday in April, the day before the gig at Vinnie's

Bernstein was to meet Vinnie at an Italian pastry and coffee shop in Corona, not far from Lemon Ice King. As the Volvo passed the famous stand, Bernstein thought of Jennifer and the many times they had enjoyed their outings there. Now he had an Italian girlfriend, and he never brought her. There were plenty of good Italian ice places in Bayside, though Bernstein and his friends swore nothing matched the King. Could it be Italians like Anna knew better? He decided he ought to ask if she was interested.

Vinnie was seated when Bernstein arrived at the pastry shop. He smiled when he saw Bernstein and stood, right hand extended. Vinnie wore an expensive-looking custom tailored suit, a pale blue shirt, and a dark maroon tie. If Bernstein was inclined to think of mobsters dressing like Damon Runyon—raincoats and fedoras, violin cases concealing machine guns—Vinnie Calamato disposed of that myth. He looked like he owned a Mercedes dealership.

"I appreciate the invitation," Bernstein said. "It's always a pleasure to meet with you. I really enjoy our talks."

"I'm a straight-shooter, Jack. I wouldn't say it if it weren't one hundred percent true. I've been in the music business a long time, hiring bands for my clubs. I've been dealing with managers since I got back from the War. Most are crooks, dipshits, or both." Vinnie paused and reached into the inside pocket of his jacket for a metallic tube, from which he withdrew a long thin cigar.

"Mind if I smoke?" he asked. "And if you'd like one…"

Bernstein thanked Vinnie and politely declined. Vinnie looked in the direction of the woman at the counter. She saw him and returned to the table with an ashtray that contained two small objects. One was a lighter, the other a cigar cutter called a guillotine, as it was a miniature version. Vinnie used the latter to slice off the sealed end of the cigar. He lit the open end and drew in, creating a fiery red glow. The woman left them alone as soon as she saw the smoke flowing from the corner of Vinnie's mouth.

"Gave up cigarettes a few years ago," Vinnie explained. "I enjoy a good cigar every now and then, but not at home. My wife would kill me if she ever smelled cigar smoke in the house. Took this from my humidor when I left home. Tube keeps it from drying out."

He treats his cigars the way I treat my weed, Bernstein thought.

Vinnie waved the smoke away from Bernstein.

"Jack, I don't want to be telling a pro like you how to do their business, but sounds like you've done such a good job with Max and that band, it may be time for them to start playing the big gigs. After my little club, they're playing at Sonny's. Two good, solid clubs, but just the start for a band that's going to make it. I think you might want to use those three spots you squeezed from me and Crane to showcase my nephew's band. It's not like you have any other groups in the wings. Sonny tells me they're just about ready, will be fine by the first performance, and from one club owner to another, that counts."

Bernstein wasn't sure he heard correctly. "You know Sonny? You guys talk?"

Vinnie waved his cigar in the air as he spoke.

"What do you mean, do we talk? How many serious club owners you think there are in Queens? We help each other out. I need a musician, I call Sonny. One of us comes across a band that's not good for one but is for the other, we call. Sonny needs some security, I send some. We're all in this together, Jack. Like they say, in unity there is strength."

Have I smoked too much Magical Moroccan? Bernstein asked himself.

"No offense, Vinnie, but I really didn't see you and Sonny moving in the same circles and being so close."

Vinnie sneered at Bernstein. "What, because he's a colored guy you think this dago can't accept him? Who do you think convinced me you were right, and I should let them play at Club Rego?"

"I'm sorry," Bernstein mumbled. "I shouldn't have opened my big mouth."

Vinnie's sneer turned to a smile.

"No problem, Jack. Most people would think the way you did about a guy like me, and most of the time they'd be right. But Jack, I told you I was in the War. I didn't tell you my platoon was one of the first to come upon the camps."

"The camps?" Bernstein asked, then, red-faced, he understood.

"I don't want to talk about it," Vinnie said softly. "But after that, I don't want to hear any racist talk. But I do want to talk about you. You can't believe how happy me and my sister are that you forced Max out of that damn Macbeth Heights. Making him ditch those jerks was the best idea anyone came up with."

Bernstein recalled Max also saying he thought he could now pay his rent from his band earnings, which raised a question.

"Doesn't Max have a job? He could always pay rent. I never figured out why he didn't."

"Because he was a lazy good-for-nothing freeloader until you took over," Vinnie said. "And he doesn't have another job. He gave notice today. He's giving all his time and effort to the music. That's your work, Jack. The Calamato family will never forget this. Anything I can ever do to help you, just let me know."

Vinnie motioned to the woman behind the counter. He let his cigar go out in the ashtray. Moments later, she carried a tray of pastries to their table. She promptly returned with two double espressos. Vinnie loved to order for Bernstein and explain every food item in detail. No surprise he owned a few restaurants around Queens. *Probably owns this place*, Bernstein thought.

Vinnie painstakingly went over every piece of pastry, delineating their nuances. Bernstein learned to appreciate the strange combination of bitter almond and sugar in the small amaretti biscuits, crunchy on the outside, soft within. Bernstein had eaten cannoli on many occasions, but he learned for the first time how the Sicilian treat is prepared by frying dough until crunchy then filling it with a sweet creamy concoction made of ricotta cheese. He never before tried zabaglione, a cup of fruit in alcohol-laden sweet cream. He struggled to find room for the coffee-flavored and custardy tiramisu and was relieved to learn the final dish was gelato, Italian ice cream he allowed to melt in his mouth and drip down his throat. Between courses, he followed Vinnie's lead and sipped from his double espresso.

The woman from the counter came by again carrying a tray with two small aperitif glasses filled with a clear liquid. Vinnie relit his cigar.

"A little early in the day, but I do want to toast you and the band," Vinnie explained. Each man took a glass, clinked, and swallowed. Bernstein tasted licorice as the syrupy drink made its way to his belly. A burst of warmth followed, and then a mild lightheaded feeling. They sat there for a minute or two enjoying Frank Sinatra singing "In the Wee Small Hours of the Morning" on WNEW.

"Actually, Vinnie, since you offered, there might be something you could help me with. I'm thinking about moving out of the basement I'm renting right now and getting a real apartment. My girlfriend's been pushing me. Her mother's my landlord, and Anna also lives upstairs in the main part of the house."

Vinnie blew out a large smoke ring, followed by a smile.

"I'm with you, kid. Can't imagine what it must be like to have your girlfriend's mother in your life twenty-four/seven. These Jewish mothers must be as bad as the Italians!" Vinnie let out a loud laugh.

"Vinnie, this mother is Italian. Last name is Bardoni."

Vinnie took a short puff on the cigar, exhaled quickly, and placed it in the ashtray.

"Hey, Jack, that's good! An Italian girl! Now you'll get a better idea what it's like to be me!"

Please, never let that happen, Bernstein struggled to not say.

"I'm glad you found out," Bernstein said. "Good to know you're okay with it."

Vinnie looked at Bernstein, palms on the table edge, body leaning forward.

"Why wouldn't I?" he asked.

"I don't know, Vinnie. I figured, you know, you're like getting close to my parents' age, and they think people should marry someone just like them."

Vinnie relit his cigar and drew on it until the end glowed bright red again. He signaled the woman to bring him two more aperitifs.

"Most people feel that way, Italians, Jews, Irish, Colored, Spanish. But you know, they're all wrong. Take my sister. Love her dearly, but let's face it, she married a wop, and what a winner he turned out to be. Can't even have a decent Italian name. When it came time to help Max, he's nowhere to be found. Lets his son live in Macbeth Heights! It's you and me, Jack. We're the ones saving the Calamato family from the shame of having a useless idiot like Max. Where would he be without you?"

"Does that mean you can help me find a place?" Bernstein asked.

"Of course," Vinnie replied. "I know a lot of landlords. Just got a nice place for Max, which you know. You know, while I'm thinking, it might be a good idea to have you in that same building. Keep an eye on Max, make sure he don't get sidetracked and screw up this music thing."

The thought of living in such proximity to Max didn't enthrall Bernstein, but he couldn't reject it out of hand. He couldn't insult Vinnie, and so far, the relationship had worked out better for him than anything before. In fact, there really wasn't anything before Vinnie.

"What kind of upfront money do you think the landlord is going to want?" Bernstein asked. He could handle paying the same rent Bardoni was squeezing from him, but in light of his pressing debts and meager income, anything beyond that was out of reach.

"From my friend? Nothing except the rent!" Vinnie roared. "I say a man is good for the rent each month, that's the best credit rating anywhere." He paused in reflection then continued. "If you're going to have a broad with you, you're going to need a one-bedroom. What's the most you can pay?"

Bernstein gave the figure he paid Mrs. Bardoni. Vinnie took

another puff of cigar and told Bernstein that sounded about right. "Next time you pick up Max, he'll have the keys for your new apartment. Now I have to go, and I'm sure you do too."

"I have to make sure my band is in shape," Bernstein said with a smile. "I think we both agree that since Max has never played before a real live audience, it's a must before he steps on your stage. In fact, it was your excellent idea. My good friend Sonny comes through again. He's getting some local people over to his club later today for that very reason. What's on your plate?"

Vinnie shook his head. "You don't want to know, Jack. Believe me, you don't want to know."

Before Bernstein headed for the door, Vinnie embraced him for a few seconds. "You take care of my nephew, there's nothing I won't do for you. Can't stand the little prick, but I love my sister."

IT WAS A QUARTER TO NOON, and Bernstein wasn't due at Walter's office until one. There was a small park down the block from the pastry shop and a candy store along the way. Bernstein stopped to purchase the *New York Times* and get change for the calls he needed to make. He found an empty bench at the other end of the park from where old Italian men played dominos on stone table boards. He read the paper, enjoying the warm mid-seventies temperature and the clear blue skies.

The governor of Ohio defended the National Guard, calling the murder of the four Kent State students necessary. Nixon's Department of Justice argued that the real wrong was the theft of the Pentagon Papers, not the lies it exposed. A new Jane Fonda movie, *Klute*, opened at the Cinerama, about an actress who moonlighted as a call girl. Or was it the other way around? Rick Wise, a previously unimpressive pitcher for the Cincinnati Reds, threw a no-hitter against the Phillies and hit two home runs along the way. The Mets meanwhile were struggling to play .500 ball. They had no offense, but their pitchers, especially starter Tom Seaver and reliever Tug McGraw, were at the top of the league. There was a general acceptance that Bill Graham was really going to close the Fillmore, and some said the nearby Electric Circus was on life support. *Just when I'm about to get there,* Bernstein thought. *Well, if the action moves to Queens and Nassau, I'm in good shape.*

At half past noon, Bernstein walked back to the candy store and called Clayton on the payphone. The guitarist was at home, running through his chords and riffs. In a few hours, the New Plateaus were going to play before a live audience randomly pulled off the streets of South Jamaica. Max's first time before a real audience. Even if it wasn't a real show, it would be a real audience, and Bernstein would see how they related to Max and vice versa. *A tough audience, but Max has to face one before he steps on Vinnie's stage in Rego Park. Score one for Vinnie. It was a good idea to require this.*

"Just keep the volume down," Bernstein advised. He recalled a lead guitarist who missed a gig because he practiced so loud the neighbors called the police, and when the musician opened the door, the whiff of weed smacked the cop in the face. Bernstein couldn't bail him out in time for the show, but he was able to persuade Ed Stern to make a rare live appearance. Bernstein nearly suffered a nervous breakdown, but now it seemed almost funny; except that a few months after the incident, the guitarist, known as Flash, dropped out of community college and was promptly drafted. That was back in late sixty-nine, when Bernstein was just beginning to pursue his dream full time. Six months later, young Flash found himself in Vietnam with a supposedly safe office job, assigned because of his prowess with a keyboard, which he developed as a college student who learned to type term papers. A few days before he was supposed to fly back to the States for discharge, he stopped off for an after-work beer at a Saigon café favored by Americans. He was seated at a curbside table when two Viet Cong passed by on a motorbike, and the passenger sprayed the cafe with a captured M16. Flash probably never knew what hit him. He was twenty years old.

That band fell apart when Flash was drafted. He was their only talent; he was as good as Ed Stern, who knew him and readily admitted it. The name Flash proved prophetic; his flame burned so briefly. Sometimes when Bernstein was really stoned and on the edge of sleep, he wondered what might have been if Flash were not killed in that damn war.

~

PICARELLI WAS SMOKING A CIGARETTE, feet on top of his desk, when he waved Bernstein in.

"Walter's running a little late, as usual," Picarelli said as Bernstein sat in a client chair. "Would you like me to call up for some coffee? The kid who works there knows me, and he'll bring it up. Tip him a quarter and he's happy."

"No thanks," Bernstein said. "I spent the morning with Vinnie drinking espressos and stuffing myself with pastries."

"Yeah, that's right. I already told you I'd be coming to Vinnie's club in Rego Park to see your band play their first gig. What's their name again?"

"The New Plateaus."

"Well, the New Plateaus are going to have one fan in that audience," Picarelli replied. "And make sure you introduce me to Vinnie Calamato and tell him what a great criminal lawyer I am. Just like I'm going to make sure Eddie Brigati of the Rascals gets your card."

Bernstein heard footsteps coming up the stairs and saw Walter lugging an overstuffed briefcase into his office.

"There's the man," Bernstein told Picarelli. "See you tomorrow night, and the introduction is a done deal."

Picarelli smiled, flashing his perfect white teeth.

"The pricks are up to ten thousand dollars right now," Walter said. "I walked out and told them to call me when they're serious."

Bernstein took a large gulp of air. "They raised their offer so soon, and you walked out on them?"

"Of course. They're running scared."

Bernstein sat up straight when he heard Walter tell him this. *Walter was right. They were all talk.*

Keep going," Bernstein said. "I haven't been getting enough good news lately."

Walter leaned back in his chair. Bernstein saw the beginning of a paunch. Walter had been an athlete all his life, but lawyering wasn't leaving time for sports.

"They're in the business. They know what's going on. They know who Vinnie is and about his clubs. Believe it or not, they know about Sonny's. The word is out about a hot new band you manage and Sonny's involved with that's a crossover or a fusion, whatever you want to call it, of Motown and pop. So maybe this time they tried to jerk around the wrong guy. It's going to be hard to argue you screwed up here. The whole picture makes them look really bad. Breaking the contract, refusing to pay as agreed, thinking you were going nowhere and would take the five hundred. Now they're going to pay many times over."

"Do you have a number in mind?" Bernstein asked.

"Sure," Walter replied. "Not a penny under fifty grand. You're going to walk away with at least thirty after my fees and expenses."

I'd have to sell seventy pounds of Magical Moroccan to make that much, Bernstein thought.

TRAFFIC WAS light in the mid-afternoon, but being a Friday, it would soon grow. Bernstein took advantage of the off hour to drive over the Triborough Bridge to the Bronx. He had called Barry from Walter's office, and when he arrived, he saw Barry had completely set up the apartment. All the furniture was in place, and he had a box of Entenmann's chocolate donuts on the dining table.

"For when we're stoned," he explained.

"How's the dealing coming along?" Bernstein asked.

"Oh, it's going fine," Barry said. "I can only call on so many people a day. I have to smoke with every one of them, and after three or four visits, I'm too wasted to go on."

"Why do you have to smoke with every single person you see?" Bernstein asked. "After the first or second stop, you must be stoned out of your mind. This is great stuff. We don't want to waste it, and we want to move it fast."

Barry smiled.

"Jack, you know as well as me that protocol demands you smoke with the person you're trying to sell to."

"Who made up that rule?" Bernstein asked.

"Come on, Jack, when was the last time you sat by and watched someone else smoke hash? Buying, selling, hanging out, everyone takes a few hits. Looks suspicious if you don't. Like maybe you're an undercover cop."

"Who thinks you're an undercover cop?" Bernstein asked.

"No one," Barry answered. "Because I always get stoned with them."

He pointed to a small wooden pipe and lighter and a pile of crumbled hashish on a small tray set on the kitchen counter. He reached over and put it down in front of Bernstein.

"Do the honors," he said.

Ten minutes later, the pile was gone. The scent of hashish filled the apartment, and both men felt as if they were floating—not tired, but not in full control either. Barry suggested the sugar in the donuts would shake the high from them, and they quickly ate two each.

"Anna thinks we're smoking too much of this stuff, and we may not make any money," Bernstein said.

BARRY SHOOK HIS HEAD. "Nah, we got plenty. I can give you the money next time we get together with Ed. Then you'll have it all."

That sounded like a good plan to Bernstein. They would hang out, smoke a few bowls, and Bernstein would be ready to pay Mitty and the pawnshop. If he were a few dollars short, he could make it up with his share of the upcoming gigs. He had two weeks.

≈

BERNSTEIN'S final stop was Sonny's. It was hours before normal opening time, but the streets were filled with parked cars. When Bernstein entered the club, he saw a crowd of at least a hundred people. Most were Black and young, but there was a healthy sprinkling of Whites, Latinos, and even a few middle-aged folk. The New Plateaus were set up, and Max stood in front of the microphone. Sonny was off to the side, bass strapped on. He nodded at Bernstein. *Max's test drive*, Bernstein thought. He motioned for Sonny to join him over at the side of the stage.

"I know you didn't want the band to play here until they proved themselves at Vinnie's," Bernstein said. "I really appreciate what you're doing right now."

"It's fine, Jack," Sonny said. "No one's paying to get in, and folks around here love to hear live music. Some may have never been here, and hopefully they'll come back."

Unless Max screws up, Bernstein thought. He watched Sonny rejoin the band.

Max was steady as a statue at the mic. His eyes had a vacant look as if he were oblivious to the crowd before him. Bernstein waited for Max to greet the audience before the first number. After twenty-five seconds, Max had said nothing. Finally, Clayton's deep voice boomed through the room, even without a microphone.

"Friends, we're the New Plateaus, and I think you all know me, Mickey, and Sonny. Now you're gonna meet our singer, the great Max Flugel. Special private rehearsal only for the neighborhood. You ain't heard singing till you heard Max."

Max relaxed his stiff posture and turned to Clayton.

"Thanks for that intro," Max said. Bernstein was unsure if he was truly ready to sing.

Sounds nervous, but doing a good job hiding it.

Clayton and Sonny played the opening bass and melody lines of "My Girl," Max's most polished number. Bernstein held his breath as he waited for Max's voice to kick in.

Max sang in perfect tune and reached every note, but he seemed less confident than when he rehearsed without an audience. The word "spunk" ran across Bernstein's mind. *Needs more.*

Max finished the song without a mistake, and the audience clapped politely, if not with great enthusiasm. *Maybe they just don't want to disappoint Sonny*, Bernstein thought.

He didn't screw up, a good sign. Nervous, as expected, which makes him seem detached from the band and audience. He can't be nervous tomorrow night, and I hope that crowd is more than just polite. Good isn't enough. We need to be great.

The next number was "Denise," played with the band's signature blend of doo-wop and rhythm and blues. Max started off as unsure as in the first song, but three lines into the first verse, he sang just as he did in practices, and the audience loved it. They clapped, hooted, some did a few dance steps. When the number ended, the band received a rousing applause. They played one of the originals Clayton and Mickey wrote for Max, a bluesy love song made for his voice. The audience demanded an encore, and the band gave them "Tracks of My Tears," which got the biggest applause of the event.

"Hard work pays off," Sonny said to Bernstein as he was leaving the club.

"Tell you tomorrow night," Bernstein replied.

Chapter Thirty-One
Last Saturday in April, 1971

S aturday morning Bernstein woke to the sound of WBAI blasting from his clock radio. He wanted time to fix any last-minute problems before the eight o'clock start time that night. On his to-do list—call the musicians, make sure their equipment was ready for set-up, make sure Max was ready at five.

Bernstein made and plastered posters throughout Queens and Nassau, promising "An Evening of R&B and Soul." They didn't see a lot of that in Rego Park. Vinnie's Club Rego offered groups aspiring to be the next Four Seasons or Jay and the Americans, unaware those ships sailed out when the British sailed in. The club's base was locals who didn't want to make the trip to Manhattan. Vinnie's staff would collect the three-dollar cover charge at the door and provide security.

Bernstein walked two blocks to his local candy store. He ordered to go a toasted corn muffin with butter and a container of coffee. He usually made coffee at home, but this was a special day. He also bought the *New York Times* and the *Queens Ledger*.

Bernstein hurried home so his muffin and coffee would stay warm. When he was secure in his basement, he set his breakfast before him and pored over the papers. The first one he opened was the *Ledger*, turning to the entertainment section.

There it was, as Vinnie promised—an eighth-of-a-page ad announcing the New Plateaus at Club Rego that night. Even more impressive was the line above the band's name—"Jack Bernstein Presents." He called Walter, remembering his lawyer explaining how Bernstein's success undercut Tennessee Eddie's claim he couldn't have succeeded with him. He got the answering service, and Walter called back five minutes later.

"Does this help?" he asked Walter.

"Immensely," Walter replied. "Focus on the show, and we'll talk next week."

"You and your wife don't have to pay the cover charge," Bernstein said. "Love to see you there."

"Not my thing, but I wish you all the best. Dan Picarelli is my ambassador."

Next Bernstein called Barry and Ed Stern to check on the progress of their sales. Both reported no trouble and expected to have everything sold by midweek. Bernstein told them they would meet in his place for a celebratory bowl. They wouldn't have to worry about Mrs. Bardoni because he was moving. He told Barry how Vinnie made it happen. Barry remained cynical of anything to do with Vinnie.

"That's how these mob guys get their hooks into you. First you manage his nephew, then your gigs are at his clubs, then you live where he decides. You haven't gotten to the bad parts yet."

"What bad parts?" Bernstein asked, a queasy feeling in his stomach.

"You know my father grew up with Mitty the Mole. That's why you got a loan. What do you think happens if someone doesn't pay up? Why do you think hardly anyone is late? What do you think happens to someone when they say no to Mr. Vinnie Calamato? Especially if the guy saying "no" got money and a place to live at bargain rent?"

Bernstein shuffled in his chair. "Barry, I don't know if Vinnie's mobbed up. If he is, he just owns some clubs, and in the entertainment business it's impossible to completely avoid the mob. There are a lot of Vinnies out there with the ability to make or break careers by who they book and promote. Maybe they give preference if a name is whispered in their ear by certain people. Whether it's Frank

Sinatra or Jack Bernstein, we have to deal with them. No doubt they put some mobsters on the payroll to show a source of legal income, but that's not the same as hurting people."

"Wait until they ask you to put some thug on the payroll. Maybe even worse. Guys like Vinnie never act out of altruism. He collects favors and calls them in."

Bernstein gripped the arms of his chair.

"I'm useless to him," he told Barry.

"Vinnie doesn't feel that way. He gave you a personal problem to solve for him. Let me tell you something, Jack. My father says when Mitty needs tough guys, he gets them from Vinnie."

Bernstein recalled the tough, beefy men hanging around Vinnie's gay club the night he met Crane. He'd seen them lounging around Vinnie's clubs and in the restaurants where they met. *Having guards to protect patrons at a gay night club I can understand, but why does Vinnie need these guys around other times?* The thought could be disturbing, but Bernstein wasn't frightened.

"Well, isn't that good news for me?" Bernstein said. "If Mitty knows I'm tight with Vinnie, he wouldn't ask for muscle, and if Vinnie knew Mitty wanted them for me, he wouldn't send them."

"Don't be so sure on either account," Barry said.

ANNA WAS WAITING at the Volvo. She left the house ten minutes before Bernstein to throw off any suspicion her mother might have about their departures.

"Sooner or later you're going to have to let her know about us," Bernstein said as he fiddled with the choke, getting it right the second time. "She is your mother, and it's not like we're committing a crime."

"As soon as you're moved out, I'll tell her we started seeing each other. For us to live together, I'd need a good cover story. She's too much of a Catholic to accept living in sin, especially with a Jew. I was thinking maybe I could tell my mother I'm living with my friend Teresa, and she'd know what to say if my mother ever started getting nosy."

"What about if your mother calls you? Even worse, wants to come by and visit?"

"I'm sure Teresa would play along if Mom ever visits," Anna explained. "As for the phone, I was thinking we each get our own separate phone. You need the phone a lot for business, and I like to talk on the phone a whole lot."

"I like it," Bernstein said, and he did.

BERNSTEIN DIDN'T KNOW Sunnyside very well, and it required several missteps and directions shouted by a mail truck driver to find Max's new place.

The building was on a residential block of turn-of-the-century brownstones, all well maintained with clean and unblemished facades. There were six apartments in Max's building, his on the second of four floors. He buzzed them into the lobby, and they took a small but elegant elevator with dark wood paneling. Max was waiting at his door. Bernstein introduced Max and Anna.

Max's apartment was bare, save for a mattress in the sleeping alcove, a television on a stand in the living room, a chair ten feet away, and a small round table in the dining room with two chairs.

"I can move the television chair to the table and we can sit, or I can show you your new place," Max said.

"Let's see the new place," Anna said.

Their new apartment was on the top floor, and the living room window included a slice of the Manhattan skyline on the far left. The place was bigger than Max's and bare, except for several boxes piled up in a corner of the living room. The names on the boxes were the finest stereo equipment—a Technics turntable, four-foot-tall Bowers & Wilkins speakers, and a McIntosh integrated amplifier and receiver.

"Vinnie left it for you. A housewarming gift, you being in the music business and all. Beats what I got packed away. I'll be up a lot to listen to music. You know, get some ideas for covers."

"I'm just overwhelmed," Bernstein said. "How can I thank Vinnie, besides making you a star?"

"Don't feel too overwhelmed," Anna said. "Vinnie probably had it hijacked off a truck."

Max laughed loudly. "Hey, looks like this little Italian girl knows my uncle Vinnie."

Bernstein walked around the apartment, pleased by its size and the perfect cleaning it had undergone in anticipation of his occupancy.

Anna was examining the kitchen appliances as Max sidled up to Bernstein. "I'm impressed with your girlfriend," he said at a near whisper. "Just be careful. You don't want to piss off a guinea girl."

Bernstein looked to make sure Anna was out of hearing range.

"Thanks for the advice, Max. I may need more when it comes to her mother. But listen, you guys were only joking about Vinnie hijacking this equipment, right?"

Max took time to light a cigarette before answering. "Don't know how he got it, but we can be pretty sure he didn't pay for it. Guys like my uncle hardly ever pay for anything. But don't get me wrong, it's the thought that counts. Vinnie doesn't give away expensive stereo stuff to just any person. You matter to him."

"Max, maybe it's you who matters to him, and I'm the guy that will make it happen for you."

Max exhaled a cloud of smoke and shook his head. "Not me, Jack. Vinnie can't stand me or my father, who he wishes never married his sister. It's only because I'm his sister's son that he even tries. But Jack, I've known Vinnie my whole life; I know how he feels and thinks. I'm telling you, Jack, Vinnie really likes you, and he wants you to succeed, even if it means making me a big success." He blew out another cloud of smoke.

"Hey, can you not smoke in my apartment?" Anna called out. "I don't want the smell of smoke, and I definitely don't want ashes on my floor!"

"See what I mean?" Max whispered. "You're in for a hell of a ride."

As long as we can smoke weed in this place, I don't care.

ANNA DECLINED Max's offer to let her have the front passenger seat.

"You're the star tonight, and you and Jack need to talk," she said.

Max looked at Bernstein and nodded in approval. He opened the rear door for Anna, who smiled in return.

Max set the radio to WWRL. "Now that I'm doing all this kind of music, I need to listen to it," he declared. "It's half my act now."

"Should we stop and pick up some dinner?" Anna asked. "Maybe call and see if the other guys want anything?"

"That's nice to think of us," Bernstein said. "Vinnie told me he's got a little room for the acts, and he always provides food for before the show, during the break, and after the show. Maybe we don't make the most money tonight, but we eat the best."

Like most small and medium clubs in Queens and Nassau, save for The Action House, a cover charge was split with the band getting the lion's share. It didn't match the four-figure fees at the Fillmore, the Circus, Westbury, or even Stony Brook, but it was enough to live on if it was regular. The food at Vinnie's club however was sure to be the best in the business. *The man loves good food.*

"Yeah, Anna, what kind of Italian invites people over and doesn't have food?" Max chimed.

～

VINNIE'S CLUB was tucked away on a side street off Yellowstone Boulevard. Bernstein turned the Volvo off of busy Queens Boulevard. The sun was just starting to drop, casting Queens in a gauzy yellow-orange light. Vinnie had told him there were a few private parking spots in the rear of the club, and one was for him. Another was for Clayton, Mickey, and Sonny, who would arrive in Sonny's van.

A thick, well-muscled young man in a black T-shirt and matching chinos and pointy boots guarded the door. When he saw the trio approach, he asked if they were with the band.

"I'm Max, the singer. This is Jack Bernstein, my manager, and Anna, his fiancée. My uncle is expecting us." The tough guy turned slightly red.

"Of course." He opened the door. "Sorry I didn't recognize you, Mr. Calamato."

"It's not Calamato," Max corrected. "The last name is Flugel, but I might have to change it."

The guard scrunched his face as he stood aside.

"Take it easy, *paisano*," Max said, and the beefy guard relaxed, smiled, and patted Max on the back as he entered.

"Thanks for making me his fiancé," Anna whispered to Max when the three of them were in the building.

Vinnie was waiting inside, and the instant he saw them he hurried to Bernstein and embraced him. Bernstein detected the scent of Pinaud Lilac. Vinnie had gotten a haircut for the occasion.

"It's an honor to have you present in my little club," he said.

"The pleasure is all ours," Bernstein replied.

Vinnie gave Max a light hug. "You do what Jack Bernstein says and you'll be a big star. Remember when you were a little kid and I'd come over to your house and we'd sit around that big set I got your mother and watch Julius La Rosa singing on Arthur Godfrey? That's how it's gonna be for you."

"For our age group, may be better to talk about watching the Beatles on Ed Sullivan," Anna said.

Vinnie looked at Anna, then broke into laughter. Bernstein noticed Vinnie's laugh was similar to Max's, but stronger and more confident. When Max laughed, there was always a hint of uncertainty in his voice. There was never any hesitation in Vinnie Calamato's.

"This must be Miss Anna Bardoni. My friend Jack has told me all about you, only the best things. Let me just say that if Jack Bernstein cares about someone, so does Vinnie Calamato. *Capice?*"

"I don't speak much Italian," Anna said. "Not Sicilian either. But I know what *capice* means, and yes, I understand." She wasn't smiling.

Vinnie was.

"Good. Because it means you ever have a problem, any problem, you come talk to Vinnie. In English or Sicilian. Oh yeah, I also speak that dialect the other Italians use because Sicilian is too hard for them."

"Let's stick with English," Anna said.

Vinnie shook his head, still smiling. He turned to Bernstein. "You got a live one here, and that's real good. You don't need me or Vito," he said, pointing to the door where the guard stood. "Anyone wants to get to you, they got to go through her, and they ain't getting through."

He then turned to Anna. "But if you ever need help, you know who to call."

The door opened, and the other New Plateaus walked into the club. Clayton and Sonny carried their instruments, and Mickey had large, round cases that looked like oversized hatboxes in each hand.

"We need to get the amps and the rest of the drum kit out of the van," Sonny called.

"I can get a guy to help," Vinnie yelled across the club.

"Okay for the amps, but Mickey never lets anyone touch his drums."

Vinnie called out, and a skinny young man emerged from the rear of the club. Vinnie told him to help as needed. Sonny and Clayton walked toward the others as Mickey went to get his drum set. They clapped Max on the back and shook hands with Vinnie and Bernstein. Mickey joined them a few minutes later.

While the musicians set up, Vinnie led Max, Bernstein, and Anna to the bar. The bartender wasn't on duty yet, so Vinnie went behind the bar and took the drink orders. They agreed to share a bottle of wine to start. "Just one drink for Max, because we don't want him getting on stage drunk," Bernstein said. He turned to Max. "One glass will loosen you up for the show, but no more until your performance is over."

Max lit a cigarette, and Vinnie cut and lit a cigar. The bar area was quickly enveloped in smoke. Anna waved her hand, clearing the smoke from in front of her face. The sound of the guitar and bass tuning up echoed through the club.

"I have to admit I'm a little nervous," Max said. "Before yesterday I never played in front of an audience. This one's gonna be bigger."

Bernstein swirled the wine in his glass, which he had hardly touched.

"Don't be," he told Max. "You guys did the thing that makes all the difference in the world—you practiced. You worked up a great set. They're going to love you, I'm sure."

"You know if I screw up in front of my Uncle Vinnie it's only going to make him even more convinced I'm useless."

"Well, that is definitely not going to happen, Max. I've been listening to you sing with these guys for the last month. I've dropped by for a bit at every rehearsal. I talk with Sonny all the time, and he tells me the band has full confidence in you. Your voice is perfect for the songs. You're on key, you carry the tune, great timing thanks to working with Mickey. The chemistry between you four is perfect."

Seems to be going fine, but I've felt that way before and things went sideways.

Max stubbed out his cigarette in an ashtray and took a sip of wine. He looked at Bernstein. "You really think so? You really think I'm that good? Or are you just saying it to make me feel good?"

"Hey, Max," Bernstein replied. "How long did it take me to fire those two morons from Macbeth Heights? You think I waste my time on failures?"

Max flashed a wide smile and patted Bernstein on the shoulder. "You're the man, Jack. I'll never get there without you."

Let's hope it's true this time, Bernstein thought.

Chapter Thirty-Two

Vinnie had set up an Italian spread in a dressing room behind the stage.

"Hope you like it," he said as the band members filled their plates with lasagna, gnocchi, veal Parmesan, calamari, and garlic bread.

"Only sodas for the band from now until after the show," Vinnie announced. "After that, we all drink as much as we like."

Anna pressed close to Bernstein, while Vinnie was on the other side of the room filling a plate of his own.

"He's not as big a jerk as I thought," she whispered into Bernstein's ear.

"Max or Vinnie?" he asked.

"Max is sweet in a sort of annoying way, but he is sweet. Vinnie just doesn't fit the picture of a mob guy. Look how nice he treats everybody, even Black people."

"Yeah," Bernstein said. "Except for the suits, the cigar, the night club, and the tough guys at the door, there's nothing about Vinnie that says 'mob'." He glanced at the clock on the wall. It was 7:50.

"The doors open in ten minutes. I have to get out and mingle once that happens." As he was speaking, the band left the room to prepare for their opening. Vinnie, who had been relighting his cigar as needed, placed it in a big ashtray at the end of the bar.

"Showtime," he said, and the three of them walked out onto the floor of the club.

The doors opened at exactly eight. Bernstein stood off to the side, estimating the size of the crowd. A young woman sat at the door collecting the three-dollar cover charge. People were still filing in when he stopped counting at fifty. Vinnie greeted those he knew and occasionally those he didn't. Ed's wife was with him—unusual, as she normally stayed away from anything to do with Ed's musical world. They stopped by to greet Bernstein and Anna and Ed assured them the evening would be a success.

"I've seen this guy Clayton play clubs for years, and he's really good. With the right break, he can carry a band pretty far. Mostly R&B, but he can play anything."

Vinnie came by as Bernstein's friends were about to move on. Introductions were made, and Vinnie told them to enjoy a drink on the house. They all walked to the bar, leaving Bernstein and Anna. "Have a drink with them," he told her. "I need to see if I can get the ear of any writer or musician who can help get out the word about the New Plateaus."

A half minute later, Bernstein spotted Danny Goldstein, former deejay at the Queens College station, now with a rock and roll show on a radio station in Westchester County. Bernstein remembered seeing him at Tennessee Eddie's gig at Max's Kansas City. Bernstein had intended to call him the next day and talk about Eddie, but that next day he was no longer Eddie's manager. He wondered what Danny knew. *Probably everything.*

Bernstein made his way to Danny, who stood at the best spot to watch the band. Danny acted like he recognized him, but Bernstein wanted to make certain he knew his name. He did.

"Jack Bernstein," Danny said as they shook hands. "Haven't seen you since college. I hear you're in the business as well. Also heard about Tennessee Eddie. Too bad. Saw him at Max's. Great show. Great performer. Watch your back, Jack. In this, game everyone's a shark."

Bernstein shook his head at the mention of Tennessee Eddie.

"That's all behind me," he told Danny. "This is my new band, and they're great. Found the singer wasting his time in Macbeth Heights, of all places. Hooked him up with Clayton and Mickey and got my old pal Sonny to pick up his bass and join."

Danny was impressed.

"Wow, everyone knows Sonny. He taught at Queens, but he's actually known more for his club out in South Jamaica. Heard about it for years but never made it out there. Can you believe that? Me, a Queens boy with a show and all that?"

"If you like, I can take you out there sometime, introduce you to Sonny, maybe get you an interview with some of the acts."

"Of course I'd like it, Jack. That's what I do for a living. Talking about that, if your band is any good tonight, I'd like the chance to talk with them sometime, maybe even get them on the show."

Bernstein assured Danny he would love the band, and he guaranteed him an interview.

"An exclusive interview," he said.

Danny said that sounded promising. Before Bernstein left to meet and greet others of importance, he told Danny to catch him by the stage during the break between sets.

"I've got some dynamite hash I'd like to turn you onto. That is, if you're allowed to smoke while working."

"Smoking while working is my job," Danny replied. "See you then."

Vinnie's voice boomed through the club's speakers.

"Ladies and gentlemen, it is Club Rego's pleasure to introduce Queens' hottest new band, presented by Jack Bernstein, the New Plateaus!" Max walked from behind the stage, followed by Mickey, Clayton, and Sonny. The latter two had their instruments strapped on, and Mickey sat behind his drum kit. The crowd applauded respectfully, save for Anna and Bernstein's friends, who clapped loudly.

The band launched right into "My Girl." The song opened with Sonny's strong bass notes, soon joined by Mickey's steady and understated drumming. Clayton began strumming chords as Max took the microphone in his two hands.

Bernstein had his eyes on Max. He looked nervous, which

Bernstein expected in a singer the first time they fronted a band at a gig. He also knew that the music industry is hard and unforgiving, and second chances were not easy to come by, even with Vinnie Calamato as an uncle. *Please, no more freezing up.*

Bernstein flinched when Max missed a note in the second line of the first verse. It was not something most listeners would recognize, but any professional would, and he didn't want to read reviews about Max Flugel falling on his face thirty seconds into his act. Not with Danny and other pros judging them. Max must have known this as well, as it showed on his face. By now, Bernstein knew Max well enough to recognize he was upset with himself.

Bernstein scanned the faces of the three musicians, and they were unperturbed. They kept playing as if it hadn't happened. Bernstein was relieved and shifted his focus back to Max, who had recovered and sang intently while looking out into the audience, reminding Bernstein of clips he'd seen of Sinatra. *He learned from yesterday how to pull himself out of it.*

In the middle of the song, there was a musical break, and Clayton played a bluesy, energetic lead that slowed in anticipation of Max's resumed singing. Several people began to dance in a languid motion.

Max held the microphone and bent and swayed slightly as he sang, gesturing with and waving his free arm. *Another touch of Sinatra*, Bernstein thought. *I wonder how Frank himself would feel.* He looked into the crowd, then closed his eyes and opened them again, moving his gaze from his band to his crowd. Many people danced to the music, while others stood transfixed by the act on stage. *They sure seem to like it*, he thought.

Bernstein stood to the side of the stage, taking it all in. A finger tapped his shoulder. Dan Picarelli, wearing the same kind of close-fitting, Italian-cut suit he wore to the office, held a drink in one hand and kept the finger-tapping hand on Bernstein's shoulder.

"Off to a hell of a start," Picarelli said. "This dago Max can sing, and that band is tighter than a tourniquet."

"Are you saying this because it's true, or to get me to introduce you to Vinnie and get some business?"

"All three," Picarelli replied.

The second number was "Stay," and once again Max showed himself to be disciplined enough to perform on stage the arrangement he and the band had painstakingly rehearsed. During this number, Max grasped the microphone with one hand and walked about the stage, waving and pointing with the other or gesticulating to emphasize points to himself. The audience reacted with cheers and applause, and when the song ended, the applause lasted almost a half-minute.

Before segueing into the third song, Max introduced the band. Each time he called out a name, the crowd roared. Bernstein had given all his attention to the performance and had not watched the flow of people into Club Rego. When he scanned the room, he saw many Black faces he assumed were friends of the band or regulars at Sonny's. Bernstein realized he would be able to gauge responses by both White and Black audiences before they even played Sonny's the following week.

∿

Midway through Max's cover of "The Tracks of My Tears," Bernstein spotted a familiar figure across the room. A Brooks Brothers suit sticks out in a rock club on a Saturday night. Bernstein hurried across the room to where the man stood.

"What the hell are you doing here?" he screamed at Harold Levine, the young lawyer who had come to his basement apartment to tell him he was fired as Tennessee Eddie's manager.

"I was working late and decided to have a good time listening to an up-and-coming band. Took a cab from the office. Too bad it was still daylight. Queens is so depressing to see. But back to your supposed business collapse—for a guy who claims my client ruined his career, it sure doesn't look that way."

"No, but I am going to ruin your face," Bernstein shouted as he moved closer to Levine.

Bernstein didn't see Vinnie approaching from his left.

"Stay cool, Jack. This looks like something club management can handle. May I ask what you've done to anger my friend over here?" Vinnie asked the lawyer.

"I'm here just like everyone else, to hear the music," Levine replied.

"No, he's not!" Bernstein yelled. "He's here to spy on me and do something to hurt my lawsuit. These are the guys that stole Tennessee Eddie and are trying to cheat me!"

Vinnie turned to a fireplug of a man standing five feet behind him.

"Over here, Rocco," he told the squat man. Vinnie's pit bull nodded but stayed put for the time being.

Levine didn't flinch. "Should he lay a finger on me, rest assured my firm will sue anyone within ten feet of ownership. Interested in having your deposition taken, Mr....what is your name?" the lawyer asked Vinnie.

"Mr. Levine, should you have any business with my client, which happens to be this establishment, ask them through me." Dan Picarelli handed Levine a card. Levine studied it and dropped it into a pocket.

"I see from the address you share the same office as Mr. Bernstein's attorney. How's the pizza?" he asked.

Picarelli moved close to Levine, their noses separated by less than an inch. "The pizza's good, dickhead. And one more wisecrack out of you, your face is going to look like a pizza. Wait till you feel Rocco's left hook. And we aren't worried about your fancy-assed downtown lawyers suing anybody. You're a trespasser, and we can use force to remove you, and even greater when you resist Rocco, which is what everyone here will tell the cops. See that sign? You're a trespasser." Indeed, on the wall next to the table where the cover was collected hung a sign advising, "The management reserves the right to refuse admission or to remove anyone at any time at their sole discretion."

"You should have left when you were asked," Vinnie said, pointing an unlit cigar at Levine.

"I didn't hear anyone tell me to leave!" Levine exclaimed.

"Get your ears checked after you get out of the hospital," Vinnie replied. He turned his gaze to Rocco. Before Rocco could take a step, Levine turned and ran out the front door into the warm Rego Park night.

Picarelli was laughing so hard Bernstein worried he might have a heart attack.

"Bet he doesn't tell the partners about this adventure," Picarelli said. "Wandering off their turf a bit, I'd say. The more experienced lawyers will sit him down and explain there really are some people you just don't sue, and you don't threaten to sue them, either."

"Give me one of those cards," Vinnie told Picarelli, who immediately complied. "And let's go over and have a drink together in my private office."

Bernstein stood in place for several minutes as he struggled to comprehend what just happened. His thoughts were interrupted by Anna grabbing his behind.

"Don't worry, it's just crowded enough and dim enough so nobody sees," she said. "Saw you with Vinnie and two guys in suits. So, what was that all about?"

"I'll let you know as soon as I figure it out," he said.

THE LAST SONG before the break was Max's cover of "Denise," released in 1963. Eight years later, Randy and the Rainbows were still making a living off their one hit. Randy and the Rainbows were locals, growing up not all that far from Rego Park, and there was a lot of affection for them. Max could reach the high notes of the original while inflecting it with the R&B style of his band. The crowd loved the new take on the song. There was a long applause, and when Max told the crowd the band would be back in ten minutes, more applause broke out.

Danny Goldstein met Bernstein at the appointed location, and they were soon in a small office near the band's dressing room. Bernstein lit his small wooden pipe, the bowl filled with Magical Moroccan, and passed it to Danny. The radio host took two long drags, coughed, and then bent slightly forward. Bernstein managed to grab the pipe before Danny lost his grip.

"Are you all right?"

Danny stopped coughing and stood straight. "That is strong stuff, my friend. Thanks for the hits."

"My pleasure. So, what do you think of my band?"

Danny paused for a moment as if collecting his thoughts. "They're really good…and really different. It's this weird mix of rock—which already has R&B—and blues, pop, and dare I say a bit of what the unkind might call bubblegum. But, somehow, they make it work. You saw that audience. Black and White, everyone clapping…whatever you think of their source material, Max can sing, and that band can play. I had no idea Sonny played bass at all, let alone like that. And the guitar and drums? Super. Max has himself a professional band."

"Is there anything you can think of where we might improve? Anything we could be doing that we're not?"

Again, Danny paused to reflect before he spoke. "Just keep gigging. These guys are only going to get better and better. Probably get more musically adventurous. I might suggest getting a keyboard. For a longer set or a full concert, a basic three-piece band might not hold up the whole evening. Good as your guys' version of 'My Girl' was, it would be better with a keyboard. Just give it a thought."

"More than a thought, Danny. And how about some airtime, or at least a mention?"

"Of course." He handed Bernstein a card. "Call the station Monday morning. Tell them I said to book you and the band on my show this Friday morning."

The night before we play Sonny's. Hopefully that gets a lot of people out to see us.

~

THE SECOND SET went even better than the first. The band knew "The Tracks of My Tears" in their sleep, and Max did a surprisingly good, strong, rocking version of "Gloria," basing his cover on the version by the Irish group Them when they still had Van Morrison.

Max was visibly looser and more at ease for the second set. He didn't grip the microphone as if it were a lifebuoy on the open seas. Bernstein saw Max growing more comfortable on stage, and more importantly, he recognized the need to engage the audience. He spoke to them before each number.

Great, I was wondering when he'd remember a frontman is more than just a singer. I told him that enough times.

"Thanks for coming out tonight, folks," were the first words he spoke directly to the crowd. "I'm Max Flugel, and with me are the other New Plateaus." He introduced each by name.

"I just escaped from Macbeth Heights," he said. "But don't tell anyone. I don't wanna go back." Laughter ran through the audience. Bernstein remembered what the old keyboard player turned gas station owner said about Macbeth Heights.

Red is right. Everyone pokes fun at that place.

The stunner was the closing number, a soulful cover of the Beatles "Let It Be." Clayton's haunting melodies complimented Max's slow, mournful vocals. Sonny's bass line was slow, steady, and in harmony with Clayton. A listener could barely tell Mickey was drumming, which Bernstein knew was exactly what this arrangement required. The crowd, knowing this was the last song of the night, gave the New Plateaus a full minute of applause. When they were done, Max bid them good night.

"On behalf of the New Plateaus, I thank each and every one of you for being here with us tonight."

Bernstein saw Ed Stern twenty feet away. Stern flashed a big smile and nodded his head forcefully. Bernstein knew what he was telegraphing. *This is how professionals sound.*

VINNIE HAD SET up a post-gig table, replete with the usual food and desserts. There were several bottles of wine, a tub filled with ice, beer, and soft drinks, and a big urn of coffee. Bernstein took stock of the people he expected. All of his friends were there, and Anna of course. Stern stood talking with two studio musician friends. Picarelli was with a young college girl he met on the dance floor. Vinnie sat on a chair smoking his cigar. The three musicians filled plates with food. Anna spoke with Barry while sipping a glass of Chianti. Max leaned against a wall smoking a cigarette with a dazed look on his face, as if he wasn't certain he had succeeded. As people came over to congratulate and praise him, Bernstein decided this was Max's version of an acid trip.

Danny Goldstein emerged from a knot of people and walked to Bernstein. He said he had to leave because the worst part of the job was getting stuck with the Sunday morning show.

"Who listens to rock at eight in the morning on Sunday? That's what happens when you're the new kid on the block. But don't you worry, Jack. Your guys are going on the Friday morning show for sure. Make sure you call first thing in the morning."

"Not a chance I won't," he replied.

MAX WAS quiet the entire ride back to Long Island City. When he left the Volvo, he told Bernstein if he needed any help moving, let him know.

"I don't think Max ever believed anything like this could ever happen; at least, not to him," Anna told Bernstein as they drove to Bayside for what was likely the last time. "Who thought the New Plateaus would be this good?"

"Certainly not me," Bernstein said. "At least not when I first met Max."

ANNA AWOKE at seven and went upstairs to her room. At eight thirty, after her mother left for Sunday mass, she was back in the basement, tangled up in bed with Bernstein. When they were too exhausted to engage any further, they lay back and listened *to Clouds,* by Joni Mitchell, playing on the radio. The new FM stations would often play an entire album upon its release, with ads every three or four songs. Folk-based music fit Sunday mornings better than rock.

They drove to the Island Diner for breakfast

"Last night was amazing," Anna said. "Off stage Max is a little annoying, although not anywhere as bad as you make him out to be.

Put him on stage, and the audience can't take their eyes off him. It's his facial expressions, his body language, and of course, his singing. His voice is okay, but his phrasing is all his own."

"Sounds like you're the music pro," Bernstein said. "Getting into things like the phrasing."

"I grew up listening to Sinatra, and everybody always said that about him."

Bernstein took a moment to reflect on Anna's observation. "I think I'm finally figuring out Max's appeal, if that's the right word. You see Frank Sinatra. Clayton and Mickey see Little Anthony and Smokey Robinson. Max sees himself as a cross between Frankie Valli, Smokey Robinson, and the 1910 Fruitgum Company. Max Flugel, who I first thought was a nobody, has become all things to all people."

"And what is he to you?" Anna asked.

"My ticket to success," he replied.

"That's funny," Anna said. "That's exactly how Max told me he sees you."

Chapter 33
End of April, 1971

F
ive more days until the band plays Sonny's. If the guys do well on
Danny's show, we could add a few hundred people from places we
never even dreamed of, like Westchester and Riverdale. Then two
days after that, I've got to pay Mitty and the pawnbroker.

Don't know what I would have done if I hadn't run into Ronald.

It was Monday afternoon, just after one o'clock. Today was the day
he was going to reap the benefits of selling prime hashish with Ed and
Barry and get his debts paid off. Ed didn't have to be in the studio
until the evening with one of those pretentious groups Ed called
"vampires." They insisted on sleeping all day and then working and
partying from dusk to dawn. Barry's pharmacy school classes were
Tuesday through Thursday, so Bernstein, Ed, and Barry were going to
make an afternoon of it.

Bernstein reached for the ball of Magical Moroccan he had peeled
off for personal use. He and Anna enjoyed it almost daily, but he kept
it away from the band. The two occasions he stoned them, they
couldn't practice for twenty-four hours after. The three musicians,
experienced cannabis users, pronounced the hash supreme. Max
turned up his nose at the smell and lit a Winston, declaring he
preferred the taste.

When Bernstein first took his private stash, it was the size of a plum. The piece he held in his hand was no larger than one of Duke Schwartz's marbles. He pinched off a piece with his thumb and forefinger, put it in the bowl of his pipe, went into the bathroom, closed the door, and lit it up. As he inhaled, he realized he was leaving the basement forever the following day, and it no longer mattered if the old lady finally realized he was a toker.

~

BEFORE LEAVING for Ed's house, Bernstein called his service for messages. Danny had called to confirm he booked the time on his Friday morning show. Danny's message reminded Bernstein of his advice—the band would be even better with a good keyboard player.

Danny may be an old friend, but he's also a guy on the make like me and wants to be the first to introduce my band. I have to think hard about a keyboard. Bringing in a new person this late in the game could be a problem. The band is finally tight and together, but do I want Danny and others saying I should have added a keyboard when there was still time?

Barry was already at Ed's. The little home studio reeked of Magical Moroccan and weed. Both Ed and Barry were red-eyed and sluggish. Bernstein declined a bowl.

"I'm in a bit of a hurry today. Practice tomorrow and Thursday, airtime Friday, the gig on Saturday…plus I've been thinking of adding a keyboard for Saturday night, and that takes more time. By the way Ed, what do you think of that idea?"

Ed struggled to focus his eyes and loosen his vocal cords. "Exactly what I'd recommend," he finally said. "Clayton's a fantastic guitarist, great with leads, riffs, fills, anything with melody. He's a pro who knows exactly when to leave rhythm and come in with them. It would be good to have a keyboard to play melody lines when Clayton is playing rhythm, and vice versa."

Bernstein nodded. If Ed thought a keyboard was a good idea, that carried even more weight than coming from Danny.

"I don't know how easy it will be to find one and get them ready on such short notice," Stern continued. "I could start making calls for a good studio keyboard man. They can come in cold and do anything, but that's going to cost a pretty penny."

"Which I don't have," Bernstein said. "In fact, I'm here to get the money so I can get a loan shark off my back and get my buddy's guitar out of hock."

Stern and Barry reached into their pockets at the same time as if on cue from a director. Each produced a small stack of bills, which they handed to Bernstein, who separated them by denomination and added them up in his head. When he was done, he stuffed the money in his pockets and stared at his friends with the look of a man who discovers the strange odor from the basement is a decomposing body.

"There's just a little over two grand here!" Bernstein wailed. "That's basically what I owe Ronald. What the hell happened to our profits?"

"Gone up in smoke," Barry replied.

Bernstein felt dizzy and sat down. He dropped his head into his hands, elbows resting on his knees. As depressed and disappointed as he was about his financial setback, he felt more anger about his best friends being the cause.

"How bad is it? Ed asked.

"I'm not much better off than I was before I took the hash from Ronald," Bernstein said. "If I throw in what I'm getting for my share of the gigs, and a few hundred I got scattered among different bank accounts, maybe I can come up with enough to pay Mitty. Hopefully no one buys Pete's guitar before I can come up with the dough to buy it back, but it will cost me more than if I just redeemed it now, which I can't.

"How could you guys have done this to me?" He asked Barry and Stern. "Especially knowing my situation?"

Bernstein could see from their faces that Barry and Ed were sorry, but sorry wouldn't help him.

"I can throw in some money if it comes down to it," Barry said. "I mean, after all, I did get to smoke a hell of a lot of great hash."

"I could come up with a few bucks as well," Ed Stern said.

Bernstein mulled their words. "If I needed it, how soon could you come up with the money?"

Barry told him he could come up with some excuse to get the

money from his parents, but they were on vacation and wouldn't be home for two weeks. Ed told him he couldn't raise his wife's suspicions by taking it from one of their accounts, but in two weeks he was going to be doing some studio work for a producer who paid in cash. Bernstein thanked them but explained that it would be too late.

"I'll figure something out," he said. "Or fate will figure it out for me."

~

THE TUESDAY and Thursday practices lifted Bernstein's hopes for a knockout performance at Sonny's. He saw how much Max's confidence had grown and how he reached notes easier than before. When the band set up on the stage on Tuesday, Bernstein recalled that night at Max's Kansas City when he had felt so confident. Now almost a year and a half had passed, but the pain it caused still clawed at Bernstein's heart. Galahad's betrayal didn't hurt him nearly as much, perhaps because he had become hardened, or perhaps because he knew Galahad was right that Bernstein wasn't the manager for him. On their last night together in the basement, he told this to Anna. She said not to waste energy thinking about the past. When he was able, it worked, and the bad memories retreated.

After the Thursday rehearsal, Bernstein gathered the band at Sonny's bar and explained the radio program the next morning. They would meet at the radio station at eight-thirty in the morning. Clayton would answer any questions directed to the band as a whole, and each member would answer those specifically directed to them. When Clayton asked if it were better for the singer and frontman to do most of the talking, Bernstein explained that Max's image was still a work in progress, and he didn't want him saying anything that might come back to haunt the band later on. In truth, he thought Clayton cut a better image for a rock band. He was cool, quick on his feet, and he had been knocking on the door of success long enough to make sure it opened this time. Everyone except Sonny left at seven p.m.

Bernstein and Max drove home from rehearsal in the Volvo. Anna had bought a bedroom set, which was already delivered. A queen-sized bed was set up, the mattress still covered in plastic. When Bernstein was alone in the apartment, he found the comforter that came with the bed. He threw it on top of the plastic-covered mattress, took off his shoes and pants, and lay down.

The next he knew, Max Flugel was pounding on his door and yelling for him to wake up. He looked at his watch. It was ten past seven in the morning. He yelled out to Max, telling him to hold on. He pulled on his pants, stepped into his shoes, and made a quick trip to the bathroom, where he emptied his bladder and washed his hands and face, only to realize he didn't have a towel. He wiped his hands on his shirt and ran out the door, where Max waited.

"Get your car and meet me in front of the bakery around the corner," Max said. "Two minutes."

When Bernstein pulled into the bus stop next to the bakery, Max was walking out with a cardboard tray containing two cups of coffee and a bag of pastries.

"I ran down and gave the order before I woke you from your beauty sleep," he told Bernstein as he handed him a coffee and placed the bag so it straddled the two front seats.

Bernstein took two slugs of coffee.

"Thanks, Max," he said as he reached into the bag and retrieved a cruller. He finished it in three bites, wiped his hands with a napkin, and drove off.

"No problem," Max said. "I figured you got to sleep late, and since you're doing all the driving, the least I could do is get the coffee and donuts."

"For which I am deeply grateful," Bernstein replied. "At this hour, caffeine is the drug of choice."

"As is nicotine," Max said. He opened his window before lighting his first Winston of the day.

≈

SONNY, Clayton, and Mickey greeted Max and Bernstein in the waiting room where the station's guard directed them. A large coffee urn sat on a table, accompanied by a pitcher of milk and a bowl of sugar cubes with a tiny spoon. Bernstein poured a cup of black coffee.

Danny came into the room. He explained they would be going on in a few minutes and led them to the broadcast booth. Bernstein brought his coffee.

"Just be yourselves," he advised. "Let the band speak for themselves, Jack, and at the end, if there's anything you want to clarify, go for it." Everyone nodded and then sat down and watched a series of lights flicker on in front of where Danny was seated at his microphone.

"Good morning Westchester and parts unknown. This is Danny Goldstein, and welcome to the Rocking in the Burbs Hour, every weekday morning from nine to noon. I'm going to start this beautiful Friday morning off with a song from David Crosby's solo album, released this February. It's called 'Orleans,' and I like it. Hope you do as well. It's real short, so I'll be back in two minutes with some very special guests I'd like you all to meet."

Danny turned to Bernstein and the band.

"Good for my listeners to hear about other 'burbs and their bands. I'm hoping a few make the trek to South Jamaica and watch you guys tomorrow. When I tell these folks I'm a fan, I'm not joking."

Someday, I'm going to look back on the Magical Moroccan deal as a great boost to my career, Bernstein thought, *but not three days before Mitty expects his money.* Then he remembered how Anna urged him to stop thinking bad thoughts and reminded himself he'd gotten his band on the radio the day before they were to play a serious gig in front of a serious audience.

When the song ended, Danny told the listeners how he and Bernstein were friends in college and met up again recently at Club Rego, where the New Plateaus were making their debut.

"I knew I'd stumbled across something very special. Not in Manhattan, not in Hollywood, but in Queens—the 'burbs, even if it's technically part of New York City. So it's our kind of music, and I want you to hear it and meet the guys behind it."

Clayton answered the first question about what made this band special.

"Me and Mickey, we come from an R&B background. Sonny, he's a jazzman. And Max, well, we can say he's from the doo-wop tradition. You put us all together and you get a sound no one's heard before. The musicians moved a little toward where Max was at, and he moved toward where we're at. It's a whole new type of music. We've reached some new plateaus, and that's why we call ourselves the New Plateaus."

Mickey took the tougher question about merging South Jamaica and White Queens.

"We never gave it a moment's thought. The minute we heard Max sing, we knew we all spoke the same language—music."

When Danny asked Max if it were difficult to switch from his favored bubblegum and Four Seasons style to rhythm and blues and rock, Max was ready.

"With a band like I've got, and a manager like Jack Bernstein, it wasn't difficult at all. In fact, it's been a pleasure every step of the way."

"You guys really seem to like each other," Danny commented.

"Like brothers," Sonny intoned, his only comment of the interview.

"We're going to take a little break," Danny told the audience. "When we come back, the New Plateaus are going to play for us, and I'll tell you how to go see them tomorrow. Back in a few."

When the lights flickered off, he told the band there were instruments set up in the studio next door.

"You've got about three minutes to make yourselves comfortable. Sound system is set but make any necessary adjustments on your instruments, and if you can, play something original, not a cover."

"We can play that song Clayton and Mickey wrote for Max," Sonny said. We rehearsed it a lot this week." Bernstein recalled hearing some song he didn't recognize, but he hadn't paid much attention since it wasn't on the playlist.

The band trouped off to the studio with Danny. Bernstein was confident the musicians could play well without any warm-up, but he wasn't certain about Max. He knew sooner or later all bands faced this situation. *Any band afraid of a microphone under these circumstances isn't really a band*, he decided.

The song sounded better in the radio studio than when Bernstein heard it rehearsed at Sonny's. *Is it the equipment, the engineer, or their knowing what's at stake?* When they were back in the broadcast booth, Danny played a Beatles song and chatted with Bernstein and the band.

"Listen, I really want to thank you for coming all the way up here at what I know is an ungodly hour for musicians. You guys are great, and I hope that as you gather steam it encourages the music scene up here. Your original number was mind-blowing."

"Do you ever wish you were in the city?" Bernstein asked Danny. *A fair question. We're not on the air.*

"Not at all," Danny said. "Why should I? The action is moving, Jack. Haven't you heard? Graham's closing the Fillmore East. The Sunday Allman Brothers concert on June 27th is the end. It's a hundred percent true. A buddy of mine works for Graham. And let me predict the Electric Circus is next. The East Village has become a nightmare. It's only safe if you're a Hell's Angel."

Danny saw them to the front door while the Beatles kept his listeners happy.

"Will we see you tomorrow night?" Bernstein asked.

"Wild horses couldn't keep me away," Danny said.

"And I'll make room for you at the after-show party," Sonny added.

Danny started back to his broadcast booth, then turned around.

"And Jack, what I said about adding a keyboard and being even better—that's still true. Especially with that original piece you debuted on the show. Trust me."

"A keyboard would be nice," Max said as they drove over the Triborough Bridge. "Opens up some other musical possibilities. Some songs need a piano."

"And where am I supposed to get one a day before the show?" Bernstein asked. "Who would work for what we can pay?" The mention of payment reminded him of the debts due the following week. Then a bolt of realization blasted those concerns from his mind.

"Come to think of it, I do know of someone. We're making a brief return to Macbeth Heights."

· · ·

RED FLEMING SMILED when he saw Bernstein.

"The Music Man returns. Just can't stay away from Macbeth Heights, I guess. Come on into my office and have some coffee."

When they were seated and had cups before them, Bernstein introduced Max and Red. "Max is the singer for the New Plateaus, this hot new band that's been gigging around. Playing over at Sonny's in Jamaica tomorrow night. Just were interviewed on the radio this morning. We're expecting a big crowd."

"I'll come by if there's no cover charge," Red said.

"Red, I'm not looking to see you come as a guest. I want you playing keyboards for us tomorrow."

"What was that you said?" Max asked.

"Yeah, did I hear right?" Red followed.

Bernstein explained that two very smart music people recommended having keyboards. Red said he could play anything, anytime, and could play any kind of keyboard. If that were the case, he could join them on stage the following night.

"Not as a member of the New Plateaus, but we could bill it as 'and Red Fleming' or just announce you as on keyboards and let the audience think what they will."

"Assuming I were interested, how would I get ready?" Red asked.

Bernstein wrote out the playlist. He told Red to practice those numbers. The next day, Red would meet the band at Sonny's at five, and they'd spend an hour and a half making sure Red was in synch with the others. "Anything goes wrong, you get the hook," Bernstein joked. He told Red he would split his manager's share with him.

"Heck, I should pay you," Red said.

"If that'll make you happy," Bernstein replied.

BERNSTEIN TOLD Max he had to pick up the rest of his belongings and would be back at Sunnyside in a few hours. When he was in his basement, he called Sonny at his Queens College office, and as luck would have it, the big man was at his desk grading papers. He thought it worth seeing if Red Fleming could join the New Plateaus on keyboard with an hour and a half practice.

"Actually, if he's got the experience you say, should be easy."

Bernstein went to the drawer in his nightstand and checked the money from Ed and Barry. It was all there, $2,200. It dawned on him he could use the money to pay off Mitty, redeem Pete's guitar, and pay Ronald almost half of what he owed. He allowed the thought to percolate briefly then rejected it. All he would accomplish was to shift the dishonor from one relationship to another, albeit to a relationship far less dangerous than one with an angry Mitty the Mole.

I got myself into this, and I have to get myself out of it without being a deadbeat.

He decided it was best to pay Ronald before temptation got the better of him. Bernstein dialed Ronald's number. After the sixth ring, a recorded message informed him the phone service was to terminate at the end of the day, and there was no assurance the subscriber would receive the message. Bernstein didn't like this, and he didn't leave a message. *Who knows what happened*, he thought. *Who knows who will listen to any messages I leave.*

Bernstein didn't realize how little he owned until it was time to pack up and leave the basement. Anna had helped him pack the night before, and aside from his stereo system, television, and clock radio, everything else fit into one suitcase and two cardboard boxes. He left his battered and worthless furniture for the next tenant.

Bernstein made a mental note to visit the bulletin board at the CMC at Queens College and post an index card offering to sell the stereo system. He should be able to get at least a hundred and fifty dollars for it. He could get a lot more if he sold the stereo Vinnie gave him, but that would be seen as disrespectful.

He knew that every Friday, Mrs. Bardoni left home at half past eleven to meet friends for lunch. He waited five minutes after hearing the front door close before carrying his belongings to the vestibule. After what he had heard her say about him, and his fear that she would discover his relationship with Anna, he preferred to avoid her. He went around the corner to the Volvo, pulled in front of the house, double parked, and carried up the suitcase, boxes, television, and radio. The electronics went on the back seat. All else he threw in the trunk.

The choke offered more resistance than usual. *Don't make me stay any longer than necessary*, Bernstein thought. After the Volvo started on the third try, Bernstein took a last glimpse at his home for the past two years, flipped it his middle finger, and drove off.

Chapter Thirty-Four

Bernstein spotted a phone booth on a corner along Queens Boulevard with a parking space in front. He pulled in and called Ronald again. After still getting no answer after six rings, he drove on to his new home.

Max saw the Volvo double parked in front of the building and came down to help. They managed to get everything into the elevator in one trip.

"I like Red Fleming," Max said as they sat at the small, round table in his apartment.

"Red's the icing on the cake, far as I'm concerned," Bernstein said. "Danny's going to take personal credit for the band's success, which is fine with me as long as he keeps pumping you up on the air."

Max lit a Winston. "Feel free to light up a joint if you like," he told Bernstein. "To be honest, Jack, the last few days you've looked a little worried. Take it easy. We already had our baptism at Vinnie's club, and I think we killed it on Danny's show."

"You're doing great," Bernstein said.

"Something else eating you?" Max asked.

Bernstein wished he had a joint rolled and ready to smoke. He recalled that in his pocket he had his little pipe and the last crumbs of his Magical Moroccan. Max didn't say a word as he watched Bernstein crumble the pea-sized yellow piece and tamp it into the small bowl before lighting it with Max's lighter.

"You're right, Max," Bernstein said after he exhaled a plume of smoke. "I should take it easy. Anna tells me the same."

"It's an Italian thing, you know. Haven't you heard how we're known for being cool, calm, and collected?"

"Ashamed to say, Max—it slipped by me."

BERNSTEIN WENT BACK DOWNSTAIRS, found a parking spot and went to his own apartment. He lay down on the new bed. He knew he'd been through quite a day, and it wasn't over. *For a rock and roll manager, the day began at night. Tomorrow night is my night.*

He thought how the day began with him living in Mrs. Bardoni's basement and would end in his one-bedroom apartment with a sort-of view of Manhattan. In between, he was on the air and had arranged an impromptu audition with Red, who was old enough to be his father, maybe even his grandfather. The old man claimed he once played in a band and still practiced every day. Sonny, Clayton, and Mickey would decide if that were the case.

Bernstein kept thinking of the debts with looming deadlines. He had options but all were limited and none worked very well. He ruled out stiffing Ronald while paying off Mitty and the pawnbroker. "Borrowing from Peter to pay Paul" as one of his conservative economics professors preached. Ronald was a friend, and stiffing a friend made the offense more dishonorable. Besides, who knew if Ronald, despite his nice-guy demeanor, had an enforcement wing of his enterprise. It couldn't be cheap to live in such a luxurious apartment, despite its location, and upkeep required being paid. Mitty was nice to him, so was Vinnie, but who would want to explain to either of them that a debt couldn't be paid?

He added numbers in his head. *Two hundred profit on the hash deal. One hundred dollars as my share of the door at Vinnie's Club Rego. Three hundred emergency savings. Maybe a hundred fifty as my take from the gig at Sonny's. Hopefully a hundred fifty for the old stereo. Swallow my pride and borrow a hundred from Anna. That takes care of Mitty. Maybe a veteran musician like Clayton knows how to squeeze some extra time from the pawnbroker.*

Maybe he could just tell Walter he accepted the settlement from Tennessee Eddie's lawyers. He would have the money quickly. Surely Mitty and the pawnbroker would wait a few days if they saw proof of the money. It would be blowing a chance to make a lot on the lawsuit, but it might also save his arm or leg a breaking.

All of the options caused the same uneasy feeling in his stomach.

The last of his Magical Moroccan worked as always. Bernstein first felt as if he were floating along a river with a gentle current, then he felt a sense of ease and relief, the kind he experienced when he passed a college final he was certain he failed. Then he felt and thought nothing.

BERNSTEIN WAS AWAKENED by a loud pounding on his door. He rubbed his eyes and sat up on the edge of his bed. It took him a few seconds to remember he was no longer in the basement. He went to the door.

Anna and Max greeted him, the latter holding a pizza box in one hand and a paper bag in the other.

"I've spent the past hour hanging with Max, hoping you would wake up," Anna said. "Max was kind enough to go out and get some dinner. We're hungry. Waiting for you to wake up builds an appetite."

They stood around the kitchen counter, gobbling slices and slugging soft drinks.

"Got plain, because I didn't know how you felt about anchovies."

"Pretty much the same way they feel about me," Bernstein replied. "I'll eat them if they're on my pizza, that's for sure."

They finished eating and drinking. Anna suggested going to Max's, who had a table, chairs, and a sofa. "Sorry I didn't think of that earlier," she said.

"That's okay. You see people standing up and eating in pizza parlors."

As soon as they were inside, Bernstein asked if he could use Max's phone, which had just been installed that day. Max said of course he could.

Bernstein dialed Ronald's number. Again, there was no answer, only the recorded message about termination.

Afterward they watched reruns on Max's small television. At ten o'clock, Max announced he was going to sleep.

"Want to be well rested for the biggest day of my life," he explained. "I'll be drinking tea with lemon and honey all day and trying to speak as little as possible."

That's good news, Bernstein thought.

"If you can't reach Ronald, it's okay to use the money to pay someone else," Anna said in their new apartment. They sat next to each other on the edge of the bed. He asked her what she thought of taking the settlement offer, and she was adamant he ought to hold out for more. "Use Ronald's money in the meantime," she advised.

"It's not right," he said.

"So, what *is* right?" she asked. "Mitty the Mole sends someone to beat you up? Your friend loses his beloved guitar? All because some flaky hash dealer isn't answering calls from a guy who wants to pay him? Like he's going to care if you're a few weeks late."

"I have to worry about paying Ronald and what he might do. Don't be so sure he hasn't got the means to collect what's owed. We're talking a guy who fronts pounds. He can't afford to be stiffed too many times."

"But he can this one time," Anna said. "How about this, Jack? If you can't reach Ronald by Monday, you pay Mitty and get the guitar. We can scrape together enough to pay Ronald if he calls a few days later."

Bernstein liked the way she said "we." He put his arm around her.

"Being there's no place to hang out except bed, what do you say we take advantage of the situation?" she asked. Her mouth pressed against his, precluding further discussion.

Chapter Thirty-Five

Mrs. Bardoni thought her daughter was spending the night with a female coworker. She would have been apoplectic if she knew Anna actually spent the night in bed with her recently departed tenant, who was not missed, since she promptly rented the basement to a young man in the neighborhood for more money than Bernstein was paying each month.

Anna was up and about when Bernstein opened his eyes for the first time that Saturday.

"Since we have no food, nothing to cook it in, and no place to sit down and eat it, let's look for a place to have breakfast," Anna suggested.

Bernstein agreed, and after running his hands in water, he realized he had neither soap nor a towel. Anna laughed and handed him both.

"I knew you'd never remember to unpack them first."

Anna suggested they invite Max to join them for lunch at Gus's Diner, which was close, cheap, and digestible. After knocking on his door, Max thanked them and explained he had to leave to meet the rest of the band.

"We have to go over the playlist and a few other things before Red shows up," he said. He told them he was taking the train to Jamaica, and Sonny would pick him up.

"Sounds like this band is moving in the right direction," Anna said as she and Bernstein walked to Gus's. "Don't you think?"

"I don't know what to think anymore," he answered.

It took only minutes to walk the two blocks. A sign in the window advertised a full breakfast with coffee for a dollar fifty.

"My treat," Anna said as she pulled Bernstein into the diner.

Once they were seated and served, Anna asked, "Nervous?"

"No, I'll think of something for the money, don't worry."

"No, you fool, I meant are you nervous about the band tonight? Sonny's is easily twice the size of Club Rego, and Max is singing well but has to convince a South Jamaica audience he can sing R&B."

Bernstein chewed on a piece of rye toast while he decided.

"Max can sing rhythm and blues. These guys wouldn't work with him otherwise. The question is whether the local audience likes his interpretation as much as his band does. He did fine at that little impromptu event at Sonny's, before the band played Vinnie's. No reason to think a bigger crowd from the same place won't feel the same."

"We'll find out in about ten hours," he added.

PLEASE, Volvo, don't fail me now, Bernstein prayed when the choke refused to mix air and gas to start the engine. It came to life on the second try, and Bernstein, who hadn't prayed in years, silently thanked a Supreme Being while Anna crossed herself. *It's happening too often these days*, he thought.

Sonny had reserved a parking spot in the lot for Bernstein, a big cardboard sign reading "Band Manager." Bernstein smiled as he turned off the engine. It was seven o'clock.

The band was set up and playing on the stage with Red Fleming's electric piano off to the left of Mickey's drums. When Bernstein walked in, Red was playing the opening notes of "My Girl."

"Absolutely better with keyboard," he said to Anna.

Sonny and Red wore dark suits and skinny black ties. Clayton had on a gauzy white shirt that hung over his pants; its three buttons at the neck were all open. Mickey, whose drumming would bring forth an ocean of sweat, wore another New York Mets T-shirt. Bands these days dressed in a mismatched and eclectic style, save for the Motown groups, who still carefully coordinated their wardrobes. By anyone's standards, Max stood out. He wore a tight black silk shirt, unbuttoned to a spot between his naval and sternum, several gold chains and a large gold cross dangling from his neck.

"He looks like one of Vinnie's boys," Anna said.

"Would anyone be afraid of him?" Bernstein asked.

Bernstein focused his attention on Red's keyboard playing. He was as good at his instrument as the others were on theirs. He listened to the band jam and noodle, then run through the same original song they played on Danny's show. *He was right. He can step in any time.*

Clayton signaled for the band to stop. *He's the real leader*, Bernstein thought. *That's fine. He's a good man.*

Sonny motioned to Bernstein to meet him in his office. He told Anna he'd be back shortly.

"I'm expecting a full house tonight," Sonny said to Bernstein in his office. "Clayton and Mickey have spread the word to everyone they know, and these guys have lived and gigged around here all their lives. I always draw a good crowd on weekends, no matter what. The big question is how many other people come here because they saw us at Club Rego or they heard about us on Danny's show."

"Will all those White people come to South Jamaica?" Bernstein asked. "Maybe some if they're in Queens, but Danny's show is in Westchester."

Sonny looked at his fingertips.

"If they heard us play on Danny's show, or if they actually saw us at Vinnie's place, you bet your ass a bunch of them will be here tonight."

Bernstein smiled for the second time that day.

"Sonny, right now, I don't think my ass is worth very much as collateral." *And others already have a claim on it anyway.*

"Just you wait and see," Sonny said.

"Was there anything special we should talk about before showtime?" Bernstein asked.

"Only to let you know that this Red Fleming can really play. He just stepped right into the groove with the rest of us. Since day one the whole thing about the New Plateaus is that the band is unique. Not just Black and White, but look at the White guy we have fronting. Is there anyone like Max in rock today? The worst you ever say about him is that he's a harmless idiot. And that's you calling him the idiot, not us musicians in the New Plateaus. Put him on a stage, and he becomes a genuine talent—Mick Jagger, Marvin Gaye, Frankie Valli, and Dion rolled into one. Trust me, Jack—no one is copying us. And now we're adding this skinny old White dude who's up there with Billy Preston and Nicky Hopkins but before I got him this suit he looked like he just came from his gas station. What a musician! As are the rest of us, I might add."

"Great speech, Professor. I'm sold."

When they were at the door, Sonny draped his arm around Bernstein's shoulder.

"While we're on the subject of asses, I recommend you kiss as many as you can tonight. Jack, you have this way with people. They just want to help you. Vinnie. Danny. Red. Let's not forget Mr. Crane and those big-time venues you're going to use for us."

He thinks I won Winston Crane with my charm. If only he knew.

THE CLUB STARTED to fill up, and it wasn't even eight o'clock yet. The band was to take the stage a little after eight, but at Sonny's that meant eight thirty.

Bernstein had a joint in his pocket. He decided to save it for later that evening. He spotted Anna sitting at the bar with Barry and Ed. He joined them and asked the bartender for a club soda. The others drank red wine.

"Show time in what, twenty minutes?" Barry asked. Bernstein nodded.

"I heard them on Danny's show," Ed said. "They've gotten even better than when they played out in Rego Park last week." The way Ed said "out in Rego Park" implied to Bernstein the professional musician thought it was the minor leagues. *Did that mean he thought Sonny's was the big leagues?*

"You'll love the keyboard guy we added," Bernstein said.

"Yeah, you were talking about that," Stern replied. "Where did you find this one?"

"He owns a gas station in Macbeth Heights, and I was getting a fill-up. We started talking."

Stern stared at Bernstein for a few seconds. "Wow. A gas station in Macbeth Heights? Talk about being discovered."

Anna asked if anyone had a joint. Bernstein explained that he had one, but he was planning to save it for later.

"Well, it's now later than it was before," Barry said. "Let's go to the Volvo." Bernstein was glad he hadn't mentioned the two other joints in the glove compartment.

～

WHEN BERNSTEIN AND FRIENDS RETURNED, more people had paid the cover and filled the club. The lights in Sonny's were just bright enough for Bernstein to see the crowd was evenly split between White and Black. He couldn't tell how many people were inside, but it was more than he ever saw before in Sonny's. He began to feel confident.

Dan Picarelli appeared at his side.

"Like they say, revenge is a dish best served cold. Isn't that it?" he asked.

"Picarelli, what the hell are you talking about?"

The lawyer smiled and patted Bernstein's arm.

"Your treasonous SOB of a client, that asshole Walter's suing. Supposed to play My Father's Place tomorrow night. Guess what? He won't be making that gig. Just heard it on CBS news. Busted for propositioning a minor. Thirteen-year-old girl. Catholic school kid. Busted on Staten Island of all places. They'll cut his nuts off out there. Bet you're glad to not have that headache."

The fog of the weed was thick enough that it took a few seconds to register with Bernstein.

"Tennessee Eddie in jail? A pervert? A child molester? Who would ever think he was one of those?"

"And you picked him up on the street at night and brought him home to live with you," Anna chimed in. Bernstein hadn't seen her approach.

Bernstein pictured the tall, lanky Tennessean hauled away in handcuffs and dragged into court wearing an orange jumpsuit. He smiled. Then another thought gripped him.

"What does this do to my case, Picarelli? We're suing because I lost money he would have made. Now it looks like he did me a favor."

Picarelli laughed. He paused to light a cigarette from a pack of unfiltered Lucky Strikes. *At least smoke filtered cigarettes. They have to be safer.*

Picarelli blew a smoke ring. "I'm a criminal lawyer, not a civil lawyer, so you should ask Walter. Don't worry, Jack, you're going to make more money off the New Plateaus than you ever would have off that skinny hillbilly pervert. Catch you later, pal." Picarelli sauntered off.

"He's right, Jack," Anna said. "Now you can scratch that settlement off your list of options. Ronald's money is looking better and better."

Bernstein's emotions, as well as his digestive system, were roiled by this news. Half of the emotion was joy, but the bitter joy of revenge that doesn't solve anything. The other half was the recognition that one avenue to economic relief and prosperity was gone.

On balance, I'm happier with him going down than me getting money. At least I think so. Everyone says this band is going to make it. Now they must.

The New Plateaus took the stage to respectable applause. Max began bantering with the audience. This time, he identified himself as "Max from Laurelton," right next door to South Jamaica and mostly White. Max didn't add that when he was growing up he spent more time going east into Nassau County than going west to South Jamaica. He was on the stage with three hometown music notables.

Bernstein saw the audience liked Max and laughed and applauded as he spoke. He ended his little spiel by saying how great a band he had, and he went right into the first number, a cover of "The Game of Love," the 1965 British invasion pop song by Wayne Fontana & the Mindbenders. The band covered the song as R&B, and Max came as close as a tenor can to a growl. Sustained applause greeted them at the end, and Max did a swan dive for the crowd, drawing even more cheers.

This is going to be one hell of a night, Bernstein thought.

He spotted Danny Goldstein across the room with an attractive woman at his side. Bernstein pressed his way through the audience to greet Danny and thank him for helping draw such a crowd.

"You get the credit. I'm just a messenger."

"It wouldn't be this packed without the airtime you gave us," Bernstein said.

"This is packed house plus. Locals for sure. Sonny's an institution here, and having him on bass guarantees a packed house. You're drawing from all over. I see some people I know from Westchester and people I saw at Club Rego. I notice those things. Some folks are waiting outside for the second set after people leave."

"I'm hoping people don't want to leave."

"Don't take it personally. This is a nightclub, not a concert venue. People come and go. They go club hopping or party hopping or bed hopping. The folks are coming because the band is good. By the way, let me introduce you two. Jack, meet Sally. Sally, Jack." Bernstein grasped Sally's hand briefly.

"I'm going to catch a few more numbers, then I have to leave. Sunday morning show. I'll be talking up the New Plateaus. I want them back on. They're going to be big, and the Danny Goldstein Show spotted them first. Just remember that when you're at the top."

"From your lips to God's ears," Bernstein replied. He bid Danny and Sally a good night and wandered among the crowd. People were on the small dance floor, seated at tables or at the bar, or just standing around listening to the music and chatting with friends. Bernstein had never seen so many people in Sonny's. The crowd's applause grew stronger with every song. When Max announced a twenty-minute break, Bernstein headed toward the back room where the band stayed between sets. A hand tapped gently on his shoulder. The hand belonged to a man of average height and who wore a smile on his round, pleasant face.

"Mr. Jack Bernstein?" the man asked.

"Depends on who you are."

The man's smile widened. "The employee of an admirer of the New Plateaus…and their manager. He would like to speak with you. His limousine is parked in the lot next to your Volvo."

Bernstein was unsure what to do. The night had been good to him thus far. How did this man know he had a Volvo?

"Sure, love to meet a fan," Bernstein said. When they passed the door where young ladies were still collecting the cover charge, Bernstein stopped and spoke to the guard at the front door.

"Keep your eye on me. If I'm not out of the limo in five minutes, get Vinnie." He saw Vinnie while he was with Danny, the faithful Rocco right behind him.

The pleasant man opened the limousine door and closed it when Bernstein was completely inside. Bernstein sat on a plush seat facing Bill Krumpert and Duke Schwartz.

"We meet again, Jack Bernstein," Bill Krumpert said.

"But why?"

"I could say because you're a nice guy and I like you. We don't have to get there, Jack, because I like your band." He smiled, but on Bill Krumpert smiles did not look friendly.

"Relax," Duke Schwartz said. "We're your friends. Didn't we treat you fairly? Didn't we level with you? Even offered you work?"

Bernstein had to agree with the man, even though he looked like an idiot in his yellow leisure suit.

"Speaking of relaxing, can I offer you anything?" Krumpert asked. "Beer, wine, cocktail, joint if you like. Even have a little blow."

*Coke is hardly the relaxer, but if it's free…*Bernstein was unwilling to spend what cocaine cost.

"I wouldn't mind a line," he said.

"Set it up, Duke," Krumpert barked. Schwartz pulled a small bag from his pants pocket and withdrew a little mirror, a blade, and a small vial of white powder. Krumpert spoke while Schwartz chopped.

"Let's get right to the point. You've got to see your band during the break, and Duke and I have to get home to our wives. We poked our heads in a bit earlier for a short while. Guess you didn't see us in this crowd. Some of our people caught the show at Club Rego. Duke himself lives up in Westchester and listens to Danny Goldstein's show. So here's the deal—we like what we hear. Now, what kind of ears do you have, Duke?"

"Forty-five ears," Schwartz chirped. He handed the little mirror with two thick lines of cocaine to Bernstein and then passed him a small straw. Bernstein looked at Krumpert, who nodded his approval for Bernstein to clear the mirror, which he did with two enormous snorts.

As the cocaine hit Bernstein's neurons, Duke's voice distorted, sounding for a moment like he had swallowed helium. He felt a rush of heat through his body and a rush of blood in his head, and then he felt as if he had just been told he had won the lottery, which in a sense was the case.

"This is pretty good stuff," he croaked.

Krumpert nodded. "Ought to be for what we paid. Anyway, to cut to the chase—I know you think forty-five means bubblegum, but that's not really true. It means songs that are released as singles and get played on AM. That includes Motown, Credence, the Mamas & the Papas…oh yeah, and the Beatles and the Stones. The New Plateaus have a little something for every taste. They can't miss. We want to sign them right now. You hear this?" he asked as he opened the window between their passenger compartment and the front of the limousine. Bernstein heard the distinctive clacking of a typewriter, known to every student who ever had a term paper to complete. Krumpert closed the window.

"The contract is being typed as we speak. Ten grand to sign. We get them in the studio in a month. If they need songs, we got plenty. They announce they signed with us and are cutting an album. That means more album sales and concerts that sell more albums, and on and on. We're going to make you rich, Jack. Now, you let the band play the second set, then afterwards get all of your signatures on the contract and hand it to my associate, the fellow who brought you here. He'll hand you the check. Any questions?"

Bernstein couldn't tell if it was the drug or the contract that had his mind racing at quadruple speed. Signing with Luna would certainly be the closest thing to a guarantee of success. The label had money and clout, as well as Krumpert and Schwartz, and they thought enough of Bernstein to give him a hearing with Galahad. Bernstein never felt entirely comfortable with their bubble gum presentation, but Krumpert had shown Bernstein several other types of groups. The New Plateaus were not bubblegum, yet Krumpert and Schwartz were pressuring him to sign on the spot.

They smell money, which is why they're here right now. They must think they've got an audience for my guys. I could end all my money problems and have my first record contract. Or I could go to other labels and tell them Luna is interested. But would those labels believe me? Would they be afraid to cross Bill Krumpert? My father always said a bird in the hand is worth two in the bush.

Bernstein's mind raced even faster. He slowed it down enough to ask his question.

"Any way I can get one grand of it in cash no later than Monday morning?"

Krumpert broke into a hearty laugh. He turned to Schwartz. "Get it, Duke? He's up to his neck in hock, and this is a godsend. Why would he need cash by Monday otherwise? But hey, that's me at your age. I like your spunk, Jack. It takes balls to get into hock like that." He reached into his pocket and pulled out a roll of bills. He peeled off ten hundreds and passed them to Bernstein.

"Don't you need a receipt?" he asked.

"Consider it a signing bonus from me to you. A gift. Now get out of here." The door was opened by the pleasant-faced man, who handed Bernstein the envelope with the contract. The limousine left the parking lot.

BERNSTEIN WALKED into the band's private room with ten minutes of break time left. The band members were devouring sandwiches, washed down with sodas. Bernstein told the band the set went even better than hoped, and he made it a point to thank Red. Then he helped himself to a roast beef sandwich and a can of Mountain Dew.

A minute before the break ended, Bernstein asked Clayton to have the band meet with him for a few minutes right after the gig, before partying.

"Red too?" Clayton asked.

"Not right now. This is band-only business. Maybe fifteen minutes."

After the band left for the second set, Bernstein used the phone in the room to call Walter's service, saying it was an emergency. He gave the number, and Walter called four minutes later. Bernstein told him about his meeting with Krumpert and the contract.

"I'll be there in half an hour," Walter said.

"Good," Bernstein replied. "You'll catch the last song or two."

After hanging up on Walter, Bernstein dialed Ronald. Again six rings and no answer.

I want to square all my debts on Monday. Where the hell is Ronald?

BERNSTEIN MISSED the first song of the set. After trying Ronald, he realized how energized he was from the cocaine and the contract. The whole New York City area seemed to have heard of the New Plateaus and adored them. He just left Bill Krumpert's limousine, where he snorted high-quality cocaine, and was handed a contract and a thousand dollars cash. He would soon party with his band, his best friends, his girlfriend, and a benefactor who, if not a made member of the Mafia, was at least a genuine tough guy. *You'd never know it from the way he treats me.* On top of all that, Tennessee Eddie was in jail as a child-molesting pervert.

He made his way across the crowded club floor looking for Anna.

She was at the bar with Vinnie and Rocco. He told them everything that happened with Krumpert, except the cash.

Anna hugged him so tightly he feared he would explode. Vinnie put his cigar in an ashtray and followed suit.

"Congratulations. Who would have thought anyone could make a star out of my little nephew? Everyone else in that band, I understand, they all got natural talent. But Max owes it all to you."

"Not so sure about that, Vinnie. The kid's got something."

"If you say so," Vinnie replied, reaching for his cigar. "I also have to thank you for hooking me up with that Dan Picarelli. That's the kind of lawyer I like! I tell you, he's as good as any Jewish lawyer, and you know Jack, that is absolutely a compliment."

"Who would think otherwise?" Bernstein asked. *Is there something I'm missing?*

The band ended the set with their original number, the one Danny loved. The audience applauded and demanded an encore, and the band played a cover of Credence Clearwater Revival's "Proud Mary." Ike and Tina Turner did a soul version of the song, and the New Plateaus' version was in an even funkier blues style with Max dragging out every word in respectful imitation of a Delta bluesman. *At least pretty good for an Italian American boy from Queens.*

⁓

WHEN THE ENCORE ended and the band left the stage, Walter approached Bernstein. He wore a suit and carried a briefcase. Bernstein saw the pleasant-faced man seated at the bar looking at him. Bernstein held up all ten fingers, and the man nodded. Bernstein and Walter went to meet the band in their room.

"So, what's the deal?" Sonny asked when everyone was seated and the door closed. Bernstein told them everything about his encounter with the Luna Records head and his right-hand man, leaving out the parts about the cocaine and the thousand-dollar gift. That had nothing to do with his 10 percent.

The words were no sooner out of Bernstein's mouth than Clayton jumped from his seat and embraced Bernstein.

"My man, my man!" Clayton yelled, turning to his band mates. "How many times have I told you Jack was the man, he was taking us to the top?" He released Bernstein from his embrace.

"If I ever have a son, his name will be Jack Bernstein Walker, you can count on that."

"Poor kid," Bernstein said.

Sonny joined the two and draped a thick arm over Bernstein's shoulders. "I knew Jack before he was a big name in the music biz. Success has not changed the man. He's still the same fool."

Bernstein playfully pushed Sonny and they embraced.

"Wait a minute," Mickey called out. "Why we giving Jack all the credit? He's the man when it comes to the money and making us get it all together, but let's not forget who really made the difference—Mr. Max Flugel. The rest of us were around this music business for years and never got this far. Bill Krumpert showing up at a gig in Queens to sign a band? Think he'd be here if we didn't have Max?"

The others called out their agreement. Even Bernstein shouted, "Max is the man!" *Keep him happy.*

Max blissfully ignored the conversation as he struggled to rip the cellophane off a pack of Winstons. Bernstein called his attention.

"Max, are you listening to this?"

"Give me a minute," he said.

"Max, Mickey just said you're the man, the reason we just got a record contract. Mickey is right. You're the man, not me. I'm just the manager. You're the singer, and these guys are great musicians. But we all agree it's you, Max."

"Can't we both be the man?" Max asked. "Or take turns being the man?"

"It don't work that way," Mickey said. "Either you're the man, or you're not the man. And you are the man!"

"Okay," Max replied, a big smile on his face. All the cellophane was off the pack and he withdrew a cigarette.

"Anyone got a light?" he asked.

"He's in shock," Sonny whispered to Bernstein. "Wait until he realizes what this means."

"Either that, or he's just being Max," Bernstein said.

~

WALTER READ THE CONTRACT, then reviewed selected sections more carefully. Max and Clayton smoked cigarettes. Mickey sipped a beer. Sonny and Bernstein watched Walter's face for any signs. There were none.

Ten minutes later Walter was done. He told the group it was the standard first-time recording contract, nothing out of the ordinary. If anything, Luna was being more generous by calling the $10,000 a signing bonus instead of an advance on sales, which would have to be repaid.

"I'd recommend signing. I'll take the two extra copies, if you don't mind, and make more and send them to Jack to distribute. Make sure everyone signs both of the ones you have. Jack, I'll send you a bill. We know you're good for it now."

"Before you leave, I need to speak to you in private on a totally unrelated matter," Bernstein told the lawyer. He asked Sonny if he could use the office for a minute, and Sonny said sure, handing him the key.

In the office, Bernstein told Walter what he learned about Tennessee Eddie. Walter already knew because Picarelli had called him.

"It really reduces the value of the case, no doubt about that. That's even more true now that you have a band with a recording contract and some serious gigs ahead. It's not at all a stretch to say getting fired was the best thing that ever happened to you."

"So, what should I do?" Bernstein asked.

"Authorize me to call his lawyers on Monday and see if I can get the last offer. They may laugh in my face, but they have to pay the contract amount of five grand, plus lawyers' fees because they forced us to litigate. We also sued the new manager, who has money. There's no way around it for them. After what you did with this new band, no one will believe you were so bad they could break the contract with no penalty. Take what we get, declare victory, move on, and forget about Tennessee Eddie and Galahad and everything else unpleasant."

"Now that's a deal I accept," Bernstein said. Walter declined Bernstein's offer of a drink, and Walter stopped smoking weed years ago when he joined the district attorney's office. Walter picked up his briefcase and left Bernstein alone with his thoughts.

And to think I woke up worrying about money.

~

SONNY WAS outside the door of the party room when Bernstein returned.

"We'd like to offer Red a place in the band. You were right, we needed a keyboard, and we found one. It's your call because it was your idea to use him, and you're our manager."

"How do you guys feel about splitting the band's take five ways instead of four?"

"We feel fine," Sonny replied. "Sounds like we're on the way to making some money, and those keyboards are one reason why."

Bernstein nodded.

"I'm glad to be of service," he said. "That's what you pay me for. I'll have Walter draw up an addendum to our contract, adding Red."

They went inside the room. Red was drinking beer with Mickey. Ed Stern and Barry were in a corner with Max and Anna, all four holding glasses of red wine. Picarelli had his arm around a young college girl, not the one from the week before. Bernstein went to Red, slapped him on the back, and yelled out as loud as he could, "Let's all welcome the newest of the New Plateaus, Mr. Red Fleming!" The room exploded in applause and cheers. Jack moved next to Red.

"So what do you say, Red. You in?"

Red grabbed Bernstein's forearms.

"Am I in? What kind of question is that? You know what my dream was when I was these guys' age? To do what they're doing. And now I am!" Tears welled in Red's eyes. "I knew there was a reason I never stopped practicing. The Lord works in strange ways."

Bernstein smelled cigar smoke. Vinnie stood behind him. He slung his arms around Bernstein's shoulders, and shouted, "A record deal! Airtime on Danny Goldstein's show! Knocking 'em all dead, Black, White, green, orange! Jesus Christ, this guy can walk on water!"

"Wrong religion," Bernstein said. "Maybe better if you say I can part the Red Sea."

Their dialogue was interrupted by the ringing of a wine glass struck with a spoon. It was Max, standing on a chair demanding attention. If he had been in shock over the news as Sonny believed, the shock had worn off.

"I have to say one thing, to thank one person from the very bottom of my heart. If it weren't for that person, none of us would be here right now, certainly not me.

"When I met Jack Bernstein, it was because my uncle asked him to work with me and try and make something out of me. Up until then, everyone thought I was a loser who couldn't do anything right. But not Jack Bernstein. He has that kind of vision that sees through all the BS.

"At first, I thought Jack was a real prick. He fired my two best friends, actually my only two friends, and dragged me down to South Jamaica, where I didn't know anyone. I was trying to be Frankie Valli, and he made me be myself. He hooked me up with top musicians who are great guys. We're gonna be the best band in the world, thanks to Jack Bernstein!"

Max stepped off the chair to cheers and clapping.

"That was so sweet," Anna said to Bernstein. "Do you believe me now about Max?"

"I don't know what to believe," he replied. Then he looked at Vinnie Calamato and saw a solitary tear trickling down his cheek.

Chapter Thirty-Six

Bernstein awoke early on Sunday morning, even though he was tired from the night before. He silently thanked Vinnie for the receiver powerful enough to pick up a Westchester County FM station. He unpacked his single-cup coffee materials and his bag of ground Sumatra and boiled some water. His first cup was before him just as Danny went on air. For two hours, Bernstein relaxed, sipping coffee, listening to Danny alternate between playing fine music and talking up the New Plateaus. He smoked the two high-quality joints from his glove compartment, which he forgot to bring out at the after-show party. It wouldn't have mattered as he remained high on cocaine until at least two in the morning.

Anna was still sound asleep. Bernstein wondered how long it would be before she ran out of friends and coworkers to use as covers for her mother and have to employ the Teresa roommate scheme.

When the show ended, Danny mentioned the New Plateaus would soon appear at The Action House, and congratulated Bernstein on getting such a gig. How did he know that, as it was not yet set up? *You still have a lot to learn*, he thought.

After the show and his fourth cup of black coffee, Bernstein dressed and left the apartment. He walked a few blocks until he came upon a phone booth. His and Anna's phones wouldn't be installed until the middle of the week. He could have used Max's phone, but it was still early and Max deserved to sleep in. Bernstein dropped the dime in the coin slot and called Ronald's number. Still no answer. It was becoming strange in a worrisome way. How can a drug dealer stay in business if they don't take calls? How do they stay afloat if they don't collect money they are owed? *What's going on?*

He walked back to his apartment. He wanted to be with Anna, in ways he never felt about Jennifer. Sure, the sex was great, but there had to be something more to make him feel that way. There was something special about her, something he felt but couldn't describe. It was even more weird, her being Italian and all. Then again, so were Vinnie and Max, and being around them had worked out fine so far. *Is this what love feels like?*

He needed to speak with Barry. Barry knew much more about women. Bernstein knew Barry too long and too well to think of calling him before noon, knowing he had partied hard until dawn, and not by himself. He'd seen Barry leave with his arm around a woman last night.

~

WHEN BERNSTEIN RETURNED, Anna was making coffee. Bernstein declined her offer of a cup. He told her of his discussion with Walter about the lawsuit. She agreed with Walter.

"Who's ever going to think you suffered a tremendous financial loss by losing a pervert on his way to jail and winding up managing the hottest new band in New York? Take what he gets."

She also advised him to stop calling Ronald.

"It's not like he doesn't know how to reach you," she said. "If he wants the money bad enough, he'll call you. With the money coming in, there's no problem paying him if he calls." Bernstein agreed to set aside two thousand dollars until that day came. He had the thousand Krumpert gave him, of which he told no one, not even Anna. Mitty the Mole was covered for the next day. The guitar could be redeemed with his other funds.

Bernstein didn't have to seriously worry about money for the first time as an adult. His emotions needed time to adjust.

MITTY DIDN'T SMILE or say thank you when Bernstein handed him the balance. He nodded and said, "If you ever need me again, you know where to find me." After a brief pause, he added "You're all right, Bernstein. So are those Tarpols. I like you and wish you all the luck in the world." He rolled up his window and drove away, a lingering cloud of cigar smoke the only trace he had been there.

Despite his promise to Anna, Bernstein called Ronald twice that week, once from Creamy Egg Cream, the other when the phone was installed in his apartment. There was no answer either time. Bernstein stopped calling, and the two thousand dollars sat in an envelope at the bottom of his underwear drawer in the dresser he retrieved from Ed Stern's garage with Sonny's van.

He also brought home a dining set from a secondhand furniture dealer in nearby Woodside. When Bernstein lived in the basement, he never considered it home. It was at most a temporary stop on the bumpy road to success. Now he lived with Anna, in an apartment they furnished, and it was their home. Bernstein never envisioned this when he began their relationship, but it felt good and right so far. *Go with the flow, as Galahad would say.*

Bernstein had no trouble booking the New Plateaus into the three spots he had gotten from Crane and Vinnie—The Action House, Westbury, and the State University at Stony Brook, Long Island. He now understood that when a band like the New Plateaus comes around, the top echelon of the music world knows right away and wants them. This time, his calls were taken. Bernstein's band was now more important than his connections to Vinnie and Crane.

The Fillmore East closed less than two weeks after the gig at Sonny's, just as Danny predicted. Its demise made Bernstein's bookings at quality venues even more impressive.

The pain of the betrayals gradually subsided. It hurt when he was hearing of Eddie's gigs all over the country, even worse when the radio played songs from his album, but things had taken a different turn.

Tennessee Eddie was in jail, disgraced, and Bernstein was owed several grand for his troubles.

Galahad was making a name in the spiritual music world, of which Bernstein knew nothing and cared less, but he wished him nothing but success. Galahad and his lawyers were right—Bernstein was not the right manager for him. No hard feelings. Here he was, managing a group that would soon be filling the top clubs and venues in Queens and the Island, the new places to be.

This was only the start.

Chapter 37
Six Months Later

A second album and a national tour were in the New Plateau's immediate future. Their first album went gold and spawned two top-forty hits—Max's cover of "My Girl," on the charts for nine weeks, peaking at Number Two, and the original number they first played for Danny, which charted for eleven weeks, including two at Number One. The New York and northeastern tours were financial and critical successes. Money flowed in enough to replace the Volvo and its temperamental choke with a three-year-old BMW, whose eight-track tape player allowed Anna and him to choose their own music. The car was paid for with Bernstein's share of the five thousand dollars Walter got from the lawsuit.

Bernstein didn't need an office in Manhattan. He didn't at all mind Queens. The answering service worked fine, and Sonny allowed him to use his office if needed. Since the New Plateaus played at Sonny's as often as possible, it was convenient. Most of the new acts Bernstein signed after the Luna contract were discovered through Sonny anyway. Duke Schwartz passed two of Bernstein's referrals to Krumpert, who in each case told Bernstein to do for them what he did for the New Plateaus, and a contract would be waiting. *Love the New Plateaus, but can't have all my eggs in one basket forever.*

To his relief, Vinnie mostly left Bernstein alone. Bernstein had solved his Max problem, made him a hero to his sister, and earned him money whenever the New Plateaus or another of Bernstein's acts played at his clubs.

Bernstein knew the hardest part would be to call Winston Crane and apologize. What was he supposed to tell Crane? I extorted you, scared you into thinking I'd tell people you were gay, but now that it worked out, I'm sorry? Better to let it pass, he decided. He and Crane were professionals, and these things happened. He couldn't imagine the things a man like Bill Krumpert must have done on the way up. He didn't want to think about what Vinnie Calamato had done, or paid Rocco to do.

When he was in a quandary about music, he relied on Ed Stern. Ed wasn't needed for the New Plateaus albums, but would help out in the studio with other groups and would always be Bernstein's muse and mentor on all things musical.

Bernstein occasionally reflected that when he and Anna started living together, he had no idea if the relationship would last. Now he couldn't imagine being without her. *She lets me be me*, Bernstein often told Barry and Ed as well as himself.

Anna was his chief advisor on matters of business. Every week, they sat down at their table with her copious hand-prepared charts showing how selected groups, albums, and singles she followed stood regionally, nationally, and in the U.K. Anna assured him this revealed who was on the way up and who was on the way down. Anna tracked these trends as far back as 1967 to prove she was right. She almost always was.

"Someday there'll be a machine to do all this," she said. "You'll put in the information, and it will do the work for you."

"You've watched too much Star Trek," Bernstein said.

Whatever they were doing worked. True to Krumpert's promise, Luna Records signed two groups Bernstein managed when their early performances in Queens showed promise. Bernstein grew comfortable adopting Schwartz's standards in his recruitments.

"If it won't pass Schwartz, it won't pass Bernstein," became his motto. The first time he said this to Ed Stern, the guitarist reminded him he hadn't always felt this way.

"Talk about a change of heart," Ed ribbed. "Duke has come full circle with you, from clown to guru. Oh, excuse me. After Galahad, maybe 'guru' isn't the best word for you."

"No problem," Bernstein replied, waving a hand. "It's water under the bridge. Forget and move on. Why carry a grudge, especially against Galahad? Even you thought you could make him a real rocker. We were wrong, he was right. It all worked out. If he didn't fire me, the New Plateaus wouldn't exist. There's no percentage in having enemies in this business. Duke and Krumpert taught me there's enough money for everyone. I wish Galahad the best of luck."

"So it's now about the money, not the music?" Ed asked. It sounded to Bernstein that the question was dead serious.

"It's about both," Bernstein said. *Which is what Bill and Duke were trying to tell me from Day One.*

Jennifer began seeing a dental school senior weeks after she broke up with Bernstein the first time. She just never told him. He learned this when he ran into an old friend at the supermarket. The man was now in practice, and they were being married in a month.

"I don't manage wedding bands," was Bernstein's response.

PETE'S GUITAR sat in its case in a corner of Bernstein and Anna's bedroom. Five months after he redeemed it, Bernstein received a postcard from Pete, forwarded from the old basement address. Pete was living in a commune in the woods in Mendocino County, California. They had no electricity, so Pete was strictly acoustic these days. Could Bernstein please sell his guitar and send him the money? "It's also okay to just pawn it and never redeem it if that's easier," Pete scrawled in small letters at the very bottom edge of the card. *I'll just send him five hundred dollars and keep the guitar. It's a Stratocaster... easily worth more than that.*

A few weeks after the gig at Sonny's, now music industry folklore, Bernstein called Ronald's number one last time. The recorded voice merely said the number had been disconnected. He took a cab to the Lower East Side. When the cab stopped in front of Ronald's building, Bernstein handed the driver a ten-dollar bill, saying he would also pay double the meter if he waited. The cabbie grinned and agreed.

The same guard from his last visit said no Ronald Hickman lived there. Bernstein handed him a ten and said he only wished to speak with the elevator operator. The guard pocketed the cash and called the old Chinese man, who denied ever seeing Bernstein before and or knowing anyone with that name. When Bernstein told him the apartment number, the old man said he must be mistaken as an elderly couple had lived there for over twenty years. Bernstein asked if he could speak with them. The old man stared at him and told him to leave, or he would call the police. The stern look on the guard's face suggested it was wise to comply.

The cabbie had waited as promised. Bernstein felt the old man's eyes drilling into the back of his head as he entered the cab. The radio was tuned to the New Plateaus' latest single, their original number. The cabbie raved about them and turned the music louder.

Bernstein was pleased to see his music bringing joy to so many people, and doing so from Queens. He was given backstage passes at any venue, including Manhattan. The first time he and the New Plateaus entered the back room at Max's Kansas City, they were awestruck. Now they expected such treatment. Bernstein was proud to have crossed so many bridges and created a band with such appeal. It was bound to happen. He knew what people wanted and how to get it to them.

I've got forty-five ears.

Afterword

The Fillmore East, Electric Circus, Max's Kansas City, Gaslight Cafe, Action House, My Father's Place, Stony Brook and Westbury were real music venues in the late sixties and early seventies. Sonny's and Vinnie's clubs are the author's creations.

Bayside, Flushing, Corona, Forest Hills, Sunnyside, Astoria, Middle Village, Lauerlton, Lower East Side and Alphabet City are all real neighborhoods in New York City.

There is no such place as Macbeth Heights.

Acknowledgments

It is impossible to thank everyone who deserves acknowledgment for their assistance in completing this novel, and if I omitted anyone, it was certainly not intentional.

Over fifty years ago, as a young twenty-something, I stood in Bernstein's shoes (or Frye boots). I prepared a demo tape for an artist I was managing and got some prominent labels to give it a listen. Once we get past that, everything else is made up.

Here's a shout to the talented musicians who played on that tape and the many others I encountered during my brief career in rock management. Deep gratitudes to Barry Weissman, my friend of more than fifty years, a former professional drummer whose band opened for the Rascals back in the day. Barry double-checked all my references to music, equipment, and musicians to make certain they were accurate.

Special thanks also to my lifelong friend, Brian Ritter (Barry Tarpol in the book) who discussed the novel with me every step of the way as a check on accuracy and authenticity of the time and place.

My daughter Liz was kind enough to proofread the introductory materials and several of her astute recommendations were followed.

As always, heartfelt thanks to Keybangers Bangkok, my primary writing group, sounding board, critics and muses, who took the time to review and comment on the first several chapters.

A debt of gratitude is due my principle editor, Nate Bowler. There isn't one aspect of my writing that didn't improve thanks to his sharp eye and brilliant sense of what goes where and when.

As always, the deepest gratitude is due my dear wife Josie, who as always, endured having an obsessed novelists as a husband. Her support is what always gets me across the finish line.

About the Author

Stephen Shaiken practiced criminal law in for more than thirty-five years, the first four in Brooklyn, and the rest in San Francisco. He is a graduate of Queens College and Brooklyn Law School, and earned an MA in Creative Writing from San Francisco State University before starting his legal studies. He and his wife Josie are residents of Tampa, Florida.

Stephen lived in Bangkok, Thailand for several years and has authored three novels in the acclaimed NJA Club Series, best described as exotic noir thrillers. The three novels-*Bangkok Shadows, Bangkok Whispers* and *Bangkok Blues*-feature American expat lawyer Glenn Murray Cohen and his eclectic friends from Bangkok's mysterious NJA Club as they face intrigue and danger.

Queensborough Rock is a different kind of novel, set in New York City in the late sixties and early seventies. The protagonist is a young rock and roll manager struggling to break out of the second-tier Queens rock scene into the glamor and stardom of Manhattan. The novel was very loosely inspired by Stephen's brief career as a rock manager in 1970-71.

When he isn't writing, Stephen enjoys travel, gardening, yoga, guitar, and following politics and current events with a passion. He's a voracious reader of fiction and nonfiction in too many genres and subjects to list. He has a special love for apocalyptic and dystopian science fiction, hard-boiled detective fiction, literary work by an endless list of authors he loves respect and admires, but at the top of his reading list at the moment are Paul Auster, Ward Just, Cynthia Ozick, Louis Auchincloss, Joan Didion, Philip Roth, Walter Mosley, Philip K. Dick, Jennifer Egan.

Follow Stephen on his blog and on Twitter, and sign up for his newsletter, to receive advance notice of Stephen's future novels and short stories. His blog contains short stories, travel tales and photos, and comments on the state of the world.

Follow Stephen's blog
http://www.stephenshaiken.com/

Follow Stephen on Twitter
https://twitter.com/StephenShaiken

Receive Stephen's newsletter
http://eepurl.com/dBomIX